**Danica Winters** is a multiple-award-winning, bestselling author who writes books that grip readers with their ability to drive emotion through suspense and occasionally a touch of magic. When she's not working, she can be found in the wilds of Montana, testing her patience while she tries to hone her skills at various crafts—quilting, pottery and painting are not her areas of expertise. She believes the cup is neither half-full nor half-empty, but it better be filled with wine. Visit her website at danicawinters.net

A true Renaissance woman, **Deborah Fletcher Mello** finds joy in crafting unique storylines and memorable characters. She's received accolades from several publications, including *Publishers Weekly*, *Library Journal* and *RT Book Reviews*. Born and raised in Connecticut, Deborah now considers home to be wherever the moment moves her.

Discover more at millsandboon.co.uk

# WINTER WARNING

## DANICA WINTERS

# COLTON'S
# BLIZZARD HIDEOUT

## DEBORAH FLETCHER MELLO

MILLS & BOON

First Published in Great Britain 2024
by Mills & Boon, an imprint of HarperCollins*Publishers* Ltd
1 London Bridge Street, London, SE1 9GF

www.harpercollins.co.uk

HarperCollins*Publishers*
Macken House, 39/40 Mayor Street Upper,
Dublin 1, D01 C9W8, Ireland

*Winter Warning* © 2024 Danica Winters
*Colton's Blizzard Hideout* © 2024 Harlequin Enterprises ULC

Special thanks and acknowledgement are given to Deborah Fletcher Mello for her contribution to *The Coltons of Owl Creek* series.

ISBN: 978-0-263-32238-5

0724

This book contains FSC™ certified paper and other controlled sources to ensure responsible forest management.

For more information visit: www.harpercollins.co.uk/green

Printed and Bound in the UK using 100% Renewable Electricity at CPI Group (UK) Ltd, Croydon, CR0 4YY

# WINTER WARNING

## DANICA WINTERS

Thank you to all who put their lives on the line
to help others.

# Chapter One

The skier had been missing since last night. In these sub-zero temps, death had likely found the skier long before Search and Rescue had even been notified.

Ty Terrell could count on his fingers the number of times they had managed to pull people off the mountains alive after that amount of time. If he had to guess, the skier had gone off path and found themselves in a slide. Avalanches happened with striking regularity in the Spanish Peaks outside Big Sky, Montana.

If this missing skier had gotten wrapped up in a chute, then they wouldn't be found until the snowmelt next spring—if then.

He blinked and an image of the last body he'd found in the thaw popped into his mind. The guy had been discovered still frozen, looking like a Peruvian mummy with his lips curled tight above his teeth, his eyes sunken and his skin browned by the ravaging effects of prolonged cold. He'd looked nothing like the pictures of the fifty-three-year-old man they had been sent to find. Aside from being freeze-dried, the guy had been in pristine condition. His wallet had even been in his back pocket, which had made identification that much easier.

Hopefully this SAR mission would be different, and it wouldn't be a recovery, but a rescue—even if the feeling in his gut told him it was likely the former.

He checked to see that his black Trunab go bag was in the back seat of his pickup as he started the rig. It was a long drive up to the trailhead, one made longer by slick roads, which may or may not have been plowed this week. It had snowed last night, which would make this rescue even harder, but hopefully they could still pick up a track at the location where the skier had put in and then simply follow the ski marks.

The drive up to the Beargrass Trailhead normally only took about ninety minutes from his place, but today it took closer to two hours, even driving faster than he should have. Thankfully, until the last half mile or so, he had been able to keep it out of four-wheel drive even though the snow was more than two feet deep in some spots. Someone else had cut tracks through the fresh powder and as long as he stuck to them, he'd been good to go.

At the trailhead, Cindy DesChamps, Chad Tenley and George Dolack—who everyone lovingly called "Moose"—were already sitting there waiting for him with the sleds as he pulled up. They looked annoyed, or maybe it was that they were amped to get working and each passing second was another heartbeat closer to their victim expiring.

He pulled his truck up in front of their rigs, making sure not to block the trailers so they could get in and out as they needed. Moose walked up to his window. "I didn't know I needed to call my mother to drive your ass up here." He slapped his hand on the edge of the open window. "Could you have gotten here any slower?"

"Hey, man, you're lucky I made it here at all. I just got off work," he said, picking up his Search and Rescue beanie and slipping it over his slightly too long brunette hair. He needed to get it cut—if he ever had any down time.

"Did you get all the texts about our vic?" he asked.

In all honesty, he'd just heard they were looking for a woman who'd gone missing while skiing. That's all he'd needed to hear. "Of course." He waved Moose off.

Moose rolled his eyes but didn't bother to ask questions. He knew Ty well enough by now that he didn't have to worry. Ty always completed his mission. "A few members are already out there, working the bottom line."

"I swear, I got here as quickly as I could."

"Just because you're some fancy-pants detective, you think it's some kind of excuse for being half-informed and late," he huffed, with a teasing laugh. "I see how it is."

"You know I would much rather spend time talking to you and Cindy than chasing down felons and doing high-risk stops."

"Yeah right, *high-risk stops*," Moose repeated with a laugh. "The only high-risk stuff you've done in the last six months is testing your stomach at the little taco truck near the ski hill."

"Those tacos are *amazing*." He rolled up his window. The guy wasn't entirely wrong. He'd been spending far too much time in his squad car serving warrants and answering repeat offenders' assault calls. It was all pretty routine, although he would still have to say that every-thing he did came with inherent risk. Though, it wasn't anything close to what most people saw on cop shows on television.

Big Sky was made up of mostly ski bums in the winter, hunters in the fall and fish heads in the spring and sum-mer. Crime always came with people, but his little town didn't have an abundance of either. He had to admit that he liked life just as it was.

He stepped out of his warm pickup and the cold stung his face. It was going to be a long day on the mountain. Going to the back of his rig, he grabbed his snow gear and donned up. There was no such thing as cold, there was only having the wrong clothing to deal with condi-tions. That being said, he hoped he'd brought the right coat and pants. According to the radar, it was supposed to dip into the double-digit negatives tonight and tomorrow, which would only be compounded by the wind speed on their sleds—it would easily feel at least fifty below in a matter of minutes. Hopefully they'd find this skier before having to worry about the nighttime temps.

The team had the machines unloaded and he clicked on the comms, which fed directly into his helmet. Cindy was on her sled and, after testing to make sure they could all hear each other, they hit the trail.

He turned on his heated gloves, trying to keep up with Cindy who was riding fast and hard on the ridgeline. Ac-cording to the map, the ridgeline ran flat then gradually descended into the valley below. If a person was profi-cient, they could work the line basically back into town, though it would take about a day.

Maybe the skier was just going slower than anticipated. Or, she had gotten started later than she had intended.

They moved to the side of the tracks as the trees grew thicker. If the skier had been in this thick stuff the entire way, he and the team would have to work around the main area where she had disappeared, making large circular swaths where they could look for exit points instead of sticking exclusively to the trail. It would make their search far harder, but they would do what needed to be done.

If all else failed, they would have to come in on their skis, but it would make any sort of recovery more difficult. If things went that direction, he wouldn't be surprised if they had to call in the helo team to airlift out their victim.

"I'm going to take the middle trail," Moose said, motioning to the right with his hand. "I'll meet you guys at our first waypoint."

"You got it," Cindy said. "We will expect you there in one hour. Let us know if you need assistance."

"Roger." Moose tipped his hand in acknowledgment before running his sled toward the bottom of the far tree line.

The run he was taking was far more treacherous than Ty was comfortable with, but he could understand Moose's thinking. It was a perfect chute for a skier who wanted or needed to make a faster descent. Even though there was solid logic behind his decision, he didn't like that Moose was going alone, but Cindy was the boss. Besides, Moose was the most experienced rider of the group, and if anyone was going to make that run, he was their best choice.

Thanks to the sound of his own engine, he could barely hear the roar of Moose's sled as he rode off into the distance, but everything would be fine. Expanding their search perimeter was the best thing they could do, regardless of his personal feelings. They could get to Moose pretty quickly if they needed to; Ty just needed to stop being overly cautious.

He took a breath of the exhaust-scented air and pushed forward behind Cindy and Chad. These two had been dating for a while now, and they weren't about to leave each other's sides. He loved that level of commitment. He'd kill to have that kind of relationship, someday. He'd have to meet the woman of his dreams first, and to this day the only woman who'd ever come close was his very first girlfriend, Holly Dean.

They'd been fifteen when they started dating and they'd been together for most of high school—until she had decided to run off to college and leave him behind. He'd tried to fight the fight and tell her that he'd follow her, but she hadn't wanted him. That had been that.

Everyone had told him that time would heal that wound, but all it did was serve as a reminder that losing love was the worst kind of pain.

He found the thoughts reawakening parts of him that were best left dormant, and he pushed the memories down.

After thirty minutes, the tracks reappeared near the base of the copse of trees. Cindy radioed, "Looks like we're back on trail."

"Roger," Moose answered, "meet you below."

He had definitely been overly cautious. Maybe he'd seen too many injuries and his line of work was taking a toll on him. Though crime wasn't too bad around Big Sky, just last week he'd been first on scene for a man who had been smoking while installing a propane tank in his grill. It hadn't ended well for his nose or his fingers. Hopefully the guy didn't need all ten digits for his job.

Maybe Ty simply needed a vacation—somewhere tropical.

As he dreamed of palm trees the snow drifts grew around him, and to his left there was a large subalpine fir with a tree well so deep he didn't dare to approach. If he had to guess snow here had to be at least ten feet deep in some spots. They were over the bottom limbs of the trees now. It was wild.

The tree growing by the large fir shook violently. He slowed down, braking. That was odd. As he looked closer, the base of the small tree was covered in something red. It wasn't just red...no, it was ruddy and pink. *Blood.*

He stopped his sled. "Cindy, we have movement back here," he radioed.

He didn't want to move too close to the fir, and if there was someone stuck at the base of the shaking tree, he didn't want to cause a cave-in. They'd have to be dang careful as to not cause further issues than those they already faced.

He turned off his engine and pulled off his helmet. As soon as he did, he heard a muffled woman's cry.

"Ma'am, I'm on my way. I hear you!" he called, not so loud as to cause problems with avalanches, but loudly enough that he hoped she would know help was on the way.

He put his helmet down and climbed off. After grabbing his pack and his shovel, he did one last check that everything was there and easily reachable if there was a cave-in or other emergency. Her muffled cry grew louder.

Cindy and Chad turned to come back to him as he slowly moved toward the woman's call.

He started to dig about six feet back from where the woman's cry sounded. Cindy radioed Moose and the lower team to let them know they'd located their vic. Moose didn't answer—they'd have to update him when they met at the waypoint.

After making the calls, Cindy and Chad parked back by his sled and grabbed their shovels. As they all set off to work, it didn't take long for them to be waist deep in the snow pit. Cindy talked nonstop, reassuring the woman that they were coming and everything would be alright.

It was amazing how just simple communication could help ease a victim's terror.

The woman's voice grew louder as he neared her. He put his shovel to the side and started to scoop back the snow with his gloved hands. Two purple-gloved fingers poked through the snow to him. He took hold of her fingers and pushed back the snow. The woman's helmet came into view. Even though her face was mostly covered, he recognized those blue eyes—Holly.

Before the shock of seeing her could settle in, he had to stay focused on the job at hand. "I've got you." He'd always had her. Even when he didn't.

She nodded, but her eyes grew wide as she recognized him, as well. "Thank you, Ty."

"Don't worry, we are going to get you out of here and to the hospital for care," Ty said, trying to bring her comfort in this time when she needed it the most.

He reached down under her arms and pulled her back from the tree and into the pit his team had created. She fell back into his lap as he landed in the snow.

"How are you feeling? Are you hurt?" he asked, panicked.

She shook her head. "I'm fine. A little cold, but I'm okay."

"Were you skiing alone?" Chad asked.

Holly was shaking, but he wasn't sure if it was from hypothermia setting in or from the adrenaline of being found. She tried to remove her helmet, but her hands were barely functioning, so he helped her pull it from her head.

"It…being alone…it was a mistake." Tears welled in her eyes. "I knew better."

When she sat back, blood poured from her thigh. They had to get her to the trucks and warmed up and her wound looked at as quickly as possible—though they had found her, her life still hung in the balance.

## Chapter Two

Holly had never been any good at following directions, especially when people told her to be quiet, to step back and let others take the lead, or to stay in her lane. To listen was to have her soul silenced, which was far worse than being reprimanded for having a voice. However, this was a lesson in humility.

She should have listened.

However, the conditions were perfect for the day on the slopes. Fresh powder and sunshine. What more did a person need?

Her co-owner at Spanish Peaks Physical Therapy, Stephanie Skinner, had told her that the slopes were looking treacherous, but *no*...she had to be headstrong.

Well, that had definitely come back to bite her right in the butt.

Now she was waiting on a Search and Rescue team to return in the passenger seat of her ex-boyfriend's truck—the same ex who had just come to her rescue—while holding a compress to the outside of her thigh. Plus, she had broken her ski. Altogether, this was going to cost her *big*.

Her thoughts moved to the movie *Pretty Woman* and the moment Julia Roberts said the word.

A giggle escaped her lips. The sound pulled Ty's attention and he glanced over at her, making her realize how ill-timed her laugh had likely sounded. He'd once called her emotionally unstable when they had been together. Her wayward laugh likely only reminded him of how unstable she really was...validating his past accusation.

*Gah... I have already given him enough ammunition to use against me*, she thought. *Then again, he can think what he wants to think.*

No matter how good-looking he was, or how, when she looked over at his pink lips, she could still recall the way he kissed—slow and hungry and so full of passion that the mere thought made her squirm—yeah, no matter what, his opinion of her didn't matter.

"You getting warmed up?" he asked, adjusting the heat vents so a steady flow of hot air poured out on her.

She was burning in more ways than one. He didn't need to know that, though.

She nodded and cupped her fingers over the other immediate heat source and let it pour into her palms until it burned, and her fingers felt as though they were being stung by bees.

"Thank you, again," she said, not quite sure what to say to the man from her past who had risked his life to save hers.

"I'm glad we got to you in time. We had been told you were missing since last night," he said. "I didn't even know your name. Your coworker had just reported that you had failed to show up for work and he had been told you'd been skiing."

That sounded about right, Robert Finch would make an emergency call like that without talking to others. But in this case, his overprotective nature had been to her benefit. When it came to her, he was less than rational. Lately, though, his attentions had been moving toward their administrative assistant—who he cared about *a little too much.*

"I meant to go out yesterday after work, but I waited until this morning instead. I'd told my co-owner, Dr. Skinner, I wouldn't be in the office today, but Robert mustn't have heard." She pressed her warm hands against her chilled neck, and it made goose bumps rise on her skin. In what seemed like seconds, her hands were cold again and she pressed them back over the heater.

She hated being cold, but she couldn't complain after how close she had come to turning into an ice cube.

"Wait." She paused, looking over at Ty. "So you didn't know it was me you were looking for?"

Ty shook his head. His dark hair was longer than the last time she had seen him, and it fell into his chocolate-colored eyes. She had always thought he had the most beautiful hair of any man she'd ever seen—it was unfair, really. Why did dudes always have the best hair when all they had in their showers was a steadily shrinking bar of green soap?

"No, like I said, I didn't." He gave her a look that wasn't exactly soft but made it clear that he didn't mean to come off as a jerk, either. It was like his coming out there to rescue her was just *business.*

She didn't know if she should ask him the question that was nagging at her, but she couldn't help herself. "Would you have come if you *had* known it was me out there?" She motioned toward the hillside where he had dug her free of the snow.

He cringed slightly like he was trying to dodge a wayward bullet.

She was nothing if not direct. It had been one of the reasons why they hadn't worked. He was far more passive while she dealt with things as they popped up—who knew such a thing could be a fatal flaw?

He sighed, like he was thinking about the same thing and was reminded of why they would never work out—even though many years had passed since the last time they had spoken. "My job requires that I do what is needed of me. And, if you remember correctly, I wasn't the one who broke things off between us. I don't have any hard feelings."

He was lying. There was no way he hadn't resented her for her saying what they had both been thinking at the time—things between them just weren't what they needed to be in order for them to move forward as a couple. At the bottom of it, in high school, they both still had some growing up to do.

Now, well…maybe he'd changed. Maybe he really didn't have any hard feelings and she was the one who was still living in the past.

"Let me take a peek at your leg," he said, changing the subject and pulling her out of her world of whodunit and whys. Some hatchets were best left buried.

She pulled back the gauze, exposing a long slash on

the inside of her thigh where her ski had snapped and cut through her snow pants. Now that the bleeding had slowed, she could tell that it would have been well-served with a couple of stitches, but regardless of whether she chose to get them or not, the wound would heal. She hated stitches.

"It's going to be all right—I can tough it out."

He leaned over and pushed back the edges of her black snow pants so he could get a better look at the semi-staunched cut. "We will have the doctor look at it—though it looks like you didn't hit the femoral artery. When we first got you out, I was a little worried. It looked like you lost quite a bit of blood."

"You know it often looks way worse than it is." She replaced the gauze and pulled her pants back over her cut, covering her skin.

"It looked like you would have died without me." He sent her a strained grin.

She wanted to deny the truth and tell him that she would have been fine, but when she closed her eyes and paused for a moment, she was struck by the terror of being under the weight of the snow. She could still feel the pressure of it on her chest.

Her breathing quickened at the mere thought.

Being suffocated by snow had always been one of her greatest fears. She thought about the heaviness of the snow on her chest and the inability to struggle free of the concrete-like icy snow every time she had been out skiing, but thankfully it had never stopped her.

She wondered how she would feel the next time she skied, or if there would even be a next time.

"Are you okay?" he asked.

Dammit if he didn't always have a way of knowing exactly what she was feeling right at the moment she was feeling it. It was like he could pick up on her emotions even better than she could sometimes.

"Yeah." She sounded airy, even to herself.

"You went through a lot today. I'm sorry if I made you feel badly about it." He messed with the heater vent again, more out of some need to expend nervous energy than it was to help either of them, she assumed. "I... I was just surprised to see you. And, for your information, I would have kicked myself if I had not come out here and then found out it was you who needed help after the fact."

She forced a smile. He was only playing nice. "You don't have to say that, but I appreciate the sentiment."

He frowned and there was an uncomfortable silence between them that made her realize what a misstep she had made and how she had sounded.

He opened his mouth to speak, but she raised her hand to silence him. "I didn't mean that... I'm sorry."

His eyes widened.

"I really am grateful it was you out there. I am humiliated that I even found myself in that situation. I'm a better skier, I know not to get close to the trees, but..." She ran her hand over her face.

"Nature and life have a way of humbling us all." The corner of his mouth quirked up in a tired, c'est la vie grin. "You did see your skis, right?" he said, motioning to the broken ski in the back of his truck.

The sight brought a tear to her eye as she nodded.

She could understand humility, but she hated being constantly humbled in front of this man.

His handset crackled and there was a garble of sound as a woman spoke. Strangely, he seemed to understand, but to her it was nothing more than women's tones and static.

"I'll be waiting," he said, letting go of the button on his handset as he stared at her. His eyes were wide and for a brief second, he looked...well, *lost*.

"What happened?" she asked, fear creeping up within her.

"Moose, the other member of my team, hasn't checked in. He was going to meet us at the end of the draw at Beargrass. Cindy and Chad have been sitting there waiting for him, but he's still not arrived." There was a crack in his voice.

"When was he supposed to be there?" she asked.

He glanced at his watch. "Almost an hour ago."

She didn't want to ask if he thought something had happened to his teammate; it seemed ridiculous. Of course, something had gone wrong if the man wasn't showing up on time. These people were professionals, and they were known for their promptness and higher level of communication if, and often when, something went awry.

"Hand me some duct tape." She motioned toward her pants.

"You can't go out there with me. You're cold, hurt, not trained, and I don't have room on my sled." He sounded adamant.

He could keep her plenty warm.

"Look, you guys were out here for *me*. Make room on your sled." She opened up his glovebox and inside was a roll of tape. "Ha! Some things really never change."

"It's simply planning ahead," he said, sounding almost annoyed.

She took a piece of the tape, ripped it free and closed the gap in her pants. "Let's go. Your friend needs help. I'll be fine."

Even as the words left her lips, she felt the falseness in them. She wouldn't be fine, not as long as she was forced to be so close to the man from her past. Every second with him was a second her heart was in danger.

## Chapter Three

Ty had to be out of his mind. There was no way he should have let her get on his sled with him, but there they were...him driving the sled with her sitting behind him with her arms around his waist. He could think of a hundred reasons why this was a bad idea, but the single reason to say yes—that his best friend was missing— was enough to make him act against his better judgment.

Besides, Holly was the most stubborn woman he'd ever met. If he tried to argue against it, he'd spend the next hour talking and she'd still probably get her way. It was better to just bite the bullet and put Moose's needs ahead of his own.

He glanced back at Holly, who was tucked down behind him to lessen the wind on her face. It was smart, but somehow her blond hair flipping around annoyed him.

Then again, most things about her annoyed him. Spending time with Holly was akin to nails on a chalkboard. Everything she did drove him up the wall. She was hardheaded, brusque and always thought she was the only one who had the right answer. With her, it was her way or the highway.

Truth be told, though, when her mask fell away, she was also one of the most caring and giving people he had ever met. And even now, after all these years, he couldn't deny the fact that she was stunningly beautiful. A piece of her hair caught the wind, and he watched it flip around as he drove. He could still remember how soft it had felt the nights he had run his fingers through her locks.

"You doing okay?" he asked, slowing down and tapping her on her uninjured leg to get her attention. She was wearing his helmet and it was a little big, but he hadn't allowed her on without at least some level of safety gear that covered her entire head. They had already saved her once; he didn't need to put her life in danger any more than necessary once again.

She nodded, the helmet loose and wobbling on her shoulders so much that she stilled it with her hand.

It was cold without his helmet, but as long as she was good, so was he. He pulled his beanie down farther over his ears.

He sped up, trying to follow the tracks in the snow in front of them in his bouncing headlights. Riding at night was always fun, but it came with an entirely different set of dangers—sticks became lances and cracks in the snow were like steel traps. Added to that danger was having her on his back, which affected the sled's balance and stability in the deep snow.

He tried to control his nerves. From the get-go on this call, things had just been *off*. Maybe he was the one who had caused this all to go a little sideways.

*It will be fine. Moose is going to be okay.* He tried to talk himself down off the ledge.

He and Moose had been friends since they had gone to the law enforcement academy together. Moose hadn't risen up the ranks like he had; he had jumped around from department to department because his wife at the time hadn't loved living on the east side of the state. She needed mountains, or so Moose said. They'd ended up here, but as soon as Moose had gotten a house, the wife had served him divorce papers.

Now he'd been working in Big Sky for about a year and the divorce had finally been settled.

For the last six months, Moose had been going through what Ty could only call Moose's groupie phase. He'd taken more women home in the last few months than Ty had in his entire life. That was, until recently when, according to Moose, he'd found a good one.

How good? Well, this was Moose he was talking about so that was up for debate.

He slowed as they started down the steep grade at the end of the ridgeline, near the location where they had found Holly.

*Holly.*

She squeezed him as they passed by the area where he and his team had found her. He wondered how it made her feel. If it had been him, he would have been embarrassed, relieved and grateful. He kind of got those vibes from her, but there was something else there that he couldn't quite put his finger on.

Her arms loosened around him and, as they did, he found he had almost liked them tighter. He was tempted to turn and tell her to hold on more, but he restrained himself. Things between them were already weird enough without him making things worse.

As they drove, and he cut back and forth on the mountain, he couldn't believe he found himself this close to her once again. She was one girlfriend who hadn't left his thoughts, but he had never imagined running into her. She was out of his league, and always had been.

The last time he heard anything about her, she had been dating an anesthesiologist out of Bozeman. The guy had been jet-setting around the globe with her, and he'd seen a few pictures on her social media of them standing on the different islands around the Pacific Rim between ski trips in Vale and Whistler.

If she was dating those kinds of guys, he wasn't sure why she had even come back to make her home in Big Sky. On a positive note, she was working as a physical therapist at a local place. Maybe she liked to keep a certain level of her own autonomy and independence without being beholden to some jackass anesthesiologist.

Whatever it was, and whether or not she was still with the dude, it was none of his business. He needed to simply keep his mind on watching the overhanging branches and downed logs—though, he had a feeling that those weren't the only dangers he faced.

Cindy and Chad were parked at the first location, and as he pulled up, he found them munching away on protein bars and energy gels like they knew, just as well as he did, that it was going to be a long night.

"Hey," Cindy said, watching Holly as she took off his helmet and slipped it under her arm. "I'm glad to see you were up for a ride. You must be feeling better. How's the cut on your leg?"

"It's just a flesh wound. Nothing major." Holly smiled, reassuringly. "Thank you for everything. Seriously, I'm sorry for what happened."

Cindy waved her off. "It's what we do."

Chad, Cindy's boyfriend, nodded. "Besides, we love coming up here. It's fun...until something like this happens. Though—" he paused, looking over at the trail leading from their location "—I'm sure we will find Moose. Knowing him, he ran out of gas or something. He *was* in charge of his own sled today. You know how he can be."

Ty chuckled, but the knot in his gut didn't go away.

"The other team we had working the bottom are heading home," Cindy said.

"How many were there?" he asked, trying to play it cool. That was what he got for being late this morning and not asking more questions.

"There are four on the other team. Frank Vallenti, Valerie Keller, Dan Wood and Smash—don't ask how he got the nickname, you know it involves women." Cindy put up her fingers like she was counting.

He liked the other members of SAR, but he hadn't worked with Valerie or Dan much. Smash was hilarious and, on a few occasions, they had put some down at Stockman's Bar. He didn't drink much anymore, but if Smash invited him, he was going to be there. The guy had a way of speaking that reminded him of a Southern grandpappy, especially when he had a ZYN nicotine pouch under his lip.

"They haven't heard from Moose, either," Cindy continued. "We were waiting for you guys to catch up, then we are planning on everyone working the face of the mountain. We will meet at the bottom in two hours. If you find Moose, radio in. Cool?"

"Make sure you stay in contact. We don't want anyone else going missing," Chad added.

Ty nodded, watching as Holly slipped on his helmet and pushed her blond curls under the edges. She really was beautiful.

He grabbed his extra set of goggles from under the seat and put them on his head. His cheeks were still exposed, and they would get cold, but it was better than nothing and at least Holly was going to stay warm.

They hit the slopes again, working around the side of the mountain and into the timber. He drove slower than he normally would, taking his time especially around the trees as he made sure not to get anywhere near their bases. If he turned off the engine and came to a stop, he was sure that he would have been able to feel Holly's heart thrashing in her chest. After all she had been through, she was taking this getting-back-on-the-horse thing like a real trouper.

The snow started to fall, and the wind picked up, making it appear like they were in a shaken snow globe thanks to his headlights. It was so dark and the world around them felt muffled, even dampening the roaring sound of their engine.

Holly tapped his shoulder and he pulled to a stop. He turned. His face was achingly cold, and his lips were starting to chap. He looked back at her. "Everything okay?" he asked, wondering if something had come over the comms or if she was hurting or something.

She pulled up the helmet so he could hear her. "Do you have a flashlight?" she asked.

He reached into his chest pocket. "I have a headlamp," he said, pulling it out. "Why? Did you see something?"

"I just need a minute," she said, reminding him that she was human.

He handed her the light, clicking it on. "I'll step over here," he said, motioning to the right. "Don't go too far. The snow is soft in places. I don't want to have to dig you out, again."

She didn't laugh. Instead, she gave him a little nod as she affixed the lamp and stepped off the sled.

Walking out into the storm, he thought about how he had been wrong in teasing her. It was too much, too soon. If she remembered anything about him at all, it was that joking around was how he tended to deal with anything uncomfortable. It was what made his job as both a SAR member and a detective bearable. If anything, he wished he could be funnier—like Moose.

When they found him, Moose was going to be the butt of the jokes around the unit for a while. The last time Moose had done something foolish was when he'd taken a header off the team's raft and had lost his radio and a myriad of other electronic gear at the bottom of the river. They had called him the million-dollar baby for months, even after their divers had managed to retrieve some of the lost gear.

He figured he'd take advantage of the moment while Holly was doing the same and climbed off the sled. He moved to unzip his pants, but as he did, something caught his eye. There, near the base of the fir, was the tip of a ski. It was yellow and at a strange angle, and he recognized it as the bottom of one of the SAR unit's sleds.

"Moose?" he asked, calling out into the blizzard.

There was no answer.

The knot in his stomach moved up into his throat and, as he tried to call his friend's name again, it came out as a croak. He moved nearer to the exposed ski on the machine. He pulled out his cell phone and turned on the light, exposing the world around him. About ten feet past the downed sled, lying under a slowly melting patch of snow, was a body-shaped lump.

Moose's blue jacket was sticking out and a few feet from his right hand was his helmet.

He moved toward his friend, instinctively knowing what he was about to find.

Even in his wildest imagination, he couldn't have been prepared for this...

Moose's head was nearly cut off. His eyes and mouth were opened wide as though he had been frightened to death and he was forever left screaming.

Ty was forced to look away.

He looked toward Moose's feet. Even under the fresh snow, he could see the pink tinge of blood; it was nearly everywhere he shone his flashlight. Moose hadn't been dead long—just over an hour at most.

If only he had gotten here sooner. However, even if he had, in the case of an injury like this, there would have been nothing he could have done for his friend.

He took a series of photos with his phone, making sure

to get the entire area around the body. He even took a shaking video. In an environment like this, where there was fresh snow coming down and windy conditions, it wouldn't take long for the entire scene to be covered and any evidence destroyed.

He continued rolling the video as he moved to his best friend's body and brushed off the thin layer of snow from his jacket. His jacket was cold and the heat from his body had dissipated. The coat was covered in blood and nearly black. In the bright light of his flashlight, it was hard to see, but it didn't really look like he'd sustained any other injuries. However, until they got the coroner in, it would be hard to say with absolute certainty and he wasn't about to disturb the scene any more than required.

After confirming his friend was deceased, he took a step back and said a silent word in honor of him. It helped the pain in his chest, but nothing could make that heartache go away.

The snow beneath Moose had soaked up the blood and melted from the warmth of the liquid, but it appeared to have gotten chilled enough that everything sat still—and the only sound was of the falling snow and the wind.

Thanks to the melting of the snow, Moose's head was tilted back at a strange angle, exposing the sliced flesh. He could make out the rubbery edge of the severed windpipe. Thick red clots of blood had pooled at the edges of the cut and had slithered down his trachea like deathly red snakes.

The angle of the cut was nearly perfectly straight, no

slashing or sawing. It was almost as if Moose had run into a wire…or, someone had wanted him unquestionably dead.

# Chapter Four

Holly tried to control her breathing, but as she took in a long inhale, the taste of blood filled her mouth with its coppery tang and she slammed her lips shut. *This…this man's death…* It was her fault.

She'd left the privacy of the trees only to stumble upon this scene. Now she glanced down at the nearly decapitated body, then quickly turned away.

Yes, there was no denying he was dead.

Her stomach roiled, threatening her with a wave of nausea, but she tried to swallow it back.

Why couldn't she have just gone to work? Instead, she had been selfish and decided to take the day off and play. Look what it had cost the world around her…

"Ty…" she said, barely whispering his name.

He looked over at her, but there was a vacancy in his expression that made her wonder if he was really even hearing her or if he was acting on instinct alone.

"Ty, I'm so, so sorry." She didn't know what to say, or how to say it. She was rattled by her role in his friend's death. "I wish… I wish I could bring him back." *And take back this entire day.*

This was all something out of her worst nightmare. She'd always feared getting hurt on the slopes, but even in her terror, she had never imagined that it would be followed up with something like this—an innocent man losing his life.

Ty grunted, looking away.

He was so reserved, but even in his stoicism, she could feel his pain radiating from him. Or maybe it was anger.

She clamped her mouth shut. Anything she could say to him now, well…she was worried that it would only make things worse.

His handset crackled to life as Cindy said something over the comms. Ty frowned and as she caught his eye, he turned away, shielding himself from her gaze. It bothered her more than she cared to admit.

"We located Moose. DOA." There was a metered stoniness to his voice.

Cindy said something on the other end of the mic, and though Holly couldn't make out the words she was saying she could hear the sadness in her tone.

This wasn't just Holly's worst nightmare—it was all of theirs.

TY WAS TRYING to hold back all the rage that filled him. He wanted to yell at the sky and tell the world what a screwed-up place it was. How could this have happened?

He had to get his act together. Anything he was feeling would have to wait.

Ty exhaled, long and hard, collecting himself. He was a detective first and a friend of Moose's second.

He couldn't fall for the torrents of anger that raced

through him. For Moose's sake, and for the sake of his family, Ty needed to handle this situation with as much professionalism as possible.

That meant, for right now, until he knew more about what had actually happened, he needed to treat this area and the body like it was a potential crime scene. Which meant he needed to notify the sheriff and let him know what had happened. Hopefully, Sheriff Sean Sanderson would make the call to Moose's mom, Rebecca. However, if anyone should notify her of Moose's death, it should be him. He was his closest friend and he'd eaten dinner on many a Sunday at Rebecca's home. They were close, so close in fact that she sometimes called Ty her adopted son.

He found himself getting choked up thinking about the woman who, just like him, was now alone in this world.

*Knock it off,* he reminded himself, closing off the door to his emotions once again.

There were some things and some aspects of this that would have to wait.

*One step at a time.*

He turned to Holly. "Are you okay?" He should have asked her before, but like a jerk he'd been so caught up in the hierarchy of needs that she'd had to wait.

She nodded, but he could tell by the darkness in her eyes and the slump in her shoulders that she was lying to him. While he appreciated her attempt to shield him, he was the one who should have been shielding her.

"Why don't you walk over here with me, if you'd like?" he asked, holding out his hand.

She turned to his gloved hand with a slight look of surprise, but then slipped her hand into his.

Their footfalls crunched in the hard, frozen crust of the snow beneath them. The wind was kicking up, causing the temps to plummet. He led her just far enough away that she couldn't see the body but to a point that was still visible from a headlamp's light beam.

"First, none of this is your fault." He took her other hand and made her face him.

She wouldn't meet his gaze.

"Look at me, Holly," he ordered.

She shook her head and from the trembling of her hands, he could tell that she was struggling to keep her emotions under control—he knew that feeling all too well.

Something about her struggle made him steel his resolve. Holly needed him to be the strong one. For her, he would.

She looked into his eyes, her gaze filled with guilt and pain. "You are okay." He tried to calm her.

"I'm... This... It's my fault." Her voice was strangled. "I should have just gone to work."

He took hold of her hands, and the action was so unexpectedly comfortable that it caught him off guard and he struggled to keep his train of thought. "Moose is... *was*...a good friend of mine." He motioned his head in the direction of the man's dead body. "I can promise you that he wouldn't want you to take responsibility for this."

"Someone will. I'm sure his family and his *wife* will want answers." She choked on the word *wife*.

He couldn't help the little chuckle that escaped him at

the thought of Moose still married. Moose would have had all kinds of colorful words at that kind of talk.

However, the thoughts of Rebecca once again gave Ty pause. "His mom is one of the kindest and most generous women I know."

"That doesn't make me feel any better..." She paused and looked down at their entwined hands. "Not that I should."

"That's not where I was going." He wanted to pull her chin up, to make her see his face and know he was telling her the truth, but things between them were already more intimate than he intended. There were some things he just couldn't deal with today, and not having a clear head with this woman was one of them. "Look, seriously, we don't even know what has taken place here. We need more answers before you can start condemning yourself."

His handset crackled to life and Cindy's voice pulled him from Holly. He'd have been lying if he said he wasn't a bit relieved. It was hard to console her and tell her not to feel guilty for her role in this, when he was feeling the same kind of culpability within himself. He was the one who had let Moose go out on that trail alone. He'd even questioned it at the time. If only he had spoken up or agreed to ride with him. Sure, the trail he'd taken was more challenging, but if Ty just hadn't been a wimp Moose might still be alive.

Cindy was two minutes out. He was relieved, but he wished he could stop anyone else from feeling the same way that he and Holly were. As soon as they showed up, he held no doubts that they would be as troubled by Moose's death. Moose had been a friend to pretty much everyone in their unit. This was going to hit the team *hard*.

He needed to talk to the sheriff.

"Holly," he said, squeezing her hand, trying to comfort her as best he could. "I need to make a phone call. I don't want you going near the remains, okay?"

She nodded, but she said nothing. Her silence did little to help the stone in his gut.

"I'll be right back. Cindy is on her way."

She nodded again but let go of his hand and moved to sit down on the top of the snow at his feet. In all reality, she probably needed the rest. She'd had one helluva day. He could only imagine all the things that she was thinking and feeling—and compounding it all had to be hunger and sheer exhaustion. He should have never brought her back on the mountain. However, choices had been made, and things had turned to this. There was no going back, there was only moving forward. And maybe that was what he should have said to her about her guilt. Hell, it's what he needed to tell himself, but he wasn't about to take his own advice to heart.

He pulled out his cell phone. Surprisingly, given their location in the backcountry, he had service. He tapped the contact for Sheriff Sanderson. Without a doubt the man was going to hate hearing from him this late at night— a call at this hour only brought bad news, and a whole helluva lot of work.

"What's happening?" Sanderson answered the call on the second ring, not bothering with the niceties that most outside of the law enforcement community abided by and considered polite.

"There's been an incident." He tried to sound placid and cool, not giving anything more than what was required.

There was the rustle of what sounded like bedding in the background of Sanderson's call. "What kind of *incident*?"

He swallowed back the lump that had moved into his throat and threatened to choke back his words. "Well, we found the missing skier, but Moose didn't make the waypoint. We went back in and looked for him... I'm sorry to tell you, sir, but Moose is dead."

There was a long pause. "What happened? Do you know, yet?"

"Not yet. We located his body and got a positive ID. His head was almost perfectly severed...too neatly to have been an accident. I was hoping that you could call in an agency assist." He treaded carefully, not wanting to step on Sanderson's toes by telling him in even the slightest way how to do his job.

"On it. Send me your exact coordinates. I'll have a coroner there as soon as possible. Where is the rest of your unit?"

"We sent everyone home who wasn't needed. I figured they could get some rest." Ty sent his commander their location.

"Good." The sheriff sounded tired.

"You should have our pin."

There was a click and the sound on the other end of the line changed as if Sanderson had put him on speakerphone so he could operate his phone and talk clearly at the same time. There was a buzz. "Yep, got it." There were a few thumps, like Sanderson was tapping on his phone. "Coroner has been dispatched to your location. I'm going to call our partners at DCI to see if they would be willing to handle the investigation. I'll be in touch."

"Yep."

"Terrell," Sanderson said.

"Yes, sir."

"Don't you dare move. And I don't want a word of this leaking out, at least not yet."

The man hadn't needed to tell him. He was in his position for a reason, but he appreciated that his superior wanted to keep this under wraps.

# Chapter Five

As Holly sat on the ground and stared out at the snow, there were soft murmurs behind her as Cindy and Ty spoke. They were probably talking about how she shouldn't have been here, and what a burden she had become.

*No... I need to stop feeling sorry for myself,* she chastised. *I caused this man's death. I just need to take responsibility and make amends.*

How could she make amends, though. There was no bringing this man back or telling his family that time would heal all wounds. She knew all too well that such an old adage was nothing more than an attempt to mollify those who needed to feel more than anyone else. Besides, time did nothing more than add distance from the sharp pain of immediacy. It did nothing for the memories or the soul-crushing moments when the losses unexpectedly took over in full force.

She knew that feeling of all-encompassing loss too well. She'd lost both of her parents in a car accident on I-90 just five years ago. The thought of their deaths still haunted her. And in moments like this, where she was facing death, it brought all the memories of losing them rushing back.

She stared vacantly at the snow-encapsulated world around her as she thought about how much she missed her mother's gregarious laugh—a laugh she would never have the chance to hear again. And her father, he used to love to drop dad jokes like they were going out of style. She loved to hate them when she was a teenager, but now she would have given anything to hear him make a crack.

The snow glistened in the moonlight, sparkling like her mother's eyes when she had laughed at her father, and it made her heart ache.

The trees were covered in a layer of snow that made them appear exactly as their namesakes—snow ghosts. She stared vacantly at two stripes in the snow. They led off into the distance over the hill and disappeared into the darkness of the night. There was a snow sled track in the center of the ski marks, reminiscent of a tank track.

She followed the marks toward Moose's body, expecting to find his machine at the end. However, instead there was a spot where the machine had been parked and someone had gotten off. The footprints in the snow headed toward the body, and in the snow was a well-packed area and then Moose's sled ski.

The marks were *strange*. It almost looked as though two sleds had been in the area. Yet, she didn't recall Ty saying Moose had been working with someone else.

The wind kicked up the cold, powdery snow, making it spin like someone had shaken a snow globe with her sitting at its center.

The only people who knew they were in the area were

the people who had been looking for her. Did that mean that someone from this guy's team had murdered him? Or, at the very least, played a role in his death?

The thought tormented her.

Her negligence had brought this man up here, which made her complicit in this man's death.

She was never going to forgive herself.

She tried to shake off the feelings, though. Self-flagellation was only going to take this thing so far and none of it would be in the right direction.

Besides, there was no way one of his teammates would want him dead. So far as she knew, the Search and Rescue team was just a volunteer group. If someone hated someone else, then why would they stay and keep volunteering? And all of these people had to be the type who were selfless—they were donating their time, bodies and equipment to rescuing people like her for nothing more than a "thank you" and a "good job" at the end of the day. They hardly fit the profile of killers.

This had to be nothing more than a horrible accident. Nothing else made sense.

Ty walked over toward her, his footfalls crunching in the snow as he approached, and he cleared his throat like he was afraid of interrupting her thoughts. "Holly?" he asked.

She turned to face him. "Hmm?"

"You ready to head back to town?"

She frowned. Not long ago, he'd made it clear that he hadn't wanted to leave the scene, but now he was ready to ship her out.

"If you want. We can go." Though part of her wanted

to stay and help, she wasn't sure what she could do, and she was getting more tired by the minute.

"Actually, I'm going to send you out of here with Cindy. I can't leave the scene unattended." His face was barely visible in the thin moonlight, but she could see the tiredness in his eyes and hear it in his tone.

"I can wait. There's no need to make Cindy pack me out. I'm fine."

"I know you are okay, but I need to make sure you're fed and that you stay safe. I'm sure you're aware, but it gets cold out here at night. I bet your adrenaline from the day has worn off." He knelt down next to her. "I can see you shivering."

Until he'd said that, she'd not really thought anything of it. In fact, she'd barely noticed. She must have been going through an adrenaline dump. Though she had seen others go through them after especially painful or intense physical therapy sessions in her clinic, she'd never gone through something like it herself. She held a newfound appreciation for her patients—heck, maybe she'd go a little lighter on them the next time they came in for their appointment.

She looked over at Cindy, but as she did, Cindy looked her way and blinded her with her headlamp.

"If we go…you'll be here alone." She tried to control the quaking that was starting to intensify throughout her body.

He looked back in the direction of Moose's remains. "I appreciate your concern, I really do. But this is what I do, Holly." There was a tenderness to his voice that she hadn't heard come from him in many, many years and it tore at her.

He was hurting and there wasn't a thing she could do about it—even if he'd wanted her to stay by his side. It only served as a reminder of how out of each other's lives they had become and would likely continue to be.

She nodded. "I get it."

There was an unexpected tightness in her chest, almost as if by leaving him on this hillside she was once again excising herself from his life.

Her feelings didn't make sense—even to her. They had broken up. They weren't *anything*. Yet here she was yearning to be by his side. What was she doing?

She glanced one more time out at the tracks as he helped her to standing. Her gloved hand fit perfectly in his and it only made the confusing feelings within her intensify.

"Did you see those?" she asked, nudging her chin in the direction of the tracks.

He looked over and his head moved to the side, reminding her of a cute puppy. The likeness of which didn't help her mixed feelings about him.

"That's strange..." He looked at the tracks that led over toward Moose's machine. He pulled out his phone and started to take pictures of the scene like she had watched him do with the body.

"I'm surprised you didn't notice them," she said, not really thinking about what she was saying. "I mean you're a detective. I thought you'd have noticed them right away."

The cuteness in his demeanor shifted and a darkness that had nothing to do with the night filled his eyes. Instead of saying anything, he turned away.

Her stomach clenched. That had come out all wrong. That's not what she'd wanted to say... It was just that she never thought he'd miss such a thing given his profession. She cringed at her thought. Of course, she'd meant what she'd said, but why did she have to be so tactless sometimes? Why couldn't she have simply been helpful and left it at that. Instead she had to run a sliver under his fingernail.

She watched him walk away, but she didn't call after him—there was nothing for her to say that could fix what she'd just fractured between them. It was really no wonder that he had broken up with her those many years ago. She'd never really had a way with words, but apparently time hadn't changed that as much as she had hoped.

A few minutes later, Cindy came walking over and handed her what she knew, thanks to the red markings and "Terrell" stenciled on the back, to be Ty's riding helmet. She thought about not taking it, or maybe refusing to ride back, but she accepted it and followed Cindy as she directed her to her sled and motioned for her to get on.

As Cindy started the engine, Holly looked back at Ty who was watching them. He gave her a stiff nod and she slipped on his helmet, fully aware that this was their last goodbye.

# Chapter Six

He watched as they placed Moose's remains into the coroner's van. This would be the last time he saw his friend,
and the realization broke him like he would have never
thought possible. With Moose gone...he was on his own.
Moose had been his greatest friend. They had spent so
many years hunting, fishing and drinking beer together
that without him, Ty wasn't sure he wanted to do any of
their favorite things ever again.

To do it without Moose, it just didn't seem right.

The doors slammed shut, pulling him from what he
now realized were inane thoughts. Here he was staring at
the body bag and thinking about standing on the banks
of the Madison with the man whose body was growing
ever colder.

Those memories and choices could wait, even if the
thoughts wanted to press through and take him to the
best moments he'd once had with his friend.

He dropped his head and closed his eyes as the van
took off down the icy road, careening slightly as the back
tires worked to find grip. The van spewed black smoke
like it was some kind of pissed-off bull.

Anger filled him as he listened to the van's tires slip and the engine rev—if they weren't in such a hurry, they would have been able to navigate the ice without issue. While there wasn't anything else that could happen to Moose that could make him more dead, it struck him as wrong that the coroner was so irreverent. On the mountain, he and his team had treated Moose with absolute veneration and care and to see the coroner fishtailing and spinning his tires tore at him.

He turned toward his truck and trailer, his sled already loaded, and he was ready to go. It had been a long day.

Getting in his pickup, he pulled onto the slick road, careful to ease on the gas and not repeat the moves that the coroner's van had made. The thought of the coroner's driving made him shake his head again.

Then, how could he judge the guy when he hadn't been perfect on this call, either. He had basically dismissed Holly—and that was after he had agreed to let her come along to find Moose. Had he known things would have gone so sideways, there was no way he would have brought her along. However, the last thing he had ever expected was to find Moose like that…with his head nearly completely severed. Who had done this? And why?

As he envisioned the blood-soaked snow, he pressed the gas pedal a little too hard and he was forced to slow down. He tried to think about anything other than all that blood. It had been everywhere…everywhere except near his sled.

That fact could mean any number of things, but one likelihood rose above all the rest—Moose hadn't been sliced on his sled. His death had to have come after he'd stepped off.

He had searched around in the dark, but he hadn't seen anything obvious on scene that fit an object capable of what he had found. Hell, he hadn't even found a stick.

The last time he had been called out to a death reminiscent of Moose's was when he had been a deputy. A man had run into a wire while riding his mountain bike and the results had been nearly identical. Which made him think that there had to have been something out there that he simply hadn't seen.

There had just been so much blood.

He ran his hands over his face and picked up his phone as it buzzed with a series of emails and messages from the unit and the sheriff's office. Everyone was texting him and sending their condolences. He wanted to tell them that they were sending them to the wrong person—they needed to be talking to Moose's mom.

Then again, he needed to talk to her first—he'd have to be on her step at dawn so no one would make a mistake and have to bear the weight of tearing down a mother's world.

He looked at the sleeves of his jacket. Though he'd been wearing nitrile gloves while working on the scene, he'd still somehow managed to get his friend's blood all over his arms.

It was hardly the first time he'd had blood on him from a crime scene; he was constantly covered by the detritus of crime and death, and the sight of it didn't bother him. If anything, it felt...well, *not right*, but somehow cathartic. If anyone in the world should have been out there on the mountain taking care of Moose in his final physical form, then it was him.

He wasn't into the woo-woo stuff, but he couldn't help but wonder why Holly had come back into his life at the same time. It had to be some kind of message from the universe or whatever.

It was strange that on all the calls in all the years he had been doing this kind of thing, he'd never worked with an ex, and he'd never before lost a best friend. It had to be more than a coincidence, though he couldn't make sense of what else it all meant.

Not long after they'd broken up he'd been lost, and it was then when he decided to apply to work at the sheriff's department. He had met Moose at the academy in Helena.

*Damn.* Holly had even been behind his meeting his best friend in the first place.

It was wild how many things in his life were connected to her and their failed relationship.

Maybe it was only right that she had been there when Moose had passed—though, she could have never known all the threads that connected them. In fact, she probably hadn't even known Moose. She hadn't said anything to make him think she had, but she had been through so much that anything was possible.

Hopefully she was going to be okay—emotionally and physically. She was pretty tough. Heck, if he had to guess she had never gone to the hospital or gotten stitches.

The thought made him almost smile and huff a laugh, though he couldn't have told anyone why. Maybe it was the fact that she was exactly what every Montana woman was bred to be—tough as nails and capable of handling everything from a blown-out head gasket to a rattlesnake in the garage. Then again, they were also the kinds of women who, when they got all gussied up, could wear Chanel and walk the streets of New York City with enough confidence that people assumed they were locals.

He had to admit he had a thing for that type—the *Holly* type.

He had only spent a handful of nights with Holly. Yet he found that when he was lonely, it was those nights which he found himself thinking about. She had been a one-of-a-kind woman when they had dated, and she had become more of everything since they had parted. She was definitely the one who got away.

It did him no good to sit here and rehash the old days, when he had so many other things that he could be dealing with. One thing was for sure, he needed to find out what exactly had happened to his friend. As far as he was concerned, that was where all of his attention needed to be focused.

However, it wouldn't hurt to swing by Holly's place and check on her on his way home. That way, he could find out whether or not she had arrived safely and if she had in fact gone to the hospital. He owed her that much. Heck, he didn't even need to stop—hopefully, she'd be sleeping by now and a porch light would be on or something. If he did stop by, would it be weird? It kind of felt weird.

He tried to reassure himself by repeating the fact that he simply wanted to make sure she was safe. He would have done it for anyone. It just happened to be that this *anyone* was Holly.

It seemed like she was an exception to a lot of his rules—or maybe it wasn't rules, but comfort zones.

Once he had heard that comfort zones were where the human spirit went to die. Maybe she was being sent to him or placed back in his life to be some cosmic reminder that he needed to grow as a person. He just wasn't sure which direction.

As he drove the miles back into town, his mind did double backs and somersaults as he thought about how he should approach things with Holly, or *if* he should approach things. He was making a huge assumption that she would even want to have him back in her life. She hadn't seemed like she did. Yet she had touched him. That had to have meant something.

As he entered town, he thought about getting her number on their database and texting her, but he didn't even know what to say.

Hey, how are you doing? No.

Doing okay? No, too clipped.

Worried about you. Too much.

His best bet was just to swing by.

He exhaled, hard. He resigned himself to the fact that there was no right move here, there was only doing what his heart was telling him to do. He turned left down Spring Road, and toward the house where Holly had grown up and of which she'd eventually taken ownership when her parents had passed away—or so he'd heard through the small-town gossip mill.

It had started to snow harder, and he clicked his lights down to low beam so he could see through the flurries in the dark slightly better. His eyes were tired and as he eased down the road, the snow crunched under his tires.

He couldn't ignore the nagging in his gut that was telling him to turn around and that he had no business checking up on her. However, it was too late to turn back now. If he did, he'd spend all night worrying about her and second-guessing himself. It was only going to take a second and then he could get some damned sleep.

Tomorrow was going to be just as arduous as today had been—tomorrow, the investigation would go into full effect.

As he neared her house, he spotted a white King Ranch heavy-duty pickup parked across the street. It didn't look like anyone was inside.

The 1970s-style house hadn't changed much on the outside since he was a kid. The only difference had been new gray siding, which did little to mask the age of the place. It wasn't his business, but he wondered if Holly had updated the inside when she had taken over ownership of the house, or if she had left it as her parents had kept it—with the brown and white textured carpet. The carpet where they had lain on their bellies, casually touching feet while they had pretended to watch television. He kind of hoped she hadn't changed a thing.

Her SUV was in the driveway, making him wonder how she had gotten it home—the last he'd seen, it had been parked where she had gone in on the ski trail. Cindy must have made sure she'd gotten home with it, or she'd had someone drive it back for Holly.

As he drove closer, her front door came into view and standing in front of it was a man with dark hair. He was wearing a heavy winter coat and cowboy boots. Ty didn't recognize the guy, but he slowed down as he watched the man bang his fist against the door. Every time he banged his fist against the wood, the Christmas wreath hanging at its center shook violently and the glass bulbs looked dangerously close to flinging off and crashing to the ground.

The guy pissed him off. Perhaps it was his intensity to get Holly to answer the door. There was a doorbell, but the guy seemed adamant about beating up the structure.

Ty slowed his truck to a crawl.

Before he reached the King Ranch pickup, he pulled to the side of the road, just far enough to be unobtrusive and unnoticed, but still see the front door and be accessible if something was happening and she needed help.

The man wailed on the door again, this time kicking at the bottom when his knocking went unanswered.

Ty reached for his door handle, readying to go have a talking-to with the unknown man as Holly's front door opened. She appeared in the light, a dark frown on her face. She was wearing a white nightgown that hugged at her frame like wanting hands, and it made her appear almost angelic in the snowy night.

She crossed her arms over her chest, but whether it was from the cold or fear, Ty wasn't sure.

Whatever was going on here, he didn't like it.

He kept his hand on the handle of his pickup, but he didn't open his door. Before he went rushing out to save her, he needed to make sure that she was really in need of saving and that he wasn't rushing in where he wasn't needed and acting like a fool.

The dark-haired man leaned against the doorjamb, moving in closer toward Holly. She stepped back from the man, but she didn't close the door. If the man was as bothersome as Ty was assuming, he would have thought that Holly would have slammed the door in the man's face. Instead she stood there talking and as she spoke her hands lowered from her chest. She looked more relaxed, but suddenly the man she was speaking to stood up straight and waved his hands in the air—the move was aggressive.

She put her hand on the open door like she was about to close it, but the man stuffed his foot inside the door as he continued to wave his hands wildly. Ty rolled down his window, hoping to hear something to tell him whether or not his presence was justified here, or if he was just witnessing a lover's spat.

The only problem was, she hadn't mentioned that she'd had a boyfriend, or even hinted that she was in any kind of situationship or whatever. Sure, it had not been his business, but from the way they had touched, and she hadn't pulled away, he assumed that he was cleared for landing…well, not *landing* her, but at least for seeing if she wanted to go out and have coffee sometime.

The man's yelling cut through the air. "Don't you care about anyone besides yourself?"

She put her hands up and her face pulled into an even deeper scowl. "All I've said is that you can't just show up here."

The sound of the man's hand connecting with the doorjamb was Ty's call to arms. That was it. He jumped out of the pickup and raced over toward Holly.

As she spotted him, her face brightened for a split second before she took on a look of utter confusion. The man with his back to him turned. "What in the hell are you doing?" the man asked, but then as quickly as he spoke, he turned back to Holly. "Is this your new boyfriend? I should have known. You always had a thing for dumbasses."

"Are you sure you didn't catch a glimpse of yourself in the glass, buddy?" he said, nudging his chin toward the door but never taking his eyes off the man.

"Funny," the guy said, turning around to face him. He looked like he was about thirty-six, and he was pale but carried the kind of bulk that made it clear he worked out. He could still take him.

"Knock it off," Holly said, moving outside, her face coming fully into the porch light. "You need to leave. You've been drinking," she said to the guy. "And you—" she turned to face him "—what gave you the right to think you could show up on my doorstep in the middle of the night and be my knight in shining armor? Haven't you done that enough today? I think you need to leave, too."

He was taken aback. She wasn't wrong, but she sure as hell wasn't right—he was not a knight and he hadn't come here to save her. "Holly, I just wanted to make sure you were okay. I needed to know you made it home. That's all."

"I'm here. You can go, too."

"Holly—" He said her name like it was a call to her for forgiveness and a whisper of something more. It made him feel weak in front of the other guy.

The dude put his hand on his shoulder and Ty instinctively jerked away from the guy's touch. The man smirked. "You know…if you want her more than me, you can have her. She is manipulative and cruel. Pushing me away and pulling me back—"

"How dare you," Holly started.

The guy put his hand up, quieting her. "Before I go, though, let me say one more thing," he said, sounding drunker than ever, "this soul crusher is nothing but problems. I'm doing you a favor in telling you to tuck tail and head out, man."

"I've always been a man who makes up my own mind. More often than not, when someone says something like you just did, it means one of two things—you're jealous or you are angry that you'll never have a chance. In this instance, I think it must be a combination of both."

The guy moved abruptly like he was about to strike, but before he did Holly made a squeaking noise that stopped the guy in his tracks.

"Robert Finch and Ty Terrell." She said their names in a way that reminded him entirely too much of his mother. "You both need to get off my porch!" She stepped between them. "Neither of you get to pick and choose what I do with *my life*."

He stood there in stunned silence.

She looked up at Robert and then to Ty, anger flaming in her eyes. "I said *leave*."

## Chapter Seven

Rebecca Dolack answered the door in her oversize floral nightgown even though it was nearly 9:00 a.m. Ty was glad that he hadn't decided to come over in the middle of the night and wake her up to tell her the news of her son's passing. She deserved one last good night of sleep. For the foreseeable future, she would be dealing with all the things that came with death.

"Ty, good morning!" she said, touching her silver hair, which was mussed from sleep. "You should have told me you were coming, kiddo—I'm all a mess." She smiled at him for a moment, but then she must have picked up on his concern and hesitation. Her smile disappeared. "What happened?"

She glanced over his shoulder at his pickup like she was looking for Moose. He hated that she would never see him walking toward either of them ever again.

"Mrs. Dolack, I'm so sorry to have to inform you that Moose passed away last night." His voice cracked and he couldn't help the tears that started to slip down his face.

She dropped to her knees as a wail escaped her, the

sound like that of an injured animal—instinctive and so lingering that he knew it would forever haunt his dreams.

He sat down beside her, pulling her into his arms as she sobbed. He said nothing. There were no words that would make the pain she was feeling any better. Nothing could stop the agony that came from having a soul torn apart.

HOLLY HADN'T MEANT to come off like she had, but the entire situation had taken her by surprise. She had no idea why Robert showed up at her house claiming that he had been so worried about her, and he felt he needed to rush to her aid. He was constantly telling her how he didn't need her, that she was garbage and in the way. Then the next minute, he was telling her how much he loved her and needed her.

He was all over the map, but then he'd accuse her of the same thing. Yet, the only thing she had ever done was tell him no and that she wasn't interested in any kind of relationship. They worked together—and for all intents and purposes, she was his boss, though the way the company was structured it didn't feel that way. Even if they hadn't worked together, he wasn't her type.

He was always making it a point of telling her that he had more women than he knew what to do with. From what she was led to assume, there was no amount of Viagra that could keep him satisfying them all.

Thankfully, they'd seemed to finally come to an understanding a month or so ago that he wasn't interested in her or she in him. Unfortunately, the second she started getting interest from other men he'd shown back up in her DMs. He was such a creep.

No doubt his appearance on her doorstep had more to do with the liquor he'd been drinking than his actual feelings. He didn't care about her; he'd told her as much. He did, however, seem to care about the administrative assistant at their physical therapy office. Maybe she had been the one behind his calling about her being missing.

Regardless of his motivations, Robert had no business at her house. They weren't a thing and they would never be a thing. They worked together, they were civil, and that was all it needed to be.

What she really couldn't make heads or tails of was Ty.

She hadn't even known he had come down from the mountain. From the way he'd made it sound, he had intended on being on the scene for a while. Additionally, from the way things had ended between them, even if he had been back in town, she hadn't expected to see him ever again. Let alone him showing up on her doorstep. If she hadn't been so embarrassed by the situation she was dealing with, she perhaps would have taken the time to ask him why he was there.

Though he had said he was there to make sure she'd arrived home safely, she couldn't come to terms with why he thought rolling up on her and her coworker was appropriate. The only thing she could clearly see was that he had a savior complex.

She hated to admit it especially given what had happened, but it was sexy that he wanted to come to her aid even though they weren't, and would never be, in a relationship again. He was just a good guy, even if his actions weren't quite in line with her expectations or assumptions. And maybe that meant the problem lay somewhere with her.

She tried to think about the situation from his perspective. Robert had been angry. He'd been intimidating and punchy, but she knew well enough that Robert was only being demonstrative, and he'd never do her any harm. He was just bigger than life sometimes.

At least, she didn't think he'd really want to hurt her.

From Ty's point of view, she could almost understand why he thought he needed to swoop in and save her. Unfortunately, he'd caught her off guard and she had responded poorly. At the very least, she owed him an apology.

That night had been fitful, but she had tried to find some sleep before she had to go to work the next day. Her thoughts kept moving between Robert and Ty and how she needed to deal with both of them, but she was left with more questions than answers.

She probably needed to call the Search and Rescue unit and thank them for coming to her aid. However, she wasn't entirely sure that she was ready to speak to Ty or anyone associated with him. Not only was she embarrassed about last night and Robert, but she was also embarrassed for having ever needed their rescue in the first place. Added to that was Moose's death and everything else, and it was clear she had created an unimaginable situation.

She felt so guilty.

Nothing she was doing was right. She never wanted to be that girl. She was thirty years old and creating more problems than ever before in her life. Her grandfather used to say that "when you found yourself in a hole, sometimes the best thing to do was stop digging." This time, not only did she need to stop digging, but she needed someone to take away the excavator she seemed to be doing it with.

The clinic was busy this morning and so far, Robert hadn't shown up for work. According to Penny Reynolds, the assistant, she had yet to hear from him. Penny had said nothing about what had transpired between him and Holly last night, so she had to assume that Penny knew nothing about it.

She wasn't about to expose their ridiculous melodrama and cause more issues.

Besides, if Penny had been going out with him then she had to have known what kind of guy he was. He never made it a secret that he was a womanizer, even going so far as to hit on women in front of her and Penny. So far, he hadn't done it to a patient, as that would have been Holly's line in the sand. She had made that known to him, as well. What he did in his private life was his business and had been up until the point he had tried to include her. Last night definitely changed some dynamics, and they would need to face things head-on.

It was really no wonder he wasn't in a rush to get to work this morning.

After seeing her third patient of the day, an eighty-seven-year-old man with severe sciatica, Penny called her from the front desk. "There's a delivery up here for you," Penny said.

"I'll be there in a second," she said, resenting the fact that she would once again have to be close to Penny today after everything that had happened. It wasn't in her nature to walk on eggshells.

Robert was going to pay for this.

Maybe she could find a way to get Dr. Skinner to agree with her to fire him, or something. She couldn't stand being around him and her ability to withstand him was waning by the day.

On the other hand, if he hadn't acted yesterday, she wouldn't have been alive today. In a way, she owed him her life.

She made her way to the front of the clinic. There were two other, newer physical therapists working today. One was in the pool near the back, and she could hear the murmur of his voice and the splashing of water as he worked with his patient. The small therapy pool gave the place a chlorine smell, but she liked it. The aroma made her feel like they were doing more than most in their field and that they weren't afraid to do what it took to make sure their patients had the highest levels of care.

She really was proud of her business…that was, as long as she didn't delve too deeply into the personal lives of the other owners and staff.

She sighed as she neared the front desk.

Personal lives were personal; she just had to leave everything there.

"Hi, Penny," she said, forcing a smile. "You have something for me?"

Penny smiled widely, her perfect white teeth sparkling in the lights, and she nearly bounced in her chair. Though they weren't that many years apart, she seemed so much younger. "Look." Penny pointed at a large bouquet of red roses and white lilies.

The scent of the lilies wafted over her. She loved lilies. "Did you see who brought them?" she asked, her thoughts moving to Robert. He was probably sending her flowers to the office to apologize for his behavior and to soften her for when he showed up at work—eventually.

"The Peaks Floral shop just delivered them," Penny said. "But there's a card, right there. Hurry. Open it. I'm *dying* to see who they are from." She clenched her hands together and held them to her chest like a kid waiting to open their Christmas presents.

Holly was half surprised that Penny didn't just stand up and hop from foot to foot in her excitement.

It was silly, but she didn't want to open the card in front of the woman who was clearly more excited about the flowers than she was. She appreciated them, but in every bouquet or unexpected gift, there was always some kind of hidden cost. If these were from Robert, the price would be forgiveness—and she wasn't entirely sure she was ready to pay.

Maybe she was just jaded.

She'd have to watch out for that in herself. Jadedness led to bitterness. To her, there was nothing worse than a bitter person; they were toxic as their resentments and anger had a way of spreading to those around them like slow-moving cancer.

"Aren't you excited?" Penny asked, obviously noticing Holly's demeanor.

"Who wouldn't be excited for flowers?" she answered, pasting a smile on her face and trying to be nice. She walked over and sniffed the lilies, taking pleasure in them for a moment before solving the mystery of the sender and then having to unravel their intended meaning.

She plucked the white envelope from the card stand and slipped the card out. All it said was, "I'm sorry." There was no signature, and it looked as though it was in a woman's handwriting—which she had to assume was the florist who had taken the order.

She sighed.

"Oh…" Penny said. "Is it a juicy note? You going to let me read it?"

She was surprised Penny hadn't already. If she had, she was faking it well.

"Someone is apologizing." She forced a smile and turned away, leaving the beautiful flowers on Penny's desk. The last thing she wanted to do was spend the rest of the day in torment whenever she spotted them. Whoever had sent them was going to be in more trouble for not signing the card than if they had sent nothing.

If they were from Robert, she'd once again need to tell him that he held no place in her private life. If they were from Ty…well, she'd need to tell him the same thing—and then follow it up with her own apology.

# Chapter Eight

The office was buzzing when Ty rolled in. Everyone was standing around in the bullpen talking about what had happened on the mountain. Valerie, a member of SAR and who worked as an evidence tech for the department, was sitting next to their new hire, Heather Lazore, a twentysomething woman, in the corner trying—but failing—to conceal her sobbing. Her face was buried in her hands and her shoulders were rounded and bobbing as she cried. Valerie was patting her back and trying to console her, but her face was expressionless.

Ty considered going over to console the woman and take over for Valerie, but he struggled to understand this reaction. She hadn't worked there long enough to have been in Moose's bed.

Her reaction was over-the-top and he had to walk away in order to not dislike her for her outburst. When he hurt, he only wanted to be left the hell alone.

Moose wouldn't have wanted a public display like hers, a yowling false lamentation. If the tables had been turned, and he had been the one to die, Moose would have probably already been cracking jokes about his final fiery destination.

He smiled at the thought.

A lump formed in his throat as he thought about Moose. His emotions threatened to get the better of him, but he suppressed the urge to feel. Action was always the answer.

In the academy, he'd spent weeks learning that inaction only meant one thing—death. He didn't want to test that lesson.

One of the other detectives, Detective Leo West, waved at him and motioned to Ty's office. The day of closed-door meetings was about to happen. He internally moaned. He needed to be out on the hill, hitting the investigation in full force, not sitting in his office and hand-holding.

He nodded at West, putting his finger up and letting him know it would be a minute. First things first, he needed to be the leader the sheriff had wanted him to be. "Hey, guys," he said, loudly enough to get everyone's attention. He hadn't prepared to do this, but someone had to say something about what had happened and his shoulders were wide enough to bear the weight.

"As all of you have heard by now, our brother in blue George 'Moose' Dolack has died." He stopped, thinking about how much he hated the word *died*. It didn't feel right. Moose hadn't merely died, he left everyone under circumstances that none of them wished upon even their greatest enemies. "The sheriff has let me know that there is a counselor available for anyone to go to and talk about what has happened. I strongly urge you to take this opportunity to seek help and get things right within you. We are all equal members of this department and, as such, we are only as strong as our weakest member. Be strong, take care of yourself and take care of your team. If anyone needs to talk to me—" he motioned at West again "—I will be in my office and available whenever my door is open."

Heather's cry pierced the air, but she choked it back, making it sound strangled and high-pitched. She lifted her hand and excused herself from the work area with Valerie by her side.

He felt for her, he really did, but he was glad to see her go. Hopefully, she would be the first one to see the counselor about her feelings.

As he walked toward his office, he looked in the window. There was a blonde sitting in the hard blue plastic chair right across from his desk. He didn't recognize the back of the woman's head, but seeing anyone in his office and waiting for him when he first arrived made his stomach clench.

This day just kept getting better.

He turned to West who was tagging along behind him. "Looks like someone already beat you to the punch." He nudged his chin in the direction of the woman in his office.

"I need to talk to you about this Moose thing." West looked serious, but then when it came to this incident, most were. His gaze moved in the direction of the wailing Heather and Valerie.

"I'll be with you as soon as I handle *this*." He sighed.

West looked hesitant, as though whatever he wanted to

talk about was of the utmost importance and he couldn't give up easily.

"I promise," Ty added, trying to reassure the guy.

Finally, West seemed appeased.

He cleared his throat before he stepped into the doorway of his office. The blonde turned to face him, and she had a surprised expression on her face as though she hadn't been expecting him even though she had been sitting in his office.

*Holly.*

He was shocked to see her. Of all the people he would have guessed to find sitting in his private sanctum, the last person he would have predicted was the woman who had recently kicked him out of hers.

"Ty," she said, making his name sound even more clipped than it was.

"How can I help you?" he asked, walking in and closing the door behind him. His heart was racing as though he was walking into an interrogation, but the one being interrogated was him.

"I think I should—"

"Apologize?" he said, cutting her off. "Don't worry about it. As far as I can tell, you and I were always on different pages. Since we have known each other, we have never quite fit into each other's lives when and where we think we should."

She quirked an eyebrow and stared at him like she was searching his face for answers. "You think you should fit into my life? Now?"

He ran his hand over his face and stepped behind his desk, leaving his back toward her for a second longer than necessary in order to gain control over his mouth. He turned. She had a tiny smirk on her lips. "That's... I just mean you and I—"

"Just stop," she said with a smile. "I know what you mean, I only wanted to watch you try to explain yourself. I've thought about *us* since you helped me up there, too. It's normal to dredge up the past when put into situations like we were. That doesn't mean anything needs to come from our thoughts. We are old enough to know we are incompatible—at best."

He sighed, the simple action was like a pressure valve on his soul. If she thought they were *incompatible* then he didn't need to delve into any of his feelings. Things between them were not going anywhere and he could focus on everything else going on in his life. "You were always one to be direct."

"I find it can help to face some things head-on." She squirmed, like she was thinking about something, and her gaze moved to his desk.

He'd put everything sensitive out of sight and locked away, but he suddenly felt overly exposed for a variety of reasons. "By the way—" he paused, shuffling loose interoffice memos someone had placed on his desk "—who let you into my office?"

"Don't worry," she said, her smile disappearing. "I haven't been here very long and the other guys in the office never really left me alone. I don't think they wanted me touching anything. Oh, and I didn't if that's what you are worried about."

He had been concerned about that, and whoever had let her in without his being inside was going to get an ass chewing. No one needed to be in his office when he wasn't present. At least he knew she could be trusted. She wasn't the one at fault, and she certainly didn't need to feel guilty about someone else's misstep.

"That's not what I was thinking at all," he lied. "I was only wondering."

She sighed, but he didn't think it sounded like it had come with a sense of relief. "The woman at the front desk brought me back, Heather was her name I think."

"Got it." He scowled but caught it and tried to cover it up as he thought about all the things he was going to say to their new hire. "So, what brought you here today? Is there something you need my help with?"

She looked almost affronted. "I… I wanted to apologize, whether or not you wanted to hear it. And I wanted to explain about what happened last night—"

"You made it clear…we are *incompatible.* If that's the case, you don't really need to explain what happened. You and your *friend* were having an argument. I shouldn't have been there. I shouldn't have interceded. I was wrong, even if my intentions were good. It's fine. I learned my lesson," he said, shutting her down.

One thing was certain, he wasn't about to apologize. He may have made a mistake in acting on his instincts, but he would do it again if he was ever in a similar situation. The key was not to let himself get in a position where he had anything emotionally at stake, again. And that…that was easy enough if he only kept his distance from the woman who'd planted herself in his office.

"I appreciate that you acted. I do." She wrung her hands, nervously. "The guy you saw, he's not my boyfriend and he's not really interested in me, he just had way too much to drink."

"I could definitely tell he'd had too much to drink. However, the rest of what you said I don't believe. Even if you're not currently in a relationship with that guy, he seemed to think that you should be." He tried not to sound annoyed, but he couldn't stop it from entering his voice. "Regardless, it doesn't matter who he is to you. And I don't think that you need to worry about coming here and explaining your situation with him to me. Let's put it in the past. I'm sure he was worried about you, that was obvious."

"Robert has made it clear that he would like to have more than a working relationship, but I'm not interested."

*Oh, this just kept getting better.*

"Was he the guy who called you in as a missing person?"

She nodded her head. "I'm surprised he did. He has women all over him and I really thought he was over this little crush on me."

"Would you say that that kind of behavior was normal for this guy?"

She shook her head. "He really isn't a bad man. He just doesn't always think things through."

"Oh, I have to say, if this was me, I wouldn't be working with someone like that."

"Well, it's a small town, and I haven't been an owner long enough to hire and fire at my leisure."

"Are you trying to tell me that as smart as you are, you don't have options?"

She crossed her hands over her chest, the universal sign that she was done talking about this. He couldn't blame her—this was uncomfortable. Whatever she chose to do in her love life was up to her. It was none of his business. "Look, I didn't come here to be judged by you or to seek life advice."

"Then why *did* you come here? You've apologized, so…" He glanced toward the door.

He was being a jerk, but she had hurt his feelings and he couldn't help himself. He could only put up with so much, and she was testing his limits.

"I want to help with this thing with your friend."

"No." He started to move toward the door to make it clear that it was time for her to go.

"Hear me out," she said, raising her hands in a desperate plea.

He paused, though he should have kept on moving.

"I know I'm not a cop, and I know that there's not much I can do. However, your friend's death was my fault. You can't argue that. He wouldn't have been out there if it hadn't been for me. If you care about me at all, let me be a part of this. I won't be in the way." Her words flew faster and faster as she pleaded her case.

He definitely should have kept walking. When she spoke to him like that, and wore her heart on her sleeve, it pulled at him and it made him soften. He didn't like it. He let out a long sigh.

"I appreciate the offer—"

"Don't." She paused, like she was trying to find the right words to completely unlock him. "I need to do this, or I'm never going to be able to look at myself in the mirror. I can't sit by and watch you and your department struggle." She motioned toward the bullpen where the woman had been crying.

He walked back to his desk and opened up a drawer. He pulled out a waiver. "I can't have you along in any professional capacity, but you have the right as a private citizen to ride along with law enforcement. However, you have to sign this." He slid the paper across his desk and then tossed her a pen.

Her eyes brightened and a smile took over her features, making her even more beautiful and impossible to say no to than ever. This was gonna be one hell of an investigation if he had her tagging along, but he knew entirely too well how she was feeling and the weight that was bearing down on her soul. That same weight was bearing on his. They needed answers, and this was one time he hoped that having all hands on deck would lead to the answers everyone so desperately needed.

## Chapter Nine

After having Penny call the rest of her patients for today as well as the rest of the week to reschedule, Holly left the clinic. It had been a gamble showing up in Ty's office and asking to be a part of this investigation. To be honest, she was a little surprised that Ty had agreed to let her come along with him, but she wasn't about to look a gift horse in the mouth. He must have sensed how seriously she needed to be involved.

Every time she had slowed down or stopped moving, she had found herself thinking about Moose and the way his head had nearly been completely cleaved from his body. Closing her eyes, she could still see the wet, red muscles and the creamy white and grayish exsanguinated flesh.

If Ty hadn't agreed to bring her along, he must have known that she would have been out there in the woods trying to figure out exactly what had happened to Moose. Though Ty seemed to like her, he didn't seem to like her enough to actually include her, so he must have heard the desperation and resolve in her voice and known what she would have done if he said no. She doubted he was acquiescing to her request out of some act of selflessness. He had probably just thought that letting her have some token role in this would keep her from going rogue. This was probably his attempt to keep her in check.

Regardless of his motivations, she was glad to have a place at the table.

After she had signed the waiver, he had planted her outside his office while he talked to several of the other officers. The assistant who'd shown her to the office was silently crying in the corner and one of her coworkers was sitting with her, whispering.

There was the occasional ring of the phones and clatter of typing, but the office was surprisingly quiet. She wondered if that was because of what had transpired or if this was typical. Her office had been livelier than this place.

She hadn't known what to expect when she'd arrived, but she had assumed that his active investigation would not include so much desk work or her twiddling her thumbs in a hard plastic seat outside his door. Yet, here she was. Perhaps, she had romanticized this just as much as she had once romanticized him.

*Why is reality always so much less exciting than fantasy?*

She tried to listen hard to hear Ty's voice from behind his closed door, however all she could make out was the occasional rumble of his voice.

After a while, the woman who'd brought her back here stopped crying. Puffy-eyed, she'd made her way back out to her workstation and her friend had moved back to her desk. Every few minutes, the friend would look over at her with curiosity. She looked to be in her early thirties, dark-haired and toned. Holly found herself wondering if the woman was the kind Ty would have dated.

*No.* He'd made it clear in his office that he wasn't the kind to date coworkers. He also was the kind who had clear feelings on the topic. As much as it annoyed her, she hated to admit that of course she felt the same way. There was just something about him being so judgmental with her that ticked her off.

The woman looked up from her computer and caught Holly looking at her. She stood up from her desk and grabbed a coffee cup that had a picture of a sheriff's badge emblazoned on it. Then she made her way over to the Keurig near the back wall. She hit the button and then, as the coffee maker kicked on, she walked over toward her. "Hey, how's it going?"

Holly smiled. "Good. Thanks."

"I'm Valerie Keller," the woman said, extending her hand in welcome.

"Holly," she said, shaking hands.

"Dean. Right?"

*Of course, the woman knows my name*, she thought, trying to cover her initial surprise at the woman's recognition of her. She had been at the center of yesterday's callout.

She nodded.

"I'm glad to see you are up and running today. I heard you'd been hurt."

Holly waved her off. "Nothing major. Skin glue and butterfly strips were all it needed—I didn't even bother going in to the hospital after I got a real look at it at home."

That being said, it was going to leave one heck of a nasty scar.

"We didn't get a chance to meet, but I was one of the SAR members up there looking for you. My team came in from the bottom of the hill." She smiled, brightly.

Holly didn't know exactly what it was, maybe it was the woman's warmth or the fact that she had tried to rescue her, but she liked her. The woman had a spark, and given the chance, she was sure they could be friends.

"Thank you," Holly said, returning Valerie's warm smile. "I'm sorry I had everyone so upset. It was never my intention."

Valerie shrugged. "Things happen. No one ever wants to be in a situation where they need us, and yet we have jobs for a reason." She touched her shoulder. "I'm glad we got to you in time."

"Me, too," Holly said, nodding as she tried to ignore the guilt in her belly. "I'm sorry about Moose."

"Yes. I appreciate that." The woman's smile faded, and she glanced toward the coffee maker. "Do you want a cup of coffee while you wait for Ty? He might be in there for a while. West had a list of things he wanted to talk about today."

"Did he work all day yesterday, too? You know, before he had the show up on the mountain?" She gave her a sheepish look.

Valerie nodded. "Yeah, but we are used to those kinds of hours. We knew exactly what we signed up for when we chose to join Search and Rescue. If anything, we should thank you for keeping our skills on point. Plus, I must admit that it is fun to get up there on the mountain."

She was surprised by the woman given how the day had turned out, but she was grateful for Valerie making light of the situation.

The woman walked back to the Keurig and grabbed a couple cups of coffee and handed her one. She took a sip and gave the woman a thankful tip of the head.

"By the way, do you work with Robert Finch?"

Holly nodded. "Why do you ask?"

Valerie shrugged nonchalantly. "Oh, he went on a few dates with my sister, Evelyn."

*Of course, he did.*

The woman stared at her, like she was looking for answers in her face. Holly tried to remain unreadable. "Are they still together?"

"My sister said things between them were really heating up. Yet, I think Robert was still seeing a couple other women. I don't know, though. You know how dating is now. I miss the good old days when people dated one person at a time, instead of dating twenty." She gave an annoyed chuckle.

"Oh, sister, I hear you." She glanced back at the closed door. "Robert is always dating somebody new, so I feel for your sister." She didn't want to tell her about Robert's incessant calling and texting, or how he had shown up at her house.

"I tried to warn her off him. I had heard about his reputation, but Evelyn swore that she loved him."

"But she knew Robert was a sleaze?" Holly didn't get it. She wasn't the kind of woman to put up with that kind of thing, or Robert for that matter.

Maybe that was why she was usually single.

Valerie shrugged. "I love her and act as her sounding board. Unfortunately, at the end of the day it doesn't matter what I think—it's her circus, her monkey."

It didn't escape her that the woman had compared Robert to a lesser ape. She glanced back over at Ty's door. While she didn't necessarily agree with the woman's condemnation when it came to all men, she had to chuckle. Besides, it wasn't like women were any better. People were merely *people*.

Ty's door cracked open, and the other officer came walking out. He had a stony expression on his face, as though he had just gotten in trouble. Ty stepped out behind him, watching the guy as he walked away. He disappeared back into his office for a moment before reappearing with his jacket thrown over his arm.

He looked over at her. "You ready?" he asked, like he had been the one waiting for her and not the other way around.

Valerie gave her a tip of the head. "Good luck with him. He looks like he's in a mood," she whispered. "Watch out…when he's like this, he bites."

She could handle the occasional nibble, especially in bed, but she wasn't about to allow herself to get bitten by him.

She stood up and touched Valerie's arm appreciatively before turning away and looking to Ty. "I'm ready whenever you are."

He rushed past her, barely waiting for her in his hurry to leave the office. Based on his coworker's expression and his behavior, whatever had occurred behind that closed door had been unpleasant.

By the time they made it to his pickup, his gait had slowed from nearly a sprint to a simple march. She made sure to stay three steps behind and safely out of proximity of his teeth.

He opened his department-issued truck's door for her, and she hesitated to get in with him, but he was staring out into the rest of the parking lot and didn't seem to notice.

As he closed the door and walked around to the other side of the pickup, she wasn't sure what she could do or say in order to help him. She also wasn't sure if she should ask where they were going, or what he planned to do. Then again, it really didn't matter. She was here legally, as a bystander and nothing more.

While she was happy to at least have some active role in the investigation, she wished there was something more she could do to make a difference besides being a passenger princess to the snarling beast.

As he roared out of the parking lot and onto the main road, she waited for him to say something.

Was he mad at her? Or, was this solely about something that had been said in his meeting?

She waited, going down the swirling funnel of self-deprecating and questioning thoughts. Finally, just as they were about to get on the snowy road that led toward Bozeman he spoke up. "Are you hungry?"

Of all the things she thought he would say to reestablish communications between them, that had been near the bottom of the list. Or, maybe he was hangry and that was what was really bothering him.

"No, but I can always go for a cup of coffee or something, if you are."

He grumbled something under his breath.

"Look, if you are going to act like a feral animal the entire time we are together, you need to let me ride in the back of the pickup or something."

He opened his mouth like he was about to argue with her, but then clamped his mouth shut for a second. The tension sat in the air between them like a ticking time bomb. "Sorry," he clipped.

"No, you're not." She was poking the bear, but she didn't care. She didn't want false platitudes—what she wanted was honesty.

"You're right. I'm not sorry. I'm furious. I don't know why you couldn't just tell me the truth."

*What? How could he be mad at me?*

"What did I do?" she asked, completely bewildered that she was the cause of his problematic behavior.

"I heard all about your relationship with Robert. I thought you said you weren't dating him, and he wasn't your boyfriend." He stared over at her like he was tempted to stop the truck and make her get out.

She was tempted to, as it was. "I didn't have a relationship with Robert. I don't know how many times I have to tell you that. And I sure as hell don't know where you heard such outrageous lies."

"My buddy back there," he said, jabbing his thumb in the direction they'd come from, "said he is good friends with your *friend* Robert. He let me know Robert had been...what'd he call it?" He sneered. "*Bagging you* for at least the last six months."

*Oh, for the love of all... Is he kidding me?*

She nearly growled. "Robert has a big mouth."

Ty slowed the truck down, but only slightly. "So, you did sleep with him?"

"That's not even remotely close to what I said. Robert makes moves on any woman who even pays attention to him. If I had to guess, he is probably clinically a sex addict. I told you before, and I wish you'd respect me enough to believe me, but I wouldn't have a relationship with that man if he was the last person on earth."

"Has anything physical ever transpired between the two of you?" He pressed one more time.

"Detective Terrell, I do not require interrogation and I stand by my previous statement. If you continue to interrogate me, I will work on Moose's death investigation by myself." She reached down and put her hand on the door handle like she was tempted to tuck and roll out of the moving vehicle.

Ty sighed. "Okay. Okay." He ran his hand over his face like he was trying to wipe his mind clear of the thoughts about her.

She hadn't lied, but she certainly wasn't about to tell him that Robert had drunkenly kissed her at last year's Halloween costume party, or anything else. It was none of Ty's business and it held no bearing on their time together.

"Why is it so important to know about my past? What does Robert have to do with the investigation we're conducting?" she countered, meeting fire with fire once again.

This, this hard-headedness and refusal to back down,

was why they could never be together. That, and a myriad of other reasons.

Ty sighed again. "It doesn't... I just..." He gripped the wheel tight. "West only brought it up because he saw you outside my office. He recognized you. Apparently, Robert had been showing him pictures of the two of you together. I shouldn't have let it get under my skin."

"First, I don't know why there would have been pictures, unless they are ones for our practice. Second, what else did West tell you? I'll be more than happy to clear things up with Robert as soon as I see him. He has no right to talk about me or spread malicious lies about things that never occurred. In fact—" she paused, realizing that now she was the one snarling "—I'm going to do my damnedest to make sure that he doesn't have a job."

That seemed to temper Ty's rage. Though, she was still at a loss as to why he would have been so upset. Even if she had been sleeping with Robert, it didn't have any bearing on what she and Ty were doing, and he had no reason to be covetous of her.

"I know that I have no right to have a say in who you choose or have chosen to date. But I think you can do better than Robert."

She wanted to ask if he had someone better in mind, but she held her tongue. "In that, you won't find an argument with me."

Especially when the man she really wanted was the one at her side.

## Chapter Ten

Ty had been given the choice to attend Moose's autopsy or step aside and allow another detective to be present during the investigation. The thought of being there bothered him, but so did the idea of passing the duty on to someone else who knew Moose. There was only one right way to handle this—he had a duty and role in which to honor his friend.

He glanced over at Holly, who kept making her way right back into his life and into the thick of things. He couldn't deny her anything. As much as he didn't want to, he cared about her too much to ignore her feelings. She wanted to be a part of this, and he could understand why. Although she couldn't have possibly understood what she had just signed up for and how much it would cost her in the long run.

No matter what, he couldn't allow her to join him in the autopsy suite. There were things no one needed to witness unless they were required.

As it was, he was going to have to dissociate like never before when he stepped foot in there. And, though it wasn't something he could admit out loud, he was actually glad that Holly would be there waiting for him when he stepped out of those doors and away from his friend's remains.

As they neared a drive-through coffee shop on the edge of town, he slowed down and pulled in. He didn't need anything, but he also wasn't in a hurry to get to the state crime lab in Billings and the office where they were going to be performing the autopsy.

"What kind of coffee would you like?" he asked Holly, turning to face her.

"You guys really have a thing for coffee, don't you?" she said with a little smile.

He didn't understand her joke. "You mean cops? You know it. We work wonky hours and it helps—we drink a lot of energy drinks, too."

He pulled up to the window to order. "I'll take a blue energy drink, extra cream. You?"

Holly looked at the menu before ordering a plain black coffee. He added on a couple blueberry muffins for good measure.

There was a white pickup that slowly drove by. It had been behind them now for about the last five miles. He glanced over at the truck, but as it creeped past, he couldn't see the driver inside. A knot clenched in his gut, though he couldn't have said why.

The girl at the window said their total, but he barely heard her as he handed her a twenty and took their drinks and food. He didn't stop staring at the truck. It was a King Ranch pickup. He had seen one like it before in town— outside Holly's place.

He thought about asking Holly if she thought Robert

would be following them, but he changed his mind. He'd promised her that he would leave any talk about that guy at the door.

He'd grilled her enough.

It was just that Detective West had been adamant that the guy was sleeping with Holly and in a current relationship. He needed to take her word and trust her that nothing had ever happened between her and Robert. Trust, however, had never been his strong suit. He was too deeply embroiled in the world of secrets to think that anyone was above lies and using crime to get ahead.

He was making something out of nothing, and his mind was playing tricks on him. Moreover, he was on edge thanks to everything that had been going on in his life in the last day or two. He needed to relax.

He moved his truck forward just enough to get out of the way of the people behind him in line, but he pretended to pick at his muffin as he watched the King Ranch pickup turn down the road ahead of them.

"Are you okay?" Holly asked, taking a sip of her coffee.

"Hmm?" he said, glancing over at her, trying to reassure himself that some psychopath wasn't following them. If she didn't notice Robert's pickup, then it had to mean he wasn't a threat and Ty was making something of nothing. "Yeah, why do you ask?" he asked, trying to play off his behavior.

"I don't want you to be upset with me," she started, seemingly unaware of the war he was raging with his intuition. "If we are going to work together, or at least

I'm going to be your sidekick or whatever, we need to get along."

*Of course, she thinks this is about her...*

He couldn't explain it, or help her to understand, that his gut was telling him something was more than just off with Robert. And no matter what—and what he wanted more than anything—was to make sure she was safe and well protected. Especially when it came to the man who had been banging on her door.

He would never trust that man.

"Are you going to answer me?" she asked, pulling him from his condemnations.

"I agree. Sorry, I'm out of sorts. It's been a long day. I'm sure you get it. And I'm sorry about the way I've been acting. It's not you, it's me." He heard his last words fall flat in the air. They harkened back to another time and place he didn't want to bring up with her.

"I…" She paused, like she was thinking something close to what he was. "I appreciate your apologies. Let's just start over. Really. Let's leave some hatchets buried."

*Yep. We are definitely on the same page there.*

"So," she continued, "where is it that you are taking me?"

He'd been so wrapped up in his thoughts that he realized how accommodating she had been with his silence. He put his drink in the cupholder and his muffin on the dashboard before easing his way out onto the main road again. "We need to run to Billings. They are rushing Moose's autopsy and I have to be present."

"Autopsy?" she said the word painfully slow.

"Don't worry about it, you are just going to wait out-side." He smiled in his attempt to console her.

She nodded.

As they turned to go toward the highway, there was a *plink* sound. He couldn't quite put his finger on it. There was another, *plink*.

A spiderweb of cracks moved through his windshield around a tiny hole at their epicenter.

"Get down!" he yelled, reaching over and pushing Holly's head down and toward the floor for cover. "He's shooting at us!"

There was the *plink* again as another round struck the glass near where his head had been only moments before.

He slowed down and grabbed his radio, reaching out to 911 as he flipped on his concealed red and blue lights and sirens. "Shots fired. Shots fired. Near the corner of 34th and Main. Send all available deputies."

There was the crackle of the radio and the 911 dis-patcher's response. Units were on the way.

He reached behind his seat and pulled out his rifle, slapping the magazine to make sure it was seated. "Don't move. Stay low and behind cover. I don't want you get-ting hurt. You understand me?" He stared at Holly, who looked wide-eyed with terror.

"Who is shooting at us?"

He shrugged, but he had a feeling he knew exactly who was pulling the trigger—and who was about to go down in a blaze of gunfire.

He always wore his tactical vest under his uniform shirt when he was in the office. Today was one of those days he was glad he went overboard with caution. As a detective, he rarely found himself on the wrong end of a gun, but today just happened to be one of those days.

The sirens blared around them, hopefully doing their job to disorient the shooter or at least pull some of their focus away from their intended target—who was, in this case, him.

He got low, but gunned the gas and raced his truck in the direction of the shooter. They had to neutralize the threat before the shooter grew bolder or started to shoot at innocent bystanders.

In front of him, from inside the white pickup that had been following them, a person—who he assumed was Robert—was pointing a gun in their direction. *Plink.*

*The guy is shooting suppressed.*

The silencer was doing its job, but the muffled gunfire made chills run down his spine.

He pressed the gas harder, all the way to the floor, as he accelerated toward the shooter. One of them was going to die, and he doubted it would be him.

*Ping.*

Another round hit his truck and threw shrapnel on impact. There didn't appear to be any bystanders in his line of sight, but there was definitely the coffee shop girl and who knew who else inside one of the buildings near them. Robert wasn't going to stop until he killed someone.

He placed his gun by his leg, grabbed at the radio and flicked on the intercom. "Put down your weapon! If you do not put down your weapon, we will shoot!"

As he took the corner, his tires screeched on the asphalt and kicked up gravel.

The driver took off, but they were faster. He rammed

his pickup into the corner of the guy's truck with a smash. Holly lurched forward in her seat, and he started to reach over, instinctively to catch her, but his rifle was still in his hand and he was forced to just hold on.

*Damn it. This isn't good.*

He couldn't get in a hot pursuit like this with her in the car. He couldn't put her in more danger.

However, he couldn't let the guy go. He was a risk to public safety.

The guy gained control over his fishtailing rig, and he laid the pedal down. He tore off, and Ty let him gain some distance. Robert's truck was heavier than his, but if he had the chance he would ram him again. Next time, into something that could help to stop him. If he stayed on the highway, there was a line of concrete medians that could act as rams.

He called in to dispatch. "Let's get another unit ready to throw spike strips two miles out." He gave them the mile marker where they could safely neutralize the vehicle.

There were a few junctions before that point, but if Robert stayed on the highway they needed to get him stopped.

He kept a wary eye on the driver, who was constantly checking his mirrors and looking back, watching them. From where they were, he couldn't make out Robert's face for a clear identification. The driver was wearing a baseball hat and sunglasses. He was nearly positive it was Robert, but he wasn't entirely sure.

Who else could it have been? As far as he knew, that

was the only person who wanted him dead—or, who wanted Holly taken out.

He'd been hoping that Robert had just had too much to drink last night. As it was, the guy was acting like he was completely out of control.

"Is Robert's behavior…this disregard for safety and focus on you, normal?" he asked, looking at Holly, who had righted herself in her seat but was still carefully hunched below the windows.

She shook her head. "He definitely watches over me. I'd say he's even overprotective."

"Do you know if he has had any history of mental illness or breakdowns?"

She shook her head. "He has always been…not like this, but…*different*. Kind of like an extreme frat guy who didn't completely grow up. You know?"

He put his rifle down by his leg and opened up his computer and tapped away as he also tried to keep an eye on the road. "It doesn't look like he has any prior arrests."

No matter what the computer said, Robert should have been arrested for something by now. He didn't seem like the kind of guy who played by the rules.

The pickup veered hard to the right, down a logging road that went deep into the mountains. The road connected with at least a dozen more.

*Ah, hell.*

From them, he could end up anywhere from Bozeman to Wyoming.

He couldn't go on this pursuit all by himself. There was no way he could safely do this until he had more backup. On those icy mountain roads, almost as soon as a person got off the highway, they lost cell phone reception.

He carefully typed a message to dispatch on his as he drove. The other units were about twenty minutes out. Until they reached him, he decided to stay put and come up with a game plan.

He slowed his truck down and pulled to the side of the road.

"What are you doing?" Holly asked, sounding alarmed. "We can't let him go!"

He nudged his chin in the direction the truck and its driver had disappeared. "He won't hurt anyone but himself up in those mountains. Until I have more manpower, I'm not going in. And I'm not putting you at risk."

"You're putting me at risk by not stopping him now." She sounded angry as she sat up. "He just *shot* at us. You can't let him drive away."

"Who said I was going to let him get away?" he countered, though he could understand from her perspective why she would be so upset.

He was amped and ready to keep going, but he couldn't go full throttle. He had teams, teams of people who were trained for these types of pursuits. And frankly, since becoming a detective, he was not as up to date as his junior team members on tactics employed in a high-speed chase. At the top of his game, when he'd been on patrol, he doubted that the suspect would have slipped through his fingers when he'd attempted the pit maneuver.

The more he thought about how he'd failed, the angrier he became. He should have shot at the suspect. Screw trying to neutralize the vehicle.

As he put the truck in Park, he ran his hand over his face. No doubt this was going to be armchair quarterbacked and picked apart by everyone else who hadn't been on scene and making the tough calls.

The one thing he was better at, and more experienced with, was thinking outside the box. The younger patrolman could chase the driver through the woods. He could find Robert another way. He would simply have to outsmart the man who was so intent on killing.

# Chapter Eleven

Holly was furious. She just couldn't believe that Ty had simply given up the chase. In fact, he'd even seemed almost relieved when three other squad cars showed up, along with a Forest Service ranger and an on-duty game warden who wanted to help with the chase. She couldn't believe that the only person who didn't want to go after this guy was Ty. It didn't make sense.

She was so mad she could have almost spit.

He was out talking to the game warden now, some guy named Aaron. She appreciated that he was being chummy, but talking wasn't bringing their attacker to heel.

*What doesn't Ty understand? He knows this guy is trying to kill me, but he is too busy talking to do what has to be done.*

She looked over at the steering wheel and the set of keys that were dangling from the ignition of his pickup. The lady on the radio for dispatch broke the tense silence inside the cab. "Reports of a white King Ranch being seen on forest road 17890, headed west."

She continued, but Holly's attention was diverted by

the two patrol units, SUVs, that pulled around them and onto the dirt road and headed toward the mountain and what must have been the named road. One of the deputies who had taken the call said something over the radio to dispatch.

Two other deputies had already headed out. Ty and Aaron just stood there, talking.

She looked at the keys again. Maybe she could just start the truck and get his attention and gently remind him she was chomping at the bit.

As if he could sense her frustration he turned and looked at her. She put her hands up, trying not to be too much, but still getting her question of what was going on across. He gave her a thumbs-up.

She couldn't stand it; she reached over and started the pickup, hoping that it would act as some sign that she was waiting impatiently. Ty looked surprised as he glanced over at her and the running pickup. She didn't know how much clearer she could be. He said something to the game warden, and slowly approached the pickup. He walked around to the driver's-side door and opened it, looked at her. "What do you think you're doing?"

She'd screwed up.

Her impatience had won out over her logical thinking. Why did she have to be that way sometimes?

"Sorry, I was getting cold, I didn't mean to bother you." She tried to cover up her mistake.

He glanced at her warm winter clothing but nodded. "You're fine." He climbed into his seat. "I'm sorry that took a little bit—I am trying to get everybody lined up and in place. So far, none of our guys have spotted him, but a civilian just called in with a possible sighting."

She nodded, thinking about what she'd heard over the radio.

"But I did get the search warrant filed with the judge."

"Search warrant? For what?" She felt horrible for having been impatient.

"While my crew is looking for Robert up here, I am going to see if we can find anything of interest in his residence."

"What do you mean anything of interest?" Holly asked. "What are you hoping to find?"

"I think based on his behavior, that Robert may have either significant mental health issues or a drug problem. Do you think it's possible that he's been running drugs out of your clinic?" He shot her a glance, and it made her wonder if he somehow questioned whether or not she would have been involved in something as ethically and legally questionable as what he was assuming Robert was capable of.

"We don't overlap on patients, and I don't review his work, so I guess it's possible. However, he hasn't acted like this before and he hasn't been this erratic, so I'm not sure what is going on."

He sighed.

She could understand his frustration, she was feeling that way, as well. At least his life wasn't the one on the line. Well, that wasn't exactly true, Robert had been shooting at him, too. Part of her wanted to tell him to take her home, but at the same time she was probably better protected with Ty by her side. Not to mention the fact that there was something about being with Ty. Heck, he couldn't even leave her in the truck while he spoke with the game warden without her getting impatient and needing him closer.

It was quiet in the truck as Ty got them going on the logging road. He dialed the phone and held it between his shoulder and cheek. She could hear someone answer on the other side. "Hi, Doctor Schultz, I was hoping to get a report on George Dolack's autopsy. I'm sorry I couldn't be there, however we had an incident arise and I needed to stay close to Big Sky."

The medical examiner said something in the background that she couldn't quite hear. As the man spoke, Ty's expression darkened, and he gripped the wheel hard.

"Can you go ahead and send me your report when you get it written?" he asked.

There was a heaviness in his voice that made Holly wonder what the examiner had told him. It clearly wasn't good, but nothing about this situation had been thus far so she didn't know how she could expect anything different.

They spoke for a few more minutes. She watched out the window as the snow-covered timber flashed by her window while they made their way out of the woods and back toward town. As they neared the intersection where the shots had been fired, she felt her body stiffen.

He slowed down by the little coffee shop. There was a series of spray paint marks where they had been parked and where the shooter had been.

She shouldn't have been surprised, but she was slightly taken aback that so much had been investigated already at the scene of the shooting. More than anything, what shocked her was that other patrol officers had already been there and left in the time that they had been on the mountain. It didn't feel like they had been gone that long.

The shooting had been such a canon event for her, and yet the on-scene investigation had only taken a few hours. It was amazing to think that they were already done and had aggregated their findings. Then again, they were there just collecting information—not passing judgments. As such, there was little gray area when it came to the actual physical evidence.

Once they had parked back at the station, she got out and took a peek at the truck. There were four bullet holes, one in the glass where Ty had been sitting. Oddly enough, it was the only one that had been close to hitting either one of them. Either Robert was a terrible shot, or he hadn't really been trying to kill them. She had to lean toward him being a horrible marksman.

Ty hung up the phone and stepped out of the pickup. He was gritting his teeth and the color had leached from his face as he took a series of pictures of the damage to his work truck. He sent the pictures off on email to his evidence techs. She wasn't sure what to do, or if she should try to get him to talk or to let him stew in silence until he was ready. Maybe she could extend her hand. She yearned to console him.

As though he could sense her feelings, he held out his hand, palm up expectantly. As she looked at his hand, he nudged his chin toward his fingers, like he was trying to persuade a gentle horse to do his bidding. She wasn't the kind of woman to be told what to do, and yet she found herself reaching over and slipping her hand into his. He wrapped his fingers around hers and finally sent her a small smile.

He grazed the back of her hand gently with his callused thumb.

There was a sickening lump in her stomach as she thought about how close they had come to being killed. She glanced at the bullet hole in the driver's-side windshield, mere inches from where Ty had been sitting. She grabbed his hand harder. "I'm sorry."

"What are you sorry about? You've done nothing wrong." Ty turned and gave her that sexy half smile that had a way of making her feel safe.

"I'm sorry for bringing all this into your life."

"You don't need to apologize anymore. This chaos, this constant edge of the seat living, that *is* my life."

"You can't tell me that you're getting shot at every day, or that your friends get killed." She instantly regretted saying the last bit.

Why did she have to keep circling back to things that brought Ty pain? It was like she just kept having to put more salt in his wounds.

"No, but there's always something. My life is never really easy. I'm always busy. I'm always involved in some sort of investigation or sex crime or death."

She stood in silence, unsure how to respond other than to simply let him speak. She wondered if he ever just talked about the things he faced.

Though she understood the emotional upheaval that likely came with being in law enforcement, she hadn't thought about the drain it must have placed on him. Of course, things like this were part of his daily life and it threw a harsh light on her own blessed experience.

For her, an exciting day meant that one of her patients had done their exercises as prescribed and were seeing her pain-free; that was what it meant to do a good job or have a job well done. For him, a job well-done meant that he put all the pieces of a death together, or any crime, and made sense of a myriad of perspectives and stories until a condensed version of the truth was exposed.

"For now, I'm going to leave my work truck here so the evidence team can go over it with a fine-tooth comb. I hope you are okay with riding in style." He motioned toward the employee lot where a late-model Dodge Ram pickup was parked. "It ain't fancy, but she is mine."

She smiled, but the action was forced. She didn't mind riding in his pickup, just so long as she was able to continue working by his side. "I don't care about fancy...as long as we are safe and can get some answers."

He nodded, but his face became stern. "Yeah... Did I tell you the medical examiner said that Moose also had a puncture wound to his chest? He said it was consistent with likely being caused by a large knife."

She stopped walking and stood in shocked silence for a long moment. Ty kept walking, but after a moment he turned and came back for her.

"What? But on the mountain...no one had mentioned any wounds besides that on his neck."

"The coroner must have missed it. There had been a ton of blood and Moose had been wearing heavy layers. It's not unusual for the initial findings to be incomplete under those types of conditions." He slipped his hand in hers and helped her toward his pickup and then inside.

She sat staring out the window, half expecting to see the hole and cracking where a bullet had shattered the glass, but she found it complete and unmarked. Someone out there was determined to commit murder—they had completed their job once—what was stopping them from killing them? Or, what if there was more than one killer?

Ty climbed into the pickup and started the engine.

"His death was clearly no accident." She had thought it was possible that he'd been murdered, but she had held out a sliver of hope that it was nothing more than a tragic accident, but that hope had been dashed. "Who was on that mountain that would have wanted him dead?"

Ty shook his head. "I looked at the pictures we took up on the hillside, but it was hard to see anything too distinctive. There weren't any good foot tracks, but the footprints that were in the snow that weren't his were slightly smaller. They were wearing snow boots, but beyond that I have no idea as to who was wearing them."

Holly pursed her lips. "That's not a bad place to start. Whoever murdered him must likely have been shorter and smaller than him. How tall was Moose?"

Ty shrugged. "He was taller than me, but not by much so I think he was probably about six foot two."

"So, he probably wore about a size twelve and a half shoe?" There weren't a whole lot of people she could think of around town who were taller or bigger than what he was describing, but this kind of thinking made her feel as though she was grasping at straws.

"Whoever did it could have been someone he knew,

making it easier to get access to him. What I can't make sense of is who had access like that and why they'd risk murdering him in such a remote area? There had to be other times and places they could have killed him that would have been easier." Ty tapped on the wheel. "I just don't get it."

"Do you have a list of the SAR members who were out on the slopes that day?"

Ty nodded. "Of course, but there were only handful people and all of them were accounted for. No one was alone, they were working in pairs. The only person who was trying to lone wolf besides me was Moose."

"Have you talked to everyone?" she asked.

"I talked to most of the team. We've all been texting after what happened."

"But you didn't talk to any of them in person?" she countered.

"We have a scheduled debriefing tonight, but with everything happening…"

"I think you should make sure that happens. Even if they were accompanied at all times, maybe one of them saw something who could help us figure out what happened up there on the hill."

He sighed, as though he had already been thinking that and she was simply voicing his plans. She should just shut her mouth. He was the detective, and she was only along for the ride. She had to remember her place—or did she?

"I'll talk to them, too."

He nodded. "Sure, but let's work this thing together."

His reaction surprised her. It was a funny thing, sometimes she found that her worst enemies were her thoughts. The only thing holding her back was herself and her assumptions.

She squeezed Ty's hand, grateful that he couldn't hear the things that she was thinking. She didn't want him to know the battles she fought within herself, about not only her way of thinking but also about how she felt about him.

It would be a lie if she told herself that she didn't have feelings for him and that they hadn't been reawakened during this time together. She wanted him in ways she hadn't wanted a man in a long time. She wanted him to take her, to own her.

However, the desire to be owned didn't sit right with her. Men and women were to stand side by side, not to have a man in front and to take control. Then again, there were times when that was exactly what she wanted and she hated it. Perhaps what she hated most was that there was no strict duality in her thoughts and feelings. Maybe what she really wanted was for things to be easy; and for them to have the simple love and feelings that had been at the pinnacle of their youth.

It would be unreasonable to think that they could ever go back to those days and that kind of love. It was also important that she didn't get stuck in the recursive loop of yearning for moments in time and life that had slipped from her grasp like dust motes. All she could do now was to grasp the moments she had as they fluttered by and live them as fully and as greatly as she was capable.

Before she realized, they were parked in front of the chestnut-brown seventies-style house she recognized as Robert's. Ty let go of her hand and opened up his computer and tapped away at his emails. Her skin cooled from where his hand had been pressed against hers. She wanted him…more than just his hand in hers, more than just a simple touch. She wanted *all* of him.

"Did you get what you needed?" she asked, aware that she wasn't only asking about a search warrant or some email.

He looked up at her, as though he had heard something else in her question, as well. "The judge has it now. I think the search warrant will be signed within the next ten minutes or so. In the meantime, we will wait here in case Robert shows back up. We also have other units coming in from DCI to act in a supporting role in this case. You know, all hands on deck."

He looked resignedly at the computer screen like he was willing the judge to come through.

"Do you need to wait until another unit gets here or can you go in without them?" she asked, having no idea what kind of protocols he was supposed to adhere to.

He looked over at her with a slight grin and it made her want to lean over and kiss him. "Nothing about this case has been normal. In fact, there have only been a handful of cases in which we've even needed to call in other counties for partnership assists. I'm sure that the sheriff has been on the phone with DCI all morning, too."

"DCI?"

"It's the division of criminal investigation from the state DOJ. They are out of Helena, and they are the oversight unit that works across the state. In our case, the sheriff will likely request that they come in and handle the entire case as an oversight since we are using resources from multiple counties. It's just another way to create a hierarchy and accountability—especially since Moose was one of our own."

She nodded, understanding why a unit like theirs would be necessary, though she hadn't heard about them before. There was so much that Ty did that she'd never realized and she continually found herself humbled.

"So, in essence, you will be accountable to them?"

He nodded, slightly. "Yes, but I'm not concerned. I'm always accountable to a myriad of people for every choice and action I take. There's a lot resting on my shoulders."

His statement made something inside her shift. He really was an incredible man. He bore so much and was currently facing what had to be one of his largest crises yet, not to mention the personal toll of losing his friend, and he was handling it all with a level of professionalism and aplomb that was truly commendable.

"I wish we had gotten Robert back there on the road. It would have made my job easier. At least I could concentrate on Moose's death. I don't know what it is about this job, but it seems like any time something big happens, something bigger comes along. It's never one thing at a time."

Now that was a feeling she could relate to. "That's how it is at the clinic, too. If there's an emergency, then there is at least one more in the same hour."

She snorted as she thought about the last time it had happened a few months ago, when a man had come in with excruciating back pain and they had found out it wasn't stemming from his back and instead he was suffering from a heart attack. At the same time, a woman came in with neck pain and they realized she had, in fact, broken a vertebra and was lucky not to be paralyzed. Both people had to be sent by ambulance to the emergency room in Bozeman.

The EMS workers had even asked them if they were going to send another and, if they were, if they could just pick them up at the same time in order to save themselves a trip—they had really thought themselves funny.

Luckily, both of her patients had survived and come through their traumatic events.

He moved his computer out of the way and leaned closer to her. "You know...while we have a second..." His gaze met hers and she found herself only thinking about the depths of the darkness at the center of his.

"Yes?" she asked, her voice far breathier than she had intended.

He smiled brightly. "You know...when we get this all sorted out, I'd love to take you on a real date. One that doesn't include search warrants or autopsy reports."

She couldn't help but laugh. "Why do I get the feeling that such a thing would be asking for a lot?"

He reached over and took her hand again. "It would be, but for you...it would be worth it." He lifted their entwined fingers and gave her a gentle kiss to the back of her knuckles.

The unexpected kiss and the warmth of his mouth made her gasp. Her body clenched and she felt a warmth rise up from between her thighs.

He couldn't have known what he was doing to her or what he was making her feel. It wasn't fair to tease her like this...to make her want and fantasize about him doing things to her that were not going to happen.

He looked up at her again and smiled. Reaching over with his free hand, he cupped her face and drew her mouth to his. He tasted of peppermint gum as her tongue grazed his lip. As their kiss deepened, she found that her own urgency was matched by his.

He wanted her.

He wanted her just like she wanted him.

She ached as she opened her legs wide, willing him to find his way between them.

He leaned back, breaking their kiss as he looked down and saw her body waiting to receive him. He smiled widely. Her gaze moved down him, and she found that he was wanting her just as much. Her mouth watered as she looked at how hard he pressed against his pants and down his thigh.

Some things about the past and their relationship she had forgotten, but how much he brought to the bed wasn't one of them.

"Ty…" She said his name like it was a moan. "Do you know how much I missed you?"

He nodded. "Probably half as much as I missed you, Holly."

Suddenly, there was the roar of a pickup and Ty dropped his hand from her face as he jerked his attention toward the sound.

Pulling up behind him was a black Tahoe.

He sighed. "It looks like we have company."

She touched the wetness on her lips. She didn't care about company. What she cared about was Ty and what they had just started and would hopefully, someday, get to finish.

# Chapter Twelve

Ty may have made a mistake in kissing her. However, he just wasn't able to control himself. He'd had to devour those lips, to taste the sweetness on them and revel in the scent of her skin. She had smelled so good, something floral, but he hadn't been able to tell if it was from her perfume or her hair. Whatever it was, he wanted to take it deep into his lungs once again.

He hadn't got nearly enough of her, or gone to the depths of the places he'd needed and wanted to explore.

He needed to taste more of her, to lick every last drop of sweet sweat from her skin as he kissed down from her lips…

He stirred.

*No*, he reminded himself. *I definitely made a mistake.*

Not only was she somewhat the cause of his friend's death, but she was also part of an active investigation. There were so many ethically gray areas in his falling for her again that he simply couldn't take things between them any further.

The sensible part of him was relieved that the detective from DCI had pulled up behind them, ending things. If he got the opportunity to continue things with Holly tonight, or some other time, he wasn't sure what he would do. It would take a will of steel not to pull her back into his arms and show her all the things he'd missed doing to her over the years. He had thought of her so many times.

He had thought he had put all of those old feelings away; however now that he was facing her head-on and being in such close proximity, everything had just come back in waves.

He got out of his pickup, casting one more gaze in her direction as he berated himself. She looked as torn and confused as he was feeling. He took a little bit of delight in seeing that her reaction was much like his own.

"Why don't you wait here for a moment, and let me talk to this detective?"

Holly nodded, but she refused to meet his gaze.

Ty closed the door and walked back toward the waiting detective from DCI. He'd never been overly friendly with Detective Josh Stowe. They had worked together a few times before, and the man was all business and a bit too tall in the saddle for his liking.

The guy was tapping on his phone as Ty walked up. He rolled his window down. "How's it going, Stowe? I appreciate you coming our way. I'm sure you had a thousand other things on your plate today."

Stowe waved him off. "It's nice to get out of the office once in a while and deal with something fresh. I have a stack of cases on my desk I've been working on for months. Sometimes, it doesn't feel like they are going anywhere."

He could understand the feeling. "I hear you."

Stowe slapped the bottom of the window frame as he opened up the door and stepped outside. "I just talked to Sheriff Sanderson and had him give me a status report. And I called the judge. He approved our warrant. Who all's going to be working this with us from your team?"

He just knew Stowe was going to love his answer. "Just you and me."

"That's it?" Stowe looked at his pickup. "Not the officer with you, as well?"

Of course, he'd assume anyone with Ty was a LEO, it wasn't a common thing to have a detective with company. That was more of a patrol officer thing, to have a ride along.

"She's a witness and she knows our suspect. In fact, it is my belief that she is the reason he's gone off the rails."

The other detective nodded, as if this was something he had seen a ton of times. "Relationships, man. It's a wonder that any of us make it out alive." Stowe laughed.

"You're not wrong." He leaned against the back of the truck and took out his phone to look at his emails. The judge had signed off on the search warrant; he wasn't surprised, but he wondered how the other detective knew before he had. Clearly, he must have made phone calls before he'd arrived on the scene. "As I'm sure you know we've already been here doing some surveillance. So far, we haven't seen anything to indicate that our suspect is inside the residence, but enough time has passed since the shooting we believe he may have been able to deposit any weapons he may have used inside. As for his pattern of life, normally during this time of day he is at work. Today, however, that obviously isn't the case."

"What are we looking for inside the home?"

He looked in the direction of the chestnut-brown house. The driveway had been shoveled during the last snowfall; berms of icy snow were stacked on each side. The sidewalk to the front door, however, was still littered with ice and patches of snow. Clearly, the guy wasn't having a lot of guests, at least through the front door.

"Due to the nature of the shooting, we are to collect any firearms, reloading supplies, surplus ammo, bullets, magazines, or any gun-related items. We're gonna need to test them to see if they were involved in the shooting in any way."

Stowe dipped his head in acknowledgment. "I know I told you in text, but I want to reiterate how sorry I am about your friend's passing. Have you made any headway on that case?"

Ty wasn't sure how the detective had gotten from their search warrant to Moose's death so quickly, but he appreciated the guy's sentiment—it was always hard to lose a fellow brother in blue, even if a person wasn't close to them. No doubt, for Stowe, Moose's death acted as a reminder that their job brought continual danger and unknown threats.

"Nothing so far. Just got the ME's autopsy report back. Looks like he suffered trauma consistent with that made by an eight-inch-long blade."

"That's a big knife." Stowe's expression darkened.

"That's what I thought, too. Larger than a folding knife carried by most hunters or outdoorsman. It's strange, but then again everything about his death was."

"That's kind of what I'd heard." Stowe scowled. "He was a good dude, though. Funny as hell."

"I miss him already."

"As I'm sure his girlfriends do," Stowe said, with a laugh. He glanced over at him like he was checking to make sure that his joke hadn't been too soon.

Ty chuckled, trying to pacify the guy. "Moose definitely had a harem. I haven't heard from any of them. He'd been talking about settling down the last time we chatted, but who knows with him."

Stowe stared over at the house. "Do you think that any of them had anything to do with his death?"

Ty shrugged. "I can't see how. The only women on the hill, at least that I know about, were Valerie, Cindy and our vic. None of them reported having a relationship beyond friendship with him."

"What about the guys?"

Ty frowned. "I don't think Moose was dating any of them, either."

"That's not really what I meant, but that's also worth looking into."

Ty shrugged. "Not a whole lot surprises me anymore. You know how it is, you see everything."

"You think we are going to see anything interesting in this place? Anything unexpected?" Stowe asked, nudging his chin in the direction of Robert's house.

Ty stopped leaning and pressed down his shirt, nervously. He had no idea what they were walking into, but he was hoping that it would lead to some kind of answer and at least a resolution in this case. Holly needed to be kept safe and protected and out of the sites of that man.

"There's only one way to find out. Let's grab our gear and head over there." He walked to the back door of his truck, behind Holly and took out his kit.

Holly looked over her shoulder at him. Her blond hair was falling loose over her shoulders, and it caught the sun, making a halo effect around her face. He tried to control the thrashing in his chest as he looked at her. She was so goddamn beautiful that she could nearly make him forget everything else that was going on in their world.

All he wanted to do was kiss her again—mistake or no mistake, at least for those precious seconds he was exactly where he wanted to be and doing exactly what he wanted to do. Kissing her was where he belonged.

She ran her hand over her face, pushing a wayward hair behind her ear, nervously. "Can I come with you? I promise I won't touch anything. I just don't want to be sitting out here, all alone."

Her voice was high-pitched and airy, and he could hear her fear and it felt like a punch to his gut. If he had just taken Robert out on the highway when he'd had the chance, he wouldn't have been putting her back in another compromising position.

He should have killed him. He should have neutralized his pickup at the very least, but in that moment all he could think about was Holly and the situation she was in. He hated putting her in danger; and yet, here he was again, sifting through an impossible set of choices and trying to find the right answers to questions he never knew he'd be forced to face.

He unbuttoned his uniform shirt and slipped it off his shoulders.

"What are you doing?" she asked.

"Getting naked." He smirked. "Is that a problem?" he teased.

Her eyes widened and she opened her mouth to speak, but nothing came out.

"I'm kidding." He pulled his bulletproof vest off and handed it over to her. "You need to put this on."

She took his Kevlar vest and slipped it on over her head.

His body was warm where the vest had rested against his skin, and it brought him a certain amount of comfort to know that his warmth was against her. Even if it couldn't be his body, at least he was close to her.

He opened her door and helped her to pull the straps tight. "It's a little big, but I'd rather you have it on in case something happens."

She glanced up at him. "He's not in there, is he?"

He shook his head. "I don't think so, but I'm not gonna put you at risk. You keep that vest on until I tell you to take it off."

*Or I take it off for you.* Though it wasn't the most appropriate moment, his thoughts turned to him undressing her in the dark. If only things were different.

"Is it okay that I go in there? You know, with everything going on?" she asked, nibbling at her lip.

"I don't want you waiting out here alone. Just don't touch anything and please stick close to me."

The way he spoke made fear rise within her. "You don't really think that he's going to show up or anything, do you?"

It was definitely a possibility, especially if he had some

kind of tech in his house that notified him upon their entry. Weasels had a way of popping up their heads when their territory was disturbed.

"I doubt it," he lied. "This is just to make me feel better."

She smiled at him, mollified.

He held out his hand and motioned for her to step out of the vehicle. Though he was aware that the other detective was likely watching them, he helped her slip from her seat before letting go of her hand.

He closed her door and grabbed his gear from the back seat. He pulled out his spare bulletproof vest and put it on, then put on his shirt and quickly buttoned it before slipping his bag over his shoulder.

Stowe walked over to them. "Holly this is Detective Josh Stowe, with DCI. Stowe, Holly."

Stowe gave her a tip of the head but didn't offer his hand.

"Let's roll." Ty motioned for the detective to follow them as they crossed the street and moved toward the door. He knocked, announcing their presence. There was no sound coming from inside. He reached down and unholstered his weapon. "Holly," he said, turning to face her. "You stay right there. We have to clear the structure. Okay?"

She nodded in understanding.

"Stowe, you ready?" he asked the detective.

The man tipped his head. "Let's do this." He stepped around Holly, giving her a gentle reassuring smile that made Ty like the guy a little more. He might have been a bit too big for his britches, but at least he was still a good human.

He went to the door and tried the knob. It was unlocked—at least he didn't have to kick it in. He opened the door a crack. "Robert Finch, this is the Madison County Sheriff's Department, we are here with a warrant to search your residence. If you are present, come out with your hands in the air!" he ordered.

Holly sucked in a breath behind him as he reached down and opened the unlocked front door. The finding surprised him. It wasn't entirely unusual for people not to lock their doors in Montana, but it was unusual for a suspect in an attempted homicide.

The smell hit him first. It was unmistakable. The coppery-metallic odor filled his senses and settled as a faint taste on his tongue. *Blood. Lots of blood.*

He glanced back over his shoulder at Stowe as he entered the house, looking to see if the other man sensed it, as well.

"Holy—" Stowe muttered. "Are you getting that, too?"

He nodded, looking into the entryway. To his left was a living room, which led to the main area of the house. In front of him was a typical entrance, a coatrack and a closet then at the far end of the little hallway was a set of stairs. At the top step, dripping down the beige carpet was a long trail of red. From their angle it was hard to say with any certainty, but if he had to guess the blood's source was probably lying just out of sight at the top.

He considered stopping and calling in more units, but there weren't any to spare. They had to handle this.

"Robert Finch, if you are inside the residence, put your

hands up and step out where we can see you!" he ordered, louder than before in some hope that the source of the blood wasn't the man who'd gone missing.

There was no answer, not even the barking of a dog in the neighbor's yard. It was eerily quiet, so quiet that he could hear his own breathing and the racing of his heart.

He wasn't known for being nervous in these kinds of situations. If anything, he was typically cool under pressure, but Holly was throwing everything out of whack— she shouldn't have been there. He glanced behind him at her, but she was standing to the side of the open door and all he could see was the back of her hand and part of her side. It appeared as though she had her back turned to them and was peering out into the street.

He motioned for Stowe to close the door. She didn't need to witness what they were walking into. At least he could protect her from that.

He gestured toward the stairs as Stowe closed the door and kept it open just a crack. He liked the guy's style.

They cleared the living room to their left, then the kitchen and the rest of the ground floor of the house. Everything except the blood stain seemed normal and mostly well-kept. Nothing on the main floor gave him the impression that there had been any sort of struggle or fight.

His ankle cracked as he started to ascend the stairs. Nearing the top, he called out to Robert again, hoping the man would reply or appear in the event he was still alive or in the house. Again, he was met with eerie silence.

At first glance, he could make out a trail of the crimson liquid trickling down the hall and disappearing into the furthest bedroom on the left.

A giant black blow fly buzzed toward him, landing on his shoulder.

He hated flies.

Flies only meant one thing—they were nearing a death scene.

Clearing the hall and the other bedrooms, they worked toward what was a possible crime scene. As they neared the bedroom door, the drone of flies grew louder. He cringed at the sound; it was the same sound that frequented his nightmares. There was the faint aroma of decay, the kind that came with a recent death. For that, he was grateful. If they were finding death it was far better to find it sooner rather than later.

The bedroom door was closed, and he tapped on it, hoping against hope that he would get an answer. Instead, he only heard the buzzing of flies.

He reached down and touched the cold metal handle. Turning it, the door drifted open. The flies lifted into the air in a little black cloud of wings and bodies. There, on the floor in the master bedroom, next to the bed was Robert's dead body. Under his jaw was a small, tattooed edge gunshot wound. Blood was coming out of his mouth and stained the front of his white shirt and jeans. The injury was deadly, but it mustn't have killed him instantly as he may have walked from where they had initially encountered the blood trail—or, someone had moved him.

At the edge of the hole, a black fly moved. Ty waved his hand, shooing it off.

Near Robert's right hand was a Glock 19.

If he had to make a split-second judgment, it appeared as though Robert had committed suicide. However, after years working in law enforcement, he'd learned that the causes of deaths weren't always as they appeared.

## Chapter Thirteen

She couldn't believe Robert was dead. In all the ways she
imagined things unfolding with the man who'd fired at
them earlier in the day, finding him shot in his bedroom
wasn't even near the top of her list of likelihoods. Robert had always seemed like the kind of guy who loved
himself too much to commit suicide.

Then again, Ty had made it clear that until they were
done with their investigation, it wouldn't be known with
certainty whether or not he had pulled the trigger or if
someone else had.

She stood outside the house, looking at the open black
body bag and Robert's remains. Due to the state of rigor,
they hadn't been able to zip the bag all the way. Ty had
placed paper bags around the dead man's hands, explaining it had been done to keep any evidence on his hands
from being contaminated or altered while the body was
in transit.

Robert's eyes were closed and aside from the blood
and the hole, he could have just been asleep.

Ty touched her arm, drawing her attention. "Why don't

you come with me?" he asked. "Stowe is going to take this. We can get out of here and you can get some rest."

She didn't want to rest. She didn't want to leave. If anything, she wanted to make absolutely sure the man who had wanted her dead was placed in that body bag.

Robert had been a friend; they'd spent late nights in the office working out details and treatment plans and now she found herself questioning it all.

He had wanted to sleep with her, that much she had always known. However, she had also assumed he had put his feelings aside when she'd refused his advances.

Everything he'd ever done was for sex.

She was such a fool.

He was—wait, *had been*—such a creep. And somehow she had fallen for a number of his charms and allowed herself to become a victim and luckily a survivor of a failed murder attempt.

She could never trust anyone again.

It struck her how it was the people she knew best who had always proven to be the most dangerous.

At the thought, she glanced over at Ty. Maybe he was different. He cared about her. He was selfless. Maybe those perceived qualities were what made him just as gullible as her.

The coroner went to Robert's shoulders and started to move the body. The dead man let out a sigh. The sound made her jump.

Though she had known bodies did strange things after death, she hadn't heard that sound before.

Ty sighed. "Let's get out of here."

She nodded, satisfied that the man was really gone, and she wouldn't have to see him again.

Ty took her hand and led her down the stairs and out of the house, leaving Stowe and the coroner behind. She took one last look at Robert's house after she got in the truck, and they started to head down the road.

It struck her how strange her life had become. In just a matter of days, everything had come undone and her boring, normal life had turned into something she could have never imagined.

She should have never gone skiing.

Ty reached over and took her hand. "Do you want to go back to your place?"

She nodded, as the thought of all that she had experienced and felt for the last day moved through her. She was suddenly completely and utterly exhausted.

Her gaze fluttered down to Ty's hand. Something good had come from this, even if it was something she couldn't really explore. She gripped him tighter, as if that simple action would keep him in her life even though they both had to know how futile an attempt at a relationship would be between them.

It didn't take long before they were pulling into her driveway, and he was shifting into Park. She yawned, covering it with her free hand as she looked out at the dark windows of her place.

He strode around to her side and helped her out of the truck. It was such a little thing, but he'd done it earlier as well and it warmed her heart. He really was a great man. She loved that he was a gentleman and that he honestly seemed to care about what he did, the cases he was involved in and her.

As they walked toward her house and the moment they would have to say good-night, she couldn't remember exactly why they hadn't worked out before. It was all just some cloudy memory of the past, hazy and muted by time and experience.

She stepped to her front door, unsure of what to say or how to end their time together. There was always the option of inviting him in, as well. Her thoughts went to his kiss and the way she had opened to him. If she let him in, things between them would move to the bedroom. As much as she wanted him and to re-create that kiss, she wasn't sure she was in the right emotional space to make such a rash decision.

He moved beside her and took the keys from her as she went to unlock the door. "I've got it for you." He smiled at her, but there was a question in his eyes that made her wonder if he was having the same jumble of thoughts and feelings she was. He was probably questioning whether or not he even wanted to spend another second in her life.

He unlocked the door and looked back at her. "I know this is probably unnecessary, but do you mind if I clear your house before I go? I just want to reassure myself, more than anything."

"Robert…"

"Is dead. Yes. I know." He nodded. "I just can't ignore the knot in my gut."

She'd not been nervous about her safety in coming home. No, she'd been nervous about other things involved in Ty's being here, but now that he'd brought up questions around her coming back, she found she was nervous about them, as well.

"You don't think Robert like *booby-trapped* my house or anything, do you?" She frowned.

He smiled; the action was forced but somehow still reassuring. "I don't think he was that smart or had any of this planned out. When we get the toxicology reports from his autopsy, I bet that we will learn that he had some sort of chemicals rolling through his system."

"You think he was on drugs?"

"Drugs or a mental breakdown—either way..." His voice tapered off.

Either way, Robert was dead.

What he was saying made sense, but it went against his need to clear her house. If he didn't think that Robert had acted in a premeditated manner, then why did he feel the need to make sure she was still safe? She wanted to ask, but at the same time, she found a sense of relief in his wanting to stick around.

It was nice not being alone after a day like this.

She stepped in through her open front door and made her way inside. Her cat, Chubs, a gray tabby with a belly so round that it slung pendulum-like, strode toward them. He meowed loudly, protesting how much she'd been absent lately.

"That's Chubs," she said, motioning to her cat. "He likes people, but he drools when he is happy so watch out."

Ty came inside and closed the door. He walked over toward the cat and started scratching behind the little guy's ears. The sight tugged at Holly's heartstrings. There was just something about watching the sexy brunette man bending down, his jeans stretched tight over his ass as he cupped her cat's little fuzzy face in his hand. Chubs leaned into his hand and a little bead of drool started to slip from the corner of his mouth.

She laughed. "I warned you. And now that he knows you're a soft touch, good luck having an empty lap. He is a cuddler."

Ty stood up and brushed the loose cat hair off his hands. "I don't mind a lap full of kitty."

There was a lilt to his statement that made heat rise in her cheeks. She wasn't sure that he had meant it to sound dirty, but her sometimes unevolved brain went to the lowest hanging fruit.

"He may not be the only kitty in your lap, if you play your cards right," she teased, unable to help herself as she giggled.

Now, he was the one with a flush in his cheeks.

Two could play his torrid game.

"I…*er*… I won't be long," he said, turning his back as he reached up and lowered the zipper of his jacket.

She smiled, loving the fact that she had gotten to him. "You can take all the time you need."

Her house had been built in the 1970s and it was an open floor plan. The primary bedroom was isolated in the far corner of the house with a large walk-in closet and a huge en suite bathroom complete with a jetted tub and a glass-enclosed shower and an electric fireplace. Her bedroom and bathroom areas were her oasis. There was no better feeling than coming home after a long day at the office and sinking into a large bubble bath.

On really hard days, she would even have a chilled glass of chardonnay while she tried to soak the stressors of the day away.

Ty had his hand on the gun at his waist, and the way he roll stepped through her house made her think about him clearing Robert's house only hours before.

How long would it take before things would get back to normal and everything wouldn't remind her of the trauma of this day?

Probably never.

Time could heal a lot of things, but she doubted it would clear her of the memories of a murder attempt and a dead potential killer.

From the time they'd been shot at to the time he'd been found dead in his house, he could have only been down for maybe an hour.

It was strange now that she thought about it. Heck, it was cold outside. Where did the flies even come from?

Ty made his way over to the two guest bedrooms, opening the doors and peering inside. They didn't have much, a bed on the carpet and each had cheap dressers she'd picked up at IKEA the last time she'd made her way through Seattle on the way to Portland to see her college friends. That must have been at least five years ago.

"You have a really nice home."

"Thanks," she said. "I'm lucky my parents left the place to me—if they hadn't, it would have been tough to buy. Everything has gotten so expensive thanks to the great migration to the western states."

"Yeah," he said, nodding. "You are lucky."

"I always wanted to come back to Big Sky and when

I got the opportunity to be a partner at Spanish Peaks Physical Therapy, I was grateful to have a place waiting."

"Was Robert working there when you started?" he asked, walking toward her bedroom.

"He took his position two years after I bought into the practice." She walked to the kitchen, trying to control her anxiety from creeping up into her core thanks to him getting so close to her bedroom. She could only imagine how she would feel if she was leading the way through that door.

His hand tightened on the grip of his gun, his finger twitching over the release on his holster as he moved through her bedroom door and into her private oasis.

"Have you notified the staff about Robert's death?" he asked.

She shook her head. "I've been getting texts from Stephanie. It sounds like word has already reached them."

He nodded, but his face was pinched. He stepped into her room and disappeared.

She thought about the teddy bear that sat in the center of her pillows on her bed. *Oh, for the love of all that was good in this world, don't let him see the damned bear.*

It had been a gift from her late father, but she didn't want to answer questions as to why a grown woman still had a stuffed animal on her bed. It was juvenile and as far from sexy as she could possibly be.

If she'd been thinking maybe she could have sidetracked Ty long enough to pitch the furry thing under the bed before he'd cleared her room. Then again, he was *clearing* her room. There was no way that he would have let her go inside the room without him stopping her.

She heard the click of her bathroom door opening and the thud of his footfalls on her marble floor. *That bathroom.* She sighed.

He moved around the bathroom and then there was a long moment before he made his way back out to the living room, and her. His hand was off his gun like his search had revealed nothing—and the simple act was enough to make her relax.

He was almost as good as a hot bath.

She smiled thinking about their kiss in his truck. "Anything?" she asked, though she already knew the answer.

*Don't say anything about the teddy bear... Don't say anything...* She repeated in her mind.

He walked over toward her and stopped, putting his hand on her lower back. The action was so unexpected and so sexy that she felt her knees actually grow weak. Until now, she wasn't sure that she had even believed such a thing was real—especially when it was caused by a mere touch.

She turned around, letting his hand slip around to the front of her belly. It made her breath catch. His gaze was on his hand and where her T-shirt had risen and exposed a thin strip of her naked skin. His eyes moved up, and he stared into hers.

She'd forgotten she was wearing her coat until this moment. Inside it, she felt like she was boiling. A bead of sweat slipped down from the base of her hair and down her neck.

"I... I'm *hot.*" She stepped back, away from his touch and the effect it was having on her.

She pulled off her jacket and placed it on the coatrack

by the back door, which led out of the kitchen and toward her detached garage.

Glancing out toward the garage, she spotted a light shining out of the side window and reflecting off the snow. She didn't remember leaving the light on out there. In fact, if she had, it would have been on all day. It was totally possible that when she'd gone out there this morning, she'd flicked on the lights and forgotten them. It wouldn't have been the first time thanks to the dark winter days in Montana.

She motioned toward the light. "I… I need to go outside."

He looked out the window and in the direction she pointed. "Oh, I can get it for you." He smiled, but he opened and closed the hand which had just been grazing her skin. "If you want, we can have a warm drink together when I come back inside. Coffee?"

She glanced at the top of her refrigerator where a bottle of whiskey sat, dusty from the last time she'd even been tempted to have a finger. "If you want, I can make us hot toddies."

"Whiskey?" His grin widened. "You must be ready to call it a night."

"I think I earned a stiff one." The heat moved up from her core again, but she embraced her embarrassment. She wanted him to be as uncomfortable with their proximity and this night as she was.

He laughed, the sound throaty and rough. "I got it for you."

*He did not just say that.*

He motioned toward the garage. "I mean the light...
I've got the light."

She stared at him and the redness in his cheeks.

"I'm sure you do." She took a step toward him, but
he rushed toward the back door, pulling up the zipper
on his jacket.

As the door clicked shut behind him and he rushed out
into the darkness toward the garage, she couldn't help but
feel like once again she'd made another mistake. This
time, she'd come on too strong.


TY CLICKED OFF the light in her detached garage and let
the cold, wintery night air wash over his fevered skin.
Holly wanted him. There was no doubt that if he walked
back in that house that they would end up in bed together.
A bed complete with a stuffed animal.

He smiled as he thought of the bear. Then there was
Chubs the cat. He barely knew that damned creature and
he already loved it.

If he went back in that house, not only would he be
opening his heart to Holly, but he would be opening his
heart to her entire world and all the chaos that came with
it. But how could he judge her for her life when his was
far busier and all-over-the-map than hers.

No two days at his job were the same. He never really
left the office on time. His last relationship had crashed
and burned because of his deep commitment to the sheriff's department. There was always some case, some family, some investigation that required his attention. He was
pulled in so many directions.

She needed a man who would come home for dinner every night, a man who knew when he would need to work, and one who had weekends off to take her on dates. She needed a man who could hold her in his arms as they drifted off to sleep.

He would never be that man. He was married to his job.

He looked back at the house. Thanks to the darkness in her backyard, he could stare straight into her kitchen window. She was standing at the kitchen island, probably making them drinks.

*Drinks.*

*Oh, we will definitely end up in the sack.*

He stood there, staring at that kitchen window for far too long.

In fact, it was so long that he started to get cold. He was in complete darkness and he watched her search the night for him. He didn't move. He didn't want to hurt her or let her down, but he also found himself not wanting her to see he was out there.

This thing between them, whatever it was, was precarious. He had an unspoken rule about never going back to exes, but he'd already stepped in front of that train the moment he'd kissed her.

As she turned away from the window, he could have sworn that instead of concern, he saw a look of relief on her face. That was enough.

He knew what had to be done.

He slipped out of the backyard and toward his pickup. He started it up and rolled to the end of her road, just out of sight of her place. He stopped and pulled out his phone. He sent her a simple text. I'll see you in the morning.

He waited for a response, but he was met with silence.

# *Chapter Fourteen*

Holly tried to tell herself that his disappearance in the night didn't bother her. That his leaving was the smartest thing either of them could have done. Moreover, she tried to convince herself that the ache in her chest and the pain that she felt at his rejection was just a figment of her imagination. She didn't care that he'd left her. Alone. Waiting. Wanting him.

*Gah.*

She hadn't slept well. And though she was aware it was petty, she hoped he hadn't slept well, either. At the very least, she hoped that he stared at the ceiling for a while, second-guessing his choice.

She highly doubted it, though.

He was always the guy who had his act together. Always so damned perfect.

She'd never measure up to him. She'd always be the lesser if they ever thought about dating again.

Yet, if he was so *perfect* then why had he kissed her? A perfect man wouldn't have done what he'd done and then left her waiting in her kitchen for him to come back from the garage. If anything, he was a coward.

She could do better than a coward.

However, a coward wouldn't have interceded the other night with Robert on her doorstep.

*Robert.*

His body was now resting in a cooler somewhere and here she was worried about some ridiculous kiss.

Yes, that's what it was...*ridiculous.* And she was ridiculous for thinking it was anything more than some impulsive decision. Ty'd probably not even given it another thought. If anything, he was probably the kind of guy who kissed a woman whenever the opportunity arose. Opportunities she was sure came quite often. He was far too charming and entirely too handsome for women not to fall upon his feet...*or onto somewhere else for that matter.*

The thought of his assumed bedroom activities made a spike of jealousy pierce through her. How dare he be with all these other women?

Especially when she wanted him.

*Err...*

No, she didn't want him. And none of this mattered.

She slammed her coffee cup down too hard on the counter and it splashed up, all over her face. Hot coffee dripped down her cheek. A droplet had even landed on her eyelashes.

"Damn it..." she cussed, irritated with herself and her feelings and thoughts.

She was never skiing again.

But...she loved to ski.

She wiped up the coffee on her marble countertop. There was a tap on the door, the sound making her jump.

If that was Ty, she was going to give him a piece of her mind. She huffed as she flipped the kitchen towel over her shoulder and stomped toward the door.

Standing on the other side of the door was Detective Stowe.

"Detective," she said in greeting, slightly taken aback by his sudden presence in her doorway. "How can I help you?" She opened the door wide and stepped out of the way and motioned for him to come inside.

"Hello, Ms. Dean, how are you doing this morning?" he asked, stepping inside from the cold as she shut the door behind him.

"I'm fine. Surprised to see you. Is everything okay?" She paused as a horrible thought struck her and made her stomach sour. "Is *Ty* okay?"

He nodded, waving her off. "Absolutely, he's just fine. In fact, I don't even think he knows I'm here this morning. I haven't spoken to him since the last time I saw you two."

A sense of relief washed over her. So many things had gone wrong in her life, and she could have dealt with any number more, but Ty getting hurt would definitely push her over the edge.

"Would you like some coffee?" she asked. "I was just having some," she said, pointing toward the kitchen.

The detective smiled. "I can see that," he said, motioning toward her shirt and the coffee stain on her breast. "And thanks for the offer, but I already had my cup for the day."

She dabbed at the coffee with the towel on her shoulder. "*Gah.* I'm such a mess lately."

The man motioned to sit on her sofa. She gave him a nod and sat across from him in her large leather chair. She leaned on the armrest and pulled her feet up and beside her.

"So, if you didn't come here for my coffee, how can I help you?"

He scratched at the back of his neck; the action almost seemed like a nervous tic rather than a real itch for him to scratch. "By chance did either you or Ty see Robert driving yesterday?"

She looked up and to the left as she tried to recall everything that had happened when they'd been shot at. "I never saw his face, but I did see the driver once. He was wearing sunglasses and a hat."

The detective nodded. "Interesting. Can you say that you were absolutely sure it was Robert you saw in his pickup?"

She frowned. "I saw, wait *we both* saw who we believed to be Robert. Why?"

"Okay, but you never saw his face?"

She shook her head and suddenly found herself questioning everything about what had happened. She'd once watched a *Nova* science show about memory and how every time someone recalled a memory it was reformed in the psyche. When it happened, glitches occurred and mistakes were made, often in line with what a person *wished* had happened. It was an interesting science, but she had no idea how quickly it would change her memory. It had only been a day, but then how did perspective come into play?

What it all boiled down to was the fact that she couldn't

say with utmost certainty that she *had* actually seen Robert. What she had seen was Robert's truck, and someone driving it.

"If it wasn't Robert, who do you think was driving the truck? Who shot at us?"

The detective shrugged, but he couldn't meet her gaze. It made her wonder if he had an idea, but just couldn't tell her. "You know the interesting part of all of this is that I ran a check on Robert and didn't find any weapons registered to him. I have a guy running a ballistics analysis on the slugs we managed to pull out of the little coffee shop and from the body of Ty's pickup. It will be interesting to see what he comes back with."

She nodded, but all she wanted to do right now was talk to Ty so he could help her make sense of all of this. So, he could corroborate what they had seen.

"I think you need to talk to Ty." She paused, picking at a string on the cuff of her shirt. "May I ask why you came to me with these questions first? It surprises me."

The detective smiled, as though she had caught him in some kind of maneuver. "I can definitely see why Ty likes you. You're clever."

That didn't really answer her question. "And?"

She didn't mean to come off sharp or snarling with the detective, but she couldn't help it. She didn't like the feeling of platitudes and inauthenticity. She also didn't like the thought of the detective taking note of whatever was happening between her and Ty. What happened between them or didn't happen wasn't the man's business. Then again, he was a detective, and he was the one investigating the shooting as well as Robert's death. Perhaps their relationship had a direct impact on his investigation.

The thought made her stomach ache.

She could only imagine standing in front of a judge explaining what was or wasn't happening between her and Ty. She had known she was playing with fire, and she had still managed to find herself in this position. If only she had listened to her intuition and had not gotten involved physically. When she saw him again, she'd have to explain all the reasons they couldn't be together.

"I just wanted to hear things from your perspective before I reached out to Ty. I wanted..." He paused.

"What you wanted was to find deviations between his story and mine. I don't know what you think is going on, or what we did or didn't do, but we have done nothing wrong."

He put his hands up. "Whoa. I don't think that either of you had any direct role in Robert's death. I don't want you to think that for a second."

She had liked Detective Stowe, but he was making her upset. Or maybe, it wasn't he who was upsetting her, rather it was the entire situation.

There was a knock at the door. "That's probably him."

The detective nodded, then dipped his chin in the direction of the sound of the knock like she was free to answer. She tried not to be annoyed as she got up and opened her front door. Ty was standing there with his back turned to her, as he stared out at Stowe's rig.

He turned and gave her a guilty smile.

She was suddenly all too aware that he'd left her waiting last night, but now wasn't the time for them to talk about it. She pointed at the detective's Tahoe. "Obviously, your buddy is here." She motioned for Ty to come inside and close the door behind him.

Stowe stood up and extended his hand to Ty as he walked into the living room. "Hey, Ty, how's it going this morning?" Detective Stowe asked as they shook hands.

"Good, but I could ask you the same question." Ty frowned.

Ty instinctively stepped in front of Holly like he could shield her from harm. She had been right in being concerned that the detective had come here before speaking to him first.

"I was going to give you a call as soon as I left."

Ty crossed his arms over his chest and the simple action made him appear bigger than he had two seconds before. His pecs were pressed against his shirt, and she found herself wanting to touch them to see if they were as muscular and hard as they looked.

*Not now.* She shook off the thought.

"I'm sure I was on your mind."

*He is certainly on mine.* Her mouth had watered so much that she was forced to swallow. *I'm being ridiculous.*

She felt warmth move up into her face as Ty looked over at her and winked. He must have noticed her staring.

Detective Stowe stepped away from the couch. "I was going to call and tell you about Robert's remains and the initial assessment we got back from the medical examiner." He pointed toward the kitchen. "Do you want to talk with me, privately?"

"Just talk, unless you think one of us had something to do with it." He lifted a brow in a challenge.

Stowe sniffed. "No. I don't have reason to believe anything of the sort. So far, it does look like his death was a suicide. However, the time of death has left me with a great deal of questions."

"Okay?" Ty countered. "Why?"

"Well, according to the ME, Robert died in the early hours of the morning."

The strangeness of the time of his death wasn't lost on her. He had killed himself not long after they'd fought on her doorstep.

If Detective Stowe learned about their altercation, would it change his mind about Robert's death being a suicide?

If she told him about what had transpired, she would quickly become his number one murder suspect. She looked to Ty who gently nodded, like he was also thinking about what had happened with Robert on her doorstep.

He leaned closer so only she could hear him as he whispered. "Tell him."

She took in a gulp of air, feeling that in some ways it could be her last as a free woman. "Detective Stowe?" she started, sounding meeker than she would have liked.

"Yes. What is it?" he asked, tenting his fingers as he looked intently at her.

"Robert came over here…the night that I was found on the mountain. We had a fight."

His eyebrows rose, but his expression was neutral. His

gaze remained on her face. "Do you mind telling me what the fight was about?"

She glanced over at Ty. "He… I…"

"He was infatuated with her," Ty said, speaking for her.

Stowe looked over at him with a touch of condemnation on his face for Ty's interference. "Were you there?"

Ty cleared his throat uncomfortably. "I witnessed them on the front porch when I rolled by after the callout. I wanted to make sure she had made it home safely." He picked at the edge of his shirt cuff, but quickly stopped himself and held his hands together. "Robert was angry. He was hitting the doorjamb and yelling in her face. I knew that I needed to step in before the situation escalated."

Stowe nodded. He opened up his phone and took down a series of notes. Watching him made her gut ache.

He turned back to her. "What was Robert upset about?"

"He…" She hated that she had to say it all out loud. "He wanted to be with me. I kept saying no, but he wouldn't listen."

Stowe tapped on his screen and then looked between Holly and Ty. "I hope you two know that this makes things a bit more complicated—you may be the last people who saw Robert alive."

## Chapter Fifteen

Ty watched from the window as Detective Stowe pulled out of Holly's driveway and hit the road. He'd made sure the door hadn't hit the guy on the way out, but he hadn't been sad to see him leave.

He couldn't believe what the detective had told them. If Robert had been dead long before they'd been shot at, there was no way that he had been the one to pull the trigger. But who else would want them dead?

As an officer of the law there were certainly a number of people who didn't like him. However, he hadn't received any credible death threats and, while he was working on a variety of cases, most people seemed to understand he was just doing his job.

One of the mothers he'd recently worked with had come to pick up her son's belongings after he was found dead in the woods. She had been angry that they hadn't gotten to him when he was still alive, but he had taken the time and once again explained that their being in the woods had happened as rapidly as possible.

That case had been a tough one.

As it had turned out, the kid had decided to take his own life after a girl had broken his heart.

Understandably, his mom had been distraught and had a tough time processing the circumstances that had contributed to her son's death.

He'd never forget when he'd initially told her what happened. She had hit her knees and yelled and screamed and damned him, but it had just been her agony talking.

"Holly...is there anyone from your life who would want to hurt you?" Ty asked.

She chewed at her lip. "Not that I can think of...but everything in my life has been turned upside down."

"And I know I've asked you before, but..."

Her entire body tensed.

"Was there any kind of relationship between you and Robert? The only reason I'm asking is that it is *highly* unusual for someone to act like he had when there'd been no previous *romantic* relationship."

She couldn't meet his gaze.

Her inability to look at him told him that he'd been right...there was something she had been hiding.

"Did you sleep with him?" he pressed, knowing he had hit on something, even if it was something he didn't really want to hear.

"I... I let him kiss me. It was a few months ago. Things went further than they should have. And, well..."

"He thought it was true love?"

She shrugged, but from the way her shoulders hunched, she agreed with his assessment.

"You should have told me before." He hated the fact that she had tried to conceal anything from him. Especially something like her relationship with Robert. It was critical to the investigation.

If she could lie about something so important, what else was she capable of lying about?

"I just didn't think it was that important."

"Were you talking to him all the time? Texting or whatever?" He had to push the issue. He had to know what else she wasn't telling him.

Her chin dropped lower to her chest. "We worked together. We were friends. I made it clear I wasn't interested in a romantic relationship."

"But you were talking to him daily?"

She nodded, not looking at him.

"Multiple times a day?"

She nodded again, her chin now resting on her chest in shame.

"Okay, got it." He huffed a sigh.

"I wasn't trying to string him along. I wasn't interested in him like that." Her voice quaked. She finally looked up at him as she spoke.

"But you knew he wanted something more and you continued to talk to him?"

She furrowed her brows. "What happened... It wasn't my fault. He was the one who wouldn't take no for an answer."

He stared straight into her eyes. "Never...not for one second...would I think that what has happened was *your fault*. I think Robert had some issues. Unfortunately, he targeted you."

She shook her head. "That's what I don't understand

though… I know for a fact that he would go out with other women. He was a player."

"How do you know?"

Anger flickered over her features. "He would tell me about all these women who he'd gone out with."

"And it upset you?"

She huffed. "No. I saw it for what it was—some kind of manipulation tactic to show me how desirable he was, and what I was missing out on."

"I can safely say that I don't think you were missing out on a thing with him." He tried not to let his anger slip into his voice, but he wasn't sure it was working. "Do you remember any of the women who he said he was seeing?"

"It would be easier to ask who he *wasn't* claiming to date in the town."

"But you don't think he was actually going on those dates, or do you?"

She grabbed her empty cup and moved to take it to the kitchen. "I think that he was willing to do anything in order to attempt to get under my skin."

"Or in your bed."

She nodded, as she sat the white porcelain cup on the top of the couch and looked at him. "I don't understand men." She ran her finger over the rim. "Did he really think that his being with other women would make me want to run into his arms?"

"I think he just wanted your attention—negative attention is better than none at all." He thought about the last run-in he'd had with Robert when he'd been at this house. "I mean, just look at his display on your front porch. He *had* to have known that wasn't going to advance your relationship, but that didn't stop him from making a scene."

She tapped the cup with her fingers, making a hollow sound. "It also didn't stop him from taking his own life." She glanced over at him, and he could see the pain in her eyes. "Why is death following me?"

"It's not following you; we are both at its epicenter."

She nodded. "Have you ever heard that these things always happen in threes?"

He'd heard the old wives' tale, but he didn't know how much he believed the adage—death was a constant in his world. At this point the body count in his life was more in the hundreds than the single digits. "I have, but I don't put a lot of stock in it."

"I hope there's nothing to it." She picked up the cup and walked to the kitchen. "I don't want one of us to be next," she said the last line so quietly he was sure he wasn't supposed to hear.

He sure as hell wasn't going to let something like that happen.

As she disappeared into the kitchen, he pulled out his phone and texted Stowe.

Do you have a list of the last numbers Robert had called? I'd like to look into the women in his life.

Stowe texted back almost instantly. working on it. Will get u the list as soon as judge signs off.

Holly came walking out of the kitchen, there was a towel still draped over her shoulder and he wondered for a moment if she had completely forgotten about it.

"I was thinking…what did the medical examiner say about Moose's lacerations? You kind of said something about it with Detective Stowe."

Ty nodded, but his stomach clenched as he thought about how their meeting had ended—and how their necks were close to the chopping block. "The ME emailed me the report this morning."

It struck him as odd that Holly would call Moose's cause of death lacerations; it sounded more like something he would have said. However, she'd been around him so much that he wondered if she was starting to pick up on his mannerisms.

In relationships and courtships, one of the common indicators that people had been together a long time, or they were very interested in one another, was that they mirrored each other. In effect, they would adopt mannerisms and gesticulations of their mate or desired mate, in order to create the bond.

Holly was likely doing this unintentionally, but whether it was intentional or not, he liked it. However, they were already bonded. They'd been bonded ever since they were young, foolish and flirting with the idea of dating like mature adults. It was just recently that their bond had truly intensified and moved past the puppy love they'd once shared.

He watched as she swept her blond hair back and away from her face. As she turned her neck, all he could think about was how he wanted to kiss the small hollow by the base of her ear. He could trail his lips down…

She didn't need to do anything else to make him want

her more. As screwed up and as complicated as it was, he wanted her for everything that she embodied.

His mind went to what she had revealed about Robert.

It really wasn't her fault that a man had taken an interest in her—and an unsafe one, at that. He wasn't even upset that Robert had made a move—though the thought made him slightly nauseated. What he was upset with was her failure to be candid.

He should not have judged her for the kiss or the texting, but he *did*. He knew it wasn't okay, but it was hard not to feel like she had played a role in leading Robert on by continually texting.

If he'd been in her shoes, what would he have done?

They *were* coworkers. And based on what he did know about Robert, the dude had probably drawn her in—likely talking about something at work and then subtly testing his boundaries by flirting. He'd likely grown bolder until he was inappropriate, and she'd been forced to say something.

If that was the case, he could understand. And he could also understand why she wouldn't have wanted to admit what had happened—Robert had groomed her.

For now, the best thing he could do was get over his feelings of betrayal. This really wasn't her doing and she needed him to help her understand that and to help her work through her feelings.

"What else did they say?" she asked, pulling him from his turbulent thoughts.

"Who?"

"The medical examiner. About Moose?" she asked, sounding concerned by his lack of focus.

"Oh." He lifted his phone like she could read the email through the black screen. "They sent a little bit more information about the knife wound. It appears that the blade itself was about eight inches long and consistent with what would be a butcher knife shape."

Holly frowned. "A butcher knife? They're really big."

"I know, it's weird. Why would someone have a butcher knife on a mountainside?" He clicked on his phone and opened up the autopsy report, more so that he could control his feelings and thoughts of Holly and to concentrate on something he could better understand.

Holly walked over and sat on the couch, so close to him in the chair that their knees actually touched.

He didn't know if she was touching him on purpose, but regardless, he liked it.

"Did they find any other clues as to who would have killed your friend?" she asked, leaning down and putting her elbows on her knees.

As she leaned forward, he could see down her blue V-neck shirt. The tops of her breasts were right there. So close... His mouth watered.

Clearing his throat, he stood up. He couldn't look at her like that. All willpower would be lost, and he had a job to do. Plus, she had lied to him.

He tried to remind himself of that as he turned around and realized he could see even farther down her shirt from his new vantage. "I'm going to go grab a glass of water. Do you need anything?"

She shook her head. As she moved, so did her breasts. Damn those breasts.

"I just can't stop thinking about that knife," she said as he walked away from her.

He wished he was thinking about a knife right now and not the places his mouth could be exploring.

"Oh?" he said, stepping into the kitchen and leaning against the wall while he tried to regain his composure.

"It's a strange knife and not very functional in the woods."

"Yeah, I agree." He straightened his shirt, pressing out invisible wrinkles. "Most of the people in my SAR unit only carry small fixed-blade knives or folding knives that are around a blade size of three inches or so. A butcher knife would be hard to carry, hard to conceal and hard to use in the event of taking down an animal or butchering. Something like that is more of a statement piece or something someone would use in more temperate climates for bushwhacking."

"Do you think that someone was just trying to scare Moose and things got out of control?" she called from the living room.

He grabbed a glass out of the cupboard and poured himself some water. He chugged it down like it could extinguish the flames of lust that coursed through him. Chubs bumped against his leg and he gave the cat a little scratch behind the ear.

"I have a hard time believing that Moose was murdered. I mean, I know he was, I just…" He sat the glass down and stared at the ripples on the surface of the remaining liquid. "He didn't have any enemies. He wasn't in a location where anyone could have gotten to him easily. And now this knife? Nothing about his death makes sense."

As he spoke, he gave Chubs one last scratch and stood up. Near the stove was a large knife block. One of knives was gone.

He opened the dishwasher and placed his glass on the top rack. The machine was empty, as was the sink—except for his glass and her cup.

*Odd.*

He closed the machine and glanced around the kitchen. The knife was nowhere to be seen. As he neared the black plastic block, he could read the name of the one that was missing—*Butcher Knife.*

He had a sinking feeling that the woman who had him seeking refuge in the kitchen, the woman he'd rescued and protected, could very well be the person who was responsible for his best friend's murder.

## Chapter Sixteen

Ty was acting strange. Ever since they had talked to the detective, Ty had been off. One minute he was touching her and smiling and the next he was physically as far away from her as he could be without going outside, and he wouldn't meet her gaze.

She wanted to ask him what was wrong, but she already knew the answer—she had kept the truth of her and Robert's past a secret. It would be false to think she hadn't omitted details on purpose. She had certainly not intended on telling him everything—she had been afraid that if she told him everything, he would turn away from her and think that she had more with Robert than what had been there.

By not telling him, it had compounded the effects of her fears and made everything a thousand times worse. She should have told him the truth from the very beginning. If he hadn't liked her, or if he had judged her for the mistakes in her past, then he wasn't the man who was supposed to come into her life and remain. She just hadn't trusted that he would see past her faults.

Now, her faults were all he could see.

At one point, she had assumed that when she became an adult, life would get easier and *simpler*. Unfortunately, here she was trying to find love with the right man while also trying to escape the ravaging effects of love inflicted upon her by the wrong one.

She thought she'd handled things well, that she had done what was best to keep anyone from getting hurt— and yet, everyone in her life had either ended up dead or figuratively bloodied.

She didn't know what to do, or how to fix her mistakes. All she knew with any certainty was that she couldn't bring Robert or Moose back.

Maybe there was something about how Ty kept running away—not that he would call it that. However, when things got tough or they were growing closer, he had a way of just *disappearing*.

It seemed to have worked for him, maybe it would work for her, as well?

She glanced toward the kitchen and the back door that led out to the garage—the same place where Ty had disappeared when they'd been about to take things between them to the next physical level.

She'd forgiven him—heck, she'd even understood it. Why couldn't he come her way on this?

"Ty..." she started.

He twitched like she was striking him.

She hated the response and instantly wished she hadn't spoken his name.

"Yes?" he countered, but his feet were pointed directly at the front door like he was ready to run.

"I swear I was never interested in Robert and I'm sorry I didn't tell you everything from the beginning. I know you're mad, but I don't think it's okay for you to punish me."

He looked at her, his expression confused. "What?"

*Is that not what he is upset with?* she wondered, slightly taken aback.

She didn't want to repeat her statement if he didn't know what she was talking about. She didn't want to compound whatever problem they were having by adding more weight.

"You're obviously upset. What did I do?" she asked, earnestly.

His gaze flashed to the kitchen, but then he looked at her. He let out a long sigh. "I... Nothing. Don't worry about whatever happened between you and Robert—that guy was a real piece of work and I understand how you got in trouble with him." He walked toward the door.

She didn't know what he was doing, or where he was going, but it looked like he was once again running away. This time she wouldn't let him. Grabbing her coat, she followed in step behind him.

"What are you doing?" he asked, opening the door and moving to walk outside.

"I'm going with you. We started this investigation together, we are going to finish it together." She stood tall in her resolve. "After we are done, if you don't want to talk to me ever again then that's up to you."

He looked out at his pickup and then back at her. "Fine. Whatever."

THERE WERE ANY number of reasons that the butcher knife would have been missing from the knife block in Holly's kitchen. Ty wasn't entirely unreasonable. Yet, he couldn't stop thinking about the knife and what it *could have* meant. He thought about asking her about it and its absence, but he didn't want her to think that he was looking at her as a potential suspect or that she was complicit with the murder in any way—she was already struggling.

Holly wasn't a killer. She hadn't called in her own disappearance, and nothing pointed at her being involved in Moose's death—other than being the reason Moose had been on the mountain.

He had to be realistic, even if he was still freaked out.

His intuition told him something was very wrong and that the missing knife meant something. However, everything was just coincidental at this point. Everyone had those types of knives in their home, or at least most people did, and it's very possible that it had just been simply mislaid or put away in a drawer and he hadn't seen it. But there was just something in his gut that told him he needed to look deeper.

Then again, from the very moment he had brought Holly back into his life he'd been looking for reasons not to fall for her again. He'd been keeping her at arm's length, and now he was keeping her at blade length, as well.

As he drove toward the sheriff's department and his office, he made sure to keep his eyes on the road. He didn't want to give away his myriad of feelings and questions to Holly. It could hold. Maybe the knife would just show back up, too.

He pulled into his parking space in front of the department.

Holly hadn't said a word since they had gotten into the pickup. He appreciated it.

He got out and opened her door for her.

She looked at him with questions in her eyes, but he tried to ignore them. "Are you going to tell me why you're upset before we go inside? Or am I gonna have to play the guessing game until I figure it out for myself?" Holly asked.

He shut her door and locked his pickup. "I'll get over it. Don't worry about it."

Darkness took over her features. "I don't like this, Ty. I don't like not knowing what is going on inside you. At least give me a clue as to if I am in trouble with you or not. Is there something I can do to make things better between us? Did I say something?"

Her questions made him actually feel bad. Of course she would be questioning herself and all the things that she had done. To her, his coldness had to be strange.

"Seriously, I'll be fine. I just have a lot on my mind."

She frowned, clearly not believing him.

Before she could grill him further, he made his way to the doors leading to his office and went inside. She followed behind him in close step. As he used his badge to gain access to the authorized area, several of the office ladies took interest and stared in their direction. Of course, they would be curious. Since Holly had last been in here, the women of the office had probably learned exactly who she was, and thanks to the small-town gossip mill, they probably also knew about his and Holly's past relationship.

Nothing stayed a secret very long—especially when it came to the office drama.

He gave the ladies a small tip of the head in acknowledgment as he made his way back to his office and his waiting stack of papers.

They could think whatever they wanted. Holly was a blast from his past and now a possible suspect. If they wanted to think anything besides that, it was on them.

He closed his office door behind them and motioned for Holly to take a seat across from him at his desk. "I'm going to go over everyone who was on scene the day of Moose's death. Most people work in and around here, but it may take a few hours to go through everyone."

She nodded in understanding. "What can I do to help?"

In truth, he wanted to see her reaction so he could tell if there was anything to the knot in his stomach.

"Listen... Maybe you can find something I'm missing." *Or, something* you *are*, he thought, but he quickly rebuked himself.

He pulled up the list of SAR members and the report his boss, Cindy, had written about their callout. All the names on the list were familiar and he knew all the people so well that it felt obtrusive and a touch like madness as he started with the first name on his list—Cindy herself.

As he moved to call her, he looked over at Holly. "I know it's a big ask, but would you run down the hall and grab me a drink?"

He was fine, but he needed a minute of privacy.

As though Holly saw right through his ask, she nodded. "I'll give you some time." She motioned to the hall. "I'll be right outside when you're done."

He wanted to tell her that she was wrong, but he couldn't lie. "Thanks," he said with a weak smile. "It won't take me long on the phone here."

She stood up and gave him a terse nod before stepping out of his office and closing the door.

Cindy answered her phone on the first ring. Probably recognizing his office number, she bypassed the niceties. "Did you figure out what happened to Moose?" she asked the second she came on the line.

He huffed. "I was hoping you had," he joked, trying to ease the tension between them and make light of what had happened as much as possible.

"I've been going through everything that happened out there. It just doesn't make sense." There was the sound of cars, like Cindy was driving while she was on the phone.

"I hear you. It's a strange ordeal, the whole thing." He paused. "I read over your report of the callout. You did a nice job. Thorough. Detective Stowe is using it to help conduct his investigation into the death, as well."

"You aren't handling this in-house?" she asked.

"No, too many problems if we did." That was an understatement. If he conducted the investigation, it would be a conflict of interest. And, if this thing was never solved, then he would have to bear the weight of their not knowing what had actually happened to his friend for the rest of his life.

Moose's mother, Rebecca, would never forgive him.

"So, I did a little digging around, about our friend

Moose. According to the people at the grange, Moose had been frequenting the bar with a few different women. One of them was none other than our Miss Valerie."

The news didn't surprise him. Valerie was a member of the SAR team, but she had made a point of always saying she was never interested in dating Moose. It wasn't a secret that most of the time she and Moose barely tolerated each other. But maybe that was why they had gone out drinking together, maybe they had some kind of love-hate relationship. He didn't think they were sleeping together but he hadn't talked to Valerie directly about it.

"I'll look into that. Thanks for the heads-up."

"Do you think that Stowe can handle this? Or are you gonna run with the ball?"

"Like I said, Stowe is running with it, but I've definitely been putting in some legwork. Unfortunately, I have another new case. With everything happening, we need all hands on deck."

"I get it. If you find that you need anything else from me don't hesitate." Cindy hung up the phone.

He really did like her. She was definitely a person with no fluff or falseness.

According to the department's schedule, Valerie should be in the office soon. So, he gave her a quick call, but it went straight to her cell phone's voice mail. He left a quick message asking her just to call him back.

Though it was an interesting lead, he really did have a tough time thinking that Valerie would have let Moose into her bed. Then again, proximity, availability and the number of drinks they both had could have overridden both of their better judgments. It was something he had seen before, and as he thought about Holly, he could understand a person acting against their better judgment.

If Valerie and Moose had been a thing, it still wouldn't explain his death. Valerie didn't seem like the jealous type, and if she had hurt Moose, he was surprised that she would have done it in such an ill-conceived manner. She worked in law enforcement as an evidence tech, if she had done something like commit homicide, she would have been clean about it.

He followed up his call to Valerie by calling the rest of the team. Everyone else was helpful and Smash had even reminded him that he could pull the GAIA, their team's GPS mapping system, that each of them had used to follow their movements while on their callout that night.

To garner the information, he didn't even need a subpoena. All he had to do was reach out to their mapping expert. It would be simple to clear everyone.

He felt like an idiot for not thinking about it earlier. Yet, it wasn't something he had dealt with before. Typically, on a mission, tracking was just a matter of policy in case something went to court. It wasn't until after the fact, and in the hands of armchair quarterbacks, that it was frequently used.

He decided to give himself grace on this one. He had been dealing with a lot of events, which led to even more directions. None of them simple.

He called their mapping expert who aggregated the data, Sharon Cleaver.

"Heya, Ty, how's it going?" she chirped.

She was in her forties but when she answered his call, she sounded like an overly excited twentysomething.

"Doing fine, Sharon, but I was calling to see if you could help me out."

"Oh, yeah? What's in it for me?" she teased, but the way she spoke made him wonder if she was actually trying to flirt.

He couldn't remember if she was in a relationship or not, but even if she wasn't, it didn't matter to him.

He cast his gaze toward Holly. Out the window of his office, he could see Holly was speaking with Valerie in the hall—it was no wonder she hadn't answered her phone. Val was being chatty, and her hands were moving wildly as she spoke. She seemed to like Holly; he recalled her chatting with her the last time they had been in the office, as well.

"I'll have to send you and your team some lunch, Sharon," he said, careful not to put himself at risk for anything that was less than professional.

"Oh, okay." Sharon sounded disappointed. "I guess that would be nice."

"Perfect." He tried not to take any pride in his gentle letdown of the woman, but in his younger years he would have fed right into her advance. "In the meantime, I need to get all the data from GAIA on the other night's SAR mission involving the missing skier."

"Okay," she said, but there was a question in her voice. "Anything you're looking for specifically?"

"I just need to see the areas our teams went and get a little more data on Moose's last location."

"Oh," Sharon said, as if she had suddenly remembered she was flirting with the dead man's best friend. "I'm so sorry about what happened."

"I appreciate that." He cut her off from going any further down that rabbit hole. He didn't want to talk to her about it. "I'll be in the office for a few more minutes, so if you need anything call, but I'll look forward to getting an email with the information."

"Absolutely," she said. "I'm here to help, Ty—in any way I can."

She couldn't help herself.

"Thanks." He hung up the phone and stood up from his desk.

He needed out of this dungeon.

For the first time since Moose's death, he finally started to feel like he was getting closer to answers—even if the answers weren't what he wanted them to be.

He had to hope Valerie wasn't complicit in his death and one of their own wouldn't have acted in such a way. But there were any number of reasons that something could have gone awry and led to this outcome; especially if they had spent time together between the sheets.

And there. Right there…was another reason he couldn't fall for Holly. Relationships only brought disaster.

He walked out into the hallway and Holly looked up at him with a smile. "How's it going in there? Do you need my help?"

"Doing fine. Actually, I need to chat with Valerie for a bit." He nodded in her direction across the bullpen. "What were you guys chatting about?"

Holly shrugged. "Nothing in particular. She was asking how the investigation was going with Robert's death and if you'd found anything interesting."

Her asking was interesting. As the evidence tech, she

had access to pretty much everything he did—at least, everything that had been documented. In fact, she had likely even been on that crime scene while helping to retrieve evidence and had written the evidentiary report.

"Did she say anything about Moose?"

Holly looked at him with a questioning expression. "No. Why?"

"I'm curious, that's all." He tried to sound unconcerned.

He caught Valerie's eye and waved her over to his office before turning back to Holly. "This shouldn't take long. Then we can maybe get out of here. It's going to be a long day." He let out a long exhale as Valerie strode over toward them, weaving between the desks and the chairs that lined the hallway.

"Good luck," Holly said with a smile.

He would need more than luck—he would need a crystal ball.

Valerie made her way into his office, closing the door behind her. He sat down and waited for her to get comfortable. This was one conversation he wasn't looking forward to in the slightest.

"How are you doing with everything, Valerie?" He tented his fingers as he looked at her.

She instinctively looked down at her hands. "I'm not gonna lie, I've been better. Moose's death was really hard on me."

Though he was aware that this was a great moment for him to ask her questions about the nature of her relationship with him, he didn't feel the need to push it. She was being honest about her feelings, and he had to respect that. So instead of saying anything, he waited in silence.

"I'm sure you're not aware, but Moose and I were a lot closer than we let on." There was a crack in her voice that made him hurt for her.

Though he'd assumed that they had been in a physical relationship, he wondered if she and Moose had fallen in love. Seeing her reaction and hearing her speak, it was clear it could have been nothing else.

"He and I had been dating for about the last six months. We had been keeping it very low-key, we both knew that we were playing with fire by dating within the office." She picked at her fingernails.

He wanted to tell her that their assumption had been right. And they had been correct in not making their relationship public. Something like that would have been blood in the water. At least when it came to the gossip mill. Additionally, she would have probably been hit with an abundance of cautionary tales about Moose and his penchant for dating around.

No doubt, she knew all the rumors without anyone telling her. The amazing part was that she had still chosen to be with Moose.

He didn't know if he felt sorry for her, or if he liked her more for her ability to see past Moose's fun-seeking decisions for the great man he was. He could get how someone would have loved Moose; he'd loved the gregarious guy, as well.

"Did Moose know Holly, at all?"

Valerie looked at him, slightly confused. "No. I don't think he even saw her in person before."

The knot in his stomach loosened slightly. At the very least, Holly held no real connection to his friend and as such, no motivation to kill.

"Did you know where Moose was on the mountain on the day he was murdered?" Ty asked.

She shook her head. "I knew he was out there, running the middle line. However, that was about as close as we had come to working together that day. While we had been dating, we had been really careful not to work together in situations that could have later been picked apart by an attorney. It was one of the things that we promised each other, in an effort to avoid any potential conflicts professionally."

"That was smart." Ty thought about his burgeoning relationship with Holly. Maybe if they were careful things didn't have to go poorly.

"We really did try to avoid problems. Had I thought that anything like this would have happened while we were together…" She started to cry.

He avoided looking back at the windows where he knew Holly was watching.

"I can understand how you guys got together. I'm not here to judge you for that. However, I do need to ask you some really important questions about your relationship and your life together. Are you okay with that?"

"Are you asking as a friend, or as a detective?" She looked at him questioningly.

"Unfortunately, it's going to have to be as both."

She nodded with understanding. "Then let me clearly state that I had nothing to do with his death."

"I can appreciate that. Just make sure that you don't go

anywhere without letting me or Detective Stowe know. We don't wanna create any misunderstandings."

And just like that his interview with her was over and a whole new world of potential scenarios opened up, but one of his main concerns had subsided—Holly wasn't Moose's killer.

## Chapter Seventeen

It felt like a wild goose chase. Was this what it was always like doing his job?

For a second Holly wondered if it grew tedious, but then she thought better of it. Even though the circumstances were less than ideal, he seemed to love what he was doing. That was, she assumed so, right up until the point when Valerie left his office.

She looked battle worn and exhausted. Instead of going back to her desk, Valerie made her way out of the office, closing the door behind her. Had she been sent home?

Holly couldn't hear anything that was said in the office with the door closed, but she wished she could have.

When Ty walked out a few minutes later, he looked as ravaged by whatever had been said behind those doors as Valerie did. For a moment, he stood beside Holly, staring vacantly into space as if he barely registered that she was there.

"Are you okay?" Holly asked, worried.

He nodded, but he couldn't seem to find his voice.

"What happened in there?" she pressed.

"Detective Stowe is going to have his hands full."

She didn't know what he meant, but she didn't get the impression he wanted to tell her anything else.

"I think I'm done for the day," he said, looking down at his watch. "Do you want to get an early dinner?"

She was surprised. He'd been running on empty and going nonstop for days and after this meeting he was ready to hang up his hat. It must have gone far worse than she had even assumed.

"Sure."

"Is it okay if I cook? I have some steaks and stuff." He sounded tired as he started to make his way out of the office and toward the exit.

"Ty, if you need some rest, I can go home." The last thing she wanted to do was to become a burden.

He shook his head. "You are very welcome at my place, and I want you there. I'm sorry if I'm *off*, it's not you. I just need to come to terms with a few things."

She didn't press and they walked in silence to the truck. He helped her in. When he drove, he reached out and motioned for her hand. It was such a simple thing, but it pulled at her heart as she thought about the fact that he was turning to her for comfort.

She was dying to know what all had transpired in that office, but at the same time she was glad she didn't. If it was wearing on him as much as it seemed to be, then she couldn't imagine how she would take whatever it was that he knew. He was normally so strong and so put together that seeing him like this hurt her.

The conversation had to do with Moose, and she knew that Stowe had said that there were rumors that he and

Valerie had been an item. From what she could infer, that must have been chatted about—and found to be true.

Maybe that had a bad effect on Valerie's job and Ty had been forced to let her go. Yet, that didn't make sense. As it turned out, their relationship was no longer problematic—unless it had somehow resulted in the man's death.

Was that why Ty was so upset? Had Valerie played a role in the murder?

No, it wasn't possible, or she wouldn't have walked out of the office—she would have been arrested.

The truth was the gray area in the middle, no doubt, and it was understandable as to why Ty was acting as he was.

She would be there for him tonight, though. As questionable as their relationship was, and how much it was starting on shaky ground, she wasn't going to leave him when he needed support the most. Besides, just because they were going to have dinner at his place, it didn't mean that they were going to take their relationship further. In fact, she doubted that was what he had implied by inviting her. He needed away, and he needed a friend.

If history was to repeat itself when it came to their time together, she didn't have to worry about anything happening—he always had a way of running away when they grew closer.

She gripped his hand tighter, like her simple hold could make him stay or at least understand that when he ran away all it did was hurt them. She wasn't going anywhere and if he just stopped running, he would see that she wanted the world with him.

He pulled into his driveway and showed her into the

house. He took out the steaks from the fridge and moved around his kitchen with an easy grace.

She glanced around her as he worked. He had a charming home. It was small and tidy and what a Realtor would have called "quaint." Yet, for both of their lifestyles it was perfect. From where she stood in the small kitchen, she could see into his living room and the small dining alcove. There was a hallway and three doors. Overall, she guessed the place to be about fifteen hundred square feet maximum.

There were a few paintings on the walls of mountains, deer and elk, the kind that she had seen sold at the ranch supply store just down the road from her clinic. One of them was strikingly similar to the moose picture that sat as the centerpiece in her office's lobby.

They really were more alike than she had thought.

"Have you always lived here by yourself?" As she spoke, she realized that she really didn't know that much about his past since the time he had exited her life.

He nodded. "I bought this place from a friend around the time I started working for the sheriff's department. It was my first big adult purchase, you know." A smile finally returned to his features.

She was relieved that she had managed to help him relax and think of something else than his meeting. "Moose helped me move everything in from my apartment. He'd come over from Helena. At the time, he was married to a nurse working over there." And his smile disappeared.

She didn't want to tell him how sorry she was about Moose again; no doubt he'd been hearing a lot of that and not just from her. Guilt would ride within her forever about his friend's death. The best she could do, and the most she could hope for now, was to catch his killer, and help Ty with his grief.

"Even though he had his share of faults, he really was a good friend. I always knew that if I needed anything, I could call him. He'd show up rain or shine. It was why I was so on board with him coming to work at the station. I even talked to the sheriff for him, in an effort to help him get the job. When he was hired, it was one of the best days of our lives. We got to be *Starsky and Hutch* all over again."

This was about the most she had ever heard him speak. And she was glad that he was finding some catharsis with her.

He grabbed a pan out of the cabinet and put it on the burner, letting it heat up. "I didn't go to the bars like he did. I know too many people so going out can be exhausting—everyone wants to chat and I try to keep my work at work—but I never really chastised him for going out and wanting to be social. It was his life, and he had been through one heck of a divorce."

An idea popped into her head. "Do you think that his ex had anything to do with his death?"

Ty shook his head. "I don't think that Tracy would have sprung for the gas to come over and do it. She didn't like him, and they had a lot of pent-up hostility toward each other, but I don't think that either one of them hated the other so much that they would have turned to murder. Besides, if she was going to do that, she would have probably done it during the divorce proceedings."

That made more sense. She knew she was scratching in the dirt.

He threw the steaks on the pan, and they started to sizzle. After a couple of moments, the smell of roasting garlic, beef and spices filled the air. Her mouth watered.

"You know, I don't remember the last time a man made a meal for me." She moved to the small kitchen alcove, which hosted a two-person table. It was the cheap kind with a chipped melamine top and black plastic legs. The two chairs didn't match, and when she sat in hers it wobbled slightly.

"Well, I don't remember the last time I cooked for a woman." He smiled at her. "Be careful on that chair, it's a bit like riding a bronc. You wanna use two hands to stay on." He chuckled.

The sound of his laugh made her pulse quicken. She couldn't recall if she'd heard him laugh in the last few days, but if she had her way, she'd have loved to hear it every day.

He grabbed a couple of potatoes and tossed them in the microwave. She noticed that he had punched far too few holes in them, but she wasn't about to critique his cooking. She simply appreciated it for what it was, an act of kindness.

She'd heard people talk about their love languages in her office, quite regularly. Usually, it was women talking about their partners giving them massages and how their love language was touch. While she appreciated a good back rub or hand holding, what she had always loved most in a relationship was a man who performed acts of service. She was always in so much control and doing and going a thousand different directions that it was nice to be taken care of on occasion. However, she hadn't been pursued by a man seriously in over a year—with the exception of Robert's continuous advances.

Even now, dead, Robert was still trying to ruin her chances for love.

She really did hate the man.

"Are you doing okay with everything?" he asked, looking over at her and apparently reading her like a book.

She nodded, but it was met with a look of disbelief from him.

Apparently, they were both going to talk about their feelings. She'd not had a safe space in which to open up to anyone in so many years that she was a little uncomfortable with the idea. In the past, whatever she had told Robert in passing at work, he had always used it as ammunition to hurt her later. It was opening up to him and allowing him to believe they were anything other than colleagues that had caused the situation that had transpired.

"I'm better than I should be in some ways," she said, thinking about her grief—or lack thereof—when it came to Robert. "And in others, I will never forgive myself." She stared at the chip on the corner of the table. "I'm just going to have to learn to live with it all, though. There's nothing I can change."

He started the microwave with a series of beeps, made sure the steaks were on low, rinsed off his hands, and then walked over to her and sat down. He reached across the table and took her hands in his. "Moose's death..." He paused like he was struggling to find the right words.

"I don't know what happened, or who killed him, but it didn't happen because of anything you did or didn't do."

She looked up at him and stared into his striking brown eyes. He really was handsome, so handsome that in this moment she almost felt like she was staring into the sun, and she was forced to look away.

"What if everything that happened so far *was* because of me? What if Robert was the one who killed Moose?"

He was surprised by her query. "He could have, but why? He had no motive. But even on the off chance he did, it still wouldn't make anything that happened out there your responsibility or fault."

How had he already thought about this being a possibility, while it was earth-shatteringly new to her? In moments like this, it was no wonder he was a detective. He'd found his calling.

"Do you always have all the answers?" she asked, making sure to smile as she teased him.

He shrugged slightly, then let go of her hands and leaned back in the chair. "What can I say? I'm an overthinker."

"I can tell," she said, smiling. "I always knew you were, but I have to say that I think you've gotten better at it over the years."

"Better at it?" He smiled but quirked an eyebrow as he looked at her. "Normally, overthinking isn't what most people would consider a good quality. It leads to problems in relationships sometimes. I'm always wanting to know that the person I'm with is safe and cared for and it can come across like a red flag."

She could see how a woman would think it was. "Are you controlling?"

"Absolutely not, or I try not to be. I've just been at this job long enough that I am protective of the people I care about. Overly so, really. I'm always working on it."

She didn't think that a man taking an active interest in her welfare was overreaching or a negative, but then again, she wasn't looking for the same kind of relationships that she had experienced while young and naive. As an adult, she would expect her partner to be open and aboveboard and request the same considerations from her.

She put her hand out on the table. "None of us are perfect. We all have our idiosyncrasies. My only real dealbreaker, besides the obvious, is if a man refuses to grow and change. I want to be with someone who is always striving to be better for me and makes me want to strive to be the best I can be for him."

"Do you think you can be with an overthinker, though? They say we need the world's best communicators in order for relationships to work." He sent her a dazzling smile.

The warmth of it soaked into her heart and made her lighten. "I'd like to think I don't have a communication problem—I think the last few days can act as a testament to my ability to work through tough situations."

"But what about overthinking?"

She smiled. "Did you just overthink my response?" She giggled. "I can handle it all."

He stood up and moved to her. He lifted her chin with his finger and gave her a soft kiss on the lips. He pulled back and stared into her eyes. "Did I ever tell you how beautiful I think you are? How beautiful you've always been?"

She swooned. There was nothing like the most handsome man she'd ever known telling her she was beautiful. She couldn't help the giggle which escaped her lips. "You already got me to your house, you don't have to lay it on so thick."

He kept holding the side of her face, stroking her hairline gently with his thumb as he looked upon her. "I'd hate to think of the type of men you've been with if you think I'm not being truthful, or that I'm trying to get in your pants. I have a terrible habit of saying exactly what I mean. However, if you're game, I'd be happy to prove to you exactly how beautiful I think you are."

Heat rose in her cheeks, and she fidgeted in the wobbly chair, making it squeak loudly on the floor. "Oh," she said, embarrassed by both his candor and her reaction. "That was one heck of a pickup line." She fanned herself.

He threw his head back in a laugh. "Fair enough, that last part was a little bit close to the line of wanting to get in your pants, but can you blame a guy?"

She was sincerely surprised by his forwardness. Of all the ways she thought tonight would go, this hadn't been on the list. "Do you really want to *be* with me? You've been so hot and cold with me—you know, like the other night when you disappeared from my house. Until you texted, I was actually worried about you."

He dropped his head in shame. "I apologize for that. I do. I… It's just been a long couple of weeks—for both of us. I didn't want to muddle things between us."

"But you are okay with taking that next step now?"

She gently grazed her lips where he had touched hers. "I mean, I know that my stopping this isn't sexy, and I love being kissed, but I just want to make sure that you are thinking clearly."

He ran his hand against the back of his neck and sighed. After a second of awkward silence, he stood up and made his way over to the stove. He moved the steaks around, like they needed his full attention.

"It is ridiculous of me to want you, but the heart wants what the heart wants."

"It's ridiculous?" she countered, a pang of agony shooting through her.

"You're right, on paper *we* are a bad idea. We have already tried it once—"

"We were young, and you broke up with me," she argued, not letting him finish.

"Okay, but I didn't break up with you—you broke up with me." He smiled. "But besides that, we are going to come under the microscope. Detective Stowe already thinks we are an item, and he is going to be asking a ton of questions."

"If he already thinks we are, then what is the difference? If we are going to be judged..." She paused. "Wait, your private life is your private life. You wouldn't be the first person to have a relationship in this town or in your department. Big Sky is a small town, everyone is connected in one way or another."

He put his hand up, not bothering to argue.

"Which means that there has to be something else—" An idea struck her. "Hold up, you don't think I had anything to do with any of this? Some small part of you that is worried?"

He looked at her with a wide-eyed expression, almost like he'd been caught. "I don't, now."

She gasped. He'd told her not to feel like any of this was her fault, that she couldn't take the blame and yet, when she pushed with hard questions, she had found the truth—he thought she was in some way responsible. She should have known.

She stood up from the rickety chair and moved to leave. There was no way she could stand one more second in this man's presence. He had lied to her.

He grabbed her by the wrist, not so hard as to be threatening but with just enough pressure to hold her back from running.

He clicked the stove off. "Wait. Don't go. I don't want you to go."

"That's not what I asked," she countered, her lips trembling with anger and hurt.

"I don't think you had anything to do with it. But something had been bothering me. I have a strange question…" There was a look of trepidation as he looked at her. "This morning, when I was in your house, I noticed something."

"Okay…"

"There was a butcher knife missing from your knife block."

She let out a long, annoyed huff. "What does that have to do with…" She stopped herself. That kind of knife had likely been used to kill Moose. "But you know I was nowhere near Moose. I didn't have anything to do with his death."

"I know and that's why I didn't say anything then, but it's been bothering me since I noticed it. Do you know where that knife is?" He looked at her as if he were begging.

She shook her head. "I didn't even know it was missing. And I don't remember the last time I used the knives in my kitchen. I'm the queen of takeout and cheese sandwiches."

"So, you don't know how long it could have been gone? Has anyone else been in your house, besides me, that you know about?" He pulled her closer to him and he sat down and moved to have her sit on his lap.

She hesitated, still angry that he hadn't told her how he was feeling or what he was thinking before this. If he had just brought it up, they could have solved this and things between them would have been easier.

"I have no idea, but I hope you know that I'm not hiding anything from you, and I never want you to think that I was capable of something like murder." It tore at her that he would have even contemplated it for a second. However, he had to have known it wasn't in her nature or he would have said something before.

"I know, and I've always known that." He pulled at her, and as he did, she felt herself forgive him.

She gave in to him, sitting down on his lap. She could never really be mad at this man. He had such a way of calming the storm within her. She'd never met anyone who had the ability to do that for her. That had to mean something.

He reached up and cupped her face gently. "Look at me," he said softly. She did as he asked. "I want you. And I need you to know that no matter what happens, I'm in your corner. Do you want to be with me? If you don't want me, I understand."

She melted and she leaned into him, putting her forehead against his. "Ty, I've always wanted you. There's never been a question about that."

He pulled her in, taking her lips with his.

He kissed her in a way she had forgotten even existed. It was deep and charged, silently speaking of wants and desires, and the kind that made promises. She spread her lips open as the kiss deepened and they grew hungrier, their tongues moving faster and more manic.

"Ty... I want you..." she whispered into his mouth. "I want you inside of me."

He stood up, helping her to wrap her legs around him. He sat her on the top of the table. "I want you, too. I want you *now.*"

She reached down, feeling how badly he wanted her. Her body was aching for him. She unzipped his pants, stroking him over his smooth boxers. He was so big. Her mouth watered for him.

He kissed down her neck, cupping her breasts in his hand as he swept his kiss lower along the edge of her shirt collar. He reached down, pulling at the bottom of her shirt. He stopped kissing her just long enough to pull her shirt over her head before burying his face between the creamy mounds of her breasts.

He moaned as he kissed along her pink bra and he pushed back the fabric, exposing her pink nipple. He pulled it into his mouth, sucking on it until it was hard and tender, the sensation of his tongue flipping against her nipples made her pulse race.

She pulled at his pants clumsily until he reached down and unbuttoned them and let them fall to the floor. He reached for her and slipped her pants down her waist, kissing her stomach and down to her panties as he pulled her pants off and freed her.

He ran his tongue over the top of her panties, making her gasp and moan at the sensation of his mouth on her.

That. Feeling. It was so...amazing.

He pushed her panties to the side as he took more of her into his mouth. He flicked his tongue against her, then sucked. The sensation drove her to the edge of madness as he repeated it again and again. She threw her head back as he pressed his chin against her and flicked.

"I'm so..." But as she was about to say the last word, the wave of ecstasy crashed over her, and she called out with pleasure.

He sped up, working her until she was quivering and sensitive. "Stop..." she begged.

He leaned back with a smile on his face. Wetness covered his chin.

"Let me kiss you," she said, barely able to move.

He leaned over and she tasted herself on him. She licked her juices from his lips, and he moaned into her mouth.

Weak and shaky, she stepped back from the table and dropped to her knees in front of him, pulling down his boxers. "Now," she said, smiling up at him as they looked into each other's eyes. "It's my turn."

## Chapter Eighteen

Last night had been, hands down, the best night of his life. Ty had assumed that if he got a chance to have Holly in his bed again that it would have been incredible, but the reality was so much better than anything he could have imagined.

At one point, she'd begged him to bend her over the table. That was one memory that he would never forget. If anything, he hoped that they could re-create that on a regular basis.

That was, assuming that they were something more than a onetime thing.

He picked up his phone on the kitchen counter beside him as he stared longingly at the melamine table where so much had happened last night. He loved and hated that table. Taking his cup of coffee and his phone, he walked over to the table and gave it a light shove.

In their play, the thing had been tested to the max. It moved and swayed as he pushed against it. He would need to fix it and strengthen it if they were going to keep doing as they had.

He smiled at the thought. He would buy stronger

mounting brackets for the tabletop as soon as he got the chance. Or maybe he just needed a table with four sturdy legs.

As he thought about his options, his phone buzzed with an email, and it pulled him from his planning.

He took a sip of his coffee and put it on the table before opening up his email. Both the ME and the mapping tech, Sharon, had sent him notes. According to her findings, everyone on the mountain had been exactly where they had stated—or, at least, their tracking equipment had been

He clicked on the ME's note. They had finally managed to get the toxicology reports back from Moose's body. No foreign substances had been found. As for Robert, he'd been taking large amounts of opiates. The sedatives had only been slightly metabolized in his system—meaning that he had taken a downer in the hour or so before his death.

That was odd.

The first opioid that came to mind was fentanyl. He wasn't sure which class of drugs physical therapists had access to, but he would make sure to ask Holly as soon as she woke up.

If Robert was abusing fentanyl, it helped to make some sense of his erratic behavior. It was far more potent than heroin or morphine and just as addictive. Often, people who took fentanyl had instances of hallucinations and auditory and visual disturbances.

What was strange was that Robert had been working. It was shocking that he could be a professional by day and an addict by night.

Then again, he had seen this kind of thing many times before. Addicts came in every socioeconomic bracket. No one was immune.

He looked at the numbers. According to the report, the amount in his system wasn't enough to cause an overdose. The ME had updated the report, and the immediate cause of death was listed as a gunshot wound to the lower mandible, exiting through the top of the skull. They had left the manner of death unselected.

They were waiting for his investigation. He would need to call them. It seemed entirely too possible that it was suicide, but there was something about the entire situation with Robert and Moose that made him question everything.

He pulled up the pictures he'd taken in Robert's master bedroom where they had located his body. He stared at the first image of Robert's head. He zoomed in on the man's chin, staring at the tattooing the gunshot had made on his skin. It was dark and heavy around the wound and the barrel had even burned his flesh, which meant the gun had been pressed directly against the skin when the trigger was pulled.

According to the report, they had found gunshot residue, or GSR, on Robert's left hand, but that simply meant he was in the room at the time of the shooting. What surprised him was that they had noted that there was no obvious residue on the right hand where he would have been holding the gun to inflict such a wound.

He looked back at his phone and the picture of the Glock 19. It was on the ground near Robert's right hand. From the picture it appeared as though the moment he had died his arm and hand had gone limp and the gun had been dropped. It was consistent with most suicides he had seen in the past.

He zoomed in on the image. Something was a little off. He couldn't pinpoint what was strange about it, but there was *something* about the gun's placement that didn't feel right.

He clicked on the other pictures of the gun. From some of the angles, he could see where blood had sprayed back on the gun and dried to the hot barrel. It was undoubtedly the gun used in the shooting, though they hadn't run ballistics on the bullet they had pulled from the ceiling above the body.

As he zoomed in on the last picture, taken from near the level of the gun, he realized what was bothering him. The grip of the gun was slightly under the man's thigh.

If he had shot himself, it wasn't impossible, but it was unlikely that the body would have been atop the weapon.

He stared at the picture and scrolled through the rest in his phone. He had no idea how he had missed this on scene. However, it was barely under his body.

Then again, maybe the body had relaxed after death and moved slightly or perhaps it was an effect of rigor or some death process, which had caused the gun to appear beneath the man's thigh.

Maybe it had something to do with the fentanyl in his system.

Or perhaps he just didn't want to accept that Robert had killed himself. In a secret dark part of his brain, he hated the idea that the man had taken the easy way out of his life after he had caused so much upheaval in Holly's.

"Good morning," Holly said, pulling him from his thoughts.

He was as grateful as he was sure that those thoughts were probably some indicators that he needed therapy.

"Hi, babe," he said, shutting off his phone and shoving it in his pocket.

She looked adorable with her mussed hair and sleepy expression. He handed her his cup of coffee. "Here, you can have mine. I'll make another."

He gave her a peck on her forehead as she took the coffee from him.

"Thank you," she said, her voice hoarse. "Is everything all right? You seem *off.*"

He started to make himself another cup. "Because I gave you my coffee? Yeah, I see how you could get there." He knew exactly what she was talking about, but he was a little surprised that she could so easily pick up his emotions without him saying anything.

"Not because of the coffee. Did I do something wrong last night?" Her face was dead serious.

He realized his misstep. "It's nothing like that, I promise. I never want you to think that. Last night was perfect." He pulled her into his arms and kissed her lips. "You're perfect."

She burrowed deeper into his embrace, and he tightened his hold. A man could get used to this. He'd forgotten how good it felt to have a woman in his life whom he cared about.

"I'm far from perfect, but I'm glad you had fun."

He had a hell of a lot more than some fun.

If he had his way, he would be honored to call her perfect every single day.

"Maybe we can repeat it tonight?" he offered, a sly smirk on his face.

She giggled and the sound vibrated against his chest. He loved that feeling.

The vibrating intensified and as it stopped and started again, he realized it was coming from his back pocket. It forced him out of their embrace as he answered it. It was Detective Stowe.

"How's it going, Stowe?" he answered, slightly annoyed that the man had interrupted what was a great moment—and long awaited.

"It's going well. I was calling about the Robert Finch case. Do you have a moment?"

He grabbed his coffee. He was going to need a bigger cup. "What's up?"

"I got the phone records back from Robert Finch. I just wanted to give you a heads-up that I'm going to send them your way."

"Perfect. Did you get the ME reports? See the fentanyl?"

Stowe chuckled, dryly. "Our boy was definitely using. He had some major amounts in his blood. He'd obviously been using for a while."

Holly's eyebrows rose in surprise, making him realize he had yet to tell her about what they'd found. "That's what I got, too. Still not a factor in his death, though." He cleared his throat. "Did you notice that the gun used was sitting slightly under his thigh?"

"I did," Stowe said. "I have been looking into similar cases. So far, I've only found a couple that had matching scenarios and results. The only time they've had something like this has been when a body has been left in the heat and there's been swelling with decomposition, or if a body has been disturbed."

"Well, that or it was never really a suicide and the murderer screwed up," Ty added.

"I went there, too." Stowe paused. "They pulled prints from the gun, but they were pretty poor quality. I think someone wiped it."

Ty pulled in a breath.

"Yep, exactly," Stowe said, must having heard him. "I'm going to see if we can pull any prints from the brass."

"Let me know how it turns out."

"You got it, and I'm sending you the phone records. Let me know if anything stands out."

"Did you see anything of note?" Ty asked, looking at his phone for a second, looking to see if Stowe had sent him the records.

There was nothing.

"Actually, on his apps, it looks like he was spending a lot of his time looking into Holly Dean."

The news didn't come as a surprise. "Anybody else?" Ty asked, his gaze moving to Holly. He could tell she was listening in.

"There are a few other women it appeared he had been speaking to, but I don't know any of them personally. That's where I was hoping you'll come in and use your local knowledge." Stowe paused. "Also, I was hoping to talk to your evidence tech about Robert's body placement. What is their name?"

"No problem. That's Valerie Keller. She's in the office today, I believe." He didn't add in the part about her being hard to contact on the phone sometimes.

"Great, I'll stop by. I'll be in touch."

As he hung up the phone, he looked over at Holly, who was taking a drink of her coffee. She had a contemplative expression on her face.

"Are you okay? I realize this has to be hard on you," he said, concerned that his conversation may have been the reason she looked as she did.

She sat her coffee cup down on the kitchen counter and looked over at him. "Actually, I was thinking about the conversation I last had with Valerie. Or, I guess it wasn't the last conversation, but when I first met her." She stared off into space as she must have been thinking about it. "She actually mentioned that she had a sister who had been dating Robert."

"What?" he asked, shocked. "She never mentioned it to me."

"Well, it's not like she was dating him and at this point who wasn't Robert dating? Seriously, he was even dating Penny from the PT clinic." She forced a laugh, and it sounded almost painful.

His phone pinged with a message from the detective. He opened up the email and clicked on the attachment, which contained a comprehensive report of Robert's phone activity. According to the data, Robert had called Holly 147 times since his last billing cycle three weeks ago. In total Robert had made nearly 300 phone calls, many of them to the number he recognized belonged to the physical therapy clinic. There were only 47 phone calls which weren't somehow related to Holly.

The man was definitely a stalker.

The numbers for his text messages were of a similar ratio. However, it appeared that he had been in contact with at least two dozen individuals. His social media was interesting. He'd spent a great deal of time on one particular platform, which was photo based. There, he had been searching "girl next door," "hot physical therapists" and "how to make a woman fall for you," amongst a variety of other terms.

He really didn't like him. None of what he was finding surprised him. The guy was pathetic and a confirmed drug addict.

Holly stepped to his side, and he held out his phone so she could take a peek at the list, as well. She scanned through the pages, stopping on his messages.

"Is there a page where we can see who all these numbers belonged to?" she asked, pointing at the phone numbers he had been in contact with.

"We can pull them up on NCIC. It's the national database law enforcement uses. It basically has everything about everyone. It's actually a bit terrifying how much data is in that thing." He had used it to look into Robert when he'd been digging around after his death, but the man didn't have any real record when it came to criminal activities. As for his private information, he'd learned about every apartment and phone number Robert had ever had, as well as all of his family members' addresses and phone numbers.

"I've heard about it."

A sense of excitement filled him. They weren't any closer to finding answers to Robert's death, but at least they were getting some more information. He closed his phone and stuffed it in his back pocket. He walked toward the door and put his hand on the doorknob. "I'm going to run out and grab my computer. I left it in my pickup. We can sit down and dig into these numbers. I don't think it will take us too long to come up with the names."

She gave him a strange look, one that almost hinted at fear. Was she worried about being left alone? Her enemy was dead.

He stopped and came back to her, not wanting to see that expression on her face ever again. It pained him to see her in pain. He took her into his embrace, and he dropped his hands down to her lower back as he looked into her eyes. "Everything is going to be okay. You are safe. You will always be safe with me, babe."

She relaxed in his arms and laid her head against his chest as though she was taking a moment to listen to his heart. As she did, his heart started to ache and he wished, not for the first time, that he could get even closer to her even though they were already touching. It was an illogical thought, but it made him realize exactly how much this woman meant to him.

He was the luckiest man on the planet to be holding a woman like her in his arms. He never wanted to let her go.

After a long moment, she leaned back and looked up at him, waiting for his kiss. He obliged, moving down and giving her a kiss that he hoped she recognized as standing for something far more real and more tangible than simply lust.

She smiled, her mouth still against his, and it made him wonder if she read his kiss for exactly what he had intended. "Go grab your computer," she said, her breath warm against his lips.

He couldn't say he really wanted to go anywhere, but he let her go. He hurried outside, and as he did, he realized he wasn't wearing any shoes when his feet touched the fresh snow on the ground.

"Oh...damn," he said between gasping breaths.

He took out his keys and unlocked his pickup as he hurried through the icy snow. His feet ached with the cold by the time he reached his rig. As he opened the door, he watched as his breath made a cloud in the air in front of him.

It was barely in the single digits outside, if even that. It would have been perfect weather for being on the sled in the mountains; the snow would be great for riding. If Moose had still been alive, he would have been getting a call this morning to hit the slopes.

He really was going to miss his friend.

Thinking about Moose, he needed to reach out to Rebecca and make sure she was doing okay. She was probably having a really hard time right now, planning the funeral and waiting for the ME to release his remains to the funeral home. He felt so bad for her.

He moved to grab his computer, but as he did, he caught sight of the empty spot where he normally parked his work rig. That round had nearly cost him his life. Any of them could have—and that was to say nothing about

Holly. She had gotten down in the pickup, taken cover, but that didn't always mean that a person wouldn't take a hit.

They were both lucky to still be alive.

He'd already lost Moose; he couldn't lose another person who he cared about.

And whoever had shot at them...they were still out there. Moreover, they had probably been the ones behind Moose's death.

He picked up his computer and slid it under his arm as he shut the pickup door. His feet were so cold now that the snow around them was melting, but slowly and as it did it left fat droplets of cold water on his steadily reddening skin.

He needed to get back inside and to Holly.

Though he couldn't explain it, a strange sense of foreboding and fear filled him.

He glanced around toward the front of the house, but he was alone out here in the wintery morning. He hated that ugly wiggling feeling that started in his stomach and climbed up to his heart and made it race. It was akin to fear, and he'd only felt it a handful of times before, unless he was under fire or in direct fight or flight.

Something was wrong, but he just couldn't put his finger on it. It reminded him of the feeling he had gotten when he discovered that the gun had been accidentally moved under Robert's leg.

*Had the body or the gun been tampered with?* The thought dawned on him.

But he and Stowe were the first on scene. And he knew that they hadn't touched the gun. Which opened up the possibility that someone had been at that potential crime scene before they had—but whether someone had a role in Robert's death or if they had just disturbed the scene was a question of its own.

He walked around the side of the house and toward his garage. Just like the other night at Holly's house, the garage light was on.

*Strange. I didn't park there last night.* He looked out at his truck, which was parked in front of the garage door. If he remembered correctly, they hadn't even walked through the garage to get inside and last night the light definitely hadn't been turned on.

The fear in him roiled to something more, something resembling the tingling of burgeoning anger. Someone had been in there—or maybe they still were.

He reached down to his waist where his gun normally rested on his hip. He didn't feel his holster and realized that he was only wearing jeans and a shirt—he hadn't gotten ready for work, and he hadn't put on his gun to come out and get his computer.

His feet were burning now; they were so cold in the snow that they had started to once again feel warm. He knew the dangers that came with the sensation, but he couldn't worry about his feet. He needed to know who had been in his garage and why.

Stepping quietly, he made his way to the side door of the structure and slowly twisted the door handle. "Put your hands up!" he yelled, slamming open the door.

There was no one in his direct line of sight as he glanced through the opening, careful to keep his body behind cover in case someone decided to open fire.

"Get down on the ground and put your hands on the back of your head!" he ordered, as if there was a perpetrator inside listening to him, someone he didn't see.

He cleared the entrance and glanced inside. The place was filled with stacks of boxes, a table saw, router, lathe and his tool bench. There was only silence. He moved inside, carefully crouching down to see if someone was hiding under his old '68 Charger he'd always planned on refinishing.

He was alone.

This place was always locked up, but when he'd come through the side door, it had been open. He walked over toward the doorknob. There were fresh scratches in the brass like someone had used metal tools to clumsily pick the lock.

Everything appeared to be in its place and no boxes had been brought down from the shelves or rifled through, and if someone was looking for something of value to steal, there were plenty of expensive tools that were still sitting around. Whoever had been inside hadn't come here with the intention of robbing him. So, why would they have broken in?

And then he spotted it. The shiny blade caught the light just right and pulled his attention. He walked over toward the mysterious knife. He'd not seen this in his garage before, but as he neared the butcher knife, he had a sinking feeling he knew where it had been.

On the black handle, he wasn't completely sure, but he thought he could see the remnants of dried blood. It was brown and crackled.

Not touching it, he backed up slowly from where he

stood and didn't touch another thing as he made his way outside. The door stood open and the lights were on, but he didn't care.

He reached into his back pocket and pulled out his phone. First, he called dispatch and let them know about the break-in, asking for the closest deputies to make their way to his residence.

Next, he texted Stowe. His message was simple. I think I may have found the murder weapon.

He didn't wait for a response. Instead, he slowly made his way back to the front of the house. Outside, leading from the road were a new set of footprints. They went straight to the door. From the distance between them and the snow they'd kicked up, the person who'd left them had been running.

He hurried to the door, his fear escalating.

He grabbed the doorknob and tried to turn it, but it didn't budge. He'd been locked out.

## Chapter Nineteen

Holly was puttering around in the kitchen, looking for bacon in the freezer, when she heard the front door slam closed and the lock click into place.

"I'm going to cook us a little breakfast. I'm thinking eggs, hash browns, bacon?" she asked, not really expecting an answer.

She hummed as she found the bacon and took it to the sink. She turned on the water and let the liquid pour over the frozen meat as she removed it from the plastic. She set it on the cutting board and went back to the freezer. She pulled out a bag of frozen hash browns.

The song "Good Morning, Beautiful" was stuck in her head and she danced as she sang random words between humming. She had always liked country music. As she thought about music, she wondered what kind of music Ty liked. She didn't really remember what they had listening to in his truck when they had been together when they'd been younger. Her mind had always been on him.

After last night, she held no doubts that she would love to get the chance to be by his side more often. Daily. No, *hourly* would be best. Bottom line, no amount of him would ever be enough.

She smiled widely as she thought about his tongue on her and the way he felt when he was between her thighs.

She had found everything she had been missing in her life, and he had basically been right down the street these last few years.

If only she hadn't been so wrapped up in the chaos and drama of her life, maybe she would have found him before.

There was a slam against the front door, and then the pounding of fists.

"Holly! Get out of there!" Ty's voice sounded through the front door.

She stopped, unsure if she was hearing him right.

What happened? Why was he so upset?

She stared at the door as though she had been hearing things.

The picture on the wall near the door swayed as Ty pounded again. And it pulled her from her frozen response. She started to rush toward the door. "Holly! Holly, are you okay? Holly!" His voice was high and panicked.

"I'm—"

She stopped as someone grabbed her around the waist from behind. The force was incredible as the person hit the small of her back and their knee connected with the back of her thigh. Pain coursed through her, and she called out in shock and horror as her body dropped to the ground.

She screamed.

"Shut up!" a woman yelled at her as she slammed her in the ground so hard that it knocked the wind out of Holly's lungs.

She kicked behind her with her good leg, trying to roll over, but wheezing with pain.

Her lungs ached as they begged for air and her vision grew hazy. All she could see was the maple-colored floor beneath her face. She'd caught herself with her hands and as she moved, her left wrist popped, and a fire raced up her arm and into her shoulder.

She tried to call out, but without air all she could do was garble and wheeze.

A fist connected with her kidney, and she made a strange, warbled cry, which drove the last little bit of air from her. Her eyes widened, but she forced herself to fight. She had to fight.

She kicked wildly, her legs flying behind her as she struggled through the pain. She fought like a child stuck in a nightmare, flailing and striking at anything and everything. Her foot connected with soft flesh as someone grabbed her leg.

She used the leverage they provided to turn herself over.

Her eyes connected with the woman—she didn't know her. The woman had long dark hair; it was matted with what looked like blood in places and stray strands stuck out at weird angles around her gaunt, colorless face. The woman was speaking in gibberish.

She was muttering, but Holly wasn't sure if it was because the woman had also gotten the wind knocked out of her or if she was intoxicated.

"I... You...shhhhhh... I...sh..." The woman stared at her.

There was what appeared to be blood on her white shirt and down the legs of her pants, but it was brown with age. She wore a dark coat; its sleeves were covered in dirt and there were holes up and down the arms. Where there must have been a logo was a large open flap, which exposed the white cotton stuffing beneath.

The woman looked as unstable as she sounded.

"Who..." Holly said, finally managing to start to catch her breath.

The air felt sweet and cold in her aching lungs. Even in pain, she was grateful for that little bit of oxygen.

"Your worst nightmare, witch." The woman's voice came out ragged and as she spoke there was spittle spraying wildly from her lips. She tipped her head back in a manic laugh, and it caused the matted hair in the back to push up. It appeared like she almost had horns.

When she laughed, there was something Holly recognized about the woman's face. She looked like someone she knew, but she couldn't put her finger on it.

She pulled in a larger breath as the woman lunged forward. Holly kicked as hard as she could using every ounce of her strength and her foot connected with the woman's pelvis, where her zipper on her pants rested. She could feel the bite of the metal beneath her foot.

The woman dropped to her knees as she yelped in pain and grabbed at her crotch. She went down hard, making a thumping noise as she connected with the floor. Holly fisted her hand and drew it back. As she struck the woman in the stomach, she realized she'd never really punched anyone before in her life. Right now, that fact didn't matter. If anything, it gave her a strange sense of pride.

The woman grabbed at her belly, but rage filled her eyes. Holly wasn't afraid of the woman, only the fact that she was struggling to catch her breath.

As she went to strike the woman again, there was the sound of breaking glass in the living room and a rock landed on the floor a few feet from her. Glass had sprayed around the carpet, making it even more dangerous than before. Cold air filled the room and it bit at her nose.

The woman gave a low, guttural squeal and kicked Holly right in the back of the thigh as she tried to defend herself. The kick hurt but it was nothing like the pain she was feeling in her wrist.

Ty looked through the window, his face framed by the jagged, broken glass. "Don't you dare touch her!"

The woman looked at him and flipped him the bird. "You're just as bad as she is. You both deserve to die—and you will."

He looked around him like he was searching for a weapon, and as he drew away the woman's attention, Holly rose to her feet. She tucked her wrist against her body and searched the living room for something she could use. Near the couch was a lamp. The body of the lamp looked almost like a bat. It would be perfect.

She picked it up, jerking the cord from the wall.

She moved toward the woman, but as she did the woman saw her and instead of facing her in battle, she ran toward the back door.

"You're not going to get away that easy." Holly chased

after the woman, wrapping the cord around the body of the lamp as she prepared to battle. "You don't get to come into this house and try to kill me."

She charged toward the door after her. Readying herself to strike.

"Just let her go," Ty ordered. "I'll go around the back. Call the police."

The back door slammed as the woman ran outside.

She stopped and stared down at the weapon in her hand. Her left wrist was crooked, but it didn't hurt as much as it should have. She could still go after this woman.

She glanced toward Ty as he disappeared.

*Call the police. I need to call the police.*

Holly dropped the lamp and grabbed her phone, which was sitting on the living room table where she had left it last night.

It was dead.

*You have to be kidding me. The one time I need my phone...*

She ran toward the kitchen, and as she did, she spotted the knife block by the stove. As she pulled the butcher knife from the block, she couldn't help but feel some type of poetic justice. If this was the woman who had killed Moose, then this was the way she deserved to die.

Was she the kind of person who was capable of killing another?

Shadows filled her mind. If it was simply herself in danger, she didn't think she would be capable of being deadly. However, if this woman was hurting someone she loved it would be entirely different.

She rushed toward the door carrying the big knife.

No, she couldn't do as this woman had done. If she killed the woman, she was no better than the murderer.

And what if this was merely some random break-in, what if the woman had nothing to do with Moose's death?

Just because the woman appeared to be high, it didn't mean anything; it only meant that their town had a drug problem. Sure, Robert had had drugs in his system, but assuming this woman's guilt made Holly equally dangerous.

TY WAS BREATHING hard as he rounded the corner of the house and sprinted toward the woman in the distance. He could catch her. He had to catch her. She had hurt the woman he loved.

Anger roiled through him.

He'd never thought of himself as a dangerous man, but in this moment, there was no one more deadly.

"Get down on the ground!" he ordered.

She didn't even slow down.

As he ran, he realized his computer was still under his arm. He hadn't thought of it or about it since he had grabbed it from the pickup. He considered throwing it after the woman but knew he didn't have that kind of reach.

"This is Detective Terrell with the Madison County Sheriff's Department. If you do not stop, I will be forced to shoot!" he yelled.

She didn't need to know that he wasn't carrying a gun.

The woman slowed down and as she did, he gained ground.

She looked over her shoulder, acquiring her target,

which was him, before starting to run harder. His freezing feet ached as he moved into a barefooted sprint. He was so close he could almost reach her, but she was just outside of his grasp.

He remembered his computer. He hated the damn thing anyway.

He grabbed it with both hands and swung it at her as hard as he could. He hit her right on the back of the head.

She dropped.

In the distance were the sounds of police cars.

They weren't a second too soon.

## Chapter Twenty

Detective Stowe was sitting in the gray hard interrogation room, staring silently at Valerie Keller. Valerie's eyes were puffy and red, and her hair was loose and unkempt. A piece jutted out from the side above her ear where she had feebly attempted to gain some control over her world. She'd failed.

In the second interrogation room, sat her sister, Evelyn. This room was even more austere with nothing more than an industrial table, complete with a loop to attach handcuffs, and two plastic chairs.

Ty hated that Valerie had gotten wrapped up in this. She was a nice person, but he was struggling to come to terms with what had taken place. She had to have been involved or at least had some knowledge of her sister's intentions, but this was her chance to tell her side of the story and exonerate herself from a potential crime.

Holly was scratching at the edge of her blue plaster cast on her left arm, and he was surprised that it was already bothering her. It was going to be a long six weeks, but he would be there to take care of her and get her everything she needed.

He felt horrible that she had been hurt in the home invasion, but he was glad that he had been there and had been able to stop the woman before she had killed Holly. Another couple of minutes, and he held no doubt that the woman would have tried to beat her to death.

He'd be lying if he didn't kind of love the fact that when he had found Holly, shaking and crying after the police had arrived at his place, that she was still holding the lamp. He'd asked her what it was about, and she'd explained that she intended to take down the woman if need be.

It was funny to him that they had both gone to household objects in order to have a weapon.

He'd always heard a computer could be his best weapon, but he had never really thought of it as one as much as he did now. The thought made a smile flutter over his lips.

When he arrived in his office this morning, there had even been a little pink toddler computer on his desk, with the note that read "In case of emergencies."

His coworkers definitely thought they were a bunch of clowns. But it did make him laugh.

On the other side of the coin, when the sheriff had called him into his office after the attack, he wasn't as amused. But he really couldn't say anything as he had used the computer to stop a crime. No doubt it would end up costing the department a couple grand, but he wasn't sad or repentant. The only thing he was sorry about was the fact that he hadn't taken action against the woman before she had the chance to hurt the people he loved.

"Has Evelyn said anything?" Holly asked.

Ty shook his head. "Not since she came back from the hospital. They drew blood on her, and according to the doctor, it sounded like Evelyn was higher than a kite. High doses of opioids in her system as well as barbiturates and marijuana."

She shook her head, but she didn't look surprised. "I'm sure she and Robert were using together. It definitely helps to make sense of some of their erratic behaviors."

He looked over at her and noticed the way her blond hair was loose around her shoulders in a long cascading wave. Her makeup was on point and, aside from the cast on her arm, she seemed perfectly put together. For the first time since he'd come back into her life, she seemed to be at peace. Unfortunately, he had a feeling he was going to cause an upheaval and he didn't like himself for it. Yet, they needed to find answers and sometimes a little upheaval wasn't a bad thing.

"She'll be going through detox soon, and before she does, we need to get her to start talking." He caught Holly's gaze and sent her a wordless question.

"Seriously?" she asked, having been able to read it on his face. "You want me to go in there? Don't you think that it will send her over the edge? She's a drug addict and unpredictable."

He reached down and took her hand in his. "This isn't like before. You are in a controlled environment, she is handcuffed and I'm right here. All I want you to do is get her talking. I know it's unconventional, but I want to see her response to you."

She stared at their entwined hands like they were a lifeline, and she was on a sinking ship. He hated that look on her face. The last thing they were was sinking. No, they were rising on the tide of change and finally breaking through the storms that had ravaged her life. She was strong and together they would grow even stronger.

"If you don't want to do it, you don't have to—no pressure. If you choose to go in, I'll be right by your side."

That made her entire demeanor change. She lifted her chin and her shoulders straightened. "Okay. I just don't want to be in there alone with her. I know what she is capable of," she said, lifting her casted arm.

"If I have my way, you'll never have to do anything in your life alone again." He winked.

Her mouth dropped open and she tilted her head slightly, reminding him of a confused puppy. She was no puppy, but he loved that expression. He'd do anything to see that expression every day. There was nothing better than surprising her.

"But you haven't...you don't love me." She smiled widely as if she knew, without him saying, what he was thinking and feeling.

In this moment, he wasn't about to break that seal. He sent her what he knew was his most charming smile. "We will see about that. Besides, you're still on trial," he teased.

The door to the interrogation room opened, and Stowe walked out and into the large chamber that looked into both interrogation areas. He was shaking his head and looking dejected as he closed the door behind him. The reality of the moment pulled them from their playfulness, and Ty was reminded all too much about everything that was at stake.

If they did not get a confession from Evelyn, or something from Valerie that tied her or her sister directly to Moose's death it would be extremely hard to prove. They could get Evelyn on charges of breaking and entering and assault, maybe even more if she had been the one who had shot at them; but until they got all of the reports back from the crime lab about the knife and their findings, it would all depend on this interrogation and their ability to make her and her sister talk.

The good news was that with those charges alone, he could keep Evelyn in jail for at least as long as it would take to get the results. As such if Holly didn't want to go in there, or if she got in there and needed out right away, there was still time. However, he also knew that Rebecca, Moose's mother, was waiting on answers.

It was his hope that after today, he could go to her and tell her that the person responsible for her son's death was behind bars and would go to trial for their crime.

"Valerie's refusing to talk besides saying that she had nothing to do with the murders. The only good news is that she hasn't lawyered up," Detective Stowe said. He stepped beside them in front of the two-way mirror and looked in on the interrogation room with Evelyn.

She was staring down at her hands, where the shackles where pinched tight around her wrists. She moved her arms slightly, like she was trying to make them less uncomfortable, but they had been designed to hurt. If she hadn't been combative with Holly and him, he wouldn't have required that she keep them on, but as it was, he didn't trust her. Especially given the fact that she was on drugs.

"Is it okay if I go in and talk to her?" Holly asked. "Maybe I can get her to start talking. At least, I want to ask her why she did what she did." She looked over at Ty for reassurance, and he sent her a comforting smile.

He was proud of her for her strength and tenacity.

"She did what she did because she is a criminal, but I get what you're saying," Stowe said.

His ego must have been slightly bruised that the big-city detective couldn't get the small-town drug addict to open up and he was aware their only shot lay with Holly. Ty shouldn't have found a glimmer of joy in it, but he couldn't help himself.

"She and I will go in together," Ty said, getting in front of the man's possible arguments against them talking to Evelyn.

"If you think you can get her to talk, knock yourselves out. But do remember that the county attorney and the judges will be watching all of the footage from inside that room. Everything that happens will be heavily scrutinized." Stowe shot them a deathly serious look.

Ty appreciated what the guy was saying, but he needed no reminder. "I'm hoping that given the fact that she may have played a role in a law enforcement officer's death, that this is one trial that will go a little smoother."

"As I'm sure you know, before we make any assumptions, we need to make sure that this is the person or persons we are looking for in relation to your friend's murder." Stowe paused. "I know we've talked about it a little bit, but I still can't understand why she would have targeted Moose."

"He was having a relationship with Valerie—that's

why we brought her in to talk. She may give us some hard evidence connecting either her or her sister directly to these murders. When we brought her in, she admitted she'd been sleeping with Moose. Who knows? Maybe that's why Evelyn thought she needed to act. Maybe something in her drug-addled brain told her that her sister needed to be saved." Ty shrugged.

"Again, you're making assumptions. We need concrete evidence or the woman in there—" he motioned toward the interrogation room where Evelyn sat "—to start talking. If we don't, she may very well get away with murder."

"Let me at her," Holly said, stepping toward the door.

Stowe looked torn but gave her a stiff nod as he touched the doorknob. He pushed the door open and waited for Holly to follow Ty into the room.

Evelyn looked up from her dedicated study of her handcuffs. Her expression darkened, and her lips pulled into a twisted sneer. "Couldn't get enough of me?" she challenged.

"If I remember correctly, I put up a pretty good fight," Holly said.

"But I see you're wearing a cast," Evelyn countered, with a malicious grin.

Holly moved to the chair across from the woman and sat down. Ty stepped behind her, covering her back and giving her his support.

"How's your head doing?" he asked, motioning to the back of her head where he had smashed the computer into her. "Got a little bit of a headache?" He really couldn't help himself this morning.

"Gloat all you want," Evelyn said, a twisted smile on her lips. "I still got what I wanted." She looked directly at Holly. "Though, if I'd gotten everything I wanted, you'd be dead, too. Actually, both of you would be. If only I had killed you the first chance I had."

Holly looked at her. "What do you mean?"

"When I had Robert's truck. I should have waited and been more patient, but I had to shoot. I couldn't stand watching you two smiling together. You're the worst kind of woman. You deserve to die."

She tried to hide her surprise and hatred toward the woman who not only despised her, but also wanted her dead.

"What did I ever do to you?" Holly asked. She leaned against the table like it could support her emotionally as well as physically.

Ty dropped his hand to her shoulder, giving it a gentle squeeze and hopefully letting her know that she was doing well.

"If it weren't for you, Robert would have loved me."

Holly made a choking sound. "You do know that I was not interested in Robert in any way," Holly said, putting her hands down on the table in a symbolic gesture that she was telling the truth. "He wouldn't leave me alone and I didn't want anything to do with him romantically."

Evelyn started to rock back and forth, but Ty wasn't sure if it was because of a nervous tick or the fact that she was likely coming down off drugs.

"You're a liar." Evelyn's movements grew more erratic. "Robert told me what a liar you were. He told me all about what you did to him, and how you wouldn't leave him alone. He even showed me all the times you called and texted him. You loved him. You know you loved him." The woman's words came out faster and faster almost in tandem with her rocking.

"I talked to him because I worked with him." She paused as she pulled up memories. "He didn't take it well when I ignored him, and he would get more and more incensed the longer I went without responding." Holly sounded as though she was struggling to control the emotions she was feeling from leaching into her voice.

Ty hated that she was struggling. "Evelyn, why were you on the mountain the day of Moose's death?" He was aware that he was leading her, but this wasn't a courtroom and he simply needed her to acknowledge the fact that she had been in proximity at the time of the murder.

"Robert had told me that she was up there. He was really upset. She hadn't responded to him the night before she went missing. She's so selfish. She ruins everything." Evelyn was staring back down at her cuffs.

It didn't escape him that she was talking about Holly like she wasn't in the room.

"But why were you on the mountain? Were you looking for Holly?"

She looked up at him, anger filling her face with hard lines. "If I killed her, I could solve everything. I could do what needed to be done. Robert would be free of her, and he'd never be held accountable for her death. What I really wanted was for no one to find her body."

"So, you went up on the mountain with the intention of killing Holly?"

"Yes." Evelyn spat the word in anger. "And I would

have. If that reckless man hadn't gotten in my way. I didn't plan on using that knife on him. I wanted to make it look like Holly had gone to the woods and slit her wrists. Everything went wrong, though."

"Did you cut his throat?"

She blanched. "I stabbed him first… He tried to fight back, but I got the knife out and moved at him." She paused, looking toward the mirror. She smiled, wickedly. "It is strange how easy it is to cut someone's throat. The windpipe feels like cutting through a rubber band."

He hated this woman. She was the epitome of a criminal. She was so self-righteous and so filled with anger and hate, there was no rehabilitating her. When she went to prison for this, which she would, he'd make sure of it, she needed to never get out.

"He told me what you guys were there to do, and I knew I was too late. But I knew I'd get another chance, I just had to be patient. I just had to watch." Evelyn's rocking slowed. "That's why I went to her house… If only you hadn't been there…" She sounded aggrieved.

Her breaking into Holly's garage and his now made a little more sense. It was warm and sheltered from the elements. From within, she'd probably been able to watch anything she wanted through the kitchen window.

In fact, he wasn't sure that she couldn't have seen into his breakfast nook from nearly the same vantage point. He didn't want to ask if she had watched them that night when he'd been with Holly. He wouldn't let this mad woman steal anything from that wonderful night. She'd already taken enough from their lives.

Holly said nothing.

"Was the knife we found in the garage the same knife you used to kill Moose?" he asked, his stomach roiling at the thought but he forced himself to remain stoic.

"I thought it was a nice touch."

"Why did you leave it?" he pressed.

"I wanted Holly to know I was coming for her—and that I wasn't afraid to kill again." She looked over at Holly and sent her a vicious smile.

Holly turned away.

As much as he wanted to protect Holly, he appreciated that she was here—her presence was helping. Evelyn hated her so much that she only cared about hurting her, and in doing so she was digging herself a deeper prison sentence.

"And why did you kill Robert, if you loved him so much?" he pressed, though he didn't have a clue whether or not Evelyn had played any role in the man's death.

Evelyn threw her hands up as high as she could with them being bolted to the table. "I didn't do that. I could never have hurt him. I tried to make him stop. But all he could do was talk about her. He said she was never going to take him back. That I'd screwed everything up." Her words came out fast. "I tried to get the gun out of his hand." Evelyn's voice cracked with emotion.

The way she spoke made him think that she was likely telling them the truth.

"Before I could get the gun out of his hand, he'd had it against his chin and…" Evelyn stopped talking. "I tried to help him. I tried." Tears welled in her eyes, and a single droplet spilled down her cheek, making her appear almost human.

Ty reached for the box of Kleenex and pushed it over in the woman's direction. He knew he should have expressed sorrow for the woman's loss. He'd been present at more than one callout that had ended in a self-inflicted gunshot wound. It was grizzly. It was something that a person could not unsee. However, these two individuals, Robert and Evelyn, had been playing an evil game.

Though they had all experienced so much tragedy and loss, Ty was relieved. They finally had some answers and a path for recourse. There would be justice for his best friend's death and the attempted taking of Holly's life.

## Chapter Twenty-One

The one aspect of the case that Holly just couldn't come to terms with was the flowers that had been sent to her office. The card had been handwritten and it was a woman's scrawl, but that had likely been written by the florist and not the sender.

Evelyn wouldn't have sent those flowers. Robert may have, but she didn't know. She wanted to find out. Maybe they could go to the florist and ask questions. Then again, she wasn't sure she would want to know if Robert had sent them. If he had, it would ruin cut flowers for her, forever.

As she stood in the hallway outside of the interrogation room, her body started to shake. Ty wrapped his arms around her from behind.

"You're going to be alright," he cooed, as though he understood. "You've been through a lot today and your body is just adjusting to the stress of the environment. Sometimes I get the shakes, too. You'll be okay, though. I've got you."

He brought her so much comfort.

She turned to face him, without breaking from his

embrace. "Someone sent flowers to my office with a note that read 'I'm sorry.' They showed up the day after Moose's murder. I have no idea who they were from, but I need to know."

Ty nodded.

"I know I shouldn't be worried about such a trivial thing, but it's the one point I just can't make sense of. It could have been Robert, but he was never one to apologize to me for anything. If anything bad happened, it was always my fault. And he had to have sent them before the time of his death. Which means he may not even have known about Moose's death or what Evelyn had done."

Ty gently rubbed his thumb over her back. "What you're experiencing is totally normal. It's part of that stress response, kind of like your shaking. You're myopically focused on a detail. But don't worry, we'll get it solved. It will be easy enough to figure it out. All we'll have to do is talk to the florist and track down financial records."

She appreciated that he didn't make her feel wrong for what she was feeling and how her body was reacting. He was such a kind man. And she appreciated that he wasn't pressuring her to feel a certain way or respond a certain way. He just accepted her for who she was and what her body was capable of handling.

"Why don't I go in and talk with Valerie. I need to get to the bottom of everything that she's played a role in here, if she sent her sister out on that mountain she should be up on charges." He pulled her into his arms and took a deep breath like he was smelling her hair. The simple action helped her stop shaking. She caught her breath as he just stood there and held her.

It was so easy to love him. And now that this was all bottled up maybe they could have a real relationship. She would leave that ball in his court. This was his job that was at stake, and she certainly understood the upheaval that was occurring within his department right now thanks to the evidence tech's role in these two deaths in the community. The only good news was that it didn't appear that Valerie had actually pulled any triggers, figurative or otherwise. That had all been Evelyn.

Calming, she looked up into his eyes. "Go get this done so we can really start our lives together." Maybe she wasn't gonna leave it in his court after all. She had changed, but she'd never silently stand by when she wanted something, especially something as important as him.

As she spoke, he threw his head back with a laugh.

"Our lives together?" He gave her a cheeky grin. "You haven't even told me you love me yet."

Her face flamed with embarrassment.

"Just get your butt in there." She giggled. "Before anyone can say anything, we need these answers."

He rounded his shoulders and looked like a dejected schoolboy. He sent her a wide grin over his shoulder as he made his way into the interrogation room where Valerie sat waiting. The door closed behind him, and as quickly as the door closed his smile disappeared. She was amazed by how quickly he could go from laughing to all business. It had to come with the job.

He sat on the sofa of the soft interrogation room. The

room was far more decorated than the one her sister was currently occupying; Valerie was sitting on a leather sofa that had a coffee table in front of it complete with a stack of magazines and two boxes of Kleenex.

She watched from the other side of the mirror as Valerie reached forward and grabbed a tissue and dabbed at her nose. A fresh stream of tears poured down her face. "I'm so sorry," Valerie said, sobbing.

"So, your sister was very forthcoming with information. Do you wish to tell us your side of the story?" Ty asked.

Valerie sobbed harder.

"I know how hard this is, Valerie. But I also know that you understand how important it is to tell us the truth. Especially now, after you've been less than forthright throughout this investigation." He sighed.

As she watched him work, Holly realized how much this had to bother him. She'd been so concerned about her own feelings and the effect talking to Evelyn had had on her, but she hadn't even considered how he would feel going into that room with his coworker. Yet, if anybody was going to interview her it did make sense that it was him. No doubt the other detective would get his chance, but Valerie had always seemed to like Ty.

Unfortunately, it seemed that she had loved her sister more.

"Evelyn was using my computer, and I had no idea. She was all over that call with Holly when she went missing. She asked me a ton of questions." Valerie hiccupped and dabbed at her nose. "I didn't know Robert's relationship with Holly. Well, not until I got home that night.

Evelyn had gone off the rails. She was screaming and yelling, and she was covered in blood. I forced her to tell me what had happened, and when she told me about Moose…" Her body was rattled by sobs.

"I was so angry with her." She gulped for air. "I told her I never wanted to see her again."

"Did you have any role in Moose's death?"

"No!" she said, looking up at him through tear-filled eyes. "Absolutely not. I *loved* him. I think that was part of the reason Evelyn killed him. We were talking about getting married."

Ty put his hand on Valerie's shoulder like he wanted to comfort her in some small way. "If you knew Evelyn had been snooping on your computer, and you knew that she had played a role in your future fiancé's death, then why did you not turn her in?"

She fell forward, cupping her face in her hands in shame. Her shoulders were curled, and sobs rattled through her. "I should have. I wanted to. I just…" She sobbed. "I'm so sorry."

"Is that why you sent the flowers to Holly?"

She nodded. "I planned on turning Evelyn in. I felt horrible for your loss and what my sister had done. That's when I made the order, but I couldn't turn on my sister like that and by the time I changed my mind, they had already been delivered." She ran the back of her hand under her nose, giving up on her tissues. "I mean, I know I should have turned her in, but the damage was already done. I didn't want to lose my sister, too. She and Moose were the only people I really had in my life…in my corner."

He shook his head. "It doesn't sound like your sister was ever in your corner. In fact, it could be pointed out that your sister seems to be your worst enemy. Not only has she cost you your job, your pension, your integrity—and the man you love—but she may have cost this entire department millions. Every case you've ever worked on will now come under scrutiny."

Valerie gasped. "Oh, my God."

She covered her face and succumbed to her tears.

Holly had liked the woman, she really had. She was pleasant and sweet when they'd met earlier this week. To think this woman had basically undone all the good work of the department—even if she had done it all in the name of the love for her sister.

# *Epilogue*

It had been nearly twelve ugly and beautiful months.

Because Valerie had worked on the investigation of Moose's death, she had been convicted of obstruction of justice and accessory to murder, after the fact. Last week, she had been sentenced to three years in the Montana Women's Prison in Billings.

Valerie had gotten a reduced sentence because of her candor and willingness to work with county attorney's office in clearing her past works and limiting the effects of her criminal behavior.

Evelyn was found guilty in district court for one count of deliberate homicide. It carried a minimum sentence of life. She would never leave prison.

At least the sisters were in prison together—there, they could continue protecting one another.

Holly was just getting up for the morning when Ty walked into her kitchen. Since they'd been dating, he'd been staying over more and more often. She loved every minute of him being there with her.

He moved behind her as she cracked an egg and poured it into a bowl to scramble. Ty wrapped his arms around her and nuzzled his face into her loose hair. "Good morning, babe. I was going to make you breakfast today."

"You don't need to cook for me, babe," she said, turning and giving him a quick peck to the cheek before cracking another egg.

"I have plans for your birthday. You can have breakfast, but I am going to need you to go along with my plans for the rest of the day." He rubbed his morning stubble against the edge of her ear.

"Only if you say what I want to hear," she teased.

"I will tell you all day, every day. I love you, Holly Dean."

Her heart leaped into her throat. She would never get tired of hearing him say those words. "I love you, too."

She put down the eggshell and washed her fingers off in the sink and dried her hands. Turning around, she smiled at him. He reached behind his body and pulled out a box from his back pocket.

The little box had a red bow and there were skis on the wrapping paper.

"Ah, it's so cute," she cooed.

"You haven't even opened it yet," he said with a laugh.

"What is it?" she asked, going to the table to sit and open it up.

"It's your first present of the day."

She moved from foot to foot in excitement. "What? You didn't need to get me anything. I don't need anything more—I have you, that is the greatest gift I could get." She smiled at him as she sat down.

"You are so full of it this morning," he teased, coming over and kissing the top of her head.

"I mean it," she said, trying to sound affronted by his teasing.

"Birthday girl, I'm the lucky one." He put his hand on her shoulder. "Now, open up your present."

She pulled off the bow and slowly opened the package, taking her time.

She lifted the top of the black cardboard box. Inside was a set of ski tickets to the local resort. "Ah, babe, thank you. When are we going?" she asked.

"Today, but you're not done opening presents. Wait here," he said, putting a finger up and motioning for her to stay.

He stepped to the window and waved toward the garage. A few seconds later, Rebecca came in. She had a huge, mischievous smile and a cake in her hands. "Hi, kiddos!" she said, sounding so excited. "Happy Birthday!"

"Thank you!" Holly said, excited to see the woman who had become a major part of their life and regularly popped in with "extra" food she'd made for dinner. She loved the woman almost as much as she had loved her mom.

Ty took the cake and set it on the counter. "Thank you for doing this, Mrs. Dolack. We're glad to have you here for this." He sent the woman a wink.

"You know you can call me 'Mom.'" Mrs. Dolack waved him off. "And I'm just honored you called. I'm happy to be a part of this. Our little family," she said, her smile growing impossibly wider. "Oh, Holly, here is the best part." Mrs. Dolack reached out the door behind her. Then she lifted a new set of red Rossignol skis and handed them to Ty.

Holly set her ski passes down on the table and cupped her hand over her mouth. "Oh, guys, I love them!"

"You're welcome. I know how much you've been wanting to get back out there." Ty handed her the skis.

He really was the best man she'd ever met.

She sucked in a breath as she looked at the freshly waxed skis. "They are beautiful. We'll have to go this week. Maybe after we can go to Mom's for some hot cocoa."

The older woman nodded, but she put her hand over her mouth like she was struggling to keep a secret.

"Wait." He smiled. "First, look at the binding."

She lifted the ski to look. There at the end of her right ski's binding was a small velvet box. She stopped and stared.

"If you don't like it or whatever, I can take it back," Ty said.

She could barely move as she stared at the velvet box. Was he doing what she thought he was? If so, this was going to be the best birthday of her life.

He dropped to his knee in front of her. "Holly Dean, you are the love of my life. When we were kids, I knew I wanted to marry you, but I thought it was crazy. If only I had listened to my heart, then we could have saved so much precious time..."

She put the back of her free hand over her mouth, staring at him in front of her. Her eyes welled with tears. She had never known she could be so happy as she had been since he had come back into her life, until now.

"Holly," he continued, "we grew up together and it is my hope that we can grow old together. Will you marry me?"

She nodded. "Yes. Absolutely, yes. You are my best friend. I wanted to marry you when we were kids, too."

He opened the box. Inside was the most beautiful Black Hills gold ring that she had ever seen. It had leaves of green and pink roses in the gold. At its center was an inset diamond. It was stunning.

Ty slipped it on her finger. It fit her just as perfectly as the man who was giving it to her.

"I am yours," she said, staring at him.

"As I am yours," he said, standing. "Ski buddies, forever."

Their kiss was deeper than the meeting of lips. In that moment, the people who had lost so much over the years and had been left stranded alone by life came together as a family.

* * * * *

# COLTON'S
# BLIZZARD HIDEOUT

DEBORAH FLETCHER MELLO

## To Emma Cole

Thank you! Your patience and understanding
as I dealt with my father's illness and passing
were sincerely appreciated. You took my
challenges in stride and the many times
I fell short, you were there to
encourage and support me.
I will forever remember your kindness.

# Chapter One

"We have to find those babies! They must be here some-where," Lizzy Colton cried out. She struggled against the ties that bound her hands and feet together. "Why are you doing this?" she screamed.

The man standing above her grunted. The ski mask he wore obstructed his face, but she had memorized every detail of his dark eyes, his dismissive stare feeling like daggers of ice. He wore the same dingy slacks, red plaid jacket and brown hiking boots that he'd been in for the past few days. Lizzy wasn't certain how much time had passed since he had dragged her up this mountain, but he'd come and gone three times, throwing a bag of cold French fries and a hamburger at her feet every time he returned.

He dropped the greasy brown bag to the floor and pushed it toward her with his foot.

"I need the bathroom," Lizzy muttered, her voice drop-ping multiple decibels. "A *real* bathroom," she exclaimed as he pointed toward a large bucket positioned in the corner.

He leaned down to stare at her. His eyes danced over

her face, and when he reached out his hand to draw his fingers along her profile, she flinched. Her discomfort seemed to amuse him. He grabbed her cheeks as if to kiss her, and then he let her go, his lips lifting in a wry smile. He untied her hands, then gestured with his eyes to the bucket.

Lizzy rubbed her wrists as she pulled her body upright, stretching her legs. She flexed her arms to revive the blood flow down the appendages. She pulled against the heavy, twisted nylon rope wrapped around one of her ankles, the length only giving her enough freedom to reach the far corner. With a heavy sigh, she moved slowly in that direction, tossing him a chilly glare over her shoulder.

He grunted a second time, motioning with a large butcher knife for her to hurry. Then he turned his back to her. A cell phone in his pocket suddenly chimed for his attention. As he answered the call, she noted the stress that rose in the gruffness of his voice. He swore, a litany of profanity spewing into the chilly air. Tossing her another look, he sauntered to the cabin door and stepped outside. He whispered angrily into the phone receiver as he made his exit.

Lizzy cursed as she dropped her pants and squatted above the bucket. When her bladder was empty, she straightened her clothes and moved back to the other corner, kicking the dinner bag out of her way. Her stomach grumbled with pain, but she ignored whatever lay inside the container. She didn't trust the stranger or anything he thought to serve her.

Leaning her back against the wall, Lizzy slid down the

wood structure, easing herself to the floor. She pulled her knees to her chest and wrapped her arms tightly around herself. The last time she had tried to free herself from the bindings, he had caught her. His palm slamming into the side of her face had dropped her to the floor. The slap she could have handled, but his heavy boots slamming into her midsection had been brutal. She knew she couldn't risk another beating. She was still in pain from their last encounter and might not survive another. She settled in and waited for the man to return. Minutes later, Lizzy was still waiting.

It was only as the sun was beginning to set for the night that Lizzy realized the man had gone, leaving without retying her hands. Her abductor had retreated back down the mountain, seeming to forget that he had left her there alone. Something had pulled his attention from her and thwarted whatever plans he'd had.

With every ounce of energy she could muster, she freed herself from the leg restraints, peered out the door to be certain no one was around, and then she ran, bolting for freedom because her life depended on it.

"THE CHILDREN HAVE been found! I repeat…the children have been found! All are safe and sound!"

Ajay Wright felt a wave of relief float down his spine as he recognized his friend's voice. He took a deep breath and then another before he pressed the call button on his radio.

"Ten–four," he said to the man on the other end. "Good news is always appreciated, Malcolm."

"Happy to oblige," Malcolm Colton responded. "And

thank you. I can't tell you how much your help means to me and my family."

Ajay nodded into the radio as if the other man could see him.

Malcolm, a rancher by profession, was also a highly respected volunteer with the police department's search and rescue team. The two had been giving a public relations demonstration with both their rescue dogs when the two children were snatched. Pacer, Malcolm's shepherd-and-hound mix, had been equally invested, determined to give Ajay's dog Pumpkin a run for her money.

"I'm happy to help," Ajay finally responded.

"Everyone be careful getting back," Malcolm concluded. "There's a storm brewing, and the temperature is going to drop fast."

"Will do," Ajay replied. "Over and out."

As the call disconnected, a round of cheers rang through the chilly afternoon air, the team of search-and-rescue personnel and volunteers within hearing distance surrendering to the comfort that this time, all had ended well. There were hugs and high fives as they all began to move out of the snow-covered terrain toward the line of vehicles parked on the road below.

Ajay exhaled another deep breath. They had been searching for two small children—Justin, age four, and his sister Jane, who was only fourteen months old. Three days prior, the two had been snatched by their paternal grandfather at Fall Fest, Owl Creek's annual county fair, and many had feared the worst.

Their grandfather, Winston Kraft, had not been given custody of the children after the death of his son and daughter-in-law. Kraft had vowed revenge against the Coltons when he'd discovered that Greg Colton and his new wife, Briony, were the family who had been given the responsibility to cherish and protect those babies.

Ajay knew from past experiences that a man intent on revenge was a man capable of the most heinous crimes. The children being found safe and sound made his heart sing with sheer joy and gave him comfort knowing that for once, all things could be right in the world.

He blew a loud whistle that echoed through the late afternoon air. Tilting his head, he listened for the familiar response from his four-legged companion. He whistled a second time, his gaze narrowing as his eyes darted across the landscape. He smiled when he spied Pumpkin, his five-year-old yellow Lab, bounding in his direction.

"Good girl," Ajay muttered as the dog reached his side. He leaned to tousle his pet's fur coat. "Good girl!" He gestured with his hand, pointing the dog toward the car. He followed as Pumpkin scampered ahead of him, her tail waving excitedly.

According to procedure, Ajay double-checked that all his staff and the few volunteers with them were accounted for. He paused, watching as everyone waved goodbye and disappeared toward town. He jotted a quick note onto the clipboard that had been resting in the front seat of his new Jeep Wrangler Rubicon, the ocean-blue SUV a birthday gift to himself. He noted the date and time that the last car pulled onto the road and out of sight.

Inside the vehicle, Pumpkin settled down against the back seat. She laid her head against her wet paws, her eyes looking toward him as if she had something she needed to say.

"What's up, Pumpkin?" Ajay questioned, tossing a look over his shoulder. "Why those sad eyes?"

Pumpkin lifted her head and barked, then rested herself a second time. She didn't look happy.

"Sorry, kiddo," Ajay said. He chuckled softly. "It wasn't our save to make this time. You'll get the next one."

Pumpkin groaned, seeming to understand what her friend was saying to her. She suddenly lifted herself again and barked.

"Easy, girl," Ajay responded. "There's a storm coming in, and the wind is starting to pick up. We'll be on our way as soon as I make sure everyone else is off this mountain."

Pumpkin barked a second time, the high-pitched yelp capped with a low growl and then a grunt.

Ajay smiled, thinking if anyone could translate the conversation, they would have heard Pumpkin cursing him, not at all happy that she couldn't still be outside running about. He and his furry friend had been conversing like that since she was a puppy. He talked to her as if she understood, and she answered in kind. They were inseparable, the bond between them as thick as the blackstrap molasses he hoarded during the winter months. Molasses and his grandmother's homemade biscuits were a daily staple in both their winter diets.

His name echoing out from the shortwave radio pulled his attention from Pumpkin.

"Dispatch to Lieutenant Wright. Dispatch to Lieutenant Wright."

Ajay pressed the talk button on his radio. "Go ahead, Dispatch."

There was a swift moment of static before a voice broke through the quiet. "Ajay, this is Della."

Della Winslow and Ajay were good friends. She was his first search-and-rescue partner when he'd joined the department. She'd found Pumpkin for him and had helped to train the pup. She was one of the best dog trainers in the field, and he had great respect for her. Occasionally, people questioned their relationship, but Della was engaged to be married, and he was excited for her. Her fiancé, and the love of her life, was FBI agent Max Colton, the eldest Colton son and brother to Malcolm. Ajay and Max were acquainted through Della, but the two men didn't know each other well.

"What's up, Della?"

"We're short one volunteer. You didn't pick up any strays, by chance?"

"No, ma'am. All my volunteers have been accounted for. There's no one up here."

"We need you to do a sweep of the area between Owl Creek and the Overview Pass. We're looking for a woman. It's Lizzy Colton, Max's baby sister, and she wandered away from the group she was with. They last saw her headed up toward the back ridge. That was on the first day of our search for the Kraft children, and she's been out of contact ever since. The family just realized no one had talked to her when she didn't show up to see the kids with the rest of the family. They all thought one of them had spoken to her until they were all together and realized no one had. Doppler weather radar is now predicting this storm is going to be a beast, so we need to find her before the precipitation starts coming in."

"We might be a little late for that," Ajay said, noting the flecks of snow looking like tufts of white cotton falling from the sky. "Are we sure she didn't just head home?" he asked. They often had volunteers who quit the job after discovering just how stressful it could be.

"It doesn't look promising. Her brother Malcolm is headed to her house now to double-check. But her family swears she hasn't been seen since they started searching for the missing kids. Max is nervous, so that makes me nervous."

He sensed something in her voice as she mentioned the man with whom she would soon be united in matrimony. Something that gave him pause and put him on high alert. "Ten-four," Ajay responded. "I've got my radio. Give me a shout-out if she turns up."

"Be safe, Ajay," Della said. "It looks like it's going to get nasty out there."

The radio clicked off in his ear. Ajay sighed as he shifted his gaze up the side of the mountain. The last slivers of bright light that had shone through the canopy of trees earlier in the day were beginning to disappear. The sky had gone a dull gray, and the temperature was dropping swiftly. The snow was falling steadily, settling in for the long haul. Ajay knew it wouldn't bode well for anyone caught out in the elements unprepared.

He was familiar with Lizzy Colton through her brother Malcolm. He'd seen her that first day, frantic over the children being taken. The whole family had been at their wit's end. She'd barely glanced in his direction, anxious to be searching. She'd been impatient throughout the safety talk, barreling toward the tree line as soon as it was finished. She'd been assigned to another group, and so she'd been someone else's problem. Not his. Till now.

He blew another heavy sigh. "Let's pony up, Pumpkin," he said, the baritone in his voice echoing around them. "We're still on the clock, girl!" He grabbed his backpack, checked its contents and slung it over his shoulder.

Pumpkin jumped from the Jeep, her tail waving with anticipation. She barked twice and then took off on an easy sprint through the tree line. Ajay shifted his bag against his broad shoulders and then followed after his dog.

# Chapter Two

Ajay and Pumpkin backtracked to the festival area, meeting up with Della and another friend, Sebastian Cross. Sebastian owned Crosswinds Training, the dog training center over on Cross Road. The facility was about ten minutes from town, sitting on five acres of Cross family land. Della and Sebastian had worked with Ajay and Pumpkin to ensure their handler-canine partnership worked effortlessly. Often undertaking search-and-rescue missions together also allowed Pumpkin to engage with Della's black Lab, Charlie, and Sebastian's golden retriever, Oscar. Pumpkin was quite the diva in the presence of the male dogs.

After checking in with each other and establishing a search plan, Della, Sebastian and Ajay had all moved out in opposite directions.

Ajay had gone up and out through the thick forest of trees, following Owl Creek, which flowed down the mountain and into Blackbird Lake. An hour or so later, Pumpkin had discovered a cell phone, discarded just a few feet from the stream. Having missed the water, it was badly scratched from being tossed aside, but it still seemed to be functioning. It had no password protection and took Ajay no time at all to figure out it belonged to Lizzy Colton, the woman he was hoping to find.

Knowing she didn't have a way to communicate with anyone set him on edge. The weather had indeed turned, and there wasn't much time left for him to continue searching. He feared the worst but didn't want to consider what that might be.

Her inbox was inundated with messages from family and friends anxious to hear from her. He held the device out toward Pumpkin, palming it in his hand so she could get the woman's scent. The dog took off ahead of him, her tracking senses on high alert.

Minutes later, Pumpkin was barking excitedly, running in circles about fifty yards ahead of Ajay. Something rested beneath a tree, covered with a layer of freshly fallen snow. Ajay hurried to where his pooch now lay protectively near what she had discovered.

Reaching Pumpkin's side, Ajay knelt down beside her. The woman lying on the ground was out cold, and Ajay smiled wryly at the thought, which was not meant to be literal. But she *was* unconscious, wearing clothes that offered her little protection, and the outside elements had begun to take their toll. She'd been ill-prepared for the inclement weather, and he questioned what had happened that she was there with no coat or shoes. What had she gone through, he wondered.

Ajay knew he needed to get her to safe surroundings and get her warm, but there was no way he could carry her the distance back down the mountain side without endangering all three of them.

Ajay pulled a harness from his backpack and looped it around Pumpkin's torso. The dog whined and licked his face.

"I know, girl," he said, "but I'm going to need your help."

Her tail wagged back and forth in response. With swift precision, Ajay's backpack was secured across Pumpkin's back. She seemed content with the added responsibility.

After checking the Colton woman for broken bones, Ajay took his own jacket off and wrapped it around her torso. Then he lifted her up and over his shoulder like a sack of new potatoes.

Pumpkin started down the mountain, but Ajay called her back. He gestured in the other direction. "We need to find shelter, Pumpkin. We're going to have to ride out this storm. Let's see if we can find cover in one of those rental cabins that are so popular in this area. Pony up, Pumpkin!"

THEY HAD WALKED a good three miles when the Colton woman stirred, her arms clutching his neck tightly. Her entire body shivered beneath the shearling-lined coat he'd been wearing. Her face was buried in his chest, and she muttered something he couldn't understand.

He'd been following a map to the best of his ability. The uptick in falling snow wasn't making their trek easy, the bright white layer of precipitation blinding.

The setting sun and the requisite compass in his pocket kept him pointed in the right direction as he maneuvered forward, intent on reaching the row of rental cabins sitting on the mountain's upper ridge. He eased Lizzy higher in his arms, tightening the grip he had around her.

Her head lifted from his chest and settled against his broad shoulder. She stirred once again, but her eyes never opened. Her thin arms tightened around his neck, the hold she had on him beginning to feel like a vise grip.

He hugged her closer, hoping she sensed that he would never let her go. Not until she was safe.

THE THREE-HUNDRED-SQUARE-FOOT CABIN was luxurious by mountain standards. Its modest size boasted three rooms on the lower level and a lofted sleeping area on the upper floor. It had been over an hour since Ajay had found them refuge, and he was thankful for the fire in the fireplace and the fully stocked pantry.

Pumpkin had already consumed a can of corned beef hash, and she lay beside the woman, seeming to sense a need there that she might be able to fix.

The mattress Lizzy rested against adorned the only bed in the space. Ajay had tended to her scratches and bruises with the medical kit from his backpack. He had enough emergency response training to know that she might have suffered a head injury when she fell. He'd cocooned her in a multitude of blankets to get her body temperature back up.

She had a good case of frostnip, but the color had finally begun to return to her fingers and toes. He was hopeful that he'd found her in time to have prevented her from experiencing serious aftereffects.

Ajay wrapped his large hands around a mug of hot soup that he'd nuked in the microwave. The power had been on when they arrived, but he knew it might not last. The lights flickered as if to confirm his thoughts. He was exhausted and ready for his own nap, but sleep wouldn't be coming any time soon. They'd found shelter, but he still needed to ensure they'd be safe through the storm.

He was grateful for the working radio. He'd been able to call in their location and assure the search-and-rescue team they were okay for the time being. With the storm raging outside, though, it would be hours before anyone could get to them, and there was no way he'd be able to get Lizzy back down the mountain with that thick layer of snow impeding their trek.

The fire raging in the fireplace would only last for as long as he could keep feeding it wood, and they couldn't afford for the flames to die out. For the immediate future, they were stuck with each other, and he was responsible for her care and safety. Sleep would have to wait.

LIZZY WOKE WITH a start, her entire body tensing when her eyes opened. Her gaze shifted rapidly from side to side, skating around the room. She inhaled swiftly at the sight of the man kneeling in front of the fireplace. However, he was familiar, and she relaxed, sensing he was there to help and not hurt her.

He was ruggedly handsome with a dark beard and mustache that flattered his brown complexion. His hair was closely cropped, and his body seemed muscular beneath the long-sleeved T-shirt he wore. He resembled the actor in that Shonda Rhimes medical show she occasionally watched.

There was a fire blazing, and he was tending it with a

long metal poker. He was staring into the fire and seemed lost in thought.

She lifted her arms from beneath the covers tucked around her body, and when she did, a large dog moved beside her. Lizzy jumped ever so slightly as the animal lifted its head to stare up at her. Lizzy wasn't sure if she should be afraid, but something about her situation felt comfortable. This was definitely not like when she'd been tied to the beam in that abandoned cabin.

The dog suddenly barked, and the man turned swiftly. At the sight of her, his full lips lifted in the brightest smile.

"Don't sit up too fast," he said softly. "You suffered a head injury when you fell. You had me scared there for a minute. Let me get you some water."

Lizzy's hand went to her head, her fingers grazing the gauze wrapped around her skull. A wave of nausea suddenly pitched through her midsection, and she lay back down against the pillows.

The man rose from where he'd been kneeling and hurried to the kitchen. He filled a glass with water from a pitcher in the refrigerator. Rushing back, he knelt down beside her. He lifted the container to her lips and continued talking.

"You might not remember me, but I'm Lieutenant Ajay Wright. I'm with the Owl Creek Police Department. Their search-and-rescue team. My partner and I found you passed out a few miles down the mountain from here."

Lizzy took a small sip of the cool liquid he offered. "Your partner...?" she whispered.

Ajay smiled again and nodded. He gestured with his

head. "That beauty queen beside you is Pumpkin. I don't go very far without her."

Pumpkin nuzzled Lizzy's neck and licked her face. Lizzy giggled.

"You had a lot of people worried. Everyone has been looking for you. But they know you're with me now, and they know you're safe. A rescue team will come for us as soon as this storm passes."

"How long have I been here?" Lizzy questioned.

"Just a few hours. We had to find shelter. The snow started rolling in faster than expected. It was safer for us to find someplace to ride it out, so I carried you here."

"You carried me?"

"You sound surprised."

Lizzy wasn't sure how she sounded. She only wanted to understand everything that happened that she didn't remember. She suddenly bolted upright. "My niece and nephew. We need to find…" she started, her tone bordering on hysteria.

Ajay's voice dropped lower, his tone soothing. "They're fine. I imagine they're tucked safely in their own beds with your brother and his wife hovering over the two of them. We found them safe and sound."

Lizzy could feel the weight of the world lifting at Ajay's words. A tear puddled in the corner of her eyes. "Thank God!" she gushed, a sigh of relief blowing past her chapped lips.

Ajay nodded. "We found *them*, then the call went out about *you* being missing. Thankfully, we can report two successful recoveries."

Lizzy swiped her hand across her face. "I was so

scared," she said. "If anything had happened to those two babies, I would have been devastated." Her voice quivered, a wave of emotion wrapped around each word.

He nodded, understanding seeping from his gaze. "Can you tell me what happened out there?" he asked. "Did you get lost? I know how easy it is to get turned around in these woods."

She shook her head. There was just a moment's pause as she thought back to her last memories. "I was out searching for Jane and Justin when I spotted what I thought was the car that had taken them. It wasn't far from where they were holding the festival, so I went to see if maybe they'd been left inside. The car was empty, so I started walking around the area. Out of nowhere, someone or something hit me from behind. The next thing I knew I was in the trunk of the car, and someone was driving away. Then I passed out. When I came to, I was tied up in an abandoned cabin with someone, maybe the person who abducted me. He wouldn't speak to me or answer any of my questions. He would leave and come back, and he always wore a mask. But he was the only one who came to the cabin while I was there. The last time, he forgot to tie me back up before he disappeared— I think he was called away. When I was certain he was gone, I just took off running. At some point, I slipped and fell. That's the last thing I remember."

Ajay's brow furrowed as he seemed to process the information. Lizzy desperately wanted him to believe her. Maybe she had hallucinated after her fall, but he had to know there was something in her story that rang true. She knew she was telling the truth, but she also knew everyone else would have questions. Why had someone grabbed her? Was her being held hostage connected to the children? Clearly, she didn't have any answers. But it also seemed that something else was bothering him more.

"Why would you put yourself in danger?" Ajay queried, his question harsher than she had expected. It surprised her, and it seemed to surprise him as well. There was a wealth of emotion churning in her midsection, as she suddenly realized that he was feeling protective of her.

He drew in a deep breath, looking like his feelings had ambushed him, and then he snapped at her. "Why didn't you call for help? You could have been killed!" Her gaze never left him as he took another deep breath and held it.

Lizzy bristled at the rise in his tone. It was not how she had expected their conversation to go. There was a familiarity between them that she hadn't anticipated. It was comforting and disconcerting at the same time. Not having an answer for him that would make sense, she shifted her gaze from his and closed her eyes, pretending to fall back to sleep.

He had some nerve, she thought to herself. Besides, it wasn't like she owed Ajay Wright an explanation for anything she did.

# Chapter Three

Lizzy stared up at the ceiling, counting the rows of wood beams. That man and his animal were both sleeping soundly. One snored louder than the other. He'd positioned himself in the recliner that rested in the cabin's corner by the fireplace. A blanket lay across his chest and around his shoulders. His dog, Pumpkin, was curled up on the floor at his feet. Clearly, both had been keeping a close watch over her.

Despite his assumption, Lizzy had known exactly who Ajay was when she opened her eyes, even though she had pretended otherwise. The handsome man had been at the center of more than one conversation between herself and her best friend, Vivian Maylor. As had many of the guys who'd been friends or associates of her brothers.

Besties since they were fourteen at Owl Creek Middle School, she and Vivian had often giggled and gossiped about the boys, and men, who had passed through their lives over the years. Lizzy would have given anything to get a cell phone signal so she could call Vivian and describe in glorious detail how Ajay Wright had saved her life.

Lizzy shook the cellular device in her hand. She had lost it when that stranger had grabbed her. Ajay finding and returning it to her had been sheer luck.

Truth be told, the last few days had been the fodder of nightmares, and nothing she wanted to recall. Being rescued was the stuff of fantasies and a happy ending wouldn't hurt her feelings one bit. And who better to share that with than her dearest friend in the whole wide world?

But if Lizzy knew anything at all, she knew Vivian would be less enthusiastic, focused solely on everything bad that could have happened. Lizzy was willing to bet a dime to a dollar that now that everyone knew she was safe, Vivian was home, curled up with a book and her beloved cat, Toby, contemplating all that was wrong in the world. Despite running one of the most lucrative PR agencies around, Vivian was not the outgoing, social-butterfly type. It was why Lizzy was always trying to set her BFF up on blind dates.

Over the years, the two women had met and social-ized with many of her brother's friends. Lizzy had even dated a few, usually just the ones that irritated her three siblings most. Greg, the eldest, usually raised the most sand about her liaisons. Malcolm, the second oldest child, and then Max after him, rarely went ballistic over her antics. The two just never held their tongues, garnering great pleasure in telling her what they thought about her romantic liaisons.

She blew a soft sigh past her thin lips, and the dog lifted her head to stare at her. Lizzy smiled, and she would have sworn Pumpkin smiled back before lowering her bright eyes back to the floor and closing them.

Lizzy had never considered herself an animal person. She liked them well enough, especially when other people were responsible for them. Being raised on a ranch with all kinds of four-legged creatures, she had never had any burning desire to have one of her own to coddle and care for.

But Pumpkin had smiled back at her, and that had her feeling some kind of way. She chuckled softly under her breath.

"Are you hungry?" Ajay asked, his deep baritone voice cutting through the silence.

He startled Lizzy from her thoughts, and she found herself shaking ever so slightly. He seemed to sense she was unsettled, and he paused, allowing her a moment to collect herself. "I didn't mean to frighten you," Ajay said, his voice dropping an octave, his tone lower and deeper.

Lizzy shook her head. "It's fine. I'm not even sure why I reacted that way."

"You've experienced a trauma. You are entitled to not be okay. Please don't think you need to pretend everything's fine around me. I know better."

She nodded, quickly changing the subject. She had no interest in being psychoanalyzed by him, or anyone, right then. "Is it still snowing?"

"I think so." Ajay rose from his seat and moved to the front door. A chilly breeze filled the room as he pulled the door open. "Yeah," he said. "It's still coming down." He called for his dog. "Pumpkin, go do your business, girl, and come right back."

The dog barked and hurried outside. Ajay stood in the doorway, watching her until she rushed back in. Lizzy laughed as Pumpkin shook her fur coat, snow flying into the space around her.

"I swear she's smiling," Lizzy said.

Ajay laughed. "She does smile. You get used to it. She's a happy dog, and she loves being outside. The elements don't seem to faze her one bit."

"Happy means she's well cared for. You must be doing something right."

Ajay shrugged his broad shoulders, but he didn't bother to respond, seeming slightly embarrassed by the compliment. Lizzy felt her entire face pull into a large smile as she watched him, sensing his cheeks had heated under his warm, tawny complexion. He had the kindest eyes, Lizzy thought, a golden shimmer glistening in the cool brown orbs. His chiseled features were the stuff of high-fashion models, and she got the impression a camera would love him from any angle. She suddenly wondered just how soft his skin was, because his complexion looked butter smooth.

Ajay shifted the conversation back to his original question. "Can I get you something to eat? You have to be starving by now."

Lizzy smiled and nodded. "I could eat a little something," she said.

"Would you like to try some oatmeal? Or maybe some soup? We also have oatmeal and soup. Or if you prefer, soup and oatmeal."

She laughed. "Sounds like we're eating soup and oatmeal."

"Or oatmeal and soup." Ajay laughed with her. "Those

are two items that are well stocked up here. They have four flavors of oatmeal—plain, cinnamon, apple spice and raisin. Then there's chicken noodle soup, tomato, broccoli cheese, cream of mushroom, chicken and stars or vegetable. Pumpkin ate the last can of corned beef hash."

Lizzy feigned a frown. "I really would have liked that hash."

"Me, too," Ajay responded as he met the stare she was giving him with his own forlorn look.

The duo suddenly laughed heartily, the moment lifting the mood in the room. Pumpkin barked along with them.

Lizzy suddenly clutched her head and winced. "Don't make me laugh," she said. "I have a raging headache."

Ajay moved to her side and pressed a large hand to her forehead. "You're warm," he said. "Do you feel nauseous or anything?"

"No, not really. I just have a headache. And I'm hungry. In fact, I think chicken noodle soup would make me feel better," Lizzy said. She gave him the slightest smile.

Ajay headed toward the kitchen area. "One microwaved can of chicken noodle soup coming right up! And if you eat it all up, I have a surprise for you after."

"I don't like surprises," Lizzy said.

He tossed her a look over his shoulder. "Everyone likes surprises."

"I'm not everyone," she countered.

Staring at her for a moment longer, Ajay finally nodded, then turned his attention back to the can of soup in his hands.

Lizzy grinned, reaching out to pet Pumpkin, who'd settled down against her side.

"So," Lizzy said, anxious to continue their conversation, "do you like the snow as much as Pumpkin does?"

Ajay tossed her a look over his shoulder as he stood in front of the microwave oven. "Not really. I prefer tropical heat. Put me on an island, and I'd be a happy man."

"So you moved to Owl Creek, Idaho? Did you know that we're not remotely tropical?" The barest hint of sarcasm was wrapped around her words.

Ajay chuckled. "I had to go where employment took me. I was working in Boise when I got this job offer. It wasn't one I could turn down. The snow was an added bonus."

"Do you like search and rescue?"

"I love it. I spent time in the military after I graduated high school. That led me to law enforcement and the rest is history."

Lizzy nodded, then took a sip of the hot soup he'd passed to her.

"What do you do?" Ajay questioned.

"I'm a starving artist working as a graphic designer. Are you familiar with Bark Design Company?"

Ajay shrugged his broad shoulders. "Sorry."

"No worries. I've only been in business for two years now. My latest venture into the corporate arena. In all honesty, I'd love to be in my own tropical paradise painting landscapes. But I have a talent for graphic design, and it pays well."

"I'd love to see your work one day," Ajay said.

Lizzy lifted her gaze to study his expression. His interest felt genuine, not as if he were saying something just to be saying it.

He smiled, his lips lifting slowly.

She smiled back. "One day," she finally said. "One day."

A warm wave of quiet filled the space between them. Pumpkin stared at one and then the other. There was the slightest rumble of noise deep in her chest before she rolled over onto her side and closed her eyes.

"Tell me about your family," Lizzy said. "Unless that's too personal. I wouldn't want you to break any rules, but I figured since we're stuck here together..." Her voice trailed.

Ajay shifted in his seat. "There's not much to tell," he said. "I'm an only child. A military brat born in Germany. My father was a career soldier, and we lived on six different military bases while I was growing up. My mother was a stay-at-home mom. Now Dad's retired, tending to his gardens, and Mom is the librarian at the local elementary school where they live."

"An only child!" Lizzy exclaimed. "I bet that sucked growing up."

Ajay laughed. "Not at all. You don't miss what you never had. My mother kept me busy with sports and extracurricular activities. Since I never had a problem making friends, I had a great social life. My really good friends were as close as family. I was also very comfortable being alone with myself. I didn't have to share. All in all, I think I turned out okay."

"I guess growing up with three brothers, I never appreciated what being an only child might be like. It sounds like it had its advantages."

"There are only four of you?"

"More if you take into account our Jerry Springer history."

Ajay's brow lifted. "Now I'm definitely intrigued."

"Malcolm never told you about our family?"

Ajay shook his head. "The subject never came up, to be honest. I knew he had siblings, but I try to stay out of other people's Jerry Springer business."

"Well, keep up," Lizzy said as she leaned back against a mound of pillows. "This story's a doozy! It all started with our parents. Our mother, Jessie, has a twin sister, Aunt Jenny, who we call our Mama Jen. Even though the two are twins, they were never close and didn't much like each other."

Ajay winced as Lizzy nodded her head to emphasize her comment.

"In high school," she continued, "the two sisters both dated the star football captain, Robert Colton. After graduation, Robert chose Aunt Jenny, and the two married. This pulled the two sisters even further apart. But Uncle Robert had an older brother. And not to be outdone by her sister, Jessie married Robert's brother, Buck. Buck Colton is my father."

Ajay shook his head. "I think popcorn might be necessary here. This sounds like some serious tea. Some really good tea!"

Lizzy giggled. "Let me finish! Now, my Uncle Robert and Aunt Jenny had six kids, so I not only grew up with my brothers, but a half dozen cousins, too. My brother

Greg was the first child my parents had. He was that *oops!* baby. Then came Malcolm and after him, Max. Max worked for the FBI until recently. And of course you know Malcolm. I am the youngest and the only girl. I was their other oops baby."

"That's funny," Ajay said. "Oops!"

"To be honest, I'm not sure any of us were planned."

"Your story's not that bad. It's kind of tame, actually. I was expecting a true scandal the way you started your story."

"I'm not finished. Get another handful of that pretend popcorn," Lizzy said. She shifted in her seat. "My parents divorced when I was a toddler, and my mother left us."

"I'm so sorry," Ajay said. He leaned forward, clasping both hands in front of him. "That must have been hard for you all."

Lizzy shrugged dismissively. "It really got hard when we found out about the affair between my mother and my uncle."

Ajay's eyes widened. "Your mother, Jessie, and your Uncle Robert?"

She nodded. "Not only did they have an affair, but they had pretended to be married, buying a home a few hours outside Boise. They even had two children together. My half-brother Nathan and my half-sister Sarah. And no one knew until just recently. Surprise!" she gushed, giving him dance hands.

Ajay's eyes bounced from side to side as he put all the pieces to the Colton family tree in place. "Wow!" he exclaimed. "That also makes Nathan and Sarah your cousins, too."

"Siblings, cousins, whatever. I just know we shared the same incubator. And they share the same sperm donor with my Aunt Jenny's kids."

Ajay shook his head. "Are you all close?"

"We're all working on it," Lizzy said softly. "I imagine future family holidays will be quite interesting."

"Save a seat for me," Ajay teased. "I don't want to miss the fireworks."

"We managed to all get through Uncle Robert's funeral, and after that the truth started to come out. He suffered a stroke a few months ago. At least, that's what we've all been told."

"You don't believe it?"

"I really don't have any reason not to, but I know some of his children have had a lot of questions. Then toss in a whole other family wanting to lay claim to their share of his estate, and I'm sure everything looks fishy."

"I'm sorry to hear that," Ajay said. "Losing a parent must be difficult enough without the added drama."

"Do you have a good relationship with your parents?" Lizzy questioned.

"I do," Ajay said with a nod of his head. "My father is one of my best friends, and my mother, well... She still spoils me when she can. I love them both dearly. How about you?"

"My dad is the best. I don't know what I would do without him. My mother, on the other hand, is a whole other story." She scowled. Her eyes moved to the window, and Lizzy seemed to drift off into thought.

Ajay could feel a shift in her energy. He hesitated to ask more about her mother after everything she'd shared.

"So what's the big surprise you have for me?" she questioned, holding out the empty soup bowl. The sudden change of subject meant he didn't have an opportunity to push further.

Ajay jumped from his seat. He reached for her dirty dish and took it with him back to the kitchen counter. A moment passed as he shifted items in one of the cabinets. Stepping back toward her, he held his hands behind his back.

"Should I be scared?" Lizzy said, eyeing him nervously.

"Only if you have an irrational fear of... Twinkies!" His grin was canyon wide as he held out the cellophane-wrapped treat. His eyes met hers and held. "We actually have dessert to go with all that soup and oatmeal!"

Twinkies! Lizzy laughed heartily. Maybe things were beginning to look up after all, she thought.

"I HATED CHEESE as a child," Ajay said. "I thought it was the worst thing in the world. Now, I can't get enough of the stuff!"

"It was cottage cheese for me. I hated it then, and I despise it now." Lizzy frowned. "Please, tell me you don't eat cottage cheese."

"It's not my favorite, but I can get it down if I have to. It just requires something sweet to go with it. Like pineapple. Or strawberries."

"Yuck," Lizzy responded with a scowl.

Ajay laughed. "So what's your favorite dessert?"

"The first cake I taught myself how to make, and it came out well, was a pineapple upside-down cake. I've perfected my recipe, and it's my all-time favorite dessert to make and eat. And my daddy loves it!"

"What about your brothers?"

"They don't count. I can make a pan of boxed brownies, and that makes them happy."

"Brownies are good!"

"What about you? What's your favorite sweet?" Lizzy asked.

"I would give everything away for a perfect banana pudding with lots of those vanilla wafer cookies."

"I don't know if I've ever made banana pudding."

"It has to be the cooked pudding, not the one where you mix whipped cream and pudding mix together. Homemade pudding with bananas and vanilla cookies. I could eat that all day, every day!"

"I'll have to give that a try."

"Now don't go messing up good bananas. If it's not good, I will tell you."

"Who said I was making it for you?"

Ajay whooped, the laughter deep in his chest. "Touché!" he said when he'd collected himself. "Touché!"

His smile was wide as he stared at her. Lizzy was beautiful. Her girl-next-door glow was captivating, and her cheeks had brightened with the rise of heat in the room. Her strawberry blond hair fell in natural waves around her face and down her back. Her facial features were perfection, stunning blue eyes and the most luscious mouth. He found himself wondering about the person allowed to kiss her lips with regularity. Who were they and how had such luck befallen them?

He wanted to ask but knew to do so was unprofessional and also none of his business. A low sigh blew past his full lips.

"So, what else do you like to do to entertain yourself?" he asked. "We've ascertained you're a good cook. What else are you good at?"

"I'm very good with my hands," Lizzy said, the barest hint of innuendo in her tone.

Ajay laughed. "I'm thinking you might need to explain that," he said.

She smiled, arching her eyebrows suggestively. Then she laughed. "I like to be crafty," she said. "I like to make beautiful things from useless scraps. I'm the queen of handmade gifts."

"I would throw useless scraps in the trash. I guess I'm not that good with my hands," he replied.

Lizzy laughed. "That's a shame," she said with an eye roll.

"Let me rephrase that," Ajay said. "I'm good with my hands, but I'm not crafty. Is that better?"

"That's for you to determine, not me!"

"But you have me feeling some kind of way."

"Don't put that on me!"

"Like I didn't see that eye roll and that look you gave me. I know how to take a hint."

Lizzy giggled. "You're a little sensitive, aren't you?"

Ajay pressed his hand over his heart. "I'm extremely sensitive and I make no apologies for it."

"I like sensitive men," Lizzy said, a sly smile pulling at her thin lips.

Ajay grinned, feeling his own lips pulling wide across his face.

## Chapter Four

Lizzy Colton talked in her sleep. Ajay had been watching her for over an hour, and she had been tossing and turning and talking in her sleep the entire time. After one too many bad jokes about Twinkies and the sweet cream inside, they had chatted for a few minutes longer, the conversation mostly idle chatter about nothing of any importance. Sleep had come soon after.

There was still much about the woman Ajay wanted to know. Lizzy Colton was very much an anomaly in his little world, and he was enjoying her presence. Unlike the last woman he'd dated, she didn't take herself too seriously. She was funny and instinctively looked for the best in a bad situation. She also exuded confidence, and he had always found that kind of surety in a woman very sexy. He found himself enjoying the little idiosyncrasies that made her so intriguing.

He discovered she practiced tapping therapy or what was called EFT, emotional freedom technique. It was supposed to be a powerful stress reliever. She'd spent an hour teaching him the meridian points on his body, the acupressure points he tapped with his fingers while focusing on what was causing his stress.

He was hesitant at first, disbelieving, and she found his reticence amusing. It turned out he had only needed to be open-minded and adventurous. When he finally allowed himself to explore the possibilities, he was pleasantly surprised. She was an adept instructor, patient and skillful. There was a rhythm to what he learned, a structured dance of sorts that put him into a state of full relaxation. Then they'd both drifted off to sleep.

Now, watching her, he wished there was something he could do to ease her discomfort and help her find a semblance of peace. Because her beloved tapping didn't seem to have helped the anxiety she was clearly feeling.

Everything she'd gone through looked like it was beginning to haunt her dreams, despite her efforts to pretend like she wasn't bothered when she was awake. But Ajay knew that bottling up that kind of trauma wouldn't serve her well.

"Why are you staring at me?" Lizzy suddenly asked, her blue eyes open wide, her expression questioning.

Looking up, Ajay was taken aback. So lost in his own thoughts, he hadn't expected to get caught like his hand was in a cookie jar. "Was I staring?" he asked, feigning ignorance.

The look that crossed her face spoke volumes. Not only had he been staring, but every thought in his head could probably be read like a summer novel across his face. She must already know that he stared because he was concerned. Worried that she wouldn't be well despite his best efforts. He could keep her safe for the moment, but there was nothing he could do about the personal demons she refused to acknowledge. She was on her own in that battle.

"Okay, be like that," Lizzy said. She shifted against the mattress, sitting herself upright.

"Like what?"

"Like that."

Ajay smiled, but he didn't bother to reply. He changed the subject. "I keep thinking about your kidnapping. Do you know any reason why someone would want to take you?"

Lizzy shook her head. She blew out a soft sigh. "I really have no idea."

"Do you think it was random? That you just happened to be in the wrong place at the right time?"

"The story of my life," Lizzy muttered, seemingly pondering his question. "But no, something about it doesn't feel random. It felt like there had been some previous planning. I almost want to say he purposely meant to grab me. Showing up where I did just gave him the opportunity."

"And you're certain you never saw this man before?"

"Not that I really saw him, with the mask and all. But no. I have no idea who he is. I'd recognize his eyes, though. I'd recognize those eyes anywhere."

"Do you have any idea why he'd want to kidnap you, Lizzy? Is there anyone who has a grudge against you or who you've had beef with lately?"

She shook her head, and he could almost see her mind going through a list of everyone she knew. "No one," she said finally. "It just doesn't make sense to me."

"When you chased down the car, there was no one there, is that right?"

There was a hint of attitude in her response, as though Lizzy was beginning to feel like she was being interrogated. "I wouldn't say I chased it down. It was parked, and I went over to inspect it. I was hoping to find Justin and Jane inside, but it was empty. I started walking around the area, and that's when someone came up behind me and hit me on the head. Everything after that is really foggy. That's all I know!"

"One last question, if you don't mind. Do you remember what the car looked like?"

She nodded. "Yeah. It was an older model Nissan. A Maxima, I think." She repeated herself, needing to affirm that she was certain of what she saw. "Yeah. A black Nissan Maxima."

Ajay paused, replaying everything in his head that Lizzy had told him about being captured. He fell into thought as she pulled the blankets tighter around her torso and drifted back to sleep.

Ajay sat watching her toss and turn, her slumber restless and disturbed. He watched, almost afraid to pull his eyes away from her as if something might happen. Because clearly they were missing something, and he couldn't begin to know what that was, or if she was really safe.

WHEN LIZZY NEXT AWOKE, she was running a high fever and her chest rattled with congestion. She could barely open her eyes, and Ajay's concern rose exponentially.

It had been snowing for an entire day and didn't look

like it planned to end any time soon. It had been hours since he was last able to get a signal on the radio, and he could only hope that someone would be headed in their direction sooner than later.

Pulling on his jacket and boots, he and Pumpkin headed outdoors. He carried a stack of towels that he dropped into the freshly fallen snow, rolling the towels about until they were wet and icy. Back inside, he wrapped one of the cotton cloths around Lizzy's neck and pressed another to her forehead. He knew he needed to lower her body temperature by any means necessary.

She shivered from the sudden chill as perspiration beaded across her brow. She moaned, the guttural sound pulling at Ajay's heartstrings.

"It's going to be okay," he said, his voice a loud whisper. "I'm not going to let anything happen to you, Lizzy."

Pumpkin dropped her head into Ajay's lap. Her puppy-dog stare shifted from Ajay to Lizzy, and she licked the side of Lizzy's face before burrowing her muzzle into her neck.

"She needs to rest, Pumpkin," Ajay said. "Leave her be." He stroked the dog's thick coat and nudged her down to the floor at his feet.

Hours passed as he sat at Lizzy's side. He felt helpless, only able to watch and wait. And the waiting was beginning to take its toll. Knowing he needed to keep his composure, to keep Lizzy from fearing the worst, he remained steadfast, determined that they would soon be home, safe and sound.

Ajay gently caressed the length of her fingers, her palm like smooth satin against his own. She had drifted back to sleep again, but her breathing was still ragged. She struggled for air, and that cough had become barking. Intuition told him things were only going to go downhill if help didn't arrive soon. Time wasn't being a good friend.

Lowering his head, Ajay closed his eyes. He pressed his forehead to the back of her hand, wanting to will whatever strength he had to her. Then he whispered a silent prayer skyward, wishing for complete and total healing. He still held her hand tightly, struggling against his desire to pull her into his arms.

THE SNOW HAD finally stopped falling, but Ajay still wasn't able to get a radio signal in or out. Lizzy's fever had barely broken, but he'd been able to rouse her long enough to entice her with three tablespoons of soup and a few sips of hot tea and lemon. She'd fallen right back to sleep and seemed to be resting as well as she could under the circumstances.

With the fire burning in the fireplace and the snow-painted canvas outside, Ajay couldn't help but think that under different circumstances the cabin was probably a very romantic place for the right two people.

He found himself pondering the idea of himself and Lizzy Colton and blamed the fantasies on their current situation. With nothing but time on their hands, they'd spent some of the hours in the cabin getting to know each other before Lizzy's fever spiked. He'd had dozens of questions for Lizzy, and she'd had just as many for him. He wanted to think they'd become fast friends as they'd traded stories about their childhoods and families.

With more in common than not, they'd discovered similar interests in food, music and movies. He had watched *Titanic* as many times as she had, if not more. They both loved Italian food, and she'd promised him a lasagna dinner when this was over and they were back to civilization. Learning they both kept Amythyst Kiah, Shy Carter and Ghost Hounds on rotation in their playlists had sealed the deal on a lifelong friendship both looked forward to exploring.

LIZZY'S TEMPERATURE SPIKED twice more, and twice more Ajay wrapped her in cold towels. Without her smile and laughter, it felt like an eternity had passed before the first sign of rescue sounded in the midmorning air.

Pumpkin heard the engines first, barking excitedly as she rushed to the door. Jumping from where he sat, Ajay grabbed his coat and hurried outside. Holding both arms high above his head, he waved his hands from side to side for their attention.

The line of newly purchased search-and-rescue vehicles was truly something to behold. The Owl Creek town council had approved the budget for them the previous year, and Ajay knew this was one of the first storms to put them into full use. There were five in total, SnowTrax vehicles that could easily get off the road and maneuver into tight spots without getting stuck. They put traditional ATVs, snowmobiles and trucks to shame, maneuvering around and through obstacles the other vehicles couldn't. Snow depth was inconsequential as they literally floated above the snow. Each had been configured for a driver, an EMT and a gurney if needed. And they'd all been painted vibrant red with the Owl Creek town logo adorning the side.

Malcolm Colton jumped from the first vehicle followed by Max and Della. Emergency medical personnel pushed past them as Ajay pointed them in Lizzy's direction.

"She's suffered a head injury and minor frostbite," Ajay said. "Her fever's only been down for an hour or so, but she's having difficulty breathing. I'm afraid it might be pneumonia."

"We've got it from here, Lieutenant," the EMT said, acknowledging the insignia on Ajay's jacket.

Malcolm extended a hand in his direction. "Thank you! We've been worried, but I knew she was safe once you found her. I appreciate you getting that last message to us."

"Lizzy's a fighter," Ajay said.

He watched as the two brothers hurried inside to see their little sister. Seeing them together, there was no missing the family resemblance. It was the eyes for Ajay— all telling, sometimes brooding, most times full of light and energy.

Della moved to Ajay's side. She hugged him briefly before shifting into business mode. "Did Lizzy say what happened?" she asked.

Ajay nodded. "She was kidnapped. A man grabbed her and was holding her hostage. She was able to escape when he left her unattended, but she got turned around in the woods. She fell and hit her head. When I found her, she was passed out and suffering from hypothermia."

"Kidnapped? Did she recognize him?"

"No. He wore a mask. But he kept her in one of the

abandoned cabins not too far from here. If we can find it, forensics might be able to discover something useful."

They both paused as the EMTs carried Lizzy from the cabin, moving swiftly to the rescue vehicle.

"There's a helicopter coming to take her to the hospital in Conners," Max said as he too rushed past. "We just need to get her to the clearing on the other side."

"I can help," Ajay said, starting after them.

Malcolm slapped him on the back as he moved past. "You've done more than enough. Thank you again for everything you did. We've got it from here. You go get some rest."

"You need to let the EMTs check you out," Della said as she and Ajay both stepped aside.

Ajay shook his head. "I'm fine. I just need a ride back to my car."

"Then you're going to need a shovel, too," Della said smugly. "Your car is buried under a few feet of snow right now. I'll arrange for a tow. You really just need to go get yourself some sleep. I'll drive you home." She headed toward one of the rescue vehicles, then paused, throwing him a look over her shoulder. "Good save, Lieutenant Wright. You did good out here. My future in-laws won't forget that."

In the distance, Ajay could hear the chopper blades turning in the air. He stared in that direction until he saw the Life Flight rise above the tree line and head in the direction of the hospital.

Pumpkin suddenly appeared at his side, pushing her head against the palm of his hand. She whimpered softly.

"It's all good," Ajay said as he tousled the dog's fur.

"Lizzy's going to be just fine." His voice dropped to a low whisper. "She has to be, Pumpkin. She just has to be okay."

# Chapter Five

There was an abundance of commotion that suddenly intruded on Lizzy's rest. Familiar voices were calling her name. Voices she recognized but still couldn't identify. One of her brothers, or maybe it was all three of them. Her father and a woman who was not her mother. A stranger, whose tone was nasal and high-pitched. Someone else whose voice was soft and smooth like the brush of cotton against her skin.

Her body felt heavy and disjointed. There were people poking and prodding at her, shifting her this way and that. She wanted to tell them to stop, to leave her be, but she couldn't find the words in the murky fog that clouded her head.

She opened her eyes and was blinded by the bright lights. She closed them again, wishing away all the noise. She kept listening for one voice, and no matter how hard she tried, she couldn't hear the sweet baritone that had become a singular source of comfort for her up at the cabin. She wanted to hear the bourbon-inspired growl of Ajay Wright's seductive laugh, the rich, sweet timbre like warm caramel and sweet butter against her ears. The last time he spoke to her he was holding her hand, assuring her things would be well. She had believed him, and now all she wanted was to have him back at her side.

Their time together had been emotionally intimate in a way she would never have expected. During one of their conversations, the opportunity for a first kiss had presented itself, but Ajay had pulled himself from her, respectful of her injuries. Instead, he had tucked a second blanket around her, asking if she wanted to share the last Twinkie that had been in the box. Both had pretended like the moment never happened, and for a while Lizzy had wondered if she'd imagined it. Maybe what she wanted had nothing at all to do with what he had wanted. Maybe he hadn't given any consideration to kissing her and it had all been in her own head.

Lizzy had been drawn to the prospect of taking things further, but she had to admit, that yet again, it was the wrong place and the wrong time and, for all she knew, maybe even the wrong man. Because Lizzy's luck with men was a thing for the record books. The *boys* who always wanted her number were self-absorbed, self-centered and selfish. The few *men* she'd actually dated had been likable at the start, but things often crashed and burned before she could blink.

There was only one man who'd lasted for any length of time, and Lizzy had no desire to remember that disastrous relationship.

Lizzy heard her name, someone talking about her. Or maybe it was everyone talking about her. She wasn't sure of anything except she was missing Ajay and wished someone would tell her why he wasn't there.

"She'll sleep," a voice was saying.

"Should we be worried?" another voice questioned.

The words "...fever...antibiotics...time...rest..." floated through the air.

There was more chatter and whispered responses, none of it making any sense to Lizzy. She tried to speak, Ajay's name on the tip of her tongue. She attempted to call for him, but the words sounded foreign to her own ears.

"It's okay, Lizzy. Just rest, sweet girl." Lizzy recognized her father's voice. Only her father called her sweet girl.

It hurt to breathe, Lizzy thought, but oxygen in her nostrils made it easier. *It's okay*, she repeated over and over again in her head. *It's okay*.

Something beeped, the sound startling. She tried again to call for Ajay, and then she felt a hand gently caressing her forearm. She wanted to smile, to open her eyes one more time to see if he was there. But sleep was calling her loudly, pulling her back beneath a blanket of quiet and calm.

Everything was going to be okay, she thought as she gave into the slumber. Ajay had promised, and she knew with almost infinite certainty that Ajay Wright always kept his word.

HE DIDN'T DARE tell anyone that he was missing Lizzy Colton, Ajay thought to himself. Heaven forbid he say it out loud, even if only for Pumpkin's ears. He had only been back in his home for a week, and he was missing her as if they'd been separated for an eternity. He blew out a soft sigh as he scavenged for a meal in his very empty refrigerator. It had been so long since he'd last shopped that the pantry of oatmeal and soup up in that cabin sounded pretty appetizing right then.

He scrambled himself an egg, the last one left from a container of twelve. There was no bread, nor anything that resembled bacon, to be found. That egg and a pack of peanut butter crackers became the meal, and when he'd consumed the last bite, he sat at the kitchen table feeling lost and, for the first time, alone.

He couldn't help but wonder if Lizzy was doing well. He had called the hospital the day before to check on her, and Malcolm had been happy to tell him she was finally out of the woods. She was expected to make a full recovery and was already giving her big brothers a hard time. Malcolm hadn't said whether or not she had asked about him, Ajay thought.

Ajay wanted to call to check on her again but knew that it would probably be frowned upon. He wasn't family, no one knew him as her friend, and his position on the search-and-rescue team dictated he file his final report and move on. Officially, he could be written up for calling a woman he'd rescued. Most especially if he wanted to invite her for coffee and maybe dinner, no matter what the circumstances. Personal relationships with clients were frowned upon. Doubly so since he was also in a leadership position, and he needed to be the example other officers followed. Besides, he thought, Lizzy might not be interested in seeing him again.

Pumpkin suddenly barked, running from the room and back again.

"You don't know," Ajay muttered at the dog. "For all you know, she might have a boyfriend."

"Ruff! Ruff!"

Ajay rolled his eyes skyward. He hated it when it felt like his four-legged friend was reading his mind. He hated it more when it felt like the animal was giving him advice.

He dropped down onto the sofa, flipping channels on the television remote. As promised, Della had arranged for his car to be in his driveway, the tow truck arriving the day after she had dropped him home. He had needed to sleep, but he hadn't rested well. There was a nagging feeling in the pit of his stomach that he couldn't shake.

He didn't feel comfortable with the idea that Lizzy's kidnapper still roamed the streets of Owl Creek, and no one knew who it was or why they'd taken her. How was her abduction linked to the missing Kraft children? *Was* there any connection at all? Had they intended to lever-age her capture against the Colton family for a ransom? Had she been the next intended victim of a serial killer hunting innocent women for sport?

He still had more questions than answers and that left him feeling vulnerable. Because if Lizzy ever needed pro-tection, it would be now. At least until they were able to solve her case. And if Lizzy needed protection, then he desperately needed to be where she was. He needed to trust that she was safe. Not knowing what was going on with her didn't leave him with any confidence.

"I need to go check on Lizzy," he said out loud. He jumped to his feet and reached for his keys and jacket. He was headed to the hospital. He paused briefly to reflect on the ramifications of his decision, deciding to hell with protocol as he rushed out the door.

As Ajay made his exit, Pumpkin barked again, her tail wagging in agreement.

LIZZY WAS SO done with the hospital food they'd been serving her. She pushed whatever was on the plate in front of her from one side to the other. It looked like mashed potatoes and tasted like mush. She'd also had her fill of nurses taking her temperature and logging her blood pressure every other minute.

She was ready for a semblance of normalcy, if such a thing could ever exist again. She was grateful that her family had finally stopped hovering over her. Her brothers had returned to their jobs, and her father had finally been convinced to return to his ranch. There had been no sign of her mother, the matriarch not bothering to call or visit.

Lizzy was three years old when Jessie Colton walked out on her husband, leaving him and her children behind. Lizzy had no memory of ever calling her mommy or mother or mom. Jessie had never returned, not bothering to stay in contact with her offspring. The boys had missed her, having memories from when she'd been there to make them breakfast and lunch and take them to school. Whatever gap she'd left in their small worlds had been filled abundantly by their father, who hadn't taken the responsibility lightly. He had been, and continued to be, one hell of a father.

Jessie had missed every important moment in Lizzy's

life, and Lizzy had learned to accept not having her around. It was all she had ever known.

Mama Jen had been there in Jessie's stead, showing Lizzy how to apply makeup, giving her the birds-and-bees talk, taking her shopping for her prom gown and being the voice of wisdom when her father and brothers lacked understanding of female things. Mama Jen had been a lifeline Lizzy never knew she needed until she was there.

Mama Jen hadn't left the hospital since Lizzy arrived a week ago, supporting her father and brothers and making sure all of Lizzy's needs were attended to. She was a nurse by profession and fell into the role easily. So not hearing from Jessie Colton hadn't bothered Lizzy at all.

But she had hoped to hear from Ajay Wright, and his not calling had her squarely in her feelings. It had pushed her knee-deep into a bad mood, and she was past ready to go home and sulk without being disturbed.

She reached for the phone to call Vivian. Her friend would understand, Lizzy thought. And if she didn't, she could at least be trusted to share her ideas without holding her tongue. As she scrolled through her contacts, she was suddenly distracted by a commotion in the hallway.

Looking out the room door, Lizzy was startled by a man standing by the nurse's desk. His back was turned, and he was leaning over the counter chatting with one of the nurses. No one else was there to see what he was doing, but everything about his demeanor felt too familiar.

Lizzy shifted against the pillows, a knot tightening

in the middle of her stomach. She leaned forward for a closer look.

His clothing was neat, black pants and a matching shirt with a black overcoat. It was the hiking boots, well-worn and dingy, that grabbed her attention. Boots she'd seen before.

And then he turned, his dark eyes locking with hers. He wore a mask, his face obscured, but those eyes were all too familiar.

Lizzy was suddenly dizzy, the room seeming to spin around her. The air felt thin, and she gasped loudly, fighting to catch her breath. Dropping the telephone, she clenched her fists, digging her nails into the palms of her hands.

The man lifted himself upright, staring in her direction. His gaze narrowed with hostility. He took one and then two steps toward her.

The ear-piercing shriek that echoed down the hospital hallway was deafening. It rattled the walls like a rumble of thunder. Lizzy screamed a second time, abruptly halting the man's steps. As her room suddenly overflowed with hospital staff, the man turned and disappeared in the opposite direction, Lizzy still screaming again and again.

OWL CREEK'S EXPRESS MEDICAL CLINIC was a staple in the community, and its location near the center of town made for easy access. It was also a central point of care and support services for residents, their mission devoted to patient-centered care and education. Its reputation was stellar for its size, but more complicated cases had to travel forty-five minutes to Conners and the big hospital there.

Ajay had prepared himself for the ride, making it from his front door to the hospital's parking lot in record time. As he pulled his SUV into an empty parking space, he was instantly on edge. Several Conners police cars were parked in front of the brick building. Uniformed officers were stationed at the exits directing traffic and eyeing each vehicle suspiciously. Someone or something had put them on high alert.

His gaze shifted around the parking lot, noting those who were as curious as he was and others who had no interest at all in what might be going on. Jumping from the Jeep, he locked the door and hurried toward the hospital entrance.

Inside, the number of uniformed officers standing around made it look like the entire police department from Conners and maybe even Owl Creek, too, had been called into work. Whatever was going on was serious, and Ajay found himself racing to find Lizzy to ensure she was safe. He flashed his badge at the hospital's reception desk and then the nursing station on the third floor.

As he neared Lizzy's room, the number of officers seemed to increase. Detectives he knew and occasionally worked with were interviewing nursing staff and taking statements from a number of visitors to the hospital.

Della stood at the door to Lizzy's room. He could hear her inside, crying hysterically, and it took every ounce of fortitude he possessed not to push his way inside to get to her.

"What's going on?" he snapped, greeting his friend brusquely.

Della's gaze widened. "What are you doing here?" she questioned.

"I wanted to check on Lizzy." He suddenly felt anxious and slightly embarrassed. "Did something happen?"

Della eyed him with a narrowed gaze and a wry smile. "Interesting," she muttered.

"Don't start, Della. I just wanted to make sure she's doing okay."

Della grabbed his arm and pulled him aside. "Lizzy thinks she saw her kidnapper outside her door. They haven't been able to calm her down since."

"Did you pull the security tapes?"

"And the building was locked down as we checked everyone coming and going," Della answered with a nod of her head.

"He didn't hurt her, did he? Did he touch her?" Ajay's mind was racing, his eyes darting from corner to corner.

"No. Lizzy screamed bloody murder before he could make it to the door of her room. Apparently, the man she saw was chatting up one of the nurses, trying to get a date. The doctors think she may have been hallucinating from all the medication they've been giving her. Max agrees. Now she refuses to let them give her anything to help her calm down. The family doesn't know what to do. They're even considering sedating her completely and transferring her up to the psych ward for an evaluation."

Ajay shifted his weight from one leg to the other. He

desperately needed to lay eyes on Lizzy. He shook his head. "She'll be fine," he said as he turned toward the room and the two uniformed officers standing guard. "I need to go in to see her."

"I don't know if that's a good idea," Della said softly.

"Just be my friend," Ajay replied as he tossed her a look over his shoulder. There wasn't anything anyone could do to stop him, he thought, but he didn't say it out loud.

Della nodded for the officers to let him pass, and they stepped aside as he moved into the room.

The Colton family all turned at the same time, eyeing him warily. Silence surrounded Lizzy's low sob as they all stopped talking, their focus shifting to where he stood.

"I don't mean to interrupt," Ajay said. His gaze left her brothers and settled over her face, noting the stream of tears that trickled down her cheeks. "I just wanted to make sure Lizzy…" he started.

"Ajay!" Lizzy screamed his name, extending her arms in his direction.

He hurried to where she sat in the hospital bed. As he neared, Lizzy's expression changed from gleeful to angry. She threw a punch, hitting him squarely in the chest.

"Ouch! What the hell, Lizzy? That hurt!" He rubbed where he suspected a bruise would rise in varying shades of black and blue.

"You ghosted me!"

"I did not!"

"So where have you been?" Lizzy said, her voice raised. "You promised to take care of me."

Ajay paused, suddenly aware of all the eyes on him,

her family watching their exchange closely. "I'm here now," he finally answered, taking a seat on the side of the bed.

Lizzy threw her arms around his neck as he gently wrapped her in his arms.

"He was here," she whispered loudly. "That freak came after me here in the hospital. He was right outside my room! I saw him, and no one believes me."

"I believe you," Ajay whispered back. "And I promise, we're going to find him."

Lizzy exhaled the softest sigh, still clinging to him tightly. Her sobs had finally subsided to a recital of hiccups, but at least she was no longer shaking or railing at her family.

"We're going to step outside. Do you mind staying with her?" Malcolm asked, his question directed at Ajay.

Lizzy still clung to his neck as he nodded, his eyes lifting to meet the stare his friend was giving him.

As they headed out the door, he and Lizzy could hear the questions the family had wanted to ask the two of them.

"Who is he?" her father questioned, his voice booming.

"Did you know about this?" Max asked.

Della shrugged in response. "I don't know anything."

"I'm sure it's not serious," Jenny said. "Lizzy would have said something before now."

"Hero worship," someone else—Ajay wasn't sure who—stated. "What else could it be?"

The door closed tightly behind the last person, and with the room empty, Ajay pulled her arms from around his neck. Still holding tightly to her hands, he eased her back against the pillows.

"I'm not delusional," Lizzy snapped. "They all think I've lost my mind, but I know what I saw."

"I know," Ajay replied. "Now start from the beginning and tell me everything you remember."

As Lizzy spoke, Ajay noted the small crowd standing in the hallway. For a brief moment, he considered closing the blinds that covered the glass window to the space outside. The Colton family had gathered en masse, joining the medical personnel and the police detectives. No one seemed thrilled by the turn of events. He could only imagine what else was being said about her, and him. He took a deep breath, holding it in his lungs before blowing it out slowly.

"It was his shoes," Lilly was saying. "They were old and busted and seemed out of place with what else he was wearing. At first, I thought it was weird, then I remembered all the snow outside, so maybe he just didn't have proper winter boots. But then he turned around, and I knew it was him. Even though he was wearing a mask, I recognized those evil beady black eyes of his. I just started screaming, and he ran."

"What kind of mask was he wearing?"

"Hospital issue. One of those blue paper masks."

Ajay's head bobbed up and down as he took mental notes of everything she was telling him. He understood everyone's concern, but he believed her. He knew her family did as well but were trying to keep her calm considering her situation. He was certain Lizzy had seen the man who'd held her hostage, and he was willing to bet that if he'd come to the hospital, the man was now stalking her.

The door suddenly opened, the noise from the hall billowing into the room. Ajay didn't know the stranger who stood in the entrance with an oversize bouquet of fresh flowers. He stood as tall as Ajay, with an unkempt head of light brown hair. His eyes were bright blue, and his resemblance to the Colton family couldn't be denied. Ajay suspected they were related, but he still stood protectively, putting his body between Lizzy and the other man.

"May I help you?" Ajay asked, his deep voice a tad harsh and a lot possessive.

There was a moment of hesitation before the other man responded. "I'm Nate Colton," he said. "I'm Lizzy's... brother. Her half...brother," he suddenly stuttered, tripping over the words to explain who he was and why he was there. He gestured with the flowers as if the sight of them explained his intentions.

Lizzy sat up straighter in the bed, the slightest smile pulling at her lips. "Nate! What a surprise!" she said. She swiped the back of her hand across her eyes.

Nate smiled back.

Ajay extended his hand. "Ajay Wright. I'm a friend of your sister's."

"Nice to meet you," Nate said. "I understand you found her and kept her safe. Thank you."

"Ajay is a lieutenant with the Owl Creek Police Department. Search and rescue is his specialty. And Nate is a detective with the Boise Police Department. You two have a lot in common." Lizzy looked from one to the other, the two men standing like stone in the middle of the room. "You're both cops!"

"It's nice to meet you," Ajay said.

"Same," Nate muttered.

Ajay turned toward Lizzy. "I'll leave you and your family alone. I'll be right outside if you need me."

"I'll scream," Lizzy said, her smile widening.

Ajay chuckled as he made his exit and closed the door behind him.

NATE GAVE LIZZY a sheepish grin. "I came to check on you and to say hello before I headed back to Boise. You were completely out of it the last time I was here." He laid the flowers on the overbed table that rested in front of her.

Lizzy was sure her expression registered her surprise. "You were here before?"

"I came to help with the search when they said you were missing."

She shook her head ever so slightly. Family and friends had come and gone for days, and not knowing that Nate had visited left her feeling sad. "Thank you. I didn't know. That was sweet of you. And these flowers are beautiful."

Nate smiled, his entire face lifting with light. "I'm learning that's what family does for each other." His gaze shifted to the brothers standing outside the room. For a moment, he seemed to drift off into thought.

Lizzy smiled again, guessing what was on his mind. "It's going to get easier," she said. "For all of us."

Nate nodded. "I hope so. At the moment, it's still a lot to take in."

"How's Sarah?" Lizzy asked.

"She's good. She asked about you. She wanted to come visit you herself but wasn't sure you would want to see her."

"It's strange suddenly having a sister. I imagine it's a lot for her right now."

"Don't I know it!" Nate said with a low laugh. "We suddenly have four new sisters and six new brothers. I'm going to have to review my Christmas budget this year."

Lizzy laughed with him. "No worries. We do Secret Santa. You'll only have to buy one present."

Nate looked confused. "Secret Santa?"

"We throw everyone's name into a hat. You pick one name, and that's the only adult you have to buy a present for. It makes things super easy. And it's fun. There's always a gag gift or two tossed in with the real presents."

"You all are really close, aren't you?" A wave of sadness washed over Nate's face.

"We try. I've always had my brothers, and Mama Jen kept us connected to her kids. Chase, Fletcher, Wade, Hannah, Ruby and Frannie were more like siblings than cousins. They were always around, even when I wished they weren't." She smiled. "Kidding."

Nate shook his head. "Jessie really did us a disservice," he said, a hint of anger in his tone.

"At least you have a relationship with our mother."

"I don't have anything to do with her, especially now with this cult mess she's gotten herself into."

"Greg mentioned it briefly, but then the festival happened and all the drama with his babies. He said she's joined some church?"

"It's called the Ever After Church, but there's nothing at all Christian about it. It's some sort of shady operation, and only our mother would try to play like their leader is directly related to the next coming of Christ. In actuality he's a wolf in sheep's clothing, but she refuses to see it. It's always about power and money with her, and she thinks he has both. Her adoration for the man borders on obsessive. I'm sure it'll only last until the next schmuck captures her attention."

Lizzy shook her head. She could hear the frustration in Nate's voice, his anger rising steadily. She changed the subject for both their sakes. "Let's not talk about Jessie anymore. I can feel my blood pressure rising just thinking about her."

Nate smiled. "You don't have to ask me twice!"

"WHAT'S GOING ON with you and my sister?" Malcolm asked. He and his brother Greg stood shoulder to shoulder staring at Ajay. "That's my sister, for Pete's sake!" he exclaimed. "My baby sister."

Ajay tried to put a friendly expression on his face, and he laughed. "Lizzy and I are just friends."

"You both looked a little too cozy to be just friends," Greg interjected. "Are you sure nothing happened between you two up in that cabin?"

Ajay wished he could explain what it was between him and Lizzy, but he didn't have a single word for what he, or she, was feeling. They were definitely friends. He wouldn't argue that with anyone, but there was more to their connection that he couldn't yet define. He just knew she needed him, and he would battle hell and high water to keep her safe.

Now her family was eyeing him as if he'd been the one to take her captive and hold her against her will. They wanted an explanation, and he didn't have one to give.

He said, "Well, I could give you the dirty details, but if I did, Lizzy would probably kill me!" He tried to use humor to diffuse the moment, nervous energy fueling the chuckle that passed over his tongue.

Greg took a step in Ajay's direction, his hand balled into a tight fist. "I will break your face," he snapped.

Ajay held up his hands as if surrendering. "That was a joke!" He shifted his eyes toward Malcolm. "Call your brother off me," he said.

"He has a weak punch," Malcolm said. "It's more like a bug bite. If I hit you, I'll make sure it puts you on your ass."

"I swear, I didn't do anything with your sister but keep her safe. I was a perfect gentleman the entire time. Just ask her if you don't believe me."

They settled into a brief moment of silence, the men seeming to stand off against each other.

"He's good," Malcolm finally said. "I'll vouch for him."

"You vouched for that Brian guy, and we all remember how that turned out," Max said. He and Della had eased into the conversation, moving to stand beside Ajay.

Malcolm quipped, "Brian was Greg's friend, not mine."

"That's why I didn't vouch for him," Greg replied. "Besides, Lizzy chewed him up and spit him out. His feelings are still bruised."

"I taught her that," Malcolm said. "Don't think my sister's going to be easy to handle. She's not."

Ajay changed the subject. "Della, were you able to find anything on the security tapes?"

"Nothing that can help," she answered. "There was a man at the nurse's station. We didn't capture a good look at his face, but it was just like she described. We can't say for certain though that he was after Lizzy. In fact, it looks like he was more interested in the nurse than in her."

"So, you've talked to him?"

Max shook his head. "No, he was gone by the time we arrived, but we did interview all the hospital staff. I've had an entire FBI team on this since you found her, and they keep coming up empty."

Ajay gave him a nod. "Hopefully, FBI involvement will help."

"Especially since I don't technically work for them anymore," Max said. "My *retirement* from the agency didn't last long, but we're talking about my sister here, and I don't trust anyone else to take lead on this. I had to pull some strings and call in a few favors, but I'll keep the FBI involved as long as I'm able."

Appreciation crossed Ajay's face. He and Max exchanged a fist bump before Ajay responded. "So, it's possible it was her kidnapper?"

Lizzy's brother shrugged. "We can't rule him out, but we do have to take into consideration that Lizzy has been heavily medicated. She might not have been in her right mind."

"She has been out of it," Greg added.

"She seemed perfectly lucid to me," Ajay noted.

"Because she's refused to take any more of her medication," Malcolm said. "In fact, she's threatening to check herself out of the hospital and go home."

"Would that be a bad thing?" Ajay questioned. "She'd be able to recuperate, and you could all keep an eye on her at the same time."

The family exchanged a wave of glances, looking from one to the other.

Ajay continued, "And if someone is stalking her, putting her where she'd be hard to get to might make it easier for us to catch him. He might make a mistake and show his hand."

"I don't know if that's a good idea," Greg said. "That might be like putting her out there to be bait."

"Ajay makes a good point, though," said Malcolm. "We can keep her safe while she continues to heal and keep our eye out for anyone wanting to do her harm."

"Has anyone thought to ask Lizzy what she wants to do?" Della questioned.

The men all turned to look at her at the same time.

Her brown eyes danced across their faces as she flipped her light brown hair over her shoulder. Her gaze stopped on Max, and her brow lifted questioningly.

"We should probably ask Lizzy what she wants to do," Max said, his expression sheepish.

"That might be a good idea," Malcolm agreed.

They all turned to stare at Ajay. His eyes widened, and he suddenly felt like he was under a spotlight about to be dissected. He crossed his arms over his chest. "What?"

"Let us know what she says," Malcom said, tossing him a wink.

"We'll be downstairs in the cafeteria," Greg interjected. "Dad and Mama Jen went down a few minutes ago to grab some coffee. We'll go update them."

Della pressed her hand against Ajay's arm. "She trusts you, Ajay. And I really need to be able to have a conversation with her where she isn't calling her brothers names or cursing us all for being incompetent. The last few times I tried to question her, she went off on a rant that made that last blizzard look tame. She's very spirited when she wants to be."

Max laughed. "Aren't you being nice, honey!" he said. "I like that. Lizzy is *spirited*." He leaned to kiss Della's cheek.

Malcolm gave Ajay a look, rolling his eyes skyward. "Lizzy's a raving hellion when she's angry, and right now she's mad as spit," he said. "It looks like you're the only one she's *not* irritated with. So you're it."

"While you do that," Greg concluded, "we'll double-check with her doctors and get their thoughts about her leaving."

Ajay rubbed the tender spot on his chest. For reasons he couldn't explain, he wasn't quite sure any of them had any idea what the hell they were doing when it came to Lizzy Colton, most especially him. Taking a deep breath, he watched as her family all walked away, huddled together in conversation. Turning, he moved back toward Lizzy's room, hesitating just briefly before heading inside.

## Chapter Six

"I'm not staying here a minute longer," Lizzy snapped. "I don't care what my brothers say. I know what I saw, and I'm not going to sit here waiting around for that man to come after me again." Her voice had risen an octave, and she folded her arms across her chest.

"I agree," Ajay said, his tone even.

"You agree?" Lizzy sounded surprised.

"I think home is the best place for you to be. You can recuperate at your family's ranch."

"I have my own home," she responded. "A very nice home. Thank you very much."

"You probably need to be where there's family to help you until you're stronger. Besides, I don't want to worry about you being alone. I also don't think your father and brothers want to be worried about you, either."

"Fine," Lizzy said grumpily. "I'll stay at the ranch, but there's one condition."

"And what's that?" Ajay questioned.

"I'll only stay if you agree to stay there with me. Just for a few days. I'll feel better if I know you're there to protect me."

Ajay hesitated. He hadn't anticipated her request, and staying with her at her father's house hadn't been on the top of his list of things to do. He tossed a glance in the patriarch's direction.

Buck Colton had arrived an hour earlier, catching the tail end of Lizzy's most recent rant. He was a tall muscular man, his complexion weathered from the sun and hard work. Lizzy had inherited her father's bright smile, and there was no missing his devotion to his children.

"It's settled then," Buck said, easing to Lizzy's side to kiss her forehead. "Lizzy will come home when the hospital releases my sweet girl, and Lieutenant Wright is welcome to stay at the ranch for as long as he's needed."

"I appreciate your hospitality, sir, but I'm certain I'll need to clear it with the police chief."

"No problem," Buck said. "Chief Stanton and I are old friends. He owes me a favor or two. And if need be, I'll even clear it with the mayor."

Ajay smiled. "You're friends with Mayor Carlson?"

"He taught my boys how to ski before he retired and became a public servant."

"Small world," Ajay muttered.

Lizzy laughed. "Smaller town!"

Her father winked. "Getting the proper permissions, son, won't be a problem. I'll take care of everything. You just keep an eye on my baby girl."

Ajay nodded. "Yes, sir, Mr. Colton."

A FEW SHORT hours later, the senior Colton had arranged for Lizzy to be transferred to the family home with in-home nursing services to provide her care. Arrangements had also been made with Ajay's superiors for him to provide the Colton family with security.

Lizzy wasn't one hundred percent happy with the arrangements. She had wanted to go back to her own things, in her own space. But knowing Ajay would be where she was left her feeling a little better about the whole situation.

Vivian answered her phone on the second ring.

"It's about time," Vivian gushed. "I've been worried sick about you. Malcolm's been keeping me updated, but still…"

"I'm fine," Lizzy replied. "In fact, I'm headed home now."

"I'll meet you there," her friend said.

Lizzy shook her head into the receiver. "I need a favor. I need you to meet my friend Ajay at my house. He'll be headed in that direction in a few minutes. I need you to pack some clothes for me. I'll be staying at the ranch for a few weeks."

"Is everything okay?" Concern seeped through Vivian's question.

Lizzy smiled as if Vivian could see her. "Everything's fine now. I'm getting out of this hospital, but they're making me stay at the ranch."

"Then things aren't fine. What's going on?"

"I'll explain when I see you, but do you think you can meet Ajay? Please? You have the spare key to my house, and you know where all my things are kept. I trust you'll get everything I need without me having to make a list."

"Who is this Ajay person? Do I know him? The name sounds familiar."

"Lieutenant Ajay Wright. He's police. He's also the man who rescued me, and Vivian, he's gorgeous!"

"Is he the police officer that your brother is friends with? The cute one who looks like..."

The door to Lizzy's room suddenly opened, and Ajay peeked inside. He gave her a bright smile, his whole face seeming to lift with joy at the sight of her.

"I've got to go," Lizzy said, interrupting her friend's comment. "But come to the ranch later so I can catch you up. I promise to tell you everything!"

"You better," Vivian quipped.

"I'll text you his cell phone number," Lizzy said, "and give him yours so you two can touch base with each other."

"That's fine," Vivian replied. "Quick question before you hang up."

"What?"

"Doesn't he have a girlfriend?"

"Do you have a girlfriend?" Lizzy suddenly asked. "I don't remember you saying anything when we were at the cabin."

Ajay gave her a narrowed stare, his eyes drawing into thin slits. "Why do I feel like you were just talking about me?"

"Because I was. I was telling my best friend what a good guy you were."

Ajay's cheeks turned a brilliant shade of fire-engine red. He shook his head.

"So are you?"

"Am I what?"

"In a relationship? Do you have a girlfriend?"

"No," he answered, "but I don't think we should be talking about each other's personal lives. I'm on the clock, and I take my assignments seriously."

"That's good to know. I'd hate to have security that wasn't serious about protecting me."

Ajay chuckled. "The ambulance transport is here to take you home. I'll follow behind them."

"I need you to do me a favor and stop by my house. My friend Vivian is going to meet you there. I need clothes, and she knows exactly what to pack for me."

His brow lifted. "Now I'm running errands, too?"

Lizzy's eyes widened. "It's not like that. You and Vivian are the two people I trust most with my personal possessions. I don't even trust my brothers like that."

"I guess I should be flattered. But I don't think your family is going to be happy about that."

"My family knows how particular I am about my things. And who I do and do not trust, and why."

Lizzy didn't miss the odd expression that passed over Ajay's face. She sensed that he felt uncomfortable, and she was suddenly worried that she had made things between them awkward. That was the very last thing she had wanted for the two of them. Contrition furrowed her brow. If she could have kicked herself, she would have.

Lizzy had never been a wallflower, needing a man to take care of her. Despite growing up in a home where her big brothers babied her and her overprotective father coddled her every wish, she wasn't spoiled. She wasn't the fragile, weak female some thought her to be. With Ajay, she just wanted to be noticed and wanted, but she was behaving like a lovelorn teen desperate for a boyfriend.

But Ajay wasn't her boyfriend, and they weren't in a relationship, despite how she was behaving and how she was treating him.

"I'm sorry," she said, her voice dropping. "I should have asked how you felt about...well...everything." She took a deep breath, losing the words to explain herself.

"It's okay," he said, his smile returning. "There's just a lot happening. We need to sit and talk and maybe figure some things out. But until then, I'm fine with meeting your friend. I'll make sure someone follows the ambulance. Max and Della, maybe."

"I'm not usually so pushy," she said. "It's just...well..." She shrugged.

Ajay gently tapped her hand. "I need to go by the station first, then I'll meet your friend. After that I need to run by my own place to pack a bag and pick up Pumpkin."

"Thank you," she said. For the briefest moment, Lizzy wanted to press her lips to his, to seal their deal and move things forward. And then she remembered she was an assignment, with rules that he needed to follow. Kissing her wasn't part of the job description, no matter how hard she might have tried.

As he walked out of the room, Ajay tossed her one last smile.

THE OWL CREEK POLICE DEPARTMENT was quiet for the time of day. Quieter than he had expected. Ajay found the silence a little unnerving as he entered the building and moved past the reception desk to his office. He lifted a hand in greeting as he passed one familiar face and then another, but he didn't bother to stop for any lengthy conversation.

Inside, he shuffled through the mail that had been dropped on his desk, separating the junk from what might have been important. There were five messages reminding him that Pumpkin was due for her annual physical and that he, too, needed to schedule a date for his firearms recertification. Once he had cleared what was important, he shut off the lights and closed the door.

Heading down the hall toward the corner office, he greeted the officer sitting at a desk outside the police chief's door. She was a new hire and Ajay had only met her one time. He paused, trying to remember her name as he greeted her.

"Officer Bailey, good morning," he said finally.

"Lieutenant Wright," she responded. "It's good to see you again. And please, call me Bridget."

"Only if you promise to call me Ajay."

"How are you doing, Ajay?" she asked.

Bridget Bailey was a petite young woman with large brown eyes and a pixie haircut that made her appear younger than she was. Ajay remembered that she had graduated at the top of her class at the academy and was considered a feather in the department's cap, adding to an already impressive roster.

"I'm well," he responded. "Does the chief have a moment to speak with me, by chance?"

A booming voice called out from inside the office,

their commanding officer never missing anything that was happening in his building.

"Get in here, Wright!" Police Chief Stanton bellowed.

The young woman gave Ajay a bright smile. "I think he can see you now," she said.

Ajay laughed. "Thank you," he said as he rounded her desk and moved through the office door. He closed it after himself, his gaze meeting the chief's evenly.

"Chief Stanton, good morning."

"What's good about it? I hadn't been here for an hour before I start getting calls about you wanting to be reassigned to a private assignment. People seem to forget I run this department."

"Yes, sir," Ajay said. The chief gestured for him to take a seat and he moved to one of the upholstered chairs in front of the desk and sat down.

"So, what's going on?" Stanton asked. "Buck Colton called me. Something about his daughter needing you to be her personal bodyguard?"

Ajay took a deep breath. "Miss Colton was my last rescue and she's having a difficult time. Her family thinks that since we bonded while we were trapped during the storm that she would do better if I were to stay with the family until her kidnapper is apprehended. I also think my being there will allow me to investigate the case and hopefully catch whoever is preying on her."

The captain nodded his head slowly. "So, you think you can do a better job than my best detectives can do?"

"Chief Stanton, I think I'd be in a unique position to gather evidence your best detectives will have a harder time discovering."

A pregnant pause billowed slowly between the two men. The police chief sighed, and his tone softened ever so slightly. "Ajay, you're one of our best search-and-rescue officers. We're good now, but if I need to call you back in, I will."

"Yes, sir."

"And this assignment is temporary, so don't you get comfortable. Buck Colton is a good friend and one of the police department's biggest advocates. Our citizens need to know we're here to support them and they can always depend on us. So don't do anything to embarrass us."

"Yes, sir."

"You'll be the point person on this case and have the full support of our detective unit. Use them. As well, the FBI will also be working this investigation, but you already know that, don't you?"

Ajay grinned. "Yes, sir. I do."

Stanton grunted. "Clear this case, Lieutenant. I want it solved yesterday!"

"If I can ask for one more favor, Chief?"

Stanton's brow lifted, his gaze narrowed. He waited, not bothering to respond.

"I'd like to request that Della Winstead be allowed to work this case with me. She and I work well together, and I respect her insight. Of course, it would only be temporary, sir. Just until we can catch our perpetrator."

Stanton sighed deeply. "I swear! I think folks forget who's in charge around here."

"No, sir! Not at all."

There was another moment's pause as the police chief considered Ajay's request. Finally, he shook his head as he moved back to the pleather chair behind his oversize desk. "You better be glad I like you, Wright. Now go impress me and take Winstead with you."

Ajay smiled. "Thank you, Chief! You won't regret it."

"I better not, son. Or there'll be hell to pay around here. You're dismissed."

Backing his way out of the office, Ajay gave his commanding officer a slight nod of his head as he made his exit and closed the door.

"How'd that work out for you?" Bridget asked.

"I have my work cut out for me," Ajay responded.

"Don't mess up," the young officer said. She gestured toward the closed door with her head. "He won't be happy if you do."

Ajay sighed. "Yeah! That's what I'm afraid of."


THE PHONE RANG a half dozen times before Della answered his call. When she did pick up, she was giggling on the other end, sounding slightly out of breath.

"Hello?"

"Are you okay?" Ajay asked. "Is this a bad time?"

Della giggled again. "I was just having a conversation with Max. What's up?"

Ajay didn't mince words, getting right to the point of his call. "I just spoke with the captain about this case. Apparently, Buck Colton called in a favor, and now I'll be taking lead on the investigation into Lizzy's kidnapping."

"Good for you!" Della gushed. "Not looking to make any friends with the detective's division, though, are you? You know how sensitive those guys are."

"I'm hoping they'll see this as a good thing. That it'll take some of the load off their plates."

"Aren't you the optimist!"

"I know you'll be able to help me sell it."

"Me?"

"The captain approved you working the case with me. He also stressed that it's temporary, and that you and I will still be on call for search and rescue if we're needed."

"Me?"

"What better way to sharpen those investigative skills of yours than on a case that's important to you? Besides, I trust you and I know you'll have my back if I get in over my head. I need you, and since Max has pulled in his FBI team, it's a win-win for all of us."

"Max is only doing this because it's his sister. He'd rather be making furniture."

"Then he, too, is motivated to solve this case quickly so he can get back to what he's truly passionate about."

"Don't get me fired, Ajay! I really do like my job."

"Thank you, Della," Ajay said, a wide smile pulling across his face. "I'm headed over to Lizzy's house to meet her friend Vivian. I'll call you when I'm leaving."

"Be safe out there, please. I hate worrying about you. It makes Max jealous."

Ajay laughed. "As it should!" he teased. "As it should."

THE DRIVE TO Lizzy's didn't take as long as Ajay antici-pated. The twenty-five-hundred-square-foot property was located between the Colton family ranch and where the north end of Owl Creek met downtown. It was a quintessential 1900s Craftsman bungalow that had been completely renovated. Its captivating, historic charm was warm and inviting with undeniable curb appeal. Lizzy could easily stroll or bike through the city or return to the family homestead in the blink of an eye. It was impressive from the outside, and Ajay imagined it was equally impressive on the inside.

Admiring the architecture, he was standing outside his vehicle with his arms crossed when a silver sedan pulled behind him in the driveway. The woman who stepped out of the car was nothing like the woman Lizzy had described to him. This woman appeared timid and not as outgoing as her bestie. She wore a smartly tailored ocher-colored suit with a blouse the exact same color. The monochromatic look complemented her dark brown, shoulder-length hair and Mediterranean complexion.

"Are you Lieutenant Wright?" she asked.

He extended his hand to shake hers. "Please, call me Ajay."

"Ajay it is," she said softly. "I'm Vivian. Vivian Maylor. It's nice to meet you."

"The pleasure is all mine. Lizzy has told me a lot about you."

"That's interesting. She hasn't told me anything about you...yet."

"There's really nothing to tell," he said with a wide smile. Ajay wasn't quite sure what to make of the look Vivian gave him before she turned and headed toward her best friend's home. Ajay followed her.

Vivian suddenly came to an abrupt halt. She looked back at him over her shoulder. "The door," she said. "It's open. Lizzy would never leave her house unlocked or the door wide open."

Ajay grabbed her arm and gently pulled her back. "Call 911 and give them the address," he ordered. "And stay out here until the police give you permission to enter."

He reached for the pistol clipped to his waist and took off the safety. He gave Vivian one last look as she pulled her cell phone from her purse, then he moved through the door.

The interior of the home boasted an abundance of architectural molding, built-ins and stained-glass windows that adorned each room. Banks of grid-lined French glass reflected natural light onto original hardwood floors. The floorplan was a series of impressive yet cozy living spaces designed with generous scale and tall ceilings. Lizzy had married an eclectic mix of Bohemian and French country styles, integrating jewel tones with classic neutrals and bold floral prints. And someone had completely trashed her home, soiling fabrics, destroying furniture and leaving the place in complete disarray.

He moved past the dining room, through the living room and skirted from the kitchen to the screened-in patio and backyard. He had cleared the downstairs and was heading up to the bedrooms when a uniformed police officer came through the front door.

Ajay flashed his badge and kept his weapon pointing where he was headed. He had no intention of rounding a corner and being surprised. An officer he didn't recognize followed on his heels up the stairs. Minutes later, the Owl Creek police officer shouted down to the others, "All clear!"

Ajay recognized a familiar voice shouting orders from the floor below. He stood in the middle of Lizzy's bedroom staring at the wall above the king-size bed. When Della hurried up the steps and joined him, there was no hiding the distress on his face even if he had wanted to. Ajay shot her a quick look as she turned to stare where he was focused.

Time felt as if it had come to a standstill. Nothing moved, the air in the room blistered with the stench of something dangerous and ugly that Ajay couldn't touch or run from or keep far from Lizzy.

"This isn't good," Della finally said, her voice a loud whisper.

"We have to find this guy, Della," Ajay whispered back. "We have to find him now!"

The two friends took a step closer the wall. Someone had marred the soft blue paint with what looked like blood. It had dripped and dried, its consistency dark and viscous. Printed in bold, block letters were the words, *We're coming for you.*

# Chapter Seven

Ajay had called three times to check on Lizzy. He knew he needed to head toward her father's house, but he was anxious to hear what the forensics team found in her home. If anything at all.

When he had called the first time, she was sleeping soundly, finally settled into her bed. By the time he placed the second call, Vivian was there, and Max was explaining to Lizzy all that had happened and what little they knew. With the third call, she was still sobbing, shaken by the violation of her private space and the threat they'd found there.

They had ruled out the intrusion being a random act of vandalism. Lizzy had purposely been targeted, and Ajay still didn't know why. He didn't know who to blame or how to stop the threat. He disliked how that left him feeling. He hated the anxiety that dropped across his shoulders. He had no control, and that left him feeling vulnerable and weak. His thoughts were suddenly interrupted by one of the technicians who was collecting samples.

"This guy has a fetish for undergarments."

"Excuse me?" Dread and confusion felt like a gut punch to Ajay's abdomen. He could only imagine what he looked like, feeling as if the color had drained from his face. "What kind of fetish?"

The tech pointed to a pile of silk panties on top of the chest of drawers. Ajay had spied them earlier, but the graffiti on the wall had grabbed his attention and held it. Lizzy's undergarments had been pulled from the enclosure and laid neatly across the surface in order of color. Someone had clearly spent far too much time with them, and the technician seemed to take great pleasure in sharing that information.

"From what I can ascertain, he's spent the last few days using them for his own pleasure. He's ejaculated into each one, and he's clearly had multiple happy endings, unless there was more than one person. We'll run the DNA when we get them back to the lab to confirm how many offenders there were. With any luck, we'll get a hit in the database." The old man smirked as if he were amused. "And if she had any in her dirty clothes basket, they're gone. All her panties and bras are gone from her laundry. Except for what was left here on her dresser."

Ajay shook his head, still staring at the pile of soiled little underthings Lizzy had kept tucked away in a top drawer. He didn't know how to even begin to explain that violation to her.

The technician made another crude comment, laughing as if something were funny. It was the last straw, breaking whatever calm Ajay may have had left. He snapped, laying his frustration squarely in the other man's lap as he snatched the guy by his collar.

"I'm sorry! Sometimes you have to joke about it," the guy said, blood rushing to his cheeks. He lifted his hands to protect himself from the punch he thought was coming.

Della was standing at the bedroom door, clearly not amused after witnessing the exchange. Disgust painted her expression like bad makeup as she relieved the other man from his duties.

Ajay let him go, and he hurried out of the room and down the stairs, muttering under his breath about suing the department.

"Sorry," Ajay said. "I wasn't going to hit him. I just wanted to scare him. He really got under my skin."

"I know. That's why you need to head out," she said. "The team and I have got this."

Ajay gave her the faintest smile. "The team... You work fast."

"I called in favors this time. You told me to sell it and I did. Now, I'll call you if we get a hit on anything."

Ajay nodded. "I still need to run home and get Pumpkin. I'm headed to Colton Ranch right after that."

"Max said Lizzy didn't take the news well. The doctor wanted to give her something to calm her down, but she's adamant about not taking any more medication. It's probably going to be a long night."

As he eased past his friend, Della tapped him on the shoulder, a wave of compassion sweeping between them. With the last bit of energy Ajay could muster, he blew out a heavy sigh and hurried down the stairs to the front door.

THE COLTON FAMILY were gathered in the home's family room, everyone circling around Lizzy and trying to calm her. She had stopped crying, and now she was simply angry, fueled by fear and frustration.

When Ajay entered the family's home, Pumpkin by his side, he knew there wasn't anything he could say that could make things better.

"That was my home!" she hissed between clenched teeth.

"We'll buy you a new home," her father responded.

"I don't want a new home. I loved that house. Now it's tainted!"

"Lizzy, let the nurse give you something," an older woman was saying. "Something to help you sleep. Darling, you need to rest."

"She's right," Ajay interjected. "You need to rest."

"Ajay!" As Lizzy called his name, Pumpkin pushed her way through the crowd and jumped onto the sofa beside the woman. The slightest smile pulled at Lizzy's thin lips. "Pumpkin! I missed you!" Lizzy hugged the dog to her, gently stroking her fur coat.

Pumpkin settled into Lizzy's side, her position protective. It was clear to Ajay that she had no intention of being moved.

"Pumpkin! Where are your manners?" Ajay said. "Get down off that couch."

Lizzy laughed. "She's fine. Don't scold her."

The older woman moved swiftly to Ajay's side to shake his hand. She had those familiar blue eyes and short, dark blond hair streaked with strands of gray. Her presence was warming, and he instinctively knew she was Lizzy's favorite Mama Jen.

"Welcome to the ranch," Jenny Colton said. "We're glad to have you here."

"Thank you," Ajay said. "And I apologize for my friend there. She can be very possessive about people she becomes attached to."

"We love our animals around here, isn't that right?" Jenny said, giving Buck a nod.

"We certainly do. And that beauty is quite a specimen. I hear she was instrumental in helping you find our Lizzy."

"Yes." Ajay nodded. "I don't know that I could have done it without her."

"Then she's welcome here at Colton Ranch, too."

"Let me get you both something to eat," Jenny said, heading in the direction of the kitchen.

"Please, don't go through any trouble," Ajay replied. "I really couldn't eat a thing right now."

"One of the boys will show you to the guest room," Buck said. "You make yourself at home during your stay. We want you to be comfortable."

"Not too comfortable," Malcolm said with a dry laugh.

Lizzy gave Ajay a nod of her head as she continued to stroke Pumpkin's coat.

When he returned, Pumpkin was still in the same position, and Lizzy was arguing with Max.

"If scaring me was what this creep hoped to do, he's done a good job," she snapped. "I'm scared. He broke into my home. He touched my things. I'm officially scared to death!"

"We're not going to let anything happen to you," Max said.

"Like nothing was going to happen when I was at the hospital? The police are making a lot of promises they have a hard time trying to keep," she quipped. "And the FBI aren't much better!"

"It wasn't an FBI case," Max snapped back. "They didn't have jurisdiction, but as a favor to me, they're trying to help."

"They should be trying harder!" Lizzy yelled, her voice vibrating around the room. "What if I had been home? Or worse, if I hadn't gotten away or been saved by Ajay in the snow? Would it have been an FBI case then?"

"You can really be irrational sometimes," Max countered.

Lizzy pulled her knees to her chest, her arms tightening around Pumpkin's neck. She buried her face into the dog's neck, her tears falling for the umpteenth time.

Pumpkin whimpered softly.

"I think maybe we should squash this conversation until later. Everyone's tired, and Lizzy should probably go lie down," Ajay said, trying to keep his tone calming.

There was the briefest of pauses, then Lizzy jumped from where she'd been resting. Pumpkin jumped with her, staying close to her side as she moved toward a bedroom at the end of the hall.

The family stared after her, no one saying anything as she stormed out of the room.

"I'll go make sure she's okay," Ajay said. He turned to follow her.

Like birds being shooed away, her family suddenly took flight. Everyone moved in opposite directions, heading for their own homes and beds. There was a lot of muttering and an occasional curse uttered into the late-night air. Their vexation was palpable, each consumed with worry and concern but wanting to be pillars of strength for their baby sister.

"Good night," Jenny called after Ajay.

"Let us know if you need anything," Buck concluded.

And just like that, the Colton Ranch was as quiet as a library, not a single sound to be heard.

LIZZY HAD THROWN herself face down across the bed. She lay crossways, a pillow tucked beneath her head, her arms wrapped tightly around the pillow. She wasn't crying, instead staring into space still fuming with rage.

Ajay stood watching her, knowing there was little he could say to ease the hurt and anger she was feeling. Pumpkin lay at the foot of the bed, giving him a side-eye like he didn't belong in the space. A clock on the desk ticked loudly, and Ajay found himself counting time away in his head.

He didn't know just how long he stood watching, but when Lizzy sighed heavily, rolling over onto her side, it shook him from the daze he'd fallen into.

"Do you want to talk?" Ajay asked.

"No," Lizzy snapped. "I just want this to be over."

"I know."

She took a deep breath and held it before blowing it slowly past her thin lips. "I'm having a hard time finding balance. I think it's all going to be okay, and then boom, something else hits."

Ajay moved to the side of the bed and sat down beside her. Lizzy rolled herself closer to the center of the mattress to give him more room. Without missing a beat, Ajay lifted his legs, shifted his torso and gave himself permission to relax into the moment. He eased his body against hers, his arm falling over her waist. Ajay felt her entire body relax against him. He pressed his face into her hair, the scent of her jasmine shampoo wafting up his nostrils.

Neither spoke another word, allowing themselves to savor the intimacy of the moment. Lizzy clasped her hand atop his, their fingers entwining one with the other. Her touch was warm and gentle, and Ajay knew he would miss it whenever she let his hand go.

The room's windows were open for the fresh air, and a chilly breeze blew into the space. A full moon sat high in the deep black sky, light reflecting over the layers of snow on the ground.

An aura of peace filled the air, washing over them both like a gentle kiss pressed against an eager cheek. Ajay pulled a heavy comforter over them, the two snuggling closer beneath the warmth. Sleep came easily. Ajay had no clue who dozed off first, but in no time at all, the two of them were both sleeping soundly.

IT HAD BEEN AGES, if ever, since Ajay had heard the crow of a rooster in the early morning hours. But the familiar cock-a-doodle-doo snatched him out of the sweetest dream.

It took him a moment to collect himself, his surroundings unfamiliar. And then he remembered where he was, Lizzy still resting in his arms.

Exhaustion had finally beaten them both. He vaguely

remembered the nurse rousing them some time in the middle of the night, and Lizzy had allowed her to add a sedative to her medications. He imagined she would continue to sleep, her body reclaiming the rest that it was owed.

He, however, couldn't afford that luxury. He needed to assess the landscape in daylight and learn everything he could about the Colton family and Lizzy. It was the only way he imagined he could beat her stalker and keep her from harm.

Easing himself from around her, he lifted his body from the bed. Extending his arms above his shoulders, he stretched, leaning as far back as the tightness in his lower back would allow. He gave Lizzy one last glance. She looked peaceful with her hair splayed across the pillow around her face. Her cheeks were tinted a rosy shade of pink from the heat in the room. He wished he could climb back into the bed beside her, but there was too much he still needed to do. He turned and headed toward the door.

Pumpkin jumped up from where she'd been sleeping at the foot of the bed to follow behind him. "So, you *do* remember me," he whispered to the dog. "I can't believe you threw me over like that."

Pumpkin nudged his side and made him laugh.

EVERYTHING ABOUT COLTON RANCH reminded Ajay of how wonderful a home could be. Just north of Owl Creek, it was some eight hundred acres of working cattle ranch with plenty of fertile space to grow a variety of crops.

Lizzy's father, Buck, had built his fortune on two brands: Colton Produce, which monetized the agricul-

tural side, and Colton Beef. He'd been an astute busi-
nessman, building value in the land to pass down to his
children. Greg and Malcolm both worked on the property,
choosing to follow in their father's footsteps.

The family home was a renovated red wooden barn
with a two-story living and dining area, multiple bedrooms, quaint sitting areas and angles that gave the home
a rustic appearance. Buck's gardens in the backyard lent
character to the landscape. It was an impressive property.

From what Lizzy had told him, her mother, Jessie,
had always hated the idea of living in a barn, despite the
high-end designer renovations that made it a home. Buck
had added an Olympic-size swimming pool for the kids
and a guesthouse, where Greg currently resided with his
new wife, Briony, and their two adopted children. Not far
from the home was a working barn, horse paddock and
shared house where the ranch hands stayed if they chose
to live on site or just needed a place to lay their heads.

Ajay ran down the length of driveway that had been
cleared of snow and ice. Pumpkin ran with him, leaping
into the high mounds of snow as she played and exer-
cised her legs. He laughed at her antics, understanding
that feeling of freedom she seemed to be reveling in. It
was a good workout for them both.

By the end of the hour, Ajay had raced along the property's perimeter, crossing a short length of field that led
him past a small pond. He stopped at the barn to catch
his breath and admire the horses inside. He was about to
head back to the main house when Malcolm waved for
his attention, heading toward him on an ATV.

"Good morning," Ajay said.

Malcolm greeted him warmly. "How'd you sleep?"

"Like a log. It felt good to get some rest."

"Max followed Della to Lizzy's house. They wanted to check it out one last time before the police release it back to her."

"I don't want her seeing it like that," Ajay said. "This situation has her shook, and I think if she sees the damage the intruder did, it might break her. Can you arrange for someone to put the place back in order and give it a good cleaning before she returns home?"

"Yeah." Malcolm nodded. "I'll make sure it gets handled."

"I appreciate it. I don't want Lizzy more traumatized than she already is."

"You've got it bad for my little sister, don't you?" Malcolm's brow lifted.

Ajay's eyes darted back and forth, and he pondered his response. "I care about your sister," he finally replied.

He wasn't ready to admit that his heart was riding a roller coaster of emotions when it came to Lizzy. Despite all the warm and fuzzy feelings he was having for her, he was conflicted. This was uncharted territory for him. All his previous relationships had been casual encounters. There had been no one he went to bed thinking about and woke up missing. Lizzy had him out here like a grade schooler with his first crush. She occupied his thoughts every single minute of his day from the time he opened his eyes till he closed them again at night.

Yeah, he thought, he had it bad.

"Is that what we're calling it now?" Malcolm said with

a smirk. "You care? Dude! Just admit you have the hots for her!"

"Does it show?" Ajay asked.

"Stevie Wonder could see it."

Ajay sighed. "I'm not going to lie to you. I like your sister. I like her a lot. But I also know that this is not an ideal situation for either of us. I don't want her idolizing me because of what I've done and then thinking those feelings are something they really aren't."

Malcolm turned serious. "And what about your feelings? How do you know you're just not going through some savior complex?"

"I've been doing this job for too long and have never thought about the women I've rescued the way I think about Lizzy. Your sister is an incredible woman, and when this is over, I hope we can continue to get to know each other."

"Damn!" Malcolm said, feigning revulsion. "You know that's so not cool for a girl's brother to hear, right?"

Ajay laughed. "Sorry, guy!"

Malcolm nodded. He hesitated, mulling over the conversation before responding. "You have my blessing," he finally concluded. "But I'm not sure Max is ready to give you a green light."

"I get that. What about your father? Has he expressed any concerns?"

"Dad just wants Lizzy to be happy. Don't think he hasn't noticed the change in her disposition with you around. We've all noted the transformation."

"Then we're good. I'm sure I can win Max over once he gets to know me better. Besides, Lizzy and I are still discovering what we like about each other. For all I know, she might decide that I'm not the one, and Max can say he told you so."

Malcolm winced. "Please, don't mess up," he said with a snort. "I hate when Max is right!"

Ajay laughed. "I'll do my best!"

"Do you want a ride back to the house?"

"Thanks, but I need to finish my run. I'm still getting the lay of the land. Just in case."

"I'll meet you at the house then," Malcolm said, jumping back on his four-wheeler. "Mama Jen just got here, and she said she's making pancakes!"


"SO WHAT'S GOING on with you and that young man?" Jenny sat in the sunroom beside Lizzy. The two women were enjoying the early morning sunshine and their first cup of coffee for the day.

Lizzy took a sip of the hot brew from the mug she held, hesitating. She could feel something like joy pulling at the muscles in her face, widening the smile in her eyes.

"I don't know," she finally answered. "I really like him, Mama Jen. He seems like a great guy, and I can see myself in a relationship with him. But I can't imagine him wanting a woman who is so needy! And since we met, I've been like a need magnet. Just one blunder after another. What guy wants to be bothered with that?"

Jenny chuckled. "Obviously, he doesn't feel that way. I can tell by how he looks at you that he clearly cares a great deal about you. And his concern feels very genuine."

"Exactly!" Lizzy tossed up her hands. "He's concerned. It's like I'm a project he's suddenly responsible for, and when this is over, I'll just be a finished assignment."

"You don't give yourself enough credit, Lizzy. You're a strong capable young woman. Lieutenant Wright can see that, and I think he respects and admires that about you."

Lizzy shrugged her shoulders. "Maybe."

"No maybes. That man is very interested in you, and you are interested in him. Don't waste years of your life being unhappy when love is right beside you trying to get your attention."

"Did you do that? Waste years of your life?"

Jenny sighed. "When I married Robert, he was like a shiny new penny. After a while, that shine started to dull and tarnish. I kept trying to polish him up and shine him back up. I ignored all the dings and dents and scuff marks. Before I knew it, there were just too many blemishes for him to ever be new and pretty again."

"What about you and my dad? You both seem very cozy with each other."

"Your father and I have a lot of history together. He's a good man and an even better friend."

Lizzy smiled. "Just a friend?"

"Worry about you, Lizzy. This family has enough relationship drama to contend with. Your father and I have no interest in adding to it."

Lizzy persisted, "So you have thought about it?"

Giggling, Jenny lobbed an accent pillow at Lizzy's head. The two women enjoyed a good laugh.

"This is pretty," Lizzy exclaimed a moment later. "I don't remember it." She held the embroidered pillow out in front of her. Its watercolor-inspired design was a nice complement to the decor.

Since she'd been fifteen, her father had always allowed her free rein when it came to their home. Lizzy's love of art came from her first interior design endeavors. Buck had supported all the changes she wanted to make, cheering her on during each of her decorating stages. Art school had helped her tone down some of her choices, and now the space was a beautiful mesh of bright colors against white walls and cabinets. It still retained its rustic flair and exuded comfort in every room.

Jenny answered, "Your dad and I found two of them at the flea market back in the summer. Shortly after Fletcher returned home, if I remember correctly. I thought they'd be a nice addition to this room. I'm so glad you like them. Your taste is much better than mine."

Lizzy hugged the pillow to her chest and tried to keep the glee out of her expression. She wasn't sure how she felt about her father being with any woman, but she definitely didn't hate the idea of him and Mama Jen being together.

As if she could read Lizzy's mind, Jenny tossed her a quick glance, and the two burst out laughing for the second time.

AJAY WAS CONFIDENT that no one could get onto the property and close to the Colton home without being seen. Strangers would set off all kinds of alarms, and everyone had been given implicit instructions to ensure no one passed through the front gates without being thoroughly vetted. He had all the confidence in the world that Lizzy was safe as long as she kept close to her family home.

After a quick shower, Ajay joined the Colton family for breakfast. Jenny had prepared pancakes just as Malcolm had promised she would—light, fluffy, silver-dollar-size flapjacks dripping with maple syrup. There were also strips of crisp bacon, fresh scrambled eggs and one of the best cups of coffee Ajay could remember ever having.

The noise level in the house had risen substantially since he and Pumpkin had gone for their run. Laughter was abundant, and the conversations were loud.

Lizzy and Malcolm sat at the dining table teasing their father about his new obsession with lilies. Apparently, lilies occupied over half the garden, bulbs planted during the fall to be ready for the spring. Buck had carefully charted their placement, variety and growing needs, preparing himself for the impending growing season. His family found his obsession amusing, and Ajay was impressed with his determination.

"Have you given any thought to adding a greenhouse to the property?" Ajay asked.

"Don't give him any ideas," Lizzy said with an earnest laugh.

"That's actually something to think about," Buck said.

"And Colton Florals is born!" Malcolm teased.

"I kind of like that," Buck said. "We might be on to something!"

Jenny shook her head. "I don't think starting a new business was what retirement was supposed to look like." She giggled.

Buck winked at her and laughed. "Maybe not. But that's why I'm always open to suggestions."

Lizzy looked from her father to her aunt and back. She shot her brother a look, then turned her gaze on Ajay. He didn't miss the amusement that danced in her eyes as the two seniors fell into their own conversation. She smiled, bright white teeth blessing the moment. Ajay couldn't help but smile back.

"I need to run," Malcolm said, rising from his seat. He wiped his mouth with a paper napkin. "We need to chase down a few stray cattle that knocked down the fence on the back field. My search-and-rescue skills come in handy during times like this."

"I'd offer to help you out," Ajay said, "but my search-and-rescue skills wouldn't be handy at all."

They all laughed, everyone shifting in their chairs.

"Please, be careful out there," Jenny said as Malcolm waved goodbye and disappeared out the door. She rose from her seat, moving to clear away the dirty dishes from their breakfast.

Ajay stood to help. "Breakfast was amazing," he said. "Allow me to do the dishes."

"I can help," Lizzy said. She reached for her father's empty plate.

Ajay's gaze narrowed. "Shouldn't you be resting?" he asked, his concern rising.

"I load a mean dishwasher," Lizzy answered. "I don't think putting a few plates in the tray is going to tax my strength. Besides, the doctor says I need to start moving more. Physical therapy for my weakened muscles."

Ajay didn't look convinced.

"You two have at it," Jenny said, sitting back down. "Buck and I will enjoy one last cup of coffee."

"You do that," Lizzy said, tossing the two a look over her shoulder. She purposely bumped into Ajay as she moved through the sliding barn-style doors to the kitchen.

He eyed her curiously, noting the piercing stare in her eyes. "What?" he asked, his voice dropping to a whisper.

"Do you get the impression that those two might be enjoying a little more than coffee?"

Ajay laughed as Lizzy peered past him, watching the other couple closely. He reached for the dirty plates she carried in her hands. Easing past her, he leaned to whisper in her ear. "I'm more excited about finishing that puzzle you and I started." He winked at her. "I do good puzzle," he said teasingly.

"Lieutenant Wright!" Lizzy grinned, her smile pulling full and bright across her face. "I don't know how you do it, but that actually sounded like you were being fresh," she said as she pretended to clutch a strand of pearls at her chest.

Laughter rang sweetly between them.

LIZZY DISAPPEARED INTO her father's office. Ajay watched from the doorway, not wanting to interrupt.

She sat with a sketch pad in her lap, singularly focused on the work she'd tasked herself with. When she sat back in the leather executive's chair, her arms folded across her chest, Ajay called her name. He moved into the room to her side.

"Is this a good time?" he questioned. "I don't want to interrupt if you're working."

Lizzy shook her head. "No, I'm not working. Not my day job, at least. I just can't get that creep off my mind, so I figured I'd put my artistic skills to work for me. Della said you don't have a sketch artist on the payroll, so I've given myself the job."

She reached for a stack of paper from the corner of the desk. She passed it to him, pulling her legs beneath her butt in her seat. "This is the man who was holding me hostage. And this was the same man who showed up at the hospital outside of my room."

Ajay stared at the images she passed into his hands. He shuffled through them, clearly impressed. "How did you..." he started.

"I'm really good at what I do," Lizzy said. She sat back in the chair, her expression smug. Satisfaction seeped like water from her eyes.

An actual photograph couldn't have captured the details of the man's face better. She'd done mock-ups of him in his two masks as well as one without. Clearly, Ajay thought, it took a particular skill level and a good eye for detail to generate the images she'd created with a heavy lead pencil.

"I'll get this to Della and the detectives investigating your case. It should definitely help."

Lizzy pulled both hands through her hair, twisting it into a messy topknot. "I'm tired," she said, "and I imagine you're bored and ready to go home."

"In time," Ajay replied. "Right now, we worry about you. Not about me."

She nodded. "In that case, right now, I need a nap.

Care to join me?" Her smirk was teasing as she lifted her brow seductively.

Ajay laughed. He waved the sheet of paper at her. "I still have work to do, Ms. Colton."

"You are absolutely no fun, Lieutenant Wright. No fun at all!" Lizzy giggled.

## Chapter Eight

Ajay had settled into a comfortable routine in the brief time he'd been staying with Lizzy in her family's home. During the day, he and Lizzy were able to spend a good amount of time together. Their conversations ran the gamut from the nonsensical to the sagacious. They debated the benefits of dryer lint, discussed the world financial crisis and pondered everything else of interest in between.

Sometimes her family would join them, and sometimes they didn't. They flirted with each other unabashedly. They laughed a lot and even shared a tear or two. Every waking moment together served to bring them closer as they spent time learning each other's idiosyncrasies. What they'd proclaimed a friendship had been firmly solidified, and time had served to further cement their mutual respect and admiration for each other.

"DINNER WAS EXCEPTIONAL TONIGHT," Ajay said as he moved into Lizzy's bedroom. He dropped down to the tufted ottoman that rested at the foot of her queen-size bed.

"I told you I could cook."

"I didn't believe you. I said I could cook, too, but that didn't make it true."

"So, you lied? You can't cook?"

"That's not what I said."

"That's what it sounded like."

"Well, I can cook. I make a mean scrambled egg with cheese. There are levels to cooking. My level of expertise may not be your level. That doesn't mean I can't do it."

"You can't cook!" Lizzy exclaimed. "And my vegetable lasagna just outdid whatever egg thing you think you can cook!"

Ajay pressed his hand to his heart. "Ouch! That hurt!"

Lizzy laughed. "Not as much as discovering you are a kitchen fraud."

Pumpkin barked.

Ajay shook his head. "I can't believe you're taking her side," he said as he scratched the dog's head. "Where's your loyalty?"

Pumpkin jumped onto the bed and lay herself down beside Lizzy. She tilted her head to stare at Ajay.

Lizzy laughed again. "You tell him, girl!"

"Della and I are going to have to have a conversation about your training," he quipped, his eyes rolling skyward.

Pumpkin barked, then laid her head against Lizzy's leg and closed her eyes.

AFTER AN HOUR of watching the evening news together, Lizzy shifted her legs off the bedside to kick off her leather cowboy boots.

"Do you need help?" Ajay asked.

"If you don't mind," Lizzy responded, "I could use a little assistance."

"I don't mind at all," he answered. He reached for her foot, grabbing at the heel of her boot. Lizzy pulled her leg up toward her chest. The joint gesture helped the boot to slide off and Ajay dropped it to the floor as he reached for the other foot. When both had been discarded to the floor, he was still holding on to her heel, his eyes wide.

"Don't look at my toes!" Lizzy exclaimed as she tried to pull the appendage from his hands. "I need a pedicure!"

"You really do," Ajay said, his head bobbing in agreement.

"I don't recall asking for your opinion," Lizzy snapped, a wide smile on her face.

"I can take you tomorrow," Ajay said. He was still holding her heel, despite her efforts to disengage his grip.

"I'm not ready to go out," she said. "Besides, no one will see my feet."

"I've seen your feet!" he exclaimed.

Lizzy giggled. "I cannot believe you! There are extenuating circumstances. Give a girl a break."

"I think I need to give a girl a pedicure," he said, rising from where he sat and heading into her bathroom.

Lizzy's gaze was wide-eyed, shock and awe washing over her expression. She listened as he seemed to be rummaging in her bathroom cabinet. "What are you looking for?" she asked him.

Ajay poked his head out the bathroom door. "Do you have one of those footbath things? Or a small washtub?"

She nodded her head. "Look in the linen closet. On the top shelf."

Ajay winked his eye at her, then disappeared back into the bathroom. Minutes later he returned with a foot tub of warm water, a towel, a tube of moisturizer and the brightest pink nail polish she owned.

"You're kidding, right?" Lizzy questioned.

"Not at all. You have a need, and I can help. Why wouldn't I?"

Lizzy hesitated. She didn't really have an answer to give, so she said nothing. She watched as Ajay placed the tub at the end of the ottoman and gestured for her to take a seat. She slid from the bed to the cushioned top, easing her feet into the warm bath of water that he'd scented with her lavender bodywash.

Ajay poked her big toe with his finger, amusement dancing across his face.

"Do you know what you're doing?" Lizzy asked.

"Nope! It's my first time, but I'm pretty sure I'll figure it out. How hard can it be?"

Lizzy lifted both her feet out of the water. "Now I'm scared," she said with a laugh.

Ajay pushed her toes back beneath the suds. "You act like I run into woman with crusty feet on a regular basis."

Lizzy gasped. "My feet are not crusty! They are not that bad!"

Ajay shot her a look. "Okay," he said. "If you say so."

"Take that back, Ajay Wright!"

Ajay drew his fingers down the inside of her calf, his hands dropping into the water as he continued to caress her skin. "Nope!"

Lizzy moved as if to stomp her foot and splashed him with water. "I mean it," she said. "Take that back!"

Ajay laughed. "I will not. My feet look better than yours."

"I swear! I liked you much better before you started hanging out with my brothers. They're starting to rub off on you."

"Honesty is not a character flaw, Lizzy."

"Being mean is."

"Would you rather I send you out into the world with jacked-up feet or tell you the truth?"

Lizzy didn't respond, pretending to pout. She crossed her arms and turned her head from him. She enjoyed bantering with him, but his touch was beginning to take on a life of its own, her entire body responding to the gentle caresses. She feared her voice would crack or she would say something she couldn't take back if she spoke.

"That's what I thought," Ajay said smugly.

"Enjoy your little moment," Lizzy muttered. "I will get even. Just watch your back."

Ajay chuckled. "Duly noted."

Lizzy closed her eyes and settled into the sensations sweeping from her female center. Heat burned in every direction as she focused on his touch, his hands gently kneading the muscles in each toe, across the bottom of her foot and over the top. He twisted the appendage from side to side, gently stretching each ankle. As he massaged each sinewy muscle and caressed every nerve ending, Lizzy could feel herself falling deep into the warm sensations sweeping through her entire body. It was quickly becoming the best pedicure she'd ever had, and she could tell from his expression that he knew it.

"You are so wrong, Ajay!" she sputtered.

"What did I do?" he questioned.

"You know exactly what you're doing and it's not fair."

Ajay laughed heartily. He continued to caress and tease her flesh and she let him. Minutes passed before she suddenly snatched both feet from the bath, lifting them high in the air.

"I think they're good," she muttered.

"Are you sure?" Ajay said as he reached for the towel to pat her toes dry. "I still need to moisturize them and update your polish."

"No, that's good. I can finish them later."

"I don't mind. I want to make sure you're satisfied."

"Clearly, this has to be the devil's work. You've got me heated and now I can't even think straight."

Ajay sat upright. Amusement seeped from his eyes as he stared at her.

Lizzy pointed her index finger at him. "Don't you dare try to deny it. You've got me ready to rip my clothes off and you did it on purpose, knowing that you would have to turn me down."

"I did no such thing," Ajay professed.

The two sat staring at each other, neither speaking. Lizzy finally broke through the quiet that had filled the room.

"I really like you, Ajay. I like you more than I should and definitely more than I like any of my other male friends. I don't want to embarrass myself if the flirting and teasing is just that and not something more. So, I really need you to be honest with me about what you're feeling. Please don't leave me feeling foolish."

Ajay paused before answering. He lifted himself from where he'd been kneeling to sit on the ottoman beside her. He reached for her hand, entwining her fingers between his own.

"I like you, too," Ajay finally responded. "And you know that whatever is happening between us is definitely more than two friends casually flirting and teasing each other. It's a lot more, but it can't get in the way of me keeping you safe and finding your kidnapper. No matter what the two of us are feeling."

Lizzy blew a soft sigh. She closed her eyes and sat in the silence for a good few minutes. When she opened them, Ajay was staring at her, his eyes misted ever so slightly. Shifting her body to face him, she pulled her hand from his and pressed her palm to the side of his face. There was no need for words. His eyes danced across her face, his gaze reflecting every emotion he was feeling. She felt her heart skip a beat, and then two, the entire universe feeling as if it was syncing the two of them together.

Leaning forward, Lizzy pressed her closed lips to his, the kiss lingering ever so sweetly. Rising, she moved toward the bathroom, pausing for a quick minute before closing the door after herself. Minutes later, when she returned, Ajay was gone, and Pumpkin snored softly against her pillow.

EVERY EVENING, THEY would talk until they were completely talked out, their eyelids heavy. Ajay would send Lizzy off to her room as he double-checked the doors and windows. Most nights, Pumpkin would follow Lizzy, tossing Ajay to the curb.

With regularity, his internal clock pulled him from a deep sleep at 2:00 a.m. every night. Rising, Ajay would ease down the hall to first check on Lizzy. Most times, Pumpkin would be in her room or her bed, the two sleeping soundly. Ajay would check doors and windows a second time before returning to his own room to fall back to sleep alone.

On two occasions, her father had been sitting in the family room, sipping bourbon from a cut-crystal whiskey glass. The last time the two had talked, Buck had peppered him with questions to learn more about him.

"My daughter is quite smitten with you, Ajay." Buck's stare had been searing, pulling hard at Ajay's heartstrings.

Buck continued. "I understand these are unusual circumstances for both of you, but I wouldn't want either of you to misinterpret your feelings. Lust is a far cry from love."

Ajay had nodded. "Yes, sir. I agree."

"My sweet girl doesn't fall easily for any man, but when she does, she falls hard. I won't sit back and watch her heart be broken."

"I would never do anything to purposely hurt Lizzy. She means the world to me."

Lizzy's father eyed him sternly. "Jenny says you two are falling in love and don't even realize it."

Ajay felt his cheeks heat with color. He wasn't sure how to answer that, so he didn't say anything, allowing Buck to continue the conversation.

"Personally, I think you both realize it and are trying

hard to deny it. As a father, I can appreciate you taking things slowly. Caution will serve you both well. It will also keep me from putting my foot up your backside if you get it wrong and make my baby girl cry." Buck lifted his glass and took a long sip of his bourbon. As he swallowed, the conversation shifted like a spring breeze, the two suddenly talking about football and their favorite teams.

Ajay had great appreciation for those nights, even learning a thing or two about himself that Buck had been all too willing to point out. And his corny dad jokes were actually funny despite Ajay's best efforts to not laugh.

This night was different. As he double-checked the doors, he immediately sensed that something was amiss. It was a feeling deep in his gut, a flutter of apprehension that moved him to retrieve his service weapon from the nightstand drawer before starting his rounds.

Outside Lizzy's room, he heard Pumpkin growl, the guttural noise low and threatening. He opened the door, and the dog stood ready to pounce on any intruder.

Ajay gestured her back toward Lizzy, who was sitting upright in the bed. He knew it was on the tip of her tongue to hit him with a barrage of questions about what was going on, but she bit back the words, seeming to trust he would do whatever was needed. As Pumpkin jumped back on the bed, she wrapped her arms around the animal's neck and nuzzled her face against the dog.

Ajay moved swiftly through the home, checking each room as quickly and as quietly as he was able. Traversing the hallway toward the family room, Ajay realized someone had left one of the sliding glass doors to the screened porch wide open. The family room was cold, the icy breezes from outside intruding on the space.

When he was certain no one was there who wasn't supposed to be, he moved outside, not bothering to grab his boots or a jacket. The icy remnants of the last snow against his bare feet shocked him wide awake, leaving him no reason to think that this was an accident.

The night sky was dark. The temperature had dropped, and it felt like another storm might be brewing. He turned on all the outside lights and slowly circled the perimeter of the family's home.

Outside the screened porch, Ajay noted two sets of footprints, both from heavy boots with thick treads. He lifted his eyes to follow where they led, the darkness eventually stalling his view. Then a flicker of light in the distance grabbed his attention.

Someone had come through the gates and was headed back down the driveway toward the main road. Ajay suddenly had no doubt that same someone had been in the house. So close that any of them could have been targeted.

He turned to go back inside. When he looked up, Lizzy was watching him from the doorway. Their eyes connected and locked. Tears puddled beneath her eyelids, her lashes fluttering to keep them at bay. There was nothing he needed to explain.

"I called Max and Della," Lizzy said softly. "The police are on their way."

No ONE HAD seen or heard a thing. The intruders had come and gone under the cloak of darkness. Nothing had been taken, everything left neatly where it belonged, except for a note that had been slipped beneath Lizzy's bedroom door. She gave it to Ajay, who took it gingerly by its corner and passed it to the Owl Creek forensics team. The two sat watching as it was dusted for fingerprints, the officer noting that both had handled it.

The single-ruled note paper was nondescript, torn haphazardly from a composition notebook. Blue ink was scrawled as crudely as the tear in the paper, but the scribbled words left nothing to interpretation. *We're coming for you.*

"Pumpkin woke me up," Lizzy said, her voice calmer than he would have expected. "She jumped from the bed, and I heard her growl. Somehow, I knew it wasn't you, and then this note was pushed under the door. Whoever was there didn't stay longer than a minute or two before I heard them move away. Not long after you opened the door."

Ajay nodded. "Did they even try to enter your bedroom?"

She shook her head. "No. Not at all. I think they just wanted me to know they were there."

He felt like he had failed her. "I should have been there," he muttered.

"You were there. And you did the best you could," Lizzy whispered. "This is not your fault, Ajay." She reached for his hand, gently caressing his fingers.

Ajay slid his hand from hers, suddenly feeling self-conscious. He didn't think her family was at all concerned by her public display of affection, but he didn't feel worthy of her touch. He was taking the intrusion harder than she was, and Lizzy's calm aura had him feeling off-kilter.

"I'm installing a security system first thing in the morning," Buck said. The patriarch had spent the better part of the last hour calling every member of the family to rule out it being one of them paying a late-night visit. Despite his best efforts, they all knew the task was futile. No one in the family would have come and gone at such a late hour, sneaking around like thieves in the night. Nor would they have left Lizzy this threatening calling card.

"Who all has a key to the house?" Ajay asked. "I didn't see any forced entry."

Lizzy's eyes narrowed. "It would probably be easier to list who doesn't have a key. When my father said this would be the family home, he didn't mean it figuratively. All of us have keys, even my cousins. Everyone has always had a place to stay without needing to ask. And you can come and go as you please. There's always a stocked pantry, full fridge and an empty bed."

"Family's important to me," Buck said.

"It's important to all of us," Lizzy responded.

"Which is why we will do whatever we need to do to protect this family," Buck concluded. "Besides, all these doors still have the original locks. I never even thought to change them after your mother left. I guess now is as good a time as any."

Lizzy shook her head, tossing Ajay a look. "Even my mother probably still has keys," she said flippantly.

Buck scoffed, waving a dismissive hand in Lizzy's direction. "I'm sure Jessie tossed her keys the day she walked out. She never liked this place. Said I had her living in a barn like the farm animals."

Ajay watched as Lizzy pulled her knees to her chest

and wrapped her arms around her legs. She hugged herself tightly. He had no doubt that her father's comment hit a nerve. Lizzy was proud of their family home, believing their barn had been everything they'd needed, and more. As if reading her mind, he knew that she would never understand how anyone could have found their home, or them, lacking. Most especially her mother.

His attention shifted back to their current situation. Ajay's frustration was on a low simmer. He was finding it difficult to accept that whoever was stalking Lizzy had been so close. Being there and still not catching the man, or men, had him feeling inadequate. It wasn't an emotion he was accustomed to or one he was willing to accept.

He'd been so caught up in the joy he felt spending time with Lizzy that he'd forgotten his mission. He was there to protect her, and he knew the first line of defense was always a good offense. He needed to change his tactics, and hers, if they were going to catch this guy.

"We need to get some sleep," Ajay said. "We're going to have a long day tomorrow."

Lizzy looked confused. "I don't understand."

"You're going back to your life, and I'm going back to mine."

"I don't understand. What does that mean?"

"It means we're done hiding, and we're definitely not running. We're going to take back control."

"Does that mean you're leaving?"

"It means if I stay, it's because I want to be here. And the same goes for you. If you're ready to head back to your place, I'll support that and do what's necessary to ensure your safety. If you don't want that yet, that's fine, too."

"I don't think I'm ready yet," she muttered. "I feel safe here. I don't know if I'll feel safe back at home."

Ajay nodded. "And that's okay. We can both stay right here at the ranch until you feel comfortable."

Lizzy hesitated, seeming to process everything that had happened and all that had been said. Ajay knew she still didn't have a clue what he intended for the two of them, but she did know she could trust him. In fact, she could trust him with her life, and her heart.

RETREATING BACK TO her bedroom, Lizzy dropped onto the carpeted floor. She had thought herself safe in her own family's home, but she wasn't. There was still a threat out there, and it had been close enough to reach out and touch her. She had grown comfortable, thinking she was safe here at home with the family that loved her best. But that was a lie. She wasn't safe anywhere.

But why? She still couldn't figure out who was doing this or why this was happening to her. She wanted to scream and yell and wake up from the nightmare of it all, but this wasn't a dream, and she couldn't deny the reality of her situation.

She hugged herself tightly, curling her body around a pillow as she lay in the fetal position. She didn't want her family to know her fears. She refused to let them see that this thing had her scared beyond words. She needed them to think she was healing and would be well. And, she was desperate to keep Ajay from thinking she was weak or fragile. Even if it was only an illusion, she needed him to believe that she was strong and capable in trying situations. *Smoke and mirrors*, she thought. *Smoke and mirrors!*

The knock at the door was unexpected, and she jumped. She stared but didn't respond. Lizzy's heart began to race, and her palms were suddenly clammy. She could feel the onset of a panic attack, and she began deep breathing and tapping to quell the emotion.

Minutes passed before the second knock. This time, Ajay pushed the door open slowly, peeking inside. "I just wanted to check on you," Ajay said softly.

At the sight of him, tears began to roll out of her eyes and down her cheeks. So much for trying to be strong, she thought. She swiped at her face with the back of her hand, not wanting Ajay to see her be emotional. Lizzy shook her head, words caught deep in her chest. Whatever needed to be said rained from her eyes.

Ajay dropped down to the floor beside her. He pressed his hand against her knee, gently caressing the cool flesh.

Desperate to hold back her sobs, Lizzy was good until he touched her, and then the floodgates opened. As she cried, Ajay wrapped his arms around her torso. He didn't speak, simply allowing his presence to be a comfort to her.

As the first hint of a new day's sun began to peek over the horizon outside, he was still there with his arms around her, her tears damp against the front of his shirt.

AFTER THE COMMOTION of police and investigators in the house, sleep had been difficult for everyone. After tucking Lizzy into her bed, Ajay was still roaming the house looking for clues. He hadn't shared his thoughts with any-one, not even Della. But there was just something about the intrusion that concerned him.

How well did the interloper know the family? Who-ever it was had found Lizzy's bedroom easily, having no problems discerning her door from all the others. Why did he feel like this wasn't the first time the intruder had been in their home, by invitation or otherwise? Was the man stalking Lizzy foe disguised as a friend? Ajay was determined to find the answers.

He moved from the family room to the kitchen. Jenny sat at the kitchen table, a cup of coffee in her hand. She gave him the sweetest smile and beckoned him toward the seat beside her.

"I didn't mean to interrupt," Ajay said, his voice a loud whisper. "I wasn't expecting to find you here."

"It was so late after the police left that I just slept in the other guest bedroom. I figured if Lizzy or Buck needed me, that it would be easier if I stayed close. I heard you scurrying around and figured I'd get up to make us all some coffee. Can I pour you a cup? Or would you prefer juice? I made some green juice last night before I headed to bed. It's good!"

"Thank you," Ajay replied. "The juice would be per-fect."

"Juice it is." Jenny rose from her seat to the refrigera-tor. She lifted a large container from a shelf and brought it to the counter. Grabbing a glass from an upper cabinet, she filled it with the neon green beverage and returned the pitcher to the fridge. "It's kale, cucumber, ginger and green apple."

Ajay nodded his appreciation as he took the glass from her hand and took a sip. "It's very good," he said, genuinely enjoying the flavors against his tongue.

"And good for you! I haven't been able to convince Buck and the boys of that just yet. Slowly but surely, though."

Jenny sat back comfortably in her seat and watched him for a few moments. Ajay quickly sensed that something was on her mind, and the matriarch didn't hesitate to speak her thoughts. "Lizzy is fragile right now. She's trying to pretend that she's okay, but she's not."

"I know. This can't be easy on her. Or any of you for that matter."

"Lizzy is leaning on you for support, and I'm not sure that's a good idea."

Ajay felt himself bristle, his nerves tensing. He took a deep breath as Jenny continued.

"What are your intentions with our Lizzy? When this is over, do you plan to disappear from her life? Because that may be even more traumatic than what's happening to her now."

"I want to think that Lizzy and I have become good friends through all of this. So me disappearing isn't an option. I'm hopeful that we can explore our relationship more when we're not always worried about what might happen next. I've enjoyed getting to know her and hope we can continue that momentum. I really care for Lizzy."

Jenny nodded and paused before letting her next words drop, hitting the floor with a thunderous thud. "Lizzy has fallen in love with you. But I think you know that already. Because I think you've fallen in love with her, too. All of us really want her to be happy, and we're probably more excited than the two of you are. But I don't want her to get her heart broken."

Ajay paused, reflecting on her comment. When he looked up, the older woman was staring at him intently, studying his reaction. He nodded. "I promise you," he said, lifting his hand to his heart. He made the same promise to her that he'd made to Buck days earlier. "I won't do anything that will ever break Lizzy's heart."

LIZZY LAY IN her bed staring up at the ceiling. She'd been awake for hours, trying to process all that had happened and everything she was feeling. She was even more frightened after this last incident.

But she was equally determined not to let Ajay see her break a second time under the stress of not knowing who wanted to hurt her. From being abducted to having strangers in her personal space at her home and the family ranch, it was all chilling. It was taking every ounce of courage she possessed to stay sane.

After leaving the hospital, Lizzy had figured if she stayed close to home and shut out the rest of the world, everything would be okay. She knew that if she broke, there might not be enough that anyone could do to fix the pieces and make her whole again. She exhaled softly as she adjusted the pillow beneath her head.

Pumpkin had gone for a morning run with Ajay, and Lizzy was feeling discombobulated without her canine companion. Ajay's last words replayed over and over in her head.

*You're going back to your life, and I'm going back to mine.*

She wasn't sure she wanted to go back to her previous life. That life didn't include Ajay. She wasn't ready to see him disappear from her day-to-day existence. She had grown fond of having him around to laugh with, to tease, to sit quietly with and just be nearby. She didn't want to miss him.

Neither of them had broached the subject of what would happen to them after her stalker was found and danger no longer existed. There had been no deep discussion about relationships or feelings. Even after she'd professed her adoration, they'd gone back to business as usual.

But there was something that brewed between them like morning coffee. It was heated and necessary and perfect. It had left an impression and a longing that couldn't be denied if they were honest with each other. And Lizzy wanted more, a second and third cup that could soothe the weariness in her spirit and lift her up on a high the likes of which she had never experienced before. She would have called it love, but labeling it and having it disappear on her would be heartbreaking.

Some things were best left alone, she thought, and maybe a relationship between her and Ajay was one of those things.

When her cell phone rang, she rolled her eyes skyward. Without looking, she knew it was Vivian. Vivian seemed to have her number on repeat, dialing her every hour on the hour, but Lizzy was ignoring her bestie. Not because she didn't want to talk to her friend, but because she didn't want to hear a lecture on what she was doing wrong and needed to be doing right. Lizzy already knew and had no need for any reminders.

Vivian would *tough love* her until every thought of her and Ajay was nothing but a memory, and Lizzy wanted more than memories for as long as she could hold on. That was why she wasn't going to answer Vivian's calls or return them until she was ready. She promised herself a conversation with her friend when she was ready to let Ajay go.

*You're going back to your life and I'm going back to mine.*

What Lizzy trusted was that she and Vivian knew each other well enough that Vivian wouldn't take her disregard personally. Vivian would give her time and space, and when Lizzy was ready, the two women would pick up where they left off as if nothing tragic had happened. They would laugh and gossip, and Vivian would remind her that Ajay's kindness had been a condition of his employment. He hadn't been a summer fling to love and leave. He'd just been in the right place at the wrong time.

Her phone suddenly chimed, an incoming text message calling for her attention. Her first thought was to ignore it, too, but when it beeped a second time, she forced herself to glance at the screen. The message was from Ajay.

Get up and get dressed.

She texted him back. NO!

Get dressed Lizzy. We have to go.

Where?

Lizzy waited for a response, but none came. She asked a second time.

WHERE!

Don't worry about where. I'm leaving in 30 mins. Be ready or you can go as you are. But you are going.

Lizzy giggled. She had no doubt that he would probably sling her over his shoulder in her pajamas and slippers if he needed to. She also liked that he didn't take her crap when she was shoveling it with both hands. He was no-nonsense, straight as an arrow and everything she could have ever needed.

Rising from the bed, she headed toward the adjoining bathroom. She needed a quick shower if she were going to be ready in time. She would return Vivian's call when she and Ajay went back to their respective lives. Why give her bestie a reason to be a killjoy when she was actually having fun?

"I DON'T MEAN to be a killjoy," Della said, "but we're coming up empty."

Ajay adjusted his cell phone against his ear. "Who is this guy?" he snapped. "And why do I feel like he's always one step ahead of us?"

Ajay knew the frustration in his tone had to be off-putting. He heard Della gasp as he spewed a litany of curse words over the phone line.

"Sorry," he said. He took a deep breath.

"Don't take this the wrong way," Della said. "But maybe you should recuse yourself from the case? It's starting to mess with your head, and if you and Lizzy are in a relationship, that's not going to help."

"So, you're policing my work now?"

"I'm being your friend. We have always been straight with each other. I'm not going to stop now. This case is starting to get to you and it's getting to you because of your feelings for Lizzy. Why can't you admit that?"

Ajay shifted the conversation, not wanting to answer questions about his emotional stability. He also wasn't willing to admit that Della might be right—he was too closely involved to successfully investigate the case and find Lizzy's stalker.

"Were there any prints on that sheet of paper?"

Della blew a soft sigh. "Nothing. It came up empty."

"Did any of the cameras in the area catch anything?"

"Nothing that we can use."

A lengthy silence swelled thick and full between them. It was Della who spoke first.

"I have an obligation at Crosswinds today. I'll be there if you need me."

Ajay nodded as if the woman could see him. "I'm getting Lizzy out of the house. I'm hoping it will draw out her stalker. I know she wants to visit Ruby and Sebastian's new baby, so we might do that."

"How about we put a police tail on you just to be safe?"

"That's fine. Just make sure they keep their distance. I don't want Lizzy worrying about one more thing."

"No problem."

"We'll probably run errands tomorrow. She has a physician's appointment first thing in the morning."

"It's not anything serious, is it?"

"Just a follow-up, I think. Jenny will be going with her, too. I'm just playing chauffeur."

"Well, come see me if you drop by Crosswinds. I'll be down in the kennels."

There was a moment of hesitation before Ajay spoke. "Thanks, Della," he said softly. "I did get your message. Loud and clear."

"Whatever you decide, you know I'll support you," Della said.

"I do," Ajay answered. "And I appreciate you for being there for me."

# Chapter Nine

Ajay hadn't completely thought through their next steps, but he figured he had a better chance of catching the criminal if Lizzy were out in the open, taunting him to take his best shot. He'd spent most of the morning on the phone trying to get answers. The captain had reamed him for not letting the detective team help him and Della do their jobs, claiming Ajay's insistence on working single-handedly on the case hindered the search. Even he and Della had exchanged words, his friend claiming he was too close to the case to be of any real help.

He didn't have the words to explain how furious he was about someone getting that close to Lizzy on his watch. Maybe he had done everything he could do, but it still wasn't enough as far as he was concerned. It wasn't enough because the kidnapper was still out there. Still lurking in the shadows. And clearly hunting the woman he was falling in love with.

The air in his lungs blew out in a heavy gust of warm air. He could never say aloud what had been going through his mind about Lizzy. There was no one he could tell about the growing feelings he was having for her, not even his dog. They still didn't know each other that well, but Lizzy had grabbed a large chunk of his heart and was holding tightly to it. She'd gotten under his skin, and it felt as if he'd been plagued by a virus of magnanimous proportions. It had him feeling happy and foolish and completely out of his element. He was so enchanted with her, he was willing to fight tooth and nail for the opportunity to discover everything he could about her. He was willing to step out on the front lines and go up against anyone or anything determined to do her harm.

Her Aunt Jenny had called it love, claiming they had both fallen hard for each other. She could very well be right, but Ajay would keep that tidbit of information close to his chest until he was ready to have that conversation with Lizzy.

LIZZY RELAXED INTO the passenger seat of Ajay's ride, allowing her body to melt against the warmth of the leather seats. Pumpkin sat upright in the back seat, her head hanging out the open window. A country singer was serenading them from the radio. The sun was shining, and the air was crisp. They couldn't have asked for a more perfect day.

"Where are we going?" she questioned.

Ajay tossed her a look. "Hunting."

Lizzy's gaze narrowed. "I think that's going to require further explanation."

"We're going to find the man trying to terrorize you. When we find him, I'm going to make sure he never gets an opportunity to cross paths with you again. Even if I have to hurt him to keep him away from you." Ajay's tone was stern and straight to the point.

"I don't know if this is a good idea," Lizzy said. She shifted her body and turned to face him. "I have to be honest with you, I don't know if I'm ready. My anxiety is sky-high right now."

"You can't keep hiding. You are sitting around waiting for something to happen, and that will make you stir crazy. You need to get out, visit with your family, hang out with your friends. When's the last time you spoke with Vivian?"

Lizzy cringed, suddenly feeling like a real jerk for ignoring her bestie's calls. Vivian had stopped leaving messages, but she continued to call her like clockwork.

"I owe her a call," Lizzy said, contrition wrapped around her words. "I haven't been a good friend lately."

"Good friends are hard to come by," Ajay said.

"What if I'm putting her in danger? If anything happened because of our association, I would be devastated."

"I won't say it's not a risk. I honestly don't know. But I do know it's highly unlikely that, whoever this guy is, he's going to harm anyone else. He's had ample opportunity, and he hasn't taken it. My sense is this is more about making you his possession, either for profit or his own perverse gain."

"Well, that makes me feel better," Lizzy said facetiously. The snark in her tone was thick.

"Everything's going to be fine," Ajay said as he gave her a wide smile. "I promise."

She blew out a sigh of relief, wanting to believe because Ajay seemed both determined and certain. She turned her attention back to the road.

From the back seat, Pumpkin eased her snout over Lizzy's shoulder, nudging her. Lizzy smiled, that little gesture of comfort taming the angst in her heart.

WHEN AJAY TURNED onto Cross Road, the private drive into the Crosswinds Training Center and the Cross family home, he wasn't sure who got more excited—Lizzy or Pumpkin. He turned left past the medical building toward the kennels and training areas. The single-family home was in walking distance of the kennels, and he turned into the parking area between the two.

Both woman and dog were bouncing up and down in their seats. Lizzy squealed as if she'd won the biggest prize at the state fair, and Pumpkin whined as if she'd been given a treat for her good behavior.

Crosswinds was Owl Creek's pride and joy. The facility was owned by former marine Sebastian Cross. Sebastian was well-known in the community for his expert training and handling of search-and-rescue dogs. He also supported veterans with PTSD, providing them with service dogs to help with their healing.

Sebastian's new love, Ruby, was a Colton, Jenny's eldest daughter and Lizzy's first cousin. She owned Colton Veterinary Hospital, and her vet services surpassed all others in the area. Both Sebastian and Ruby were thriving, living their best lives. Friends and business associates, they worked well together, focused on building their respective businesses.

When Sebastian became a target, his land considered

prime real estate, no one had expected that Ruby would get caught in the cross hairs of a fanatic claiming to do God's bidding. Fighting side by side for what they believed in had given the couple a new look on what life could be like for them. Now they were celebrating the birth of their first child, a baby boy named Sawyer Colton Cross.

Lizzy hadn't seen her cousin for a little while, only hearing bits and pieces of the drama from other family members. Mama Jen had told her of the new baby's birth, but Lizzy's current situation had kept her from visiting.

There weren't enough words for Lizzy to express to Ajay how happy she was. He had made her entire world turn on its axis. She was beyond ecstatic.

"I'm going to take Pumpkin over to the kennels so she can nuzzle some of the puppies if they have any. Ruby and Sebastian are at the house. I'll catch up with you in a few minutes," Ajay said.

"Thank you," Lizzy said as she threw her arms around Ajay's neck. She pressed her mouth to his, kissing him with an intensity that bordered on ravenous.

He couldn't help but kiss her back, his lips dancing in perfect sync with hers. He tasted like mint, she thought, wintergreen, fresh and airy. When his tongue darted past her lips to tangle with her tongue, Lizzy felt like she might have dropped to her knees had she been standing.

They both pulled away at the same time. Ajay's eyes were wide, and he looked as if he wasn't certain what was expected of him next. Lizzy's palm was pressed against his chest, and she could feel his heart racing. He was visibly fighting to catch his breath.

Lizzy pressed her mouth to his for a second time, giving him a quick peck on the lips, then she jumped from the car and sprinted down toward her cousin's home.

AJAY SHOOK HIS HEAD. Clearly, he and Lizzy were headed down a path of no return. Neither was going to be able to come back from the growing tsunami of emotions swirling between them. He bit his bottom lip as he exited the vehicle, Pumpkin on his heels.

Inside the kennels, Della sat at the front desk, her dog, Charlie, resting beside her. Charlie barked in greeting, moving to Ajay's side for a scratch behind his ears. Pumpkin pressed her nose to her friend's, the two engaging in typical scratch-and-sniff doggie behavior as they greeted each other. Ajay motioned for Pumpkin to take a seat, and she lay down on the floor, curling her body against Charlie's.

"This is a surprise! I wasn't expecting to see you out and about." Della stood to give him a hug.

"I thought it would be good to get Lizzy out of that house, and she hasn't seen the new baby."

"Babies always make you feel good, and that one is a cutie!"

"How's it going?" Ajay questioned.

"Work is work. Still no news on Lizzy's stalker. It's really starting to mess with everyone's heads. It's been a minute since I've seen the team so frustrated by a case."

"Glad I'm not the only one."

"You need to let this go, Ajay."

He rolled his eyes skyward. "Didn't I just hear this lecture from you?"

"You need to hear it again. Go back to search and rescue and do what you do best. The captain has put his best detectives on the case to help you. I know how important this is to you, but you don't need to let it consume your entire life. They'll catch him."

"I think whoever it is, they're known to the family. It's someone they're friendly with and maybe even someone they trust."

"Why do you say that?"

"No forced entry into the home, which suggests they had a key, and the intruders knew exactly where Lizzy's bedroom was. They didn't waste time looking for it."

Della nodded. "I'll pass that information on. In the meantime, though, want to tell me how things are with you and Lizzy?"

Ajay's brow lifted, the question putting him on edge. "What do you mean, how things are with me and Lizzy? Things are fine."

"I saw you two swapping saliva. Things looked more than fine."

"How the hell…?" Curiosity turned to embarrassment.

Della laughed as she gestured to the security cameras. One was pointed toward the parking lot, his vehicle front and center. "Sebastian had these put in when the trouble was going on a few months back. Just to be safe." She tapped her hand over her heart. "They've been good for my voyeuristic spirit!" Her raucous laugh was teasing.

Ajay shook his head slowly. "Let's keep this between

us, please. I still don't know what's happening with me and Lizzy."

"Looked cut-and-dried to me. I mean, that was some kiss!"

"She kissed me," he said sheepishly.

"It didn't look like you were putting up much of a fight, my friend."

Ajay laughed. "I got caught up. It won't happen again."

"That's your lie," Della said with a shrug. "Tell it any way you want to tell it."

The two laughed cheerfully together.

# Chapter Ten

Lizzy and Ruby were clinging tightly to each other when Sebastian entered the small family room. He stood patiently, allowing the two women a moment that both clearly needed. Ruby kissed Lizzy's cheek. Even though she had her biological sisters, Lizzy had always been special to her. She'd been the baby girl of all the babies, and Ruby had been especially protective of her since she'd been the only girl in a house filled with yucky boys.

"I've been worried sick about you," Ruby said as she grabbed Lizzy by the hand.

"I'm fine. But you had a baby!"

Ruby grinned. "I did." She pointed toward Sebastian, who was cradling their infant son against his broad chest.

Lizzy squealed, her excitement brimming out of every pore. "Can I hold him?" she asked, her arms extended.

The noise startled the dog reclined in front of the fireplace. Oscar, Sebastian's golden retriever, sat up and looked around.

"It's okay, boy," Sebastian said as he took a step forward. His smile was bright as Lizzy reached for the baby, lifting their bundle of joy from his arms.

Lizzy moved to the sofa and sat down. The small person in her arms had chubby cheeks and suckled his tongue. His blue eyes opened and closed and opened again as he looked up at her. Lizzy declared him the most beautiful baby she had ever seen.

"He's absolutely precious," Lizzy gushed.

"He's a sweet baby," Ruby said as she unfolded a white spit cloth and laid it against Lizzy's shoulder. "I think we'll keep him!"

"I just want to know how you carried him for nine months and he comes out looking just like his father. I don't see an ounce of Colton in him."

Sebastian laughed. "He did get my good looks, didn't he?"

"I swear I think it's karma for something I did in a former life," Ruby said.

The doorbell suddenly chimed.

"Were you expecting someone else?" Sebastian asked, his eyes shifting toward Ruby.

She shook her head again. "No."

"It's probably my bodyguard," Lizzy said, nonchalantly, her gaze still locked on the baby.

The married couple exchanged a look. Sebastian moved to the front door and pulled it open. Laughter exploded as he greeted Ajay warmly, showing him into their home.

"Ajay!" Ruby exclaimed. "We heard you were pulling watchdog duty."

Ajay laughed. "Is that what they call it?"

"Whatever it is you're doing, I'm just happy to know my baby cousin is in good hands."

Ajay stared where Lizzy was sitting. There was a glow

on her face that he hadn't seen before. Her joy was palpable, filling every corner of the room. She looked good with a baby in her arms and before he could catch them, those words seemed to jump out of his mouth on their own accord.

Lizzy gave him a smile. "Why, thank you, Lieutenant Wright. That's very sweet of you to say. I hope to have my own babies someday."

Ajay could feel his face warm as he blushed profusely. Sebastian and Ruby grinned at them both.

"So, what's up with you two?" Ruby asked. "Mama says you're staying at the ranch, Ajay?"

"Just until they can get a lead on whoever has been threatening Lizzy."

"I told you I had a bodyguard," Lizzy said teasingly.

"For a small community like Owl Creek, we've had a lot going on these past few months. And not a lot of it has been good," Sebastian said. "Della and Max were telling us about what's been happening with you, Lizzy, and it's almost as wild as what Ruby went through."

Ruby nodded. "It was bad enough when we thought you were lost. But then to find out that someone had actually taken you was really frightening."

Lizzy shifted her gaze from Ruby's face to Ajay's. "Something similar happened to Ruby not too long ago."

"Turned out to be some lunatic from that new church that's pitched their tent here in town," Sebastian said. "They're called the Ever After Church. He was one of their ranking members and claimed he was ordered by God to lay claim to the property here. Setting his sights on Ruby to get to me was his first and last mistake."

"If you ever need to talk," Ruby said, turning toward Lizzy, "you just call me. I know how it feels to have someone coming after you like that. I've never been so scared."

"And you were pregnant," Lizzy added. "I can't even imagine keeping it together under those circumstances."

Ruby reached for Sebastian's hand. "I don't know what might have happened if Sebastian hadn't been going through it with me. He was my rock!"

"I guess boys do come in handy!" Lizzy snuggled the baby against her shoulder.

Ruby laughed. "Only if they're not related to you! Brothers are still butts!"

Both men shook their heads and rolled their eyes, but seemed to be amused. Ajay finally took a seat beside Lizzy, cooing at the little boy who was the spitting image of his friend. Laughter filled the room, ringing warmly through the air.

"Have you two eaten?" Sebastian asked. "I was going to toss something onto the grill for lunch. There's more than enough to share."

"We don't want to wear out our welcome," Lizzy muttered.

Ajay added, "I should probably get Lizzy back to the ranch."

"And Mom brought us a cake," Ruby interjected. "Chocolate mousse cake! If I remember, that was one of your favorites, Lizzy!"

"Besides," Sebastian added, "you're going to need a crowbar to pry my son out of her arms and that might take a while."

Ajay chuckled. There was a moment of hesitation as he and Lizzy had a silent conversation. She attempted to plead with him with her eyes.

"We'd love to stay," he finally said. "And if you have a crowbar I can borrow, it would be appreciated."

Sebastian laughed. "Steaks and a side of crowbar coming right up!"

LIZZY HADN'T STOPPED talking since they'd left Crosswinds. After spending time with Ruby and Sebastian, they stopped down at the kennels to collect Pumpkin and bid goodbye to Della. Once they were in the car, Lizzy was a bundle of joy and happiness. Her exuberance was infectious, and before Ajay knew it, he was almost as giddy as she was.

Almost.

Despite their moment of relaxation and fellowship with the other couple, Ajay was still on high alert. Still looking over his shoulder, and hers, for anything out of place. He understood Lizzy wasn't safe until they captured whoever was after her. And Lizzy's safety had to be foremost in his thoughts.

Lizzy asking him a question pulled him from his musings. "How many kids do you want?"

Ajay blinked, his lashes fluttering. "Kids?"

She laughed. "Kids! Those really small people who cry a lot. Have you ever thought about having kids of your own?"

"Not really," Ajay answered honestly. "I've always been singularly focused on my career. I hadn't considered what my future might look like with a family. I figured there was plenty of time for that."

"I want at least six kids," Lizzy said definitively.

"Six?" Ajay was incredulous. He shot Lizzy a quick glance, then shifted his eyes back to the road.

"I've always imagined I'd have a big family. When I was younger, I was determined to only have one child. But then I thought how lonely that must be, and well, coming from a big family, why not *have* a big family?"

Ajay chuckled. "As an only child, I can attest to the fact that not having a big family isn't a big deal. I could probably see myself with two kids. Maybe even three. But six? I can't wrap my mind around six."

Lizzy laughed. "I think we could handle six kids easily. Four boys and two girls. I want the boys to come first and then the girls. Big brothers can be pretty cool."

"While we're at it, why not put in an order for twins?" Ajay said facetiously.

"Twin girls! Yes!"

He shook his head. "I can't with you!" he said, laughing heartily.

"We should probably get to work on that. Don't you think?"

"I think we need to end this conversation before you say something that gets me in trouble."

"What kind of trouble?"

"The kind of trouble that makes babies," he replied.

She grinned. "Would that be a bad thing? Practice would be half the fun!"

Ajay changed the subject. "Tell me about Brian. From

what I heard, that was a devastating crash and burn for him."

Her brow lifted, surprise washing over her expression. "Who told you about Brian?"

"One of your brothers might have mentioned him. He was a friend of Greg's, and from what I hear, you chewed the guy up and spit him out."

Lizzy rolled her eyes skyward. "He was my last boyfriend. He was a real douchebag!"

"Ouch!"

"I thought he was the one. I'd already planned to name our first child Brian Junior. Then I discovered he already had a son named Brian Junior. Two in fact. And a daughter named Brianna. But he never bothered to tell me. His wife did."

"Three kids *and* a wife?"

"Three kids, a wife and a mistress."

"Greg didn't know he was married before he introduced you?"

"No one knew. Not even the mistress who named his second son Brian, too."

"What a douche!"

"Exactly!" Lizzy exclaimed, tossing her hands up in the air.

"What did you do when you found out?"

"You really don't want to know."

"No, I really do," Ajay said, stealing another glance in her direction.

"I negotiated a meetup with the other two women and their kids and invited him to a surprise party. And we met in the conference room at his job."

Ajay laughed. "Please tell me how you managed to pull that off at the man's job."

"I'd been hired to do some marketing work for his firm. I had a presentation to give. He just happened to be the star on my program."

"What happened then?"

"Before or after his wife slapped him with divorce papers?"

"I don't need to know anymore. You are ruthless, Lizzy Colton!"

"I'm not a woman to be played with. If I give you my heart, then I'm trusting you to protect it. Hurt me, and I will cripple you. And that's after I sic my brothers on you."

"And here I thought you were this nice, kind, sweet..."

She cut him off. "I'm all those things. But I'm also vicious, and I can be mean if you cross me. So don't ever cross me."

Ajay smiled. "No worries. I imagine I'll be too busy with four sons and twin daughters."

Lizzy giggled like a teenager. "Seriously, though. This thing with us..." She paused, seeming to search for the words to explain what was on her heart.

"This *thing* is scary," Ajay said. "And I don't want either of us to make a mistake. We've been thrown together under unusual circumstances. I think we really need to take things slow. Very slow."

"So no more kissing?" Amusement danced across Lizzy's face. "Because I really liked kissing you."

"I think we should table the kissing for a minute."

"No."

"Excuse me?"

"No." Lizzy folded her arms across her chest. "I like kissing. And I really liked kissing you. So, no! I'm not tabling kissing, and you can't make me. Well, you could, and of course I'd respect your decision, but still…"

Laughter billowed through the interior of the vehicle. Ajay shook his head from side to side. "Why are you making this so hard?"

Lizzy paused, seeming to choose her words carefully. She took a deep breath before finally responding. "Because I really meant it when I said I liked you, Ajay. And I think you feel the same way about me." Her tone had changed, humor shifting to something more serious. "And although I heard what you had to say about not letting what's between us get in the way of your responsibility, I don't want us to miss out on what might be the best thing that's happened to us because we're too busy trying to be proper and listen to what other people say we should be doing. I want us to follow our hearts for as long as it feels right."

Ajay turned his head to stare at her. The look she was giving him was filled with promise, the shimmer in her eyes drawing him in. He could feel himself falling head-first into her stare, and all he could do was nod. He turned back to the traffic they'd gotten stuck in.

A knot tightened in Ajay's throat as he pondered their conversation. There wasn't anything else he could say, so he didn't say anything at all. Instead, he reached for her hand, pressing his palm against hers. He entwined her fingers between his own, lifting her hand to press a damp kiss against the back. He hoped Lizzy already knew he would have moved heaven and earth to kiss her again and again.

Ajay's gaze suddenly paused on his rearview mirror. The car coming up behind them was moving too fast for the icy roads. He had seen it swerve in and out of traffic earlier but hadn't given it much thought until now. Because now it seemed to be trying to catch up to him, bearing down with disregard for everyone else on the road. He slowed, ready to maneuver defensively out of the sedan's way if necessary. It passed one last car to fall in line directly behind them.

"What's wrong?" Lizzy asked, her brow furrowed with concern.

"Do you recognize the car following us? It's been on our tail since we left the training center."

Lizzy glanced at the side mirror, then turned in her seat to stare out the back. "No," she said with the shake of her head. "I've never seen it before."

The road had cleared, only a few vehicles headed in their direction. Ajay signaled, then pulled into the right lane to allow the other car to pass by them. Instead, that car pulled right, continuing to follow him.

Despite his best efforts, Ajay couldn't see inside the other vehicle. The windows were tinted, making visibility difficult at best. The car was so close to his rear end that if Ajay hit the brakes suddenly, they were sure to collide.

"Should we call someone?" Lizzy questioned as she dug into her purse for her cell phone.

Pumpkin, who had been sleeping peacefully on the back seat, sat up, seeming to sense the tension that had risen in her owner. She barked, a low yelp as if she knew something was going on.

"It might be nothing," Ajay said. "Just hold on."

He stepped on the gas, his truck accelerating swiftly. The car behind him picked up speed as well. Ajay was driving too fast for comfort, and the other driver seemed determined to keep up.

As they approached the intersection headed away from the center of town, the car pulled up beside them. As the driver lowered the window, Ajay readied his service weapon at his side.

The other car suddenly sounded its horn, and a teenage boy hung out the window to give Ajay his middle finger. The others inside all laughed as if he'd actually done something amusing. As the light turned green, the driver hit the gas and barreled through the intersection, making a right turn directly in front of Ajay. He narrowly missed hitting another car before jetting off.

Ajay reached for his police radio and engaged the microphone. "Dispatch, ten-thirteen. Officer needs assistant."

"This is Dispatch."

"We have a ten-fifty-five in progress. It's a late model Ford sedan, license plate three, nine, eight, Adam, Zebra, Lincoln. I repeat…three, nine, eight, Adam, Zebra, Lincoln. The driver and passengers appear to be in their teens." Ajay gave the dispatch officer their location and the direction the car was headed in.

"Ten-four, Lieutenant. Traffic officers are in pursuit."

"Thank you, Dispatch. Over and out."

Minutes later, Ajay reached the front gates of the

Colton Ranch, noting the new security box that had been installed since they'd left. He pressed the call button, and Buck answered immediately.

"This thing is fancy!" the elder Colton exclaimed. "Let me buzz you in."

As the gates swung open, Lizzy finally breathed a sigh of relief. "All this excitement isn't good for my nerves," she said.

Ajay chuckled softly. At the home's front door, he reached out for her, wrapping his arms around her shoulders. Lizzy sighed as she melted against him, relaxing into his chest as if nothing had happened.

In the distance, the sun had made its descent, darkness quickly claiming its place. There was the barest sliver of a crescent moon, and the chilly air was eerily still. Their visit with Sebastian and Ruth had lasted longer than initially planned. A late lunch had become an early dinner, and dinner had ended in a round of board games with coffee and a second helping of dessert. Lizzy had held their baby, fed him a bottle, changed his diaper and ordered a bundle of baby gifts from an online app on her cell phone. Laughter had been abundant and greatly needed, and Lizzy and Ajay were able to relax in a way that felt nurturing. Both were now exhausted as the late-night hour was pulling at the last of their energy.

"Thank you for a great day," Lizzy said. "It felt good to get out. I had so much fun I'm not ready to end the day yet."

"You're welcome. But you really need to go get some rest. I can't have your people mad at me for keeping you up past your curfew!"

Lizzy giggled, her head shaking from side to side. "You worry about the darndest things!"

Ajay smiled. "One of us needs to," he replied. "I'm going to stay out here for a minute to decompress. I'll see you in the morning."

"Another adventure?"

He smiled. "Maybe. After your doctor's appointment."

Lizzy's eyes widened as she suddenly remembered the obligation. It was her follow-up appointment to get the doctor's all clear for her to return to a semblance of normalcy. "Shoot," she replied. "I forgot about that."

"I didn't. Someone needs to keep you on track."

"I hate going to the doctor," she said. "He has clammy hands!"

Ajay chuckled. "I'm sure everything will be fine. Good night, Lizzy." He leaned to press the gentlest kiss against her cheek.

"Good night, Ajay," she whispered.

Pumpkin barked, leading Lizzy into the home, and all Ajay could do was shake his head.

# Chapter Eleven

Ajay rose early the next morning. He hadn't slept well and figured he would start the new day with work. After a cup of hot coffee courtesy of the Keurig coffee maker on the counter, he'd dressed, checked on Lizzy and his dog, and then headed toward town. Driving to the police station to check in and follow up on the progress, or lack of progress, in Lizzy's case had him irritated, and it was barely light out. He needed to work out to ease his stress, and he wasn't certain when that would happen.

Today's schedule was mapped out, starting with driving Lizzy and Mama Jen to her doctor's appointment. He had a meeting with the police captain after that. Pumpkin was due at the groomers for a bath, and who knew what might blow up before his day ended.

Thinking about Lizzy had him in a strange headspace. No woman before her had been able to push him to such an emotional crux the way she did. And there had been plenty of other women. Women who passed through like the birds that settled about in the warmer season and disappeared with the cold. Women who wanted nothing from him but a few good memories, and women who wanted more than he was able to give. And now he'd fallen in love with a woman who wanted a six-man football team to go with the husband, the house and the picket fence.

He loved Lizzy. As crazy as it sounded after such a short period of time, he was in love with Lizzy Colton. Saying so felt as natural as breathing, and if he could have shouted it out to the world, he would have. For now, though, he felt like he couldn't even tell Lizzy what was in his heart and in his head, and that burdened him more than everything else.

"AJAY, HEY, DUDE! What's up?"

Ajay had been sitting at a back table in Hutch's Diner. After leaving the police station, he had just enough time to kill before needing to head back to the ranch to pick up Lizzy and Jenny for her doctor's appointment. The morning breakfast spot was a town favorite, serving the best coffee in Owl Creek. The business had been started by Hutch Maddox. After his death a few years back, Hutch's wife, Sharon, and their son Billy had taken over running the establishment. True to her husband's vision, Sharon had maintained that 1990s vibe, and the welcoming atmosphere had made the diner a staple in the Owl Creek community.

Ajay looked up to find Billy staring at him. The two men bumped fists in greeting. "How's it hanging, kid?" Ajay asked.

"A little to the left, a little to the right," the young man answered jokingly.

Ajay laughed with him.

"We haven't seen you in a while. Not getting your coffee at some other place, are you?"

"Never! Besides the coffee, I'm addicted to your mother's biscuits and gravy. No one does sausage gravy like your mom."

Billy held up a coffeepot. "Would you like a refill?"

"Thank you," Ajay said as he tilted his cup toward the young man. "How are things going with you, Billy?"

"No complaints. Work keeps me busy. Mom keeps me busier."

"Moms will do that. You're lucky to have yours."

"Everybody keeps telling me that," Billy said with a shrug.

"Everyone's telling you right."

Billy nodded, but his expression seemed to say otherwise. Ajay knew that against his mom's wishes he'd taken a gap year from college, unsure what he wanted for himself. But mom and son had always seemed content with the decision once it had been made.

"If you're still here after I make my rounds and get the orders out, I'd like to sit and talk for a minute," Billy said. "If that's all right?"

"Always," Ajay answered.

Billy turned and headed in the opposite direction. Ajay watched as the young man circled the diner, filling empty cups with fresh coffee.

The room was beginning to fill, the morning crowd looking for breakfast before starting their day. His gaze was suddenly drawn to a man sitting on the other side of the room. He looked comfortable in his seat, as if he'd been there before. But he also looked out of place in his expensive wool suit and silk tie. He didn't give Ajay tourist vibes, and Ajay couldn't think of one business in town whose employees needed to bring a Wall Street flair to their positions. Not even the local bank employees dressed so conservatively.

Under different circumstances, Ajay would probably have not paid him an ounce of attention, but he was staring in Ajay's direction and that instantly put Ajay on the defensive.

When Ajay stared back, the man nodded his head, every strand of his dark blond hair staying in place. With the horn-rimmed glasses he was wearing, he almost reminded Ajay of Clark Kent. His shoulders were broad and his physique trim, but Ajay didn't get *superhero* from him.

Ajay nodded back, the gesture polite but dismissive.

Billy suddenly plopped down into the seat beside him. "I have to be quick. We're short one waitress this morning."

"Not a problem," Ajay responded. "What's going on?"

"I've been thinking about joining the police department. I just wanted to get your thoughts about that."

"Obviously I consider it a good profession. Are you still considering school?"

Billy nodded. "Boise State University has a really good criminal justice program. They also have one of the best forensic science programs. It would keep my options open. Or do you think I should just apply to the Idaho State Police Academy?"

"There are some specific requirements you have

to meet to get into the academy. First, you have to be twenty-one years old."

"That's almost two years away."

"Sounds like college would be the best route. Plus, it'll afford you the opportunity to discover exactly where you'd like to see yourself in our criminal justice system. You may discover being a peace officer isn't for you."

"That's what my mother said."

"Smart woman, your mother."

Billy's smile spread across his face. "Thanks. I may have some more questions, so you need to come back more often."

Ajay laughed. "Deal!" He suddenly leaned forward in his seat. "Actually, I do have a question for you, Billy. Do you know the gentleman sitting in the booth there by the window? The one in the blue suit."

Billy shrugged. "He's one of those Ever After Church guys. He likes to come in and talk to people. The tourists mostly. Mom says he's a snake oil salesman. But I think he's growing on her, 'cause she agreed to go to one of his services this month."

Ajay and the man locked eyes again. This time, the man stood, carrying his cup of coffee in Ajay's direction.

"Thanks, Billy," Ajay muttered.

"Good morning, sir!" the man greeted him.

Ajay smiled. "Good morning to you."

"Do you mind if I join you? Good coffee is best shared with a new friend."

Ajay pointed toward the seat on the other side of the table. "Please, have a seat."

"Thank you," the man said as he adjusted his suit

jacket before sitting down. He extended his hand. "My name is Acker. Pastor Markus Acker. My flock and I are new to this fine city, and I'm still getting to know my way around. This establishment has become one of my favorites for breakfast and for fellowship."

Ajay shook his hand. "It's a pleasure to meet you, Pastor Acker, and welcome to Owl Creek."

"I apologize for staring at you earlier, but I could tell that you were a deeply troubled soul. And troubled souls are my specialty." His smile was charismatic, and his voice was like butter, smooth and easy.

"I wasn't aware I had any issues for anyone to be concerned about," Ajay said calmly.

The pastor suddenly quoted, "Incline thine ear unto my cry; For my soul is full of troubles: and my life draweth nigh unto the grave. I am counted with them that go down into the pit; I am as a man that hath no strength..."

Ajay nodded. "Psalm 88, verse 3."

"You've studied your Bible. I am impressed."

"As a man of faith, I'm sure you know others of faith stand on the teachings of the Bible, too. Just as you do."

"Yes, yes, yes." Acker closed his eyes, his head waving slowly from side to side. When he opened them, Ajay was watching him closely. The pastor smiled his saccharine smile. "I would love to invite you to one of our services." Acker reached into the inner pocket of his jacket for a business card, passing it to Ajay. "Our programs are open to the community so bring your family. And your friends. All are welcome."

"Thank you," Ajay said.

Acker stood, lifting his empty coffee cup from the table. "I didn't catch your name, my brother."

Ajay smiled. "Ajay. Ajay Wright. *Lieutenant* Ajay Wright with the Owl Creek Police Department."

If Ajay hadn't been studying the man so intently, he would have missed the flutter above his left eye. The pastor visibly bristled but didn't seem to allow the information to throw him completely off guard. Instead, he took a deep breath and smiled. "Well, Lieutenant Wright, it's been a pleasure. I hope that we run into each other again soon."

"Very soon," Ajay replied in a friendly manner. "Very soon."

Acker walked back to his own table. He reached into his pocket and pulled cash from a worn leather wallet, tossed the money onto the table and headed out the door.

Ajay continued to watch him through the window. Acker had only been standing outside a few minutes when he was suddenly joined by another man. One of his *flock*, Ajay mused. But when the man turned to stare into the diner, he met Ajay's gaze.

Ajay's eyes widened as he recognized the man Lizzy had drawn. The man they suspected of stalking her.

Without thinking, Ajay jumped from his seat and bolted toward the door. Not paying attention to his surroundings, he collided with Billy's mother, Sharon, knocking a tray of food out of her hands and onto his clothes. He knocked the poor woman to the floor, practically falling on top of her himself. They both cursed, an oration of profanity filling the midmorning air.

"I'm so sorry," Ajay exclaimed. "Just charge me for the meal!"

"What's wrong, Ajay?" Sharon asked.

"It's an emergency," he shouted as he clumsily helped her up. He continued to apologize as he turned back toward the door.

By the time Ajay made it out the entrance and onto the sidewalk, both men were gone, neither anywhere to be seen. Ajay looked up one side of the street and down the other. Not even a vehicle passed him by.

He pulled his cell phone to his ear, shaking off what looked like scrambled eggs from the screen. Three rings later, Max answered.

"Is Lizzy okay?" Max asked, not bothering to say hello.

"Lizzy is fine. She's at the ranch. But I think I just saw her kidnapper. I'm down here at Hutch's Diner. He's with a man named Markus Acker."

"Markus Acker?" The shock in Max's voice was thick as clabber. "Are you certain?"

"Do you know who he is?"

There was a moment's hesitation before Lizzy's brother answered, "Markus Acker is the pastor of the church Jessie recently became affiliated with."

LIZZY STOOD NAKED in front of the full-length mirror in her bedroom. Her complexion was pale, but she no longer looked ghostly. The bruises had finally begun to fade, and the bruised ribs beginning to heal made breathing so much easier.

Were she to consider getting naked in front of a man in

general, she would only be a little embarrassed. Getting naked in front of Ajay, however, was a different beast. She wanted him to see her at her very best. If the moment presented itself, makeup would have to be her very best friend. Having his attention long enough to get into bed meant pulling out all the stops to keep his attention.

She stared a moment longer, then wanted to give herself a swift kick. Ajay wouldn't care if she were perfect or not. Ajay would love her because she brought him joy and made him happy. She imagined he would look past any scars that marred her body. He would only care if he thought it important to her. And even then, she imagined he would tell her she was being silly. He would say she was beautiful, and he'd kiss each mark and touch every part of her, because in his eyes, she was perfect.

She imagined the warmth of his fingers as they trailed down the length of her arms and across her back. He'd tease one rock-candy-hard nipple and then the other, and where his fingers led, his tongue would follow.

Lizzy suddenly shook away the reverie, moisture beginning to puddle in places it had no business being. Thinking of Ajay had her heated, and she couldn't dwell on fantasy. But, if anything at all, Lizzy thought, a girl could certainly hope.

She slid into fresh panties and a bra, then dabbed her favorite perfume on all her pulse points. A hint of powder in those places where she might perspire and deodorant over freshly shaved skin helped boost her confidence. Black leggings, an oversize sweater and red Timberland boots completed her look. After pulling the length of her hair into a high ponytail, she polished her lips with a neutral gloss.

With one last glance in the mirror, Lizzy took a deep breath, then she went looking for Ajay.

"HOW THE HELL did you manage to lose him?" Max snapped.

Ajay cut a narrowed eye toward Lizzy's brother. The two men were pacing in front of the diner, looking like both had just lost their best friend.

"You act like I purposely let him go," Ajay snapped back.

"Did you?"

"Both of you need to stop," Della said, her eyes darting from one to the other. "You know Ajay didn't do anything on purpose and you know Max is just in his feelings."

"We were that close," Ajay muttered.

Frustration played like music from a violin, a slow vibrato that was mesmerizing. Max nodded. "My guys are pulling all the security footage now. With any luck, we'll get a hit and a name."

"What do you know about Acker?" Ajay questioned.

"He's a grifter. The agency has had him and his church on their radar for some time now. They just haven't been able to get anything concrete on him to take him down."

"And his affiliation with your mother?"

Max shot him a look, clearly not happy with the question. "Let's just leave Jessie out of this for now."

"I can't do that. Lizzy needs to know that her mother may be involved in this."

Max snapped, "Lizzy needs to know no such thing."

"You can't keep this from her," Ajay said, his voice rising.

"You don't get to say what we can and cannot do with regards to my little sister. I get that you care about her. And I'm fine with you wanting to protect her, but you don't know anything about her relationship with our mother. You didn't wipe her tears away when she cried herself to sleep because that woman wasn't here. So, you are not about to add any more pain to a wound that is still raw."

"I'm not going to lie to her," Ajay hissed between clenched teeth.

The two men were now standing toe to toe, looking as if they were about to come to blows.

Inside the diner, customers had taken out their cell phones, cameras recording in hopes of capturing a viral moment they could post and exploit. Della stepped between the two, pressing her palms against Max's chest.

"You two aren't going to solve this butting heads like two bulls in a china shop. Just agree to disagree and circle back to it when you've both calmed down."

"I still think she needs to be told," Ajay quipped.

"I don't really give a damn what you think," Max barked.

Recognizing they were at an impasse, Ajay took a step back. He and Max were still shooting daggers at each other as they stared.

"We're not done with this conversation," Ajay said. He turned and began walking away.

"Where are you going?" Della questioned.

"Home to change. Then I need to go get Lizzy. I'm already late."

"I'll go get my sister and take her to her doctor's appointment." Max's expression was just a tad shy of a full-blown snarl.

Ajay tossed him one last glare over his shoulder. He turned slightly to stare at the man. "Fine. I'll meet you after to pick her up. And you have until the end of the week. If we don't come up with anything by then, Lizzy will need to be told."

"Look," Max started. "You don't get to say—"

Ajay interrupted. "I'm saying. I understand you don't want your sister to be hurt. I don't want her to be hurt, either. But keeping secrets from her isn't going to help. Lying to her will only hurt her more. The end of the week," he said, and then he turned and stormed away toward his car.

LIZZY WAS NOT happy with him. Ajay could hear her frustration over the phone when he called to say that he was running behind schedule and would have to meet her and Mama Jen after her appointment at the physician's office.

She had not wanted to hear that he needed to go home and change his clothes. Nor was she happy that Max had dropped everything he was doing to fill in for him, ensuring she was protected for however long she was away from home.

Her telling him not to bother coming at all to get her had been a defense mechanism. He knew because him telling her that was fine with him had been his.

He and Max making a quasi-agreement not to tell her

about her mother didn't make him feel comfortable. Secrets had a way of coming back to bite you in the ass when you least expected. He had no intention of starting their relationship on half-truths and full-blown lies. After their semi-heated discussion, the two men had agreed to keep it between them until the end of the week. If the detectives didn't have any answers by then, Ajay would tell Lizzy everything they knew. It was a compromise of sorts, both agreeing that not hurting Lizzy or causing her any angst was first and foremost for both of them.

With Pumpkin at the groomer's, he had a moment to himself, and he needed to process all that was happening. He also needed to straighten up his home, the place looking like the aftermath of a frat party. He'd hurried out after pulling clothes from the closet and drawers, forgetting the dirty dishes he'd left in the kitchen sink and the carpet that desperately needed a date with the vacuum. He'd be highly embarrassed if visitors showed up unannounced. Realizing he needed some time, telling Lizzy he needed to be home for a minute had been necessary.

She responded exactly how he expected. Expressing her disappointment wasn't an option but keeping it out of her voice and off her face was nearly impossible.

"Whatever," she said, a hint of attitude in her tone. "It's fine."

But it wasn't fine because she was fuming. She wasn't interested in his explanation. She was just unhappy that she couldn't have her way. Then they both said some things neither could walk back.

"Lizzy, I'm not in the mood. With everything going

on right now, you're being selfish. I'm only asking for a few hours to myself."

"I said fine, Ajay. Do whatever you want."

"Why are you giving me attitude?"

"Attitude?"

Lizzy's tone was sharp, and Ajay could just imagine the unhappy expression on her face.

"Yes, attitude! You're acting like a spoiled brat right now!"

"Go to hell, Ajay. You were the one who promised to be here if I needed you. I'm not breaking that promise. Clearly, you are useless to me if you can't keep your word!"

"Useless?"

"I don't need to be surrounded by weak men, so maybe it's better you don't show up."

"Now you're calling me weak?"

"I said what I said."

"That's fine, Lizzy. Now that I know where I stand, we're good. You have a great day!"

Ajay slammed the phone down, disconnecting the call. The conversation left him cold, his stomach tied in a tight knot.

The phone rang almost immediately, Lizzy calling him back. When he answered, she was still spewing venom, still wanting to hurt him to assuage her own pain. She had called him back to curse at him some more and he disconnected the call again, throwing the phone to the other side of the room.

Two days had passed since they'd spoken. Two days that had left him feeling riddled with guilt. He'd taken his anger out on her. He hadn't tried to be understanding of her feelings. He'd allowed his disagreement with her brother to get the best of him and she had borne the brunt of his anguish. Now, every effort he made to call her back and apologize was being ignored. Lizzy had no interest in speaking with him, and he wanted nothing more than to be back by her side, everything right between them.

He thought back to the kiss they shared, her lips plush against his own. She'd tasted sweet like honey, and it had taken everything in him to stop, his desire for more surging voraciously. He wanted to kiss Lizzy and hold her and feel her skin against his own. He wanted to take her and claim her and be everything she needed him to be.

That one kiss would never feel like enough, and for that reason alone, he needed to take a step back to assess what was happening between them.

He couldn't help but wonder if Lizzy even had a clue that she had such a hold over him.

"YOU CAN'T HOLD the man hostage, Lizzy," Max said.

"No one was trying to hold him hostage. I just…" She paused, turning to stare out the window of her brother's car. Tears pressed hot against her eyelids, and she was determined not to let her brother see her cry.

From the back seat, Buck cleared his throat. "Max, leave your sister alone. Things have been hard enough for her without you boys giving her a difficult time."

Max shook his head. "I wasn't giving her a hard time. She's sitting here pouting because Ajay couldn't be here."

"No one's pouting!" Lizzy snapped, her ire rising with a vengeance.

"Everyone calm down," Mama Jen said. "You don't need to fuss at each other. We need to be celebrating the doctor clearing Lizzy to go back to a little normalcy. That will help once she's feeling safe and settled," she said. "We're just excited to see you feeling better, Lizzy."

Lizzy turned toward the back seat to meet the stare her aunt was giving her. She didn't miss how close the two elders were sitting beside each other. It made her smile.

"I'll be fine," she said. "I do feel better, and with the new security at the ranch I'm not worried about anything happening to me there. I know Ajay needs to go back to his own life." She took a deep breath. "I'm just going to miss Pumpkin," she said softly.

"We'll get you a puppy of your own," Max said. "I'll call Sebastian as soon as we get home."

"Let's just try to find one that's already house-trained," Buck said with a deep chuckle. "I'm too old to be running around with a pee pad trying to catch accidents all day long."

Max and Lizzy laughed.

Lizzy said, "You don't run around with a pee pad, Daddy. You teach the dog to go on a pee pad."

"Well, whatever. I'm too old."

"Buck Colton, I'll have you know that sixty-three is not old. Most especially if you consider the alternative." Mama Jen tapped him with newly manicured fingers. The duo giggled.

"I'm hungry," Max said, changing the subject.

"Head to the ranch. I'm sure your dad has got plenty of food. I can make us something good to eat."

"Are you sure, Mama Jen? We can always stop somewhere in town," Max said.

"I'm certain. No point in wasting good money for no reason."

Max turned his car toward Colton Ranch. He and Lizzy fell quiet as the couple in the back seat chatted with each other.

When Mama Jen suddenly giggled, Lizzy turned to look over her shoulder. Her father was whispering in the matriarch's ear, and Jenny was blushing profusely.

Lizzy smiled, then turned back to stare out the window. She was already missing Ajay, and she knew neither a new puppy, nor an old dog, was going to take that feeling away.

## Chapter Twelve

It had been one week since Lizzy last saw Ajay. One week, twelve hours, thirty-two minutes and ten seconds. But who was counting, she thought. She lay in her bed, her body curled in a fetal position. She had barely left the room since she last spoke to him. She was sure that the last conversation had not left him with the best impression of her. Even she had thought she had sounded like a spoiled child.

It had been well over a week since their family home had been invaded and her personal residence had been broken into. She knew there had been no news about her abductor, nor had he done anything else to try to get to her. She wasn't certain if that was a good thing or the calm before the next brewing storm.

When Buck knocked on her bedroom door, easing it open to peer inside, she was actually surprised. She sat upright, turning to give her father a look.

"You have a visitor," he said.

Lizzy's heart shifted into another gear. She wanted to think that Ajay had finally come to see her. "A visitor?"

Buck gestured at the person in the hallway standing behind him. "I'll just let you two catch up," he said cheerily.

Vivian eased past the man, a wide grin across her face. "Thank you, Mr. Colton."

"Anytime, young lady. It's good to see you again," he said as he closed the door.

Vivian turned toward her, that smile disappearing so quickly that Lizzy thought she might have imagined it.

"Don't be mad," Lizzy said.

"Really, Lizzy? That's all you have to say. Don't be mad? I've been calling you every day, and you haven't shown me the courtesy of calling me back. Not even a message to tell me to drop dead. Nothing! Do you know how scared I've been?"

"I'm sorry?"

Vivian dropped onto the bed beside her. "You better be glad you're my best friend. I wouldn't take that from anyone else. What's going on with you?"

Lizzy leaned her head on Vivian's narrow shoulder. "I'm just having a hard time."

"This isn't good, Lizzy. What's worrying you most? The kidnapper? Ajay? Your family?"

"All of the above. I'm a hot mess, Vivian, and I don't know what to do. I'm scared one minute. Depressed the next. Sad. Angry. Sad again. I should be over this by now."

"You've been through a lot of trauma. No one says you have to get over it in a specific amount of time. Have you talked to your doctor? You might need anxiety meds."

"I have a prescription, and I've been taking them when it gets really bad."

"Have you thought about seeing a therapist?"

Lizzy shrugged. "Mama Jen made me go see someone once."

"It takes time, Lizzy. It would probably help if you could get back into your normal routine. Have they said when you can go back to your house?"

"It's still a crime scene, but I don't know if I plan to ever go back. He was in my things! For all I know, he could have been playing with my vibrator."

"Eww!"

"Exactly!"

"What about work? Do you have any assignments you need to finish?"

"I've been able to do everything here. But maybe I could go back to the office for a few hours each day."

"Well, that would be a start. But I think what you can probably use in this very moment is a drink. Let's go to The Cellar."

The Cellar was a wineshop downtown that hosted numerous events during the week. One of their more popular events was the wine tasting and food pairing where they partnered with area restaurants for a full dining experience.

Lizzy frowned. "I don't know…"

"Get dressed. I've already reserved a table. Besides, I need to get out so I can tell you about my love life and what's not happening in it."

Lizzy laughed. "I thought you had something new to share with me."

"You and I have a lot of catching up to do. I want to know about that man, too."

"What man?"

"You know what man I'm talking about."

"I don't want to talk about Ajay."

"Too bad. I do." Vivian stole a quick glance at the watch on her wrist. She wriggled her nose, a scowl crossing her face. "You need a shower. I'll find something in your closet for you to wear. Let's go!"

"Are you saying I stink?"

"I'm saying you don't smell fresh. Now let's do something about that."

Lizzy sighed as she lifted herself from the bed. She headed toward the bathroom, dragging her feet as if she were headed to the guillotine.

Vivian called after her, "I love you, Lizzy!"

Lizzy hesitated, turning around to stare at her bestie. "I love you, too, girl!" she said. "Even if you did say I smell bad!"

BOTH WOMEN WERE LAUGHING, two glasses of wine each fueling their mood. It was live music night, and a local husband and wife duo, James and Elaine Mercy, performing as Mercy! Mercy!, were playing their guitars and singing. The indie folk music was upbeat and a nice mood lifter. The wine, a rich and spicy cabernet sauvignon, had been paired with a delectable beef bourguignon.

It was comfort food with a luxurious flair, and with each bite Lizzy was thankful that Vivian had dragged her out of the house. She was having a great time, and the two women had fallen in sync as if no time had passed since they'd last been together.

They'd been discussing Lizzy and Ajay for a good

while. Lizzy recapped every moment she'd spent with the man. She told her friend about the kiss, about them sharing time together that had been intimate without taking their clothes off and how much she enjoyed how they laughed together. There was no detail she didn't want to share.

"Correct me if I'm wrong," Vivian said, "but it sounds like you've fallen in love with the handsome lieutenant."

"I'd prefer to say I'm in serious *like* with a boatload of *lust*."

"What you'd prefer and what your reality is are two different things. You're in love, and you might as well just say so."

"I got it bad," Lizzy gushed. "And I miss him so much!"

"You can call him, you know."

"I'm embarrassed. He called me, and I didn't answer or return any of his messages."

"You really need to stop doing that, Lizzy. There are people who genuinely care about you and want to know that you're okay, and I'm not talking about your brothers or your family. You can't keep ghosting people when you feel bad. Let us be there for you!"

Lizzy took another sip of her wine. She didn't bother to respond, not wanting to acknowledge that Vivian was right. Vivian was always right when Lizzy was getting it wrong. And her not being afraid to put Lizzy in her place was a testament to their friendship. She could trust her best friend to always give it to her straight, whether she liked it or not.

Vivian continued, "You can always attribute it to your head injury. I don't think telling the man you were just being thoughtless will win you any girlfriend points."

"So let's talk about your love life now," Lizzy said. "We know I screwed mine up."

Vivian laughed. "I'm sure if I had a love life, I'd be making mincemeat out of it, too!"

"We should teach a class on self-sabotage. We're so darn good at it."

"Maybe we should plan one of those ex-bestie parties?"

"Ex-bestie?" Lizzy raised a brow curiously.

"We invite all our friends. Then they invite their ex-boyfriends and best guy friends that they would vouch for. It's a meet-and-greet to see if we can make any love connections."

"Do you really want to date any of my exes?" Lizzy asked, amused. "Seriously?"

"Not any of yours, but one of our friends might have a good guy friend we might like. You could invite your brothers."

"Which brother?"

"Not for me, but one of them that's not dating some bimbo and would interest one of the other girls."

"My brothers have dated most of my friends. Which is why a few of them aren't friends anymore."

"Okay, so scratch that bright idea."

Their laughter rang through the room, dancing with a joy that wafted like a summer breeze through the air.

"Thank you," Lizzy said as she lifted her third glass of wine. It was Vietti Moscato d'Asti, a sweet wine with notes of peaches, candied ginger and honeysuckle. It paired nicely with the winter fruit tray and the glazed berry tart they were served for dessert. "I needed this more than I realized."

"You're welcome."

For another hour, the two women laughed, cried and had a great time. They talked about Vivian's business, the Colton family scandal, a romance novel the two had both read and a potential girls trip to Bermuda after the holidays.

"What do you plan to do for Thanksgiving?" Lizzy asked.

"Come to your house."

"And Christmas?"

"Your house. Unless I'm finally in a relationship. Then I'm going to meet the family."

Lizzy laughed. "Wouldn't it be funny if that was at my house, too?"

Vivian giggled. "That would so not be funny!"

Lizzy's phone chimed, a text message calling for her attention. She read it quickly, then downed the last swallow of wine in her glass. "All good things must come to an end," she said. "My ride is outside waiting for me."

"What ride? I had planned to take you back home." Vivian turned in her seat to stare toward the front door.

"I know. But I texted Max and asked him to come get me. I didn't want to put you out any more than I already have."

"You wouldn't have put me out."

"Dinner's on me," Lizzy said, gesturing toward the waitress with her credit card.

"This was supposed to be my treat."

"Next time. I want to get it this time."

"I'm not going to argue with you," Vivian said.

"Good," Lizzy said as she signed the receipt. "Max is

waiting to walk you to your car, and we are going to follow you home to make sure you get there safe."

"That's so not necessary."

"It'll make me feel better," Lizzy said.

Rising from their seats, the two women embraced,
wrapping each other in a warm hug.

"Call Ajay," Vivian whispered into her ear. "You deserve a happy ending, and I'm going to be really pissed
if you mess this up for us."

Lizzy laughed. "Us?"

"Darn right, us! If I never find a man of my own, I'm
going to have to live vicariously through you."

"Then we're both in trouble," Lizzy concluded.

"When are we not in trouble!" her friend said with a
giggle. "Just call the man and don't forget to give me an
update once you talk to him."


"VIVIAN SAID NOT to forget to call her when you do that
thing," Max said as he slid back into the driver's seat of
his car. "What's that thing?"

Lizzy gave her brother a quick look. He had just
walked Vivian to her front door and ensured she was
safe and secure inside. He shifted the vehicle into gear
and pulled out onto the road.

They were midway between Conners and Owl Creek
and had a good few minutes before arriving at the ranch.
Lizzy hadn't said much as they had followed Vivian
home. She'd been lost in her own thoughts, trying to
figure out what her next steps needed to be. And she still
didn't have a clue.

"I think I messed up," Lizzy said. She turned to look at her brother.

Max glanced back at her. "Does this have to do with Ajay?"

She nodded, biting back the rising emotion that threatened to bend her heart and spill her tears.

"What did you do?" Max questioned.

"I got mad when he said he needed to take some time to himself. I felt like he was abandoning me, so I decided to ghost him first."

Max nodded. "Do you like that guy, Lizzy? I mean *really* like him?"

There was a moment of silence as Lizzy pondered her brother's question. When she finally answered, tears were streaming down her face. "I think I'm in love with him, Max. I've fallen in love with him. I really wanted things to be good between us. But what man would want me and all the baggage I come with? And let's be honest. Our family puts a whole other spin on dysfunction. Then I thought, what if I turned out to be like Jessie? What if years from now I was a bad wife and horrible mother? I figured he might not have wanted to take the risk of tying himself to someone who's broken. I thought it would be better if I just pushed him away." She sobbed. "So, that's what I did. I pushed him away."

Max sat and let her cry. He didn't say anything as he drove on toward the ranch. He let her cry until she didn't have any tears left.

By then he had reached the front gates of their family home. He pulled the car through the entrance before stopping the vehicle. The two sat quietly as the darkness settled in around them. Finally, her sobs turned to a barrage of hiccups.

Max shook his head. "You are such a crybaby!"

"I am not!" Lizzy exclaimed.

"Are, too! Crybaby!" Max smiled.

"You have always thought you were the boss of somebody," Lizzy said as she swiped her eyes with the backs of her hands.

"Then don't be a crybaby! Do you want me to kick his ass for you? Because I will kick his ass. And so will Greg and Malcolm. No one messes with our little sister."

Lizzy laughed. "I know how to fight! You taught me. I could kick his ass myself if I wanted to. I want you to tell me how to fix this!"

Max took a deep breath. "You need to talk to him. You need to apologize for being a brat. Then you need to tell him how you feel and what you want. After that, you need to sit and listen to everything he has to say."

"What if he says he doesn't want me?"

"Then I'll kick his ass!"

Lizzy punched her brother in the shoulder. "I'm serious, Max."

"So am I."

Lizzy rolled her eyes skyward.

Max laughed. "One step at a time, Lizzy. Talk to him. You'll figure it out from there."

AJAY PICKED UP his cell phone, eyeing it for a quick moment before dropping it back down to the tabletop.

He wanted to call Lizzy. But he didn't want to seem desperate. Clearly, she wasn't interested in hearing from him. She hadn't returned his calls or answered any of his messages. He hadn't thought it would bother him as much as it did, but if he were honest, his feelings were hurt. He pushed the phone aside and reached for the bottle of cold beer on the table.

"We tried to warn you," Malcolm said, laughing. He sipped on his own bottle of beer. "Our sister can be a handful."

Greg laughed with his brother. "Most men make the mistake of thinking Lizzy is fragile and weak and needs a man to take care of her. Lizzy might be a little spoiled because of us, but she definitely doesn't *need* a man. That's because of us, too. She can keep up with any guy and even outdo most of them. She's tough, and she can be mean as spit when she wants to be."

The trio sat at a table at Tap Out Brewery. Popular for the local brews they served and the party-like atmosphere on game nights, it was a great place to sit back and relax after a long day of responsibilities. When Malcolm had called Ajay to come and join them for a beer, he'd welcomed the opportunity to sit and relax with the guys.

Malcolm nodded in agreement. "She was so small when our mother left. We wanted to protect her, but we also wanted to make sure she could protect herself. She seems to be doing a good job of it so far."

"Except I would never hurt her. I thought she would have known that," Ajay said a little defensively.

The two brothers exchanged a look and laughed.

"Look," Malcolm said. "She's still a woman. And I haven't met a woman yet who doesn't pose a challenge from time to time. But if you care about Lizzy, then let her know. Fight for her."

Greg nodded. "Women like when you're willing to go to battle for them. At least that's what someone told me." He lifted his brow as he sipped the beverage in his glass. "And we've got your back if you need us."

"Max might not be, but we're good with you!" Malcolm said. "The two of them being the youngest means they were always super close, so he's even more protective of her than Buck is."

"What about Max?"

They all turned to see the man standing over them. Max reached for an empty chair and pulled it up to the table. "Why are you talking about me?" he asked as he sat down.

Malcolm laughed. "I was just telling Ajay that we have his back with Lizzy, but that you might not be a fan of his."

Max cut an eye in Ajay's direction. Ajay met his stare with a look of his own. The two men sized each other up.

"Exactly what are your intentions with our baby sister?" Max questioned.

"I honestly don't know," Ajay said. "I had hoped she and I would be able to take some time to really get to know each other without all the drama of what's happening now. But I think she's mad at me right now, so I'm not sure where that puts us."

"She's not mad. She's scared," Max said. "She's not used to feeling so vulnerable."

"Neither am I," Ajay muttered.

"What took you so long?" Greg asked Max. "We expected you over an hour ago."

"I had to pick up Lizzy," Max answered.

"Is she okay?" Ajay questioned. "Did something happen?" Concern may as well have seeped like water from his pores.

"She's fine. She's at the ranch."

Ajay blew out a sigh of relief.

Greg laughed. "You almost gave this guy a heart attack." He slapped Ajay on the back.

"Why are you messing with him like that?" Malcolm chuckled. "He's a good guy, and he's got it bad for Lizzy. You need to cut him some slack."

Max shrugged. "He's all right."

Ajay tossed him a look. "So we're good?"

"As long as you don't hurt my sister, we're fine."

"Lizzy was always his baby! Like Malcolm said, he's more overprotective than our father. I'm going to hate it when he has kids," Greg said.

"Like you wouldn't do the same for Jane and Justin," Max teased.

"Speaking of…" Greg said as he rose from the table, his cell phone in his hand. "I need to call Briony and make sure everyone's okay."

"How's Della doing?" Malcolm asked, looking at Max.

Max nodded. "She'll be better as soon as I get home."

"In that case, the last round is on me," Ajay said as he gestured toward the bar.

Loud cheers suddenly rang through the air. On the big screen televisions throughout the room, a college basketball game was going into overtime, and the two teams were battling hard. Malcolm headed to the bar to grab their tray of drinks from the bartender.

"Any advice you can give me about your sister?" Ajay asked Max.

"Yeah," Max answered. "Don't let her kick your ass. We will never let you live that down."

Ajay laughed.

When Malcolm returned with a tray of drinks, he grabbed one without sitting down. "I just ran into an old friend of mine. I'm going to chat him up for a minute. I'll be back," he said, tossing them a glance over his shoulder.

The two men returned to their conversation.

"Seriously," Max said as he leaned forward, folding his hands together on top of the table. "She's having a hard time, but she doesn't want anyone to know. She cares about you, and she's afraid she's blown her chance."

"I just need to talk to her," Ajay said, his frustration palpable.

"I told her that. I gave her the old communication is key speech, and I think she's still processing it all. Just give her some time."

"There seems to be plenty of that on my hands."

"You haven't been cleared back in the field yet? Since Lizzy fired you, I figured you'd already be reassigned back to search and rescue."

"I have. I'm just holding off for now." Ajay continued, "Have you heard anything about the case? Technically, I've been pulled. Della tries to keep me in the loop without risking her own access, but I haven't heard anything of value that would help us find this guy and get him off the street."

"You know I can't talk to you about this case. It's an ongoing investigation."

"Can't or won't?"

Max stared at him, hesitating briefly. "Fine, and only because I really do like you, and I think you might be good for my sister." He leaned in further, his voice dropping. "We got a hit on the DNA that was taken from Lizzy's home. It matched the DNA found in the cabin."

Ajay's eyes widened, and he leaned in closer. "Who is it?"

"His name is Tiberius Wagner. He's got a lengthy rap sheet. Assault and battery, attempted murder, rape, robbery, fraud. He's bad news all the way around."

"Why haven't you picked him up?"

"We're working on it."

"Do you know what his connection is with Markus Acker and the church?"

"From what we've been able to figure out, it looks like he's one of Acker's more devoted disciples. He's been following him around the country for years now. He's been Acker's bodyguard and his muscle in their more illicit dealings. He's bad news, but we don't know why he targeted Lizzy. That's where it gets particularly nasty."

"Why so?"

"We have evidence showing that Wagner and Jessie Colton have had business dealings together. Jessie and Acker are also in a romantic relationship. My mother is drawn to men with money and power, but she couldn't care less how they make that happen. Only that she benefits from the fruits of their labor."

Ajay didn't miss the snark in the man's tone at the mention of his mother. "Do you honestly think she might be involved with this?"

Max shrugged. "I don't want to think my mother would do something like that. It's possible she has no idea about his more illicit dealings. But I also felt that something was off with the second break-in. Like you pointed out, it's unusual for someone to gain entry like that unless they had a key. If it was Wagner, the only way he would have known where Lizzy's bedroom was located was if someone familiar with the home told him."

"But why…"

"I'll have to prove it obviously, but I think Lizzy was snatched so they could blackmail my father for money. That whole church is an unscrupulous bunch of villains and thieves."

Ajay shook his head as he pondered the news. This put a whole other spin on everything they might have believed.

"I'm trusting you to keep this to yourself," Max said. "One, we don't want him to know we're on to him. If he gets spooked, we run the risk of him leaving the state. And two, it's going to devastate Lizzy. She doesn't need that right now. It's better that she continues to think we're a bunch of incompetent fools not doing our job. She'll learn the truth soon enough, and then things really will be hell for her."

Ajay hesitated. "I don't know about that. Keeping secrets from your sister is certain to blow up in my face."

"I get it. But isn't Lizzy's well-being more important than you taking a hit if she gets mad? What I just told you is classified, and although I'm already out the door at the FBI, I'd like to make sure they don't ding my clean record. I need to know I can trust you."

"You have my word," Ajay said as he considered the ramifications of Lizzy discovering her birth mother might have purposely put her in harm's way. Learning her mom had ties to a known criminal was bad enough.

He sighed heavily and tossed back his mug of beer. Then he went to the bar to ask for one more beer with a shot of Jack Daniels.

## Chapter Thirteen

When she woke that morning, Lizzy was determined to fix what she had broken. She had practiced what she planned to say a hundred different ways. She still hadn't perfected her apology, but figured by the time she reached Ajay's home, she'd have gotten it right.

After a long shower and a breakfast of mixed fruit, granola and almond milk, she felt ready. She dressed in her favorite black jeans, a black turtleneck sweater and fuzzy Bearpaw boots, then slipped on a black leather jacket. With her hair pulled back into a ponytail, she felt cute.

Moving through the house, she called for her father but got no answer. When she reached the kitchen, she noticed Mama Jen headed out the door.

"Hey! I didn't know you were here," Lizzy said.

"Actually, I'm just leaving. I came by to drop off a casserole for dinner tonight."

"Do you know where my father is?"

"Down at the barn, I believe."

"I wanted to check with him to see if I could borrow his truck."

"He took the Range Rover, so I'm sure he won't mind. The keys are hanging on the hook in the mudroom. I'm headed down to the barn to say hello before I take off. Do you want me to tell him?"

"Please. Just let him know I won't be gone long."

Mama Jen gave her a thorough gaze, eyeing her from her head to her feet and back. "Are you sure you're okay to be going out by yourself?"

Lizzy nodded. "I'm fine. Everyone needs to stop worrying about me."

"Worrying is what we do. It comes with the job description when you have kids."

Lizzy smiled. "Good to know."

"Just be safe out there, please," the matriarch concluded before heading out the door.

"I will," Lizzy said. In the mudroom, she grabbed the keys and headed to her father's Ford F-150 pickup truck.

This would be the first time Lizzy drove anywhere by herself since she was abducted. Having other people chauffeur her around had begun to take its toll. There were errands she needed to run, shopping she would have liked to do, and she trusted she wouldn't have any problems getting around. Besides, it wasn't like she was going too far from home.

As she pulled the car out of its parking space, she felt her heart begin to race. She rolled down the window for a fresh breeze. Mama Jen's words echoed in her head, a vibration that began to feel like a jackhammer against concrete. *Be safe out there. Be safe out there. Be safe out there.*

But she wasn't safe, Lizzy suddenly thought. She

couldn't be safe until they found the man who was haunting her, or he found her first. Truth be told, she might never be safe again.

She slammed on the brakes and shifted the truck into Park. The engine was still running as she jumped from the driver's seat, fighting to catch her breath. A full-blown panic attack had her feeling like her heart was about to burst. She couldn't breathe, and everything around her was spinning.

She suddenly felt an arm around her waist and a familiar voice in her ear. Her father's tone was soothing, and she tried to focus on what he was telling her. "Breathe, Lizzy. Breathe slowly. In and out. In and out. That's it."

"Should I call an ambulance?" Max questioned.

"No," Buck answered. "She's okay. It's just a little anxiety. Once she catches her breath, she'll be just fine. Isn't that right, my sweet girl? Everything is going to be all right."

Lizzy was bent forward at the waist, her hands clutching her knees. As her breathing began to slow, she no longer felt as if she might pass out and fall over. She felt a sense of calm returning, her body shifting back into sync. She took another deep breath and held it down in her lungs before blowing it out slowly.

Buck continued to soothe her. "That's my girl. Easy peasy. In and out. In and out."

Lizzy lifted herself upright, her gaze sweeping between the two men eyeing her with concern. She nodded. "Thank you," she said. "I'm okay."

"Where were you going?" Max asked.

She shook her head. "I just had some errands to run. I thought it would be okay."

"Why don't we go back to the house?" Buck said, his arms still wrapped around her shoulders. "I think you should lie down for a minute. I can send someone to get whatever it is you need."

She shook her head vehemently. "No... I... It's important... I..." she stammered, unable to find the right words.

Max took a step forward. "It's okay. I'll drop you off."

A wave of gratitude washed over Lizzy's spirit. She clasped her hands together as if in prayer, then dropped her face into her palms. Buck pulled her to him, and she dropped her head against his chest. Her father stood hugging her until she stopped shaking, beginning to be embarrassed about causing a scene.

"I really am fine," she said. "I'll be okay."

"Are you certain?" Buck questioned.

Lizzy nodded. "Yes. I'm good."

"You make certain she gets where she wants to go safely," Buck said to Max.

Max gestured for her to get into the passenger seat of the truck. He held the door open until she was settled, the seat belt secured around her waist. Seconds later, they were pulling past the gates onto the main road.

"I'm never going to be normal again, am I?" she whispered. "I just want to be better."

Max shrugged. "That all depends on how you define normal. Will you get past this? Yes, definitely. But you need to remember that it's going to take some time. Stop trying to rush your recovery. It'll happen in its own time."

"Well, I don't have your confidence," Lizzy said.

"What I have is experience, and no, you don't have that. Now, where would you like me to take you?"

She stammered, "Well, I wanted… I need… It's only…"

Max laughed. "Got it. Did you call him first to tell him you were coming? In case he had a date or something?"

Lizzy's heart skipped a beat as she suddenly considered that Ajay could be on a date with someone. Or worse, someone was visiting with him in his home.

She tossed her brother a blank look. "I hadn't thought…"

"No worries," Max said. "I don't think Ajay is that kind of guy!"

AJAY WASN'T TOTALLY hungover from the night before, but he did have a raging headache. He was off duty for the next thirty-six hours, so he and Pumpkin planned to do absolutely nothing for the entire day. He especially wasn't going to allow himself to think about Lizzy Colton.

He figured a date with a good book would help with that, and he palmed the latest copy of a historical fiction novel Della had recommended. The author was a woman writing about people of color during the Regency period. Entwined with mystery, her story had been sitting on his nightstand for weeks, waiting for him to find time to read. Now seemed as good as any other.

He reclined on the sofa, his legs atop a leather ottoman. Pumpkin had curled up against his side, determined not to be moved. She'd been moody since she last saw Lizzy. It amazed him how quickly and how intensely their connection had been cemented. Pumpkin had been moping around as if her heart had been broken, too.

He had just turned the page on the third chapter when Pumpkin jumped up to rush toward the front door. She barked excitedly, her greeting coming even before the doorbell rang. There weren't many people who got that kind of welcome from his four-legged friend, so the list of who might be on the other side of the entrance was slim.

He was not prepared, however, when he opened the door and found Lizzy standing there. Behind her, Max stood at the curb, leaning against a truck with his arms folded over his chest. When the two men locked gazes, Max gave him a nod, climbed back into the driver's seat and disappeared down the street.

Lizzy's eyes were wide, a hint of fresh tears dancing against her lashes. She looked nervous, twisting her hands together. "My ride would only bring me one way," she said softly. "I told him I didn't think you'd mind giving me a ride back home."

Ajay smiled, hoping that his excitement didn't show on his face. "That shouldn't be a problem. Would you like to come in?"

"If I wouldn't be interrupting anything," she said, peering past his shoulder.

"Nothing at all. I was just hanging out with my favorite girl."

Lizzy's gaze narrowed, her smile fading slightly. "Oh."

"Come on in. I think she's missed you, too," he said, pointing at Pumpkin.

The yellow Lab stood patiently, her tail swishing like a windshield wiper against his hardwood floors. She jumped excitedly when Ajay signaled that she could move. Her energy was infectious, and even he had to laugh as she jumped excitedly around Lizzy.

Lizzy dropped to the floor, wrapping her arms around the dog's neck. She pressed her face into Pumpkin's fur. Her winter coat was thick and soft, and Ajay could see Lizzy relax against the animal's frame.

Quietly, he closed the front door and secured the lock, then stood and waited. Time felt as if it had come to a standstill, the moment surreal. He waited as she seemed to collect herself, and then she stood up, turning to face him.

Contrition rounded her shoulders and pinched her cheeks a brilliant shade of crimson. Her lengthy lashes batted down a rise of saline, and she held herself tightly. "I'm sorry," Lizzy said. "I acted childishly, and I apologize for my bad behavior."

Ajay stood like stone. There was a lengthy pause, silence rising between them like a morning mist.

"Oh," Lizzy added, "I promise it won't ever happen again." Her bright blue eyes danced across his face, as if searching for a sign that her apology had moved him to forgive her.

Ajay shook his head. Amused, he reached out and snaked his arm around Lizzy's waist. His fingers pressed hot against the small of her back. He pulled her against himself, the gesture sensual and possessive. He stared into her eyes, falling fast into her oceanic gaze.

Then he pressed his lips to hers, kissing her sweetly.

LIZZY KNEW BEYOND any doubt that this moment would solidify whatever it was that was between her and Ajay.

She hadn't thought it possible to be so intrinsically connected to any one person as she felt to him at that moment. It was as if he'd grabbed hold of her heart with a vise grip and intended to hang on for as long as she would let him. Whether he knew it or not, Lizzy had no intention of him ever letting go.

"I'm sorry, too," Ajay whispered against her lips. "I should never have said what I said. I should never have spoken to you that way. And I promise you that it will never happen again."

"It better not," Lizzy quipped. She kissed him again.

"You're really not very good at apologizing, are you?" Ajay said.

Lizzy smiled brightly. "Not really. I had to practice that one."

Ajay chuckled as he entwined his fingers between hers and pulled her to the living room sofa. "Can I get you something?" he asked as they settled comfortably against each other.

"No, thank you. I'm good. I just needed to tell you how much I missed you."

He slid his hand into her hair, the strands tangling around his fingers. He drew her closer and kissed her one more time. She tasted like butter rum candy and ginger. "I'm glad you came. I was going crazy without you, Lizzy. I missed you more than you will ever know."

"I almost didn't make it," Lizzy said, telling him about her panic attack.

"Are they happening often?" Ajay asked.

She shook her head. "No, not really. I've had some anxiety, but this was different. This was bad. I was petrified to step off the ranch property by myself. The fear was unbearable."

"Why are you afraid?" Ajay questioned. "You're more than capable of protecting yourself."

"Tell that to my kidnapper. He got the jump on me, and the next thing I knew I was tied to the floor in some abandoned cabin. My abilities were clearly lacking. What if that happens again? I might not be so lucky."

"First, he got the jump on you. Hitting you from behind was not a fair fight. And you were not adequately prepared to defend yourself after that. Especially after you tried to get away and he beat you. We'll make sure that never happens again. The fact that you survived cracked ribs and a head injury says more about your abilities than you give yourself credit for."

"I still feel like I'm damaged goods," Lizzy said quietly. "I just can't shake the feeling that I'm putting everyone around me at risk. Especially you."

"Why especially me?" he queried, his brow furrowing.

"Because I insisted you stay with me. Because I always want to be around you. I've been a thorn in your side, and you've just been too nice to say anything."

"That's not true. If I hadn't wanted to be there, I would have told you no. I was there because I wanted to be. I wanted to protect you and make sure no one could hurt you. And then I was there because of how I'm feeling for you. I'm falling in love with you, Lizzy."

Lizzy looked him in the eyes as he proclaimed his truth, expressing the emotion that had been such a force for both of them to reckon with since they had met. He told her what was on his heart, and then he kissed her as if he were kissing her for the very first time.

"Ajay, you make me so happy!" Lizzy said, monumental joy wrapped around the words.

Everything about the moment felt like a fairy tale, and then Pumpkin whined, sitting at their feet as she stared up at them. She gave them the slightest bark, and it felt like love had completely encompassed the room.

AJAY SETTLED DOWN on the sofa beside Lizzy. He had made them both a cup of ginger tea and had plated a small charcuterie for them to snack on. The afternoon was passing so quickly that Lizzy had begun to think someone had played with the clocks to prank them.

"This is very nice," she said.

Ajay nodded. "It is and I hate to ruin the mood, but we need to talk."

The look Lizzy gave him made Ajay chuckle.

"You're not getting out of this, Lizzy. We have to clear the air before we can move forward."

She sighed, a heavy gust of air blowing past her lips. He had mentioned their argument earlier and now his insistence they rehash her bad behavior felt like it could well be the beginning of the end. Again. She felt as if they had reached a point of no return and their next decision would greatly impact what would come next for the two of them.

"Fine. What do you want to discuss?"

"We both said some pretty awful things to each other. I know I was in my feelings and just wanted us to stop arguing. But I need to know what you were thinking because some of what you said really hurt my feelings. I'm not going to lie about that. I felt like you'd sucker punched me when you called me weak. Especially since I was already feeling inadequate about not keeping your stalker from getting close to you.

"I said what I said just to be mean. I missed you and I didn't want to hear that you wanted to do something else. It was childish on my part and I'm really sorry for everything I said."

"And I apologize for anything I said that hurt you. It was just a bad time and your tantrum hit me the wrong way."

"My tantrums have always gotten me my way. They've always worked on my father and my brothers. It's a bad habit I know I need to break," Lizzy conceded.

"You need to understand that they aren't going to work on me. I will call you out just like I expect you to call me out if I'm not on my best behavior with you. We will never be able to make this work if we're not willing to have hard conversations. We can agree to disagree, but there should be no name-calling or cursing or being disrespectful to each other. I'm not going to tolerate that, and neither should you."

Lizzy reached for a cracker and a slice of cheese. As she bit them both, she found herself feeling liberated. It wasn't often she could express how she felt without fear of condemnation. She didn't like feeling vulnerable, but letting her guard down for Ajay felt right in a way she could never have expected.

As the weight of her anxiety and his lifted off their shoulders, Lizzy knew beyond any doubt that things going forward would be everything she could ever want with any man. She shifted her hips closer to his, allowing herself to wallow in the warmth of his body heat. Ajay reached for a grape and fed it to her, a comforting glow shimmering out of his eyes.

She looked around the living space. It was tastefully decorated, although it could have used a splash of color, Lizzy thought. He'd chosen gray tones with textured fabrics, woven rugs and leather furniture—overall, very bachelor pad-like. With his permission, she was excited to explore his personal sanctuary, to discover something about him that she hadn't yet learned. She rose from her seat to look around and be nosy.

White cabinetry, gray granite counters and white tiled floors made the kitchen feel slightly antiseptic. Lizzy was already considering the changes she could make to warm up the space. Nothing decorated the walls, and it was clearly the home of a man who didn't spend much time there.

There were three bedrooms. The master featured its own tiled bathroom and an expansive walk-in closet that Ajay put to little use. That space was also a dichotomy of cool whites and various shades of gray. Ajay didn't blink an eye as she pulled open his drawers and closets to peek inside. Not even when she discovered the box of Magnum condoms tucked away in his underwear drawer.

Beside the king-size bed sat a family portrait of him and his parents. He was the spitting image of his father, but it was his mother's Blackness that had blessed him with his own warm skin tone. They stood smiling, all wearing denim jeans and bright white dress shirts against a background of lush greenery. There was so much love in the photo and pride that gleamed out of his mother's eyes.

A pang of jealousy trickled through Lizzy's insides. As she put the framed photo back on the nightstand, she couldn't help but think of her own mother and the family photos they had never been able to take.

After a midday lunch of grilled cheese and tomato soup, Ajay went back to his book while Lizzy rested her head in his lap and scrolled through her phone. Eventually, they ventured outside in the cold air to walk Pumpkin. A snowball fight ensued, and Lizzy pled the fifth about throwing the first handful of snow. Back inside, they watched a marathon of The *Walking Dead*. Dozing on and off, the two simply enjoyed the respite and the companionship. By the end of the last episode, it had grown dark out, and they were hungry again.

"Why don't we grab something to eat before I take you home?" Ajay asked.

Lizzy gripped the front of his T-shirt with two hands. She pressed her forehead to his chest. "I could always stay here," she whispered.

Ajay wrapped her in his arms and hugged her tightly. "I want to say yes, but you and I both know what will happen if you stay."

"You'll make wild, passionate, dirty love to me. How is that a bad thing?"

His laughter rang warmly through the room. "It wouldn't be a bad thing. Actually, it would probably be a very good thing, but we both know the timing's not right."

"Says who?" Lizzy snuggled closer against him.

"We both should be saying it, Lizzy. When I make love to you, nothing and no one will be able to keep us from our destiny. It'll be about our dreams and desires for each other. It'll be about planning for four boys and twin girls and the love we have for each other. There won't be any anxiety, doubts or need to explain ourselves. No one questioning why or whether or not we know what we're doing. But more importantly, there won't be one ounce of regret. No wondering if we've done the right thing. And right now, I think you'd be second-guessing your decision."

"I'd argue that the pleasure we would bring to each other would far exceed any second guesses either of us might have." Lizzy took a step back, her hands on both hips.

"You know better than I that pleasure is temporary. Regret can haunt you a lifetime." Ajay pressed a kiss to her forehead. "Any idea what you'd like for supper?" he asked, changing the subject.

Lizzy sighed. "Mama Jen made lasagna or some kind of pasta casserole. We can eat at the ranch, if that's okay with you."

"That works for me," he said.

They headed for the front door. "You do know I don't like being wrong, don't you?" Lizzy asked.

Ajay chuckled. "No one said you were wrong, Lizzy!"

"I'm just going to need you to let me win an argument every now and then."

"Only when you're right and I'm wrong."

"That's what I'm afraid of!" she said, giggling.

Ajay laughed. "You'll get used to it."

DESPITE HIS BEST EFFORTS, Ajay found saying no to Lizzy virtually impossible. She was accustomed to having her own way, and in all honesty, there was little he wouldn't do for her.

Turning down her advances the previous day hadn't been easy because he had wanted her to stay as much as she had wanted to spend the night. His grandiose speech about the right timing and their destiny had just been him stalling in order to calm the rise of nature that had him sweating. Had he not talked fast, he had no doubt the first of their four sons would be arriving some nine months from now.

Not saying no to Lizzy was why he'd awakened an hour earlier than he had planned, Lizzy at his front door with fresh bagels and large cups of coffee from Hutch's Diner. Not saying no was why he was now standing beneath a cold shower, waiting for a raging erection to subside as Lizzy worked out in his home gym in the skimpiest pair of shorts and tank top she owned.

He could already see that their relationship was going to be a battle of wills. Lizzy was determined to best him every chance she could. What he found most amusing was that he was excited for the challenge. Lizzy kept him on his toes, and he hadn't realized how much he needed that.

He slathered himself with his favorite Oribe Côte d'Azur body wash. The soap was paradise in a bottle, a luxurious gel that left him smelling like a tropical explosion of starflower oils, meadowfoam and sweet almond with the barest notes of sandalwood. He tilted his face into the warm water as the suds cascaded over his chest and down his back. His hand stalled below his pubic line, the length of his manhood twitching for attention.

Before he could consider the possibilities, there was a knock on the bathroom door. Lizzy called to him from the other side.

"Yes, Lizzy?"

"Can I come in?"

"No."

"You scared?"

"No, Lizzy!"

"Then open the door. I promise I'll keep my hands to myself."

"That's not a good idea!"

"I just want to talk."

"We'll talk when I get out."

"Are you really going to turn me away?"

"Yes, I am. Now stop giving me a hard time."

"You don't mean that figuratively, do you?" she asked teasingly.

Ajay laughed. "I'm calling your brother. I think it's time you went home."

"But I just got here!"

"Then do me a favor, please, and go walk my dog. Pumpkin needs some quality one-on-one time with you."

"Only because it's Pumpkin."

"Thank you, Lizzy!"

She giggled. "You're welcome, Ajay!"

## Chapter Fourteen

The punch Ajay threw whizzed by Lizzy's head so close that it startled her. She blinked and ducked her face into her hands. Him teaching her self-defense tactics had seemed like a good idea when she first said yes. Now she wasn't so sure, and this was their fifth lesson.

"Hey!" she exclaimed. "This was supposed to be practice. Why are you trying to kill me on purpose?"

He shook his head. "You should have been ready. I told you, never underestimate your opponent. Even if he does love you." He threw another punch.

This time, Lizzy maneuvered left and swept his feet out from under him. Ajay landed on the ground with a loud thud.

"I didn't teach you that," he said as he gasped for air.

"Brothers!" Lizzy responded, her fists high in front of her face.

She danced about like a boxer in the center ring waiting for the count against her opponent. With a swiftness she didn't see coming, Ajay grabbed her ankle and threw her off-balance. He caught her before she hit the cushioned mat.

"Hey!"

"Always finish your opponent off," he said. "You should have followed up with a head-and-groin kick. You want to make certain your attacker doesn't get back up, or worse, pull you down to his level." He swiveled his body, flipping her onto her back. He pinned both her arms above her head, dropping his weight against her torso and pelvis. He sat above her, his knees on both sides of her legs. "Try to avoid getting into this position, but if it happens, you can get yourself out."

Lizzy took a deep breath. "Even if he's bigger than me?"

"Especially if he's bigger than you. You'll need to use a transition escape to get yourself out of that situation."

"Show me," Lizzy said.

"First, try to prevent yourself from losing full control. I've grabbed both of your arms, but I want you to bend your dominant hand like you're holding a mirror in it and looking at yourself. And it's all about the positioning of that arm."

Lizzy did as he instructed.

"Second, I want you to put your foot against my hip, on the same side as your bent arm. Once you've done that, you need to push me away with your leg and pull your arm up toward your head at the same time. This gives you control and takes my leverage away. With that free hand, you can then go for an eye gouge or an ear pull."

They practiced the move a few times until Lizzy felt comfortable with it. Ajay didn't give her any slack, using his full weight to subdue her. The last time she was able to get out, she followed with a pretend kick to his chin and another to his groin.

"Excellent!" Ajay exclaimed. "Follow-through is so important!"

Lizzy grinned. She was excited to be learning techniques that could potentially save her life. She wanted to discover more. "What if that doesn't work, and he does pin me down?"

Ajay nodded as she lay back down on the floor and positioned herself beneath him. "So, say your attacker has you by the wrists, and your hands are pinned by your ears. He's sitting above you with his knees on both sides of your legs. I want you to bump your hips upward, and at the same time swing your arms down toward your ankles. This will throw me off-balance."

Lizzy did as he instructed.

"Now reach up and wrap your arms around my waist," he continued. "Hug me tight. That's it. In this position, I can't use my arms, and you want to regain your control. You're going to take your leg and swing it to trap my foot. At the same time, you grab my arm and roll."

Lizzy squealed excitedly. "That puts me back on top."

"It does, but you also need to be fast. Follow-through with a strike or two and then peel off and get out of there."

"Again," Lizzy said.

"No again," Ajay said, rolling onto his back. "You need to take a break. We've been at this all morning."

"I'm not tired."

"Well, then I need a break. You can play by yourself."

"That's no fun," Lizzy said as she rolled above him, pretending to pin him to the ground. She dropped her mouth to his and kissed him hungrily. Beneath her pelvis, she felt him tense, a rise of nature pressing firm and hard between his legs. Lizzy added fuel to the fire she ignited, grinding herself slowly against him.

With apt precision, Ajay flipped her over. He continued to kiss her for a brief moment before pulling himself away. "I'm headed to the shower," he said.

"I would think you'd have gotten tired of cold showers every morning," Lizzy said smugly.

"Cold showers are invigorating," Ajay said.

She laughed. "I hear great sex will do the same thing!"

Lizzy had been giving Ajay a hard time for days. She showed up at his home every opportunity she could, even on those days he and Pumpkin had to go to work. Her presence in his space was beginning to show in the decor that she'd added to make the home look lived in. Artwork now decorated the walls, and she'd introduced color in the throws and pillows. She'd also framed a selfie she'd taken of the two of them together, adding it to the photos in the master bedroom. With each addition, Ajay hadn't blinked an eye, seeming comfortable with her in his space.

She was genuinely awed by his willpower. She'd tried every trick in her book of tricks to try to seduce him, to no avail. He kept saying no, and she kept trying. She had immeasurable respect for his willpower.

But she knew he was right about them waiting. She wasn't ready, knowing a threat still existed. She wanted them being together to be special, not marred by her fears and the anxiety of knowing someone was still out to get her. She hated that the police were no closer to finding her attacker. But she was getting better about leaving the ranch. Even though she still needed someone in her family to be with her until she reached Ajay's side, her panic attacks had subsided. She was especially grateful that none of them gave her a difficult time about giving her a ride when she asked.

Now she enjoyed those moments of spontaneity when she could tease Ajay unmercifully. Because she knew one day, he would deem them ready, and he'd give in. The prospect of that day excited her.

So, until then she thought, she would keep teasing and flirting with him, because there wasn't an ounce of shame in her desire for the man.

"YOU REALLY NEED to focus," Ajay said. Perspiration beaded across his brow and down his face. He and Lizzy had been working out, ramping up her self-defense training. He had just run ten miles on the treadmill while she lifted weights. For reasons he couldn't begin to explain, Lizzy kept staring off into space, her focus on everything but what she needed to be doing. "What's going on in that head of yours?" he questioned.

"What happens when this is all over? With us, I mean?"

"I'm sure we'll figure it out as we go along."

Lizzy drifted off into thought again. She blew out the softest sigh, just a faint gust of air easing past her lips.

Ajay eyed her intently. He swiped a towel across his brow and chest and moved to the workout bench to take a seat. "What's got you in a mood?"

"I was just thinking how I'm having such a good time when I'm with you, and there's some creep out here who wants to take that from us. It makes me angry!" Her voice rose ever so slightly.

"I understand it's frustrating," Ajay said, "but you can't give him so much control. The more he can keep you scared, the more control he has over you. You just need to focus on keeping your strength up so that you can defend yourself if you ever need to. And you want to practice so the moves become second nature. You'll be able to throw a punch or a kick without thinking about it."

Lizzy nodded. "I just...well..." she stammered. "I just want things between us to be good. I know we play around, and you're as big a flirt as I am, but I'd like us to keep that going. And I'd like for us to share more with each other when the timing is right."

Ajay smiled. "I hope that you consider yourself my friend. Because I do, and I like to think that I work very hard to maintain my friendships with people I care about."

Lizzy moved to where he'd taken a seat and dropped into his lap with a heavy thud.

"Ouch!" Ajay muttered. "If you keep that up, there won't be much of me left for anything more."

Lizzy eased up, then sat back against him with more grace than previously. She wrapped her arms around his neck. "So really, Ajay, how do you feel about me?" she asked.

"Are you really asking me that?" Ajay's brow lifted as he stared at her.

"Indulge me, please. My insecurities are kicking in. Sometimes I'll need your reassurance."

He shook his head. "I think it's obvious. I care about you very much. And it's important to me that you're safe."

"That sounds like love to me."

"It sounds like that to me, too."

"Well, although I appreciate you wanting to be my knight in shining armor, you're going to have to step your game up. I'm not going to make it easy for you to steal my heart."

"I don't steal, but I'm willing to put in whatever work is necessary to claim what belongs to me. Most especially your heart."

"I find your confidence very sexy, Ajay Wright."

"And I find your time-wasting tactics equally entertaining. Now, you need to get back to work, and you need to *focus*," he said, emphasizing the last word. He gently pushed her up and off his lap, tapping her bottom with a flat palm.

"Tease!" Lizzy exclaimed.

"Lazy," Ajay countered.

Lizzy feigned a pout and pretended to throw a punch at Ajay's head. He threw his head back to dodge her fist, then threw his own punch.

Lizzy was quick to adjust, moving swiftly from him as she danced on her toes. She laughed.

"You're not in a boxing ring, Lizzy," Ajay said. "The likelihood of you being able to outfight a man bigger than you is slim. You also risk breaking your hands, so don't think about boxing it out. Elbows, knees, front kicks, side and round kicks are best at close range. If you can't keep any distance between you, then the best chance you have is to draw him in close and then you crush him. If you hit him in the face, hit him with the palm of your hand or rake him across the eyes with your nails. Think tiger claw."

Lizzy nodded. "Tiger claw! Got it."

Ajay spun her around and moved against her backside. He leaned to whisper in her ear. "Now crush me!"

As he eased his arm around her neck, Lizzy dipped her chin to her chest to reduce the pressure he could get around her neck. She slipped a hand between his elbow and her neck and spun herself out and away.

"Good," Ajay said.

He reached out and grabbed her in a choke hold. Like Ajay had taught her, Lizzy tightened her neck muscles, ducked her head and spun herself below his elbows. Her moves were precise, quick and exactly as he'd taught her.

"Very nice," Ajay extolled, showering her with praise.

Lizzy swept her arms out and around and took a bow. Before she could catch herself, she was suddenly lying flat on her back, the wind knocked out of her lungs. Ajay stood above her, looking down at her as she worked to catch her breath.

"Don't forget to put distance between you and your attacker. A good run beats a bad stand each and every time. So run! Don't be dancing in the end zone. That just gives him another opportunity to come back at you."

"You don't fight fair," Lizzy finally gasped.

Easing himself above her, Ajay pressed his mouth to hers. He kissed her lips, the gesture an easy caress of skin against skin.

Closing her eyes, Lizzy allowed herself to drop into the beauty of his touch, savoring the intensity of the moment. When he pulled away, she opened her eyes and smiled.

"Can we do that again?" Lizzy asked, biting down against her bottom lip.

Ajay grinned. "We should definitely practice you escaping choke holds until you're comfortable."

"As long as you kiss me like that every time," Lizzy said, "I'm good with that!"

Ajay laughed. "Just stay focused, please!"

"WHAT ARE YOU looking for?" Vivian asked. "You haven't stopped fidgeting in your seat since Ajay dropped you off."

"Sorry," Lizzy said, reaching for her glass of orange pop. "I just thought I saw someone."

Vivian looked toward the large glass windows of Tap Out Brewery. Lizzy had called her out of the blue to meet for a midday lunch of burgers and beer like old times. They had only been seated a few minutes when Lizzy jumped, certain that she'd seen someone standing by the front door, watching her.

"Do you want to call Ajay?" Vivian questioned as she tried to see what Lizzy thought she saw.

Lizzy shook her head. "I'm always bothering Ajay. It's fine. I'm sure I'm just imagining things." She knew she didn't sound convincing as she took one last glance toward the door.

"So tell me something good," Vivian said, changing the subject. "How are you and Ajay doing?"

"He's so good to me," Lizzy gushed. "That man has the patience of Job!"

Vivian waved a dismissive hand. "How's the sex?" she asked.

Lizzy leaned in as if to share something decadent. Her friend leaned in closer as well. Lizzy's voice dropped to a polite whisper. "I don't know. We're waiting until things are settled down and that creep who grabbed me is captured."

Vivian sat back in her seat, dropping her hands into her lap. Her lashes batted rapidly. Finally, she said, "You're lying, right? This is a joke?"

Lizzy shook her head. "Nope! Ajay doesn't want us to do anything that I might regret later."

"Do you think you'll regret it?"

Lizzy felt her entire face lift into a bright smile. "I won't regret a single minute that I've been able to spend with Ajay Wright. I think making love to him would be the icing on some very sweet cake."

Vivian smiled. "You two are so funny!"

"Any changes on the dating front for you?"

"Let me make you laugh," Vivian said with an eye roll. "I have a new client, and he has a very nice-looking son."

"Nice-looking is good."

"The son invited me for coffee, so I agreed. We went over to Hutch's Diner."

"Good coffee."

"We're talking. I'm enjoying the conversation, and all of a sudden, he excuses himself from the table to go and speak with a woman who's sitting alone at the counter. I'm thinking, maybe it's someone he recognizes. He comes back a few minutes later and says to me, if she stops by the table on her way out, just roll with the conversation. 'I told her you were my sister.'"

Lizzy burst out laughing.

"This fool went to get her telephone number," Vivian continued, "and when she asked who I was, he said we were family. I was so over it!"

"What did you do?"

"I went to the register and paid my bill, and as I was leaving, I told the girl what a jerk he was. I am so done with men. They're all losers and fools."

"Not really," Lizzy said, her tone consoling. "You just haven't met your man yet."

"And I'm not going to. I'm not going on another date ever."

"I'm going to find you a man."

"Nope! Focus on your own problems."

Lizzy laughed.

"I'm serious," Vivian said. "What are you going to do if you and Ajay wait and then you discover he's really bad in bed? How are you going to come back from that?"

"I already know Ajay is not bad in bed. In fact, I can say with relative certainty that he will be the best I've ever had!"

"Well, I don't have your confidence," Vivian said, laughing heartily.

The two women paused as the waiter, a young man named Darryl, delivered two mushroom onion burgers, loaded French fries and mugs of their newest craft beer, a kettle sour brew blended with orange, pineapple and passionfruit.

"Bon appétit!" Lizzy exclaimed as she lifted her mug in salutation.

"That's good," Vivian said after their toast. "This one might become my new favorite."

"I don't know. I think I still prefer their milk stout. Especially the one that gets aged in the bourbon barrels. This is nice, though."

As they ate, the conversation shifted once again.

"How are things with the new siblings?" Vivian asked.

Lizzy sighed. "Okay, I guess. I've not been a good sister if I'm honest. I could probably reach out more or something."

"It's going to take time, I'm sure."

"Did I tell you Nate came to visit me in the hospital?"

"No! What's he like?"

"He's really a nice guy. Really nice. He actually came to help search for me. When he came to visit, he brought flowers and everything. But I could see how hard this is for him and his sister."

"And the sister…"

"Sarah. She's a teacher."

Vivian nodded. "Have you spoken to Sarah?"

"Not really. Like I said, I've not been a good sister."

"In your defense, you've had a lot going on," Vivian said. "I'm sure they understand."

"I really have no excuse," Lizzy said. "I could make the time. Don't encourage my bad behavior."

An hour later, after much laughter, the two women settled their tab and headed outside. There was a chill in the air, and Lizzy pulled her coat tighter around her torso.

"I can drop you off at the ranch," Vivian said. "Or do you need a ride someplace else?" She eyed Lizzy, her brow raised, a slight smirk on her face.

Lizzy laughed. "Thank you, but I am going to run down to the gift shop to see if I can find gifts for all the kids. I need to start my Christmas shopping. I texted Ajay, and he's going to meet me there and pick me up."

"Are you going to be okay?"

Lizzy nodded. "I am. I feel good." She glanced down the street one way and up the other way. "And clearly no one is standing around waiting to pounce on me, so I should be fine."

Vivian leaned to give her a hug. "Call me later so I know you're okay."

Lizzy watched as her friend hurried to her car. The chill in the air had become a cold wind, the kind that seeped into your bones and wreaked havoc through your entire body. She pulled up her hood and zipped her coat up to her chin. Shoving both hands into her pockets, she began a leisurely stroll through the downtown area.

There was quaint charm about Owl Creek that always made Lizzy feel at home. There were no big-box stores or chain restaurants allowed within city limits. If she needed Macy's or Home Depot, she would need to drive to Conners or Boise. Tourists made the town interesting as they enjoyed the little mom-and-pop shops that added to Owl Creek's appeal. They came for the water in the summer and snow in the winter. Spring and fall were all about hiking the mountains and taking in the sights. Lizzy could never truly imagine herself living any place else.

She paused in front of an antique shop to stare in the window. There was an exquisite wall clock inside that would be perfect above Ajay's fireplace. She had just decided to go inside and inquire about it when a reflection in the glass caught her eye.

Lizzy felt her chest tighten, air escaping like helium

from a popped balloon. She inhaled deeply, desperate to calm her nerves, the cold air burning her lungs. She turned slowly to stare across the street.

Standing on the sidewalk, staring back at her, was the man who'd been at the hospital. The same man with the mask who'd taken her hostage.

Lizzy gasped, and when he suddenly darted in her direction, moving too swiftly toward her, she turned and ran.

# Chapter Fifteen

Owl Creek's Main Street was beginning to settle down for the afternoon. Most of the storefronts would soon be closing and the number of places that would stay open past six o'clock were few and far between. As Ajay headed toward the gift shop to pick up Lizzy, he was excited that she'd spent the afternoon out on her own. Lunch with Vivian and shopping after would do her good, he thought. She needed to get back to the business of feeling normal and doing normal things that made her happy.

As he turned onto Main Street, he was not prepared for the police cars parked in front. A uniformed officer was talking to an older woman with a bouffant hairdo, who was pointing down the street and talking animatedly with her hands.

A large knot tightened in Ajay's midsection. He stole a quick glance at his cell phone to make sure he hadn't missed a call from Lizzy.

"Let's just hope it was a shoplifter," he said, talking to Pumpkin, who was also staring out the window. "Or a tourist who's intoxicated and needs to be cited for disorderly conduct. Just let it be anything else and not Lizzy."

Pumpkin barked.

Ajay pulled his Jeep into a parking spot on the other side of the street. As he approached, the uniformed officer gave him a look.

"Nothing to see here," the man said.

Ajay flashed his badge. "Lieutenant Wright. I'm just here to pick up a friend."

"Your friend have a name?" There was a hint of attitude in the officer's tone. Attitude that rubbed Ajay the wrong way.

"She does, but what's going on here, patrolman?"

The woman the officer was speaking with answered Ajay's question. "A young woman ran past my store screaming for help. There was a man chasing her. I came out to see what was going on. He came back past and got into a car and left, but I haven't seen the woman, and I'm worried he might have done something to her. I called 911 for them to come look, and this young man has been difficult about doing that. He says a crime needs to be committed before they can just go off searching for someone. For all we know, a crime may have been committed!" Her voice was filled with agitation.

The patrolman glared in Ajay's direction. "I was just taking her statement when you pulled up."

Ajay nodded. "Is there anyone in your shop right now?" he asked the woman.

She shook her head. "No. In fact, it's been very quiet today. Almost too quiet. No one's been since early this afternoon."

Ajay pulled his cell phone from his pocket. He tried

to call Lizzy. Her phone rang and went straight to voice mail. "Ma'am, can you describe the woman?"

"Blonde, fair-skinned, petite. She was wearing a navy jacket and jeans, and she had her hood pulled up. I imagine because it's so cold out. But as she ran by, it blew off. That's how I know she was blond. And pretty. She was very pretty."

"What about the man?" Ajay asked.

"There was nothing pretty about him. He had on one of those full-face masks with the eyes and mouth cut out. It was black, and his clothes were black." The woman took a deep breath. "Oh, and she dropped this," she said, holding out a red knit scarf.

The knot in Ajay's stomach tightened as he recognized the scarf that Lizzy had proclaimed was her favorite. Mama Jen had crocheted it for her last Christmas, and Lizzy wore it often.

Taking the garment from the woman's hands, Ajay kneeled and held it out to Pumpkin. His dog had been sitting quietly at his side, seeming to take it all in. "Search, Pumpkin," Ajay commanded as Pumpkin took in Lizzy's scent. "Find Lizzy."

With the agility of a predator after prey, Pumpkin lowered her head and took off running. Ajay was right behind her, determined that they would find Lizzy and she would be safe and sound when they did.

LIZZY WANTED TO CRY. And maybe she was crying, she thought, her face frozen from the cold. She was cowering behind a row of trees that bordered the property behind The Tides. The Tides was a high-end restaurant on the lakefront with a large open patio. Someone had gotten married, and from where she could see inside, the crowd gathered was having a good time.

Lizzy had cut across through the property, losing the masked man in the parking lot. Ducking down behind the cars, she'd practically crawled along the property's perimeter until she could dodge into the trees without him seeing her. Now she was too afraid to move, and somewhere along the way she'd lost her cell phone in the snow. It felt like déjà vu all over again.

"This is ridiculous," Lizzy muttered out loud. "Help is right there!"

She closed her eyes and took a deep breath. She couldn't believe she was too petrified to move, scared to death that man could find her, and embarrassed that she might disturb some newlywed couple's wedding reception.

Had she only made more of a scene in the center of Main Street, in front of the shops or inside one of the stores, that man could very well be in custody already. But the fear of him coming after her, and her not being able to defend herself the way Ajay had taught her, had sent her fleeing like a terrified mouse.

"I have to move," she said, still shaking in her boots. "Please, God, help me move!"

A loud noise sounded sharply to her left. Lizzy's head snapped in that direction, the rest of her prepared to run some more. Tears suddenly rained down her face, like a waterfall.

Pumpkin rushed toward her and jumped on her excitedly as Lizzy wrapped her arms around the pup and hugged her tightly. She cried into Pumpkin's fur, a wave of relief flooding through her.

Just a minute or two later, Ajay hurried to her side.

"Good girl, Pumpkin," he said, praising his four-legged friend for a job well done. He grabbed Lizzy by the shoulders and lifted her gently off the ground. Wrapping his arms around her, he drew her close. Her entire body melted against his. "It's okay," he whispered. "I've got you."

"I saw him again. And he was chasing me. I just ran. I didn't know what else to do!" Lizzy cried, feeling like a complete and total failure.

"You did good," he said softly. "You didn't put yourself at risk, and you got yourself to safety. There's no shame in that, Lizzy. No shame at all."

"But I didn't try to fight!" she cried out.

"You didn't put yourself in a situation that may have gotten you injured. You did the right thing."

He folded himself around her, wrapping her tightly in his arms until she stopped shaking. He leaned to kiss the tears from her cheeks, pressing his mouth against hers sweetly. "Let's go home," Ajay said, as he guided her back toward the center of town, Pumpkin bobbing beside the two of them.

THE NEXT MORNING, after a pancake-and-bacon breakfast, Lizzy opted to forgo defense training. She was still feeling squirrelly after her encounter downtown and her inability to respond as she would have liked.

Ajay had let her spend the night, and he had slept on the couch in his own home, giving up his bed for her to get a good night's rest. Pancakes and bacon were the least she could do to show him her appreciation. After breakfast, he'd disappeared to the master bathroom, and she sat in the living room plotting additional changes to his home's decor.

An hour later, Ajay walked back into the living room, freshly showered and dressed. He had an appointment later that afternoon, and then he was having dinner with her brothers. Lizzy was thinking about meeting Vivian and their gang of girlfriends for an evening of ice skating. She didn't have the heart to tell Ajay or Vivian that she would have simply preferred to stay right where she was until he returned.

Ajay called her name, pulling her attention in his direction. "I have something for you," he said, a white box wrapped with a red satin bow in the palm of his hand.

At the sight of it, Lizzy grinned from ear to ear. Her rising excitement moved through the room like a drumline in the town parade. She jumped up and down elatedly, her entire being giddy with joy. "What is it? Because you know I *hate* surprises. But I do *love* a good present! Presents are everything! Can I open it?" she gushed with one big breath.

Ajay rolled his eyes skyward. "You know there's a contradiction in there, right? You hate surprises, but gifts are good."

Lizzy giggled, giving him a dismissive shoulder.

Ajay passed her the box, clearly enjoying her reaction.

Lizzy dropped to the leather recliner, tearing at the ribbon. She lifted the box top, glancing up at Ajay, her bright smile beaming, as she peeled back the tissue paper inside. She pulled a stunning beaded bracelet from inside the box.

"It's beautiful!" Lizzy gushed.

Ajay took it from her hands to clasp around her wrist. "It's also a tracking device," he said. "If anything happens, I'll be able to find you."

"How's that work?" she asked. She spun the beads with her fingers, admiring the range of colors against her skin.

"There is a small GPS chip and battery in two of the larger beads. It uses satellites to monitor your location. It's similar to the device they use for search-and-rescue dogs, and also Alzheimer's and dementia patients who might wander."

"Isn't that a little Big Brother-ish?" Lizzy asked sarcastically.

Ajay rolled his eyes. "I really want you to feel comfortable getting out more. You need to be able to go to town without an escort. Go have fun with your friends and visit your family. I don't want you to feel hampered by what might happen. And heaven forbid you get ambushed again and your defense training doesn't work, I'll still know where you are as long as you have that on."

Lizzy lifted her face to his. "Thank you," she said. "It's the best gift anyone's ever given me. And it really is beautiful!"

"I'm glad you like it. But think of it as another piece in your defense arsenal. Just like your mace, your switchblade and your training. It's one more element to keep you safe."

Ajay dipped his head to press his mouth to hers, savoring the sweetness of her lips. The touch was gentle and easy and joyful.

The doorbell suddenly chimed, ringing loudly throughout the room.

Pulling away, Ajay paused, tilting his head to listen.

"Are you expecting someone?" Lizzy questioned.

"No," Ajay responded. He grabbed his service pistol from the closet shelf in the foyer, tucking it into the holster beneath his arm.

The doorbell chimed a second time.

After peering through the peephole, he tossed Lizzy a quick glance over his shoulder, then he pulled the entrance open.

A uniformed delivery driver stood with a box in his hands. "Good morning. I have a package for Lizzy Colton," he said. He extended the box toward Ajay. "I'll just need you to sign here, please," he added as he proffered a digital signature pad.

Ajay took the stylus from the man's hand and scrawled his name across the line on the screen. As he closed the front door, Lizzy jumped from her seat and snatched the box from Ajay's hands.

"Another present! You're going to spoil me."

"Lizzy, stop!" Ajay shouted, his tone serious. "I didn't send that."

Her face dropped, her excitement deflating like a popped balloon. "Well, who did?"

"Who else knows you spend time here?"

"Besides my family, no one. And not even all of them know. I haven't even told Vivian."

"Would one of them send you a package here?"

She shook her head. "That's doubtful."

Ajay reached for his cell phone. "Do me a favor, please," he said as he dialed 911. "Put the box down and step away from it." He pointed his index finger to the floor, and then toward the kitchen.

Lizzy did as he instructed. She stepped back away from the box, grabbed Pumpkin by the collar, and the two withdrew to the other room. From where she stood in the kitchen, she could hear him asking for police backup.

Lizzy's heart began to race, the start of a panic attack beginning to rear its ugly head. She had wanted to believe that nothing bad was going to happen as long as she and Ajay were together, but even she couldn't pretend to be that naive. She wasn't safe anywhere, and wherever she was, she was putting other people in danger.

THE DETECTIVES FROM the Owl Creek Police Department were huddled in conversation while Ajay and Lizzy looked on. The bomb squad had cleared the package, and when Ajay opened the box, the entire room gasped.

The dead bird inside had been crushed in the head with a rock. The rock lay beside the bird, a note wrapped with a rubber band around it.

They all had known what it said before reading it. The all-too-familiar mantra felt like a threat of magnanimous proportions. *We're coming for you.*

Lizzy stared down at the poor bird, wondering how depraved one's soul had to be to cause such harm. She could feel them all stealing glances in her direction, waiting to see if she would break. The attention was beginning to take its toll.

Max and Ajay stood together like deflated soldiers. At first, she thought they were arguing but soon realized they were coming to a consensus about their next steps.

"She needs to go back to the ranch," Max was saying. "She's safer there."

"I agree," Ajay said.

"The FBI's forensics team will start tracing that package. If they can tie it to their suspect, I'm sure they'll go pick him up right away. Finding him has been their biggest issue. With the prints from Lizzy's house and that cabin, this case should be a slam dunk."

"I say we don't wait. We need to pick him up now," Ajay murmured.

Lizzy stepped forward. "You have a suspect? You know who's doing this to me? How long have you known?"

Ajay and Max stared at each other, clearly deciding who was going to answer her questions first. Ajay lost that coin toss.

"Your brother has been following some leads we thought might pan out."

Max nodded. "Ajay suspected whoever broke into the house at the ranch was familiar with the property. That they used a key and knew exactly where your room was."

Lizzy's head snapped in Ajay's direction. "You think someone in my family would do this to me? My brothers would never hurt me. Neither would my cousins."

"I know, but even you said it would probably be easier to look at who didn't have a key than who did. And looking at the list of who did, opened up some questions we couldn't answer. Even your father acknowledged the possibility that…"

"No!" Lizzy shouted, cutting him off. She took a step back from him. "You think it's my mother, don't you?" She shot a look toward Max. "Do you think it's our mother?"

Max took a deep breath. "I think our mother may be involved with the man who is doing this. Yes. But we don't have enough proof yet…"

"How long? How long have you known this?" she questioned, her gaze shifting toward Ajay.

"For a minute now," he answered, contrition furrowing his brow. "We didn't want to say anything until we knew for certain."

Lizzy turned from them both, doubling over as she caught her breath. Her entire body was shaking, feeling like an explosion had gone off through every nerve ending.

Ajay reached out for her, and she shook him off angrily. She didn't want to be touched. She shot Max a look that could have melted stone, so he stepped away, obviously knowing she needed a minute to collect herself. He grabbed Ajay's arm and pulled him along. The two men followed the detectives to the front yard.

Della moved to Lizzy's side, wrapping a protective arm around her shoulders. "They were only trying to protect you, Lizzy. Don't be mad."

"I'm angry! Why is this happening?" Lizzy whispered. "What did I do to deserve this?"

"You didn't do anything. This guy just gets his jollies frightening people."

"But my mother might be involved. Why would she do this to me?"

"I can't answer that, honey."

"If only I knew what he wanted."

Della shook her head. "He wants you to be afraid. Monsters like him get off on seeing their victims be scared."

"Does my mother want me to be scared, too? Does she hate me that much?"

Della shrugged. She clearly didn't have an answer that would give Lizzy any comfort.

"I'm not going to be a victim," Lizzy said emphatically. "I refuse to be a victim!"

Della hugged her tightly. Max suddenly called her name, waving for her attention. "I'll be right back," Della said softly.

"I'll be fine," Lizzy said.

As she stood there, Lizzy realized there was no getting away. The threat was real, and not even the brief moments when she and Ajay could shut out the world would change that. Moving back into the living room, she grabbed her purse and headed out the door.

Max met her at the sidewalk. "The truck's running, and it's warm," he said. "Why don't you get in and wait for me? I just need to speak with one of my agents, and then we can leave."

She nodded. "Where's Ajay?"

"I think he's inside finishing up with his statement. I'll tell him where you are so he can come see you before we leave."

"Thank you," Lizzy said, her tone void of all emotion. She glanced one last time at all the activity buzzing in and out of the home. It wasn't lost on her that she had brought this drama to Ajay's front door.

MINUTES LATER, AJAY and Max exited the house. Ajay tried to explain why he didn't want Lizzy to leave but Max clearly wasn't in agreement. Della moved toward them, and Ajay saw confusion wash over her face. "I thought you left," she said. Her eyes shifted from Max to Ajay and back.

"No," Max answered. "I'm still here."

"Where's Lizzy?" Ajay asked. Every muscle in his body suddenly tightened. He took a step, his gaze darting across the landscape.

Max said, "Where the hell is my truck?"

The trio exchanged looks, the revelation of what had just happened hitting them like a tidal wave.

Ajay swore. "Damn it, Lizzy!"

# Chapter Sixteen

They would soon be looking for her, Lizzy thought. And if they knew what she was planning, they would have done whatever they could to stop her. She couldn't begin to explain to anyone what was going on in her head. Because she didn't even have the words to make sense of the mess that had desecrated her life. One minute she was happy, feeling immensely loved, and the next minute it had all blown up, leaving her empty and hollow. If she felt broken before, it didn't hold a candle to how she was feeling now.

Lizzy still couldn't make sense of them suspecting her mother of being involved in the crimes against her. Jessie Colton was a lot of things. A horrible mother led the top of that list. But was it possible she wanted her eldest daughter harmed? Could she be involved with any man that would be so brutal toward her own child? Ajay didn't know anything about her family, but to have Max believe it cut deep. Or was Max just projecting because he resented Jessie so much?

Discovering that Ajay had suspicions that he kept from her felt all kinds of wrong. She was supposed to be able to trust him, and now she didn't know what to think. How could he have kept something like that from her? Tears began to rain from her eyes, and her heart felt like it might explode out of her chest. She took a deep breath and then another.

Her cell phone ringing startled her. She was about to turn it off when she saw it was Vivian on the phone. She pushed the talk button.

"Hello?" Lizzy's voice was raspy.

"Lizzy? What's wrong?" Vivian asked, concern flooding the connection. "What's going on? You don't sound good."

Lizzy began to hyperventilate, gasping for air. Her tears were starting to blind her view. She swiped her eyes with her hand. The truck veered left into the opposite lane and back. There was a squeal of brakes, and horns sounded loudly around her.

"Lizzy, are you driving? You need to pull over. Where are you? I will come and get you!"

Lizzy still couldn't catch her breath as she sobbed. Her body shook, and perspiration dampened her skin. She tried to speak, but her words wouldn't come, her tongue feeling like a wad of cotton in her mouth.

Pain shot through her torso, and Lizzy grabbed at her sweatshirt, letting go of the steering wheel. Suddenly everything went black, the sound of glass breaking and metal bending echoing against Vivian screaming her name in the distance.

"WHERE IS SHE going with my damn truck?" Max snapped. "She has completely lost it!"

"I told you keeping that from her was not a good idea." Ajay was pushing buttons on his cell phone.

Della glared at the two of them. "She's not answering her new phone, and I spoke to Buck. He says she's not at the ranch, and they haven't heard from her. What were you two thinking?"

Max glared. "We were thinking it was a good idea to keep Lizzy safe. That's what we were thinking!"

"I might be able to find..." Ajay started, and then he cursed again. He tossed the other two a look and bolted for his front door. Max was on his heels with Della directly behind him. Inside, Ajay went from room to room calling Lizzy's name. He suddenly noticed Pumpkin lying on the sofa, her head tilted as she stared at him. He swore again.

"What?" Max questioned.

Ajay moved to Pumpkin's side, reaching for the collar around her neck. Hanging from it like a prized trophy was the bracelet he'd given Lizzy hours earlier.

"What's that?" Della asked.

"It's a tracking device I gave Lizzy. Clearly, she didn't want us to know where she's headed." He tossed the device to the table. He paused, then he asked Max. "Where can I find your mother?"

Max's brow lifted. "Why do you want to find my mother?"

"I think Lizzy might be headed there to talk to her."

Max scoffed. "None of us have anything to do with that woman. Lizzy would never go there."

"Do you know where she is or not?" Ajay asked, filled with frustration.

Della pressed a hand to the small of Max's back, caressing him gently. "Unless something has changed," she said softly, "she still has a home a few hours outside of Boise. I can make some calls and get you an address."

"Thank you," Ajay said. He grabbed his backpack and a leash for Pumpkin. "Text me when you get that information. And can you lock my house up when they're done, please?"

Della nodded. "No problem," she said. "Let us know what you find."

As he and Pumpkin hurried to his truck, Ajay shouted over his shoulder, "I will. And if you hear from Lizzy before I get back, call me!"

THE HOME ON Wildhorse Lane exceeded Ajay's expectations, and he really hadn't known what to expect. It was a custom home in a gated estate with acreage. It sat just outside the county seat with mountain views that stretched from the Owyhee Range to Oregon to the Boise Mountains. Expansive windows gave rise to dramatic views that could easily take one's breath away.

The only thing that surprised Ajay more was the woman who opened the door, eyeing him with reservation.

Jessie Colton was quite stunning and not shy about flaunting it. She wore a teal formfitting dress that hugged her thin, almost frail frame. Her chin-length bob was bottle blond, bright and free of any gray strands. She was immediately dismissive, ready to close the door in his face, until he flashed his badge and identified himself. After that, she was far more amenable to having a conversation.

"How can I be of assistance, Lieutenant Wright?" Jessie asked. "It must be serious for you to come all the way from Owl Creek." She batted lengthy lashes and gave him a bright smile. There was no missing the bright blue eyes that Lizzy had inherited.

"I'm here about your daughter. I was wondering when you last saw her?"

Jessie suddenly looked annoyed. "Has Sarah done something I need to be aware of? You raise your children to be upstanding citizens, but you never know what they do once they are out of your sight and your home."

"I'm here about Lizzy Colton," Ajay said.

The woman visibly bristled. "Why would you come here about Lizzy?"

"You are her mother, is that correct?"

She smiled again, seeming to think how she should answer. "Lizzy lives in Owl Creek with her father, Buck. I've not seen her in years. Divorce is so difficult for children, especially when one parent fights to keep the other away. Buck Colton was not the father some people think he was. He ripped those children from me when they were small and made it difficult for me to be a good mother to them. As you can see, I successfully moved on with my life. God has blessed me immensely."

Ajay nodded. "Are you acquainted with a man named Tiberius Wagner?" He studied her expression intently, noting the rise in her eyebrows and the slight quiver above her top lip.

She shook her head. "No. No. The name's not familiar."

"I understand he's affiliated with the Ever After Church. You are also a member, is that correct?"

She smiled brightly, the glaze in her eyes shifting. "Pastor Acker is a wonderful man of God. His ministry has many followers. I, personally, do not know them all. Now if you have no further questions, I need to prepare for Bible study."

"I appreciate your time," Ajay said. He passed her one of his business cards. "Should you hear from Lizzy, I'd appreciate if you'd give me a call please."

That smile pulled full one last time. "I don't anticipate hearing from her," the woman said sternly. She closed the door between them.

As she moved past the door's sidelights, Ajay watched her shred his business card into small pieces and drop them into a trash can.

Ajay blew a gust of stale air past his lips. He'd hit a dead end, but he was grateful to know that Lizzy hadn't reached her mother and that he'd been wrong. But he needed to find her in case she was still considering a family reunion. After meeting Jessie Colton, he could tell that such a get-together would not go well for Lizzy.

Now, he needed to find her more than ever.

WHEN LIZZY OPENED her eyes, she didn't know where she was, how she'd got there or how long it had been. She vaguely recalled the car accident, being on the phone with Vivian and then blacking out as she tried to maneuver her brother's truck to the side of the road. She had no recall of anything after that.

It was cold and someone had taken her coat and shoes.

Again. She suddenly had a déjà vu moment, memories of that cabin flashing before her like Polaroid pictures.

She struggled to sit upright, realizing her feet and hands had been bound with zip ties. Again. All that was missing was the rope that had tethered her to the floor. This time, though, she lay across a metal cot. Her hands were locked around the metal bed frame. The mattress smelled of urine and sweat. A wool blanket had been tossed across the foot of the cot, but she refused to let it touch her skin if she could avoid it. What looked like blood darkened one end, and dirt and filth soiled the other.

The room was small and smelled of dampness and mildew. Lizzy assumed it was a basement. There were no windows, and the concrete walls and floor were weathered and stained. A single lightbulb hung from the ceiling, casting more shadows than light around the room. There was a single steel door leading into and out of the space, and Lizzy was alone.

She slowly assessed her situation, reminding herself of everything Ajay had taught her. Although she was scared to death, she knew she needed to stay as calm as possible. She assumed the door was locked, and she would have to pay attention when someone entered or exited. There was a commode and sink in the corner, but nothing that could easily be used as a weapon.

Until she understood the severity of her situation, there was little she could do but sit and wait. She suddenly regretted the rage that had moved her to toss away the tracking bracelet. She only hoped Ajay wouldn't give up on her, because she needed to trust that he would go to hell and back to find her, whether he told her about it or not.

Ajay was coming. She just needed to be ready to fight if he didn't get there in time.

AJAY HAD ALMOST made it home when his cell phone rang. He snatched it from the console, praying that Lizzy had listened to one of his many messages and was returning the call. But it was Max on the other end.

"Hey, where are you?" Max asked.

"About thirty minutes from Owl Creek. Have you heard from Lizzy?"

Max hesitated, and the sudden quiet put Ajay on edge. "What's wrong?"

"There's still no sign of Lizzy, but they found my truck. It was involved in a single-vehicle accident about thirty miles from your house. Someone drove it into an embankment. The airbags deployed, but there was no sign of the driver. All signs indicate she walked away from the accident unscathed, but there might have been another car onsite. Tire tracks show one leaving the scene. We're pulling camera footage now to see if we can figure out what happened."

Ajay swallowed hard, fighting the sinking feeling in the pit of his stomach. "Do you have any idea where she might have gone, Max?"

"We checked the medical center and called the hospital in Conners. There's no record of her being admitted to either. She was on the phone with Vivian when the accident happened, but Vivian didn't know where she was. She did say she heard someone talking to Lizzy before their phone line was disconnected. We've come up empty trying to identify who it might have been. The local cops have put patrol cars outside her house, your house and the ranch."

"Where the hell could she be?" Ajay muttered. He was worried before, but now he was genuinely scared for her safety.

"I'm here at the police station," Max said. "Swing by and pick me up."

"Where are we going?" Ajay asked.

Max hesitated one last time. "We need to find Wagner. Ring camera footage from one of your neighbors put him in the area at the time of her disappearance."

This time Ajay paused, pondering what they knew. It wasn't enough to get them to Lizzy before any harm could come to her. Time wasn't on their side. "I'm on my way," he said finally.

LIZZY WOKE WITH a start. This time both of her arms were free, and she was no longer tied to the bed frame. A metal chain had been wrapped around her ankle and latched tightly with an oversize lock. And she wasn't alone.

She sat up slowly, gauging the damage to her body. Although she felt bruised, she didn't think anything was broken. Her head still hurt, and she imagined her face slamming into the airbag had probably blackened both of her eyes and maybe even broken her nose. She probably wasn't pretty, she thought, but she could move when it was necessary.

The beady-eyed man stood in a corner by the door. He turned to give her a look, his smile twisted perversely.

He wore no mask this time, no longer caring if she saw his face or not. Lizzy knew that didn't bode well for her in the long run.

A greasy bag of food rested on the floor beside her foot, and she knew without looking that it was more than likely a burger and fries.

She looked to the door that had been left open. It seemed to lead into a hallway or perhaps another basement room. She wondered if he would keep it locked and where he kept the key. There was still nothing that could be used as a weapon, and she shook her wrist to see if the bed frame might be easily loosened.

"Who are you, and why are you doing this?" she asked. She did her best to keep the hysteria out of her voice.

The man didn't respond. Instead, he stood staring at her. Time ticked by slowly, and then he moved out of the room, closing the door after himself.

Lizzy pulled her knees up and folded her body into a tight ball. She leaned against the concrete wall. The cold had taken on a life of its own, and it coursed down the length of her spine throughout her entire body. She was shivering, and she could already feel her chest starting to tighten.

If she knew nothing else, Lizzy thought, she definitely knew she was in trouble if Ajay didn't find her soon.

# Chapter Seventeen

Ajay and Max stood together in the situation room at the police station. Papers and files decorated the conference room table, and a team of detectives, patrol officers and FBI agents were poring through the entire lot.

"What do we know?" Ajay asked.

Max led the way to a big monitor connected to a computer. Ajay took a step closer as a video began rolling on the screen. The view was his home and the street he lived on. Police had rolled deep, patrol cars parked haphazardly in the road.

He watched as Lizzy sauntered to her brother's truck, her hand resting on the passenger-side door. There was a moment of hesitation, and then she seemed to change her mind. She walked around the front of the truck and paused a second time. She looked one last time toward the house before jumping into the driver's seat. After sitting for a good few minutes, she suddenly engaged the transmission and pulled off down the road.

Ajay glanced at Max, shooting him a look that mirrored her brother's frustration. He turned back to the monitor.

Almost immediately, an older model black Nissan pulled onto the road behind her. It was identical to the car Lizzy had described after her first kidnapping.

Max hit the pause button. "He was watching. He's been watching her for weeks. After sending her that dead bird, I'm sure he knew we would move her from your house to somewhere else. I don't think he anticipated she would be alone. We've also spotted the car on traffic cameras between your house and the accident. There's no way he missed what happened. For all we know, he may have run her off the road."

"What do we know about the car?"

"Nothing, other than there are one hundred and thirty-six cars identical to it registered in a one-hundred-mile radius of Owl Creek, and not one is registered to Wagner."

Ajay clasped both hands together over his head. He leaned back, trying to stretch the knot out of the center of his lower spine. "Do we have any idea where this man is right now?"

Max shook his head. "The FBI raided his home address an hour ago. The place is empty. Doesn't look like anyone has lived there for the past year." He took a deep breath. "I dropped the ball. I should have moved on him days ago, but I needed to know how my mother was involved."

Ajay ignored his comment, not needing to say he'd told him so. "Is it possible that car is registered to someone else close to him? Markus Acker, by chance?"

"We didn't get a hit on any of his known associates."

Ajay tried to consider other options. He suddenly turned and looked Max in the eyes. "See if there's a black Nissan Maxima registered to Jessie Colton at her current address."

Max frowned. "I don't think…"

Ajay stared at him. Understanding swept between them, a silent conversation conveying both men's fears.

Max looked over his shoulder. "Who's working on that Nissan?"

A young woman in uniform raised her hand. "I am, sir!"

"See what's registered to Jessie Colton." He gave the girl the address.

Ajay nodded. "It's a shot in the dark, but we need to take everyone we can. Lizzy's life may depend on it."

Max nodded.

Minutes later, the young woman rushed over and passed Max a sheet of paper. "There's a black Nissan Maxima that's been registered to Jessie Colton for the last two years. But it's registered at a different address."

Max snatched the paper from the woman's hands.

Ajay looked over his shoulder to read it. "Is the address familiar?"

"No, not at all."

"Let's go," Ajay said, rushing for the exit. He called out. "Someone wake up the judge and get me a warrant!"

"We need backup," Max yelled. "I want cars rolling now! And send a unit to pick up Jessie Colton. We need answers, and we need them now!"

LIZZY STARED UP at the ceiling, taking notice of a large spider and its web in the corner. She felt cold, but she was sweating profusely. She knew it had to be a fever. *Just my luck*, she thought, *first I get abducted, then I catch pneumonia again. If it's my time*, she mused, *let me die from this damn cold before that creep gets a chance to torture me.*

*You're not going to die. I won't let you.*

Lizzy's head snapped to the side, her eyes darting back and forth. She could hear Ajay's voice in her ear, and it surprised her so much that she actually started to laugh with joy. She whispered his name, hoping he would answer, and then she realized she'd been dreaming.

Damn, Lizzy thought. How was it possible that she was in this situation and how was she going to get herself out of it?

*Stay focused.*

*You stay focused*, Lizzy thought, a pout twisting her lips. *Always giving someone orders.*

She heard Ajay laugh, and then he kissed her. She liked his kisses. Butterfly wings fluttering against her lips. His touch was like silk passing over her skin. He was teasing her sensibilities. He liked to tease her, and he was good at it.

"Save me, Ajay," she whispered out loud.

*I will*, he answered. *But let me help you save yourself.*

A loud cough rumbled in her chest. It came and settled somewhere behind her breast.

*I'll take care of you, Lizzy.*

"Come get me, Ajay! Please?"

*I'm here, Lizzy. Don't you worry.*

"I have to tell you something," she said. She reached her hand out to press her fingers to his chest.

*It's okay. I know.*

"But I need to say it!" Lizzy could feel her muscles tightening. It was only three little words, and she couldn't remember if she had ever said them aloud. If Ajay had ever heard them roll off her tongue and past her lips. Just three little words.

Ajay laughed again. *I know. It's okay.*

"I'm dreaming, aren't I?"

*Yes. This is a dream.*

Lizzy opened her eyes. The room was dark, that one dim light bulb extinguished. Her arm was extended toward the ceiling as if she were reaching for the sky. She dropped her hand to her side and tightened her fingers into a fist. She took a slow, deep breath and then another.

*I'm still here!* Ajay called out to her. *I'm still here, Lizzy. I'm not going to leave you.*

So she closed her eyes, wanting to dream of Ajay one more time.


*BLOCK. PUNCH. ELBOW. Drop. Punch.*

*Block. Punch. Elbow. Drop. Punch.*

*Block. Punch. Elbow. Drop. Punch.*

*Focus, Lizzy! Focus!*

"My head hurts," Lizzy muttered. "I'll practice later."

*You need to fight, Lizzy! Block. Punch. Elbow. Drop. Punch.*

"I'm tired, Ajay. Please, come save me!"

*I'm here. Just stay focused.*

"Stay focused. I have to stay focused," she whispered out loud.

The door creaked, and Lizzy opened her eyes to see

the beady-eyed man moving into the room. He was muttering under his breath.

She struggled to focus. She needed him to get closer. *Block, punch, elbow, drop, punch.* Ajay's voice had become a mantra, the words spinning over and over in her head. All she had to do was focus, she thought. Focus and run. She pulled herself upright, leaning back against the concrete wall. Focus and run, she thought.

"Please," she begged. "Can I have some water please?" *Draw him in close*, she thought. *Then drop him hard.* "Please!"

The man turned and stared at her. Then without speaking, he backed out of the room and locked her inside.

"Next time," Lizzy muttered. "I'll be ready next time."

SOMETHING HAD CHANGED between Ajay and Max. Max was now his brother, too, despite their differences. And his brother was hurting. He owed it to Lizzy to be there for Max as much as he would be there for her.

"I'm sorry," Ajay said, his car careening toward the address logged into his GPS.

Max tossed him a questioning look. "About what?"

"About your mother. I'm sorry for what you and your family have had to go through with her. What you are still going through. It's not fair."

Max turned to stare out the window at the landscape whizzing by. He didn't respond, as if he had no interest in the conversation.

Ajay continued, "I met Jessie. And you were right for wanting to shield Lizzy from her. Lizzy doesn't deserve that kind of hurt. But neither do you." He drove down the center of the road, his lights flashing. His sirens were silent, not wanting to forewarn anyone they were coming.

Max broke the silence. "I appreciate you being there for Lizzy."

"Always," Ajay replied. "She's my heart."

The two men punched fists in solidarity.

In front of them, the road narrowed as they began to climb the mountain, far from Blackbird Lake. The road suddenly turned right, still heading upward. Two quick turns and a lengthy driveway opened to a clearing in the woods. A small home sat centered on the lot, and parked in front was a Nissan.

Ajay had cut his lights one turn back, so everything was pitch-black, with the exception of a single light in a front window.

"Guns blazing?" Max asked.

"Shoot first, figure it out later," Ajay replied.

Max sat reading a message on his cell phone. "Backup is ten minutes away, and we got our search warrant."

"I'll knock on the front door," Ajay said.

Max nodded as the two men exited the vehicle. "I'll go around back," he whispered.

Pumpkin was glued to Ajay's leg, watching his every move in order to figure out her own. Approaching the home, he could see how dilapidated the structure was. It didn't appear that anyone had lived there for a long while, but a radio was playing loudly inside. The station was local. One of the Christian stations at the University of Idaho Boise.

At the front door, Ajay tested the handle, surprised

when it turned and opened. He slowly pushed the door and stepped inside.

It took a quick minute for his eyes to adjust to the darkness. The home was devoid of furniture, nothing to impede his search. His service weapon was drawn, and he swung left and then right, stepping carefully as he checked for whomever was in the house.

A pot rattling in the kitchen led him in that direction. With the precision of a cat stalking prey, Ajay eased his way down a short hall and peered into the room.

Wagner stood over a small Bunsen burner, boiling a small pot of water. He was humming along with the radio, declaring his love for Jesus.

Ajay braced his body and announced himself. "Owl Creek Police! Tiberius Wagner, you are under arrest. Put your hands up!"

Wagner turned, surprise blanketing his face. He froze, his beady eyes shifting as he contemplated his next move. His gaze shifted from the pot of hot water to the large butcher knife resting against the table and then to the door. He wasn't prepared when Max moved in behind him and pressed his weapon against the back of his head.

"Give me a reason," Max said. "Get on your knees."

Wagner slowly lifted his hands in surrender. He dropped to his knees.

Ajay holstered his weapon. He moved behind the man and secured his hands. Then he lifted him back to his feet and pushed him into the only chair in the room. "Where's Lizzy Colton?" Ajay asked.

Wagner didn't reply. He dropped his head against his

chest and closed his eyes. He began to pray, an invocation designed to give him absolution for his sins.

Max was racing from room to room, searching for his sister. When he came back into the kitchen, he shook his head, coming up empty.

"Where is she?" Ajay asked again.

Wagner opened his eyes to stare up at Ajay. "She is with our heavenly father. She is blessed."

Ajay felt his breath catch in his chest. "And where might your father be hanging out today?"

"How dare you mock our faith! You will never understand."

Max punched him. Hard. Sending the man back down to the floor.

Ajay knelt down to stare at him. "I understand that if you don't tell me where she is, you very well may meet your heavenly father sooner rather than later."

Wagner closed his eyes and began praying again.

Sirens sounded in the distance. The cavalry coming to render aid.

"You got this?" Ajay asked Max.

Max nodded.

A large flashlight lay on the counter, and Ajay picked it up and turned it on. The light was bright, illuminating a wide area of space.

Ajay whistled, and Pumpkin jumped, her stance tight. "Find Lizzy," he said. "Go get your girl!"

With her head down, Pumpkin raced through the home and returned to the kitchen. She scratched and barked at the back door. Ajay opened it and rushed behind her as she took off into the woods. He raced after her, passing two uniformed officers headed inside. "You two with me," Ajay yelled.

Pumpkin darted across the cleared expanse back to the tree line. She was determined as she led Ajay along a trail that had been recently cleared. Less than a mile ahead, Pumpkin came to a stop and sat down, barking once for Ajay's attention.

At the end of the trail was a concrete structure with a single door. Someone had built what appeared to be a bomb shelter, hidden behind piles of melting snow and stacks of lumber. There was a lock on the door, and Ajay fired his weapon, ripping into the metal. He snatched what remained of the lock away, tossing it to the ground.

Inside, steps led them down to another locked door. This time the lock was a dead bolt. Pumpkin had followed him, and she barked excitedly.

Opening the second door, Ajay was thrown off by the darkness. There was a single light and switch, but the bulb had blown. He pointed the flashlight inside, slowly moving it from one corner to the other, and then he called Lizzy's name.

She lay in the fetal position, her body curled tightly against a metal cot. Even in the dim light he could see that she wasn't well, every ounce of color drained from her face. She was shivering and all he could think was to get to her side and wrap himself around her. He suddenly realized that if anything happened to Lizzy, there would be hell to pay. No one and nothing could stop him from enacting revenge against whoever was involved in doing this to her. Even if one of those persons was Jessie

Colton. He turned to the man behind him before rushing forward.

"I need an ambulance. Now!"

LIZZY COULDN'T IMAGINE her dreams being any sweeter. Ajay held her hand and caressed her cheek. There were more kisses and gentle touches, and she knew that nothing could ever break their bond. Not even her own bad behavior. He was her friend first, and one day, he would be her lover and maybe even her husband and the father of her babies. One day when all this bad business was finished with. She could hear him in her ear, and she smiled.

*You came!*

*I promised you I would.*

*Will you save me?*

*I'm right here.*

*We should name the twins Hope and Faith.*

*Hope and Faith.*

*Those are good names, right?*

*Very good names.*

*I was ready to save myself so I can be a good mother to your sons.*

*You will be a great mother. And I'm here now to save you.*

*You promise?*

*I promise!*

Lizzy opened her eyes, the sweetest dream fading in the chilly air. She was being lifted onto a stretcher, warm blankets tucked around her body. Something licked her cheek, and she frowned. Then the softest whimper in her ear lifted her smile. She murmured, her voice barely a whisper, "Pumpkin!"

Ajay leaned down and kissed her forehead. "Hey, there! Everything's going to be okay. I'm right here, too!"

"Ajay!" Lizzy's smile widened. "I have something I need to tell you!" She gushed, happiness spilling over each word. "I love you!"

Ajay pressed his cheek to her cheek and whispered into her ear, "I love you, too!"

# Chapter Eighteen

Tiberius Wagner was arraigned at the Owl Creek courthouse on charges of kidnapping, stalking, assault and obstruction. Ajay testified before the grand jury to secure his indictment and would be there front and center when he went to trial.

Testifying in detail about all that had happened and sharing what had happened at his interview after Wagner's arrest only served to make Ajay angry. Reflecting back on it, he was once again ready to punch something.

"Why Lizzy Colton?" one of the detectives had asked.

Wagner's smile was arrogant and condescending. "I did as my Lord and Savior commanded."

"So God told you to terrorize and kidnap her?"

"She is a gift to he who is a true believer."

"And you are a true believer?"

"I am a man of faith. I honor the commands as they are given to me."

"Help me understand," the detective said as he scooted his seat up closer to Wagner. "You were commanded by God to kidnap a woman as a gift to yourself for being a believer?"

"My God is a kind and generous God. You have only to trust in his word and follow his law, and you, too, will be blessed abundantly."

Standing on the other side of the two-way mirror, Ajay and Max had both been ready to go in and tear the man's head off. The questioning had continued, but when he was asked about Markus Acker and the Ever After Church, as nicely as he'd been ready to share before, Wagner shut down, refusing to utter another word. He had not spoken to anyone since, not even to his attorney to assist in his defense.

Markus Acker and the Ever After Church had disavowed any knowledge of Wagner's actions. They proclaimed him a once-loyal brother who had gone rogue. Pastor Acker had been eager to offer prayer for Lizzy and counsel for the family if they had need of his services.

Jessie Colton had also distanced herself from Wagner, proclaiming no knowledge of him using her property for any illicit dealings. Her car, her keys and that dilapidated building had been stolen with her having no knowledge of when or how. In fact, she was adamant that she had never met the man. Publicly, she asked for prayer for her daughter. Tears dampened a tissue when she gave a statement to the local media. Privately, she still hadn't bothered to check on Lizzy's well-being.

AJAY ENTERED THE hospital in Conners, meeting Malcolm and Max as they were making their exit. They both greeted him warmly.

"Lizzy said you pulled a double shift last night," Malcolm said.

He nodded. "Some hikers got lost on the trails leading to the other side of the mountain. It was a good rescue. How's my girl?" he asked.

"Mean!" Malcolm quipped.

Max laughed. "She's ready to be out of this place and home with you."

"I offered to stay at the ranch with her, but she's insisting she's not going back unless it's just for Sunday dinner."

"That's what she told us."

"We hate it for you," Malcolm teased.

"How's it going?" Ajay asked Max. "I heard you're leaving the FBI officially for the second time." He chuckled.

"I'm gone for good this time. No special assignments. No favors. Nada. Nothing. I'm past the point of being burned-out and I'm ready for a change. They have my badge, my gun, and I've signed all my pension papers. It doesn't get any more official than that."

"He's going to make furniture," Malcolm said as he rolled his eyes.

"And maybe I'll work an occasional search and rescue with my wife."

"Sign me up," Ajay said.

"Lizzy said you plan to take some time off when they release her?"

"I'm thinking the two of us could use a vacation. Maybe a tropical paradise somewhere warm."

"Don't tell, Della," Max said. "She's been aching for a beach trip somewhere since I met her."

Ajay laughed. "That's where I got the idea!"

The two brothers turned toward the hospital exit. "You take care," Max called out. "We'll talk soon."

"Christmas Day soon!" Malcolm interjected. "And don't forget to bring me a big present."

AJAY SMILED AS he moved on to Lizzy's room. At the door, laughter rang loudly into the hallway. Buck was telling one of his famous dad jokes, and Lizzy was giggling like a third grader.

"Whenever I try to eat healthy, a chocolate bar looks at me and Snickers."

Lizzy giggled. "Daddy, that is so bad."

"But you laughed, sweet girl!"

"I did!" Just then, Lizzy's eyes widened as she saw Ajay standing in the doorway. "Ajay! I was beginning to think you forgot about me."

"Not in this lifetime or any other," Ajay replied as he leaned to press his lips to hers. He shook hands with her father. "How are you doing today, Buck?"

"I'm doing good, son. Happy to see my baby girl happy. You need to keep up the good work."

Ajay grinned. "You can count on me, Buck! Where's Mama Jen? Did I miss her?"

"She's babysitting this evening. Greg and Briony are having a date night. I'm headed over to give her a hand. They like my jokes."

Lizzy giggled. "I like your jokes, too, Daddy!"

"We'll come check on you tomorrow, sweet girl!"

"I'll be at Ajay's house tomorrow," Lizzy said.

Ajay eyed her with a raised brow. "You will?"

Lizzy nodded. "They're releasing me. The doctor said I could go home as soon as my ride got here!"

Ajay and Buck laughed.

"I guess that's you, Uber Wright," Buck said with a hearty chuckle.

"I guess it is, sir! I guess it is!"

BUCK SAID HIS GOODBYES, promising to run by Ajay's house to make certain she was settled. Visiting hours were coming to an end, and Lizzy was getting restless waiting for her discharge papers.

"Are you certain you don't want to go to the ranch?" Ajay asked.

"I'm positive. Unless you'd prefer I not impose on you?"

"It's not an imposition. You know how much I want you there. It makes it easier for me to keep an eye on you."

"How did things go in court?" Lizzy asked, her tone losing that joyful lilt.

"Bail was denied. He is never going to set foot outside of a jail cell ever again."

She blew out a sigh of relief. "I started therapy today, and I really like my therapist."

"That's great! The healing process is going to require a lot of work on your part, but it's nothing you can't handle."

Lizzy smiled. She twisted the beaded bracelet on her arm, feeling safe with it on and having vowed to never take it off as she had done weeks earlier. "I think we should go home and celebrate."

"Anything in particular you think we should do to celebrate?"

She lifted her eyebrows suggestively, and Ajay laughed. "Something tells me you're going to be insatiable," he said as he eased into the hospital bed beside her.

"I'm a lot to handle, but I think you'll do just fine."

They shared a kiss, melting slowly into the moment like freshly lit candles. Ajay's hands danced across her back and settled against the curve of her buttocks. His fingers burned hot against her skin, the warmth spreading throughout her entire body.

Lizzy suddenly pulled herself away from him. "I had the most interesting dreams about you," she said, matter-of-fact.

His smile lifted his eyes, his gaze dancing over her face. "The doctors said it was the fever."

She nodded. "If you say so."

"I do."

"I've been thinking about our future babies."

He laughed again. "Four sons and twin daughters, correct?"

"I was thinking about names."

Ajay shook his head. "That was definitely the fever," he said teasingly.

"Maybe, but out of curiosity, what names would you give our twin girls?"

"Really, Lizzy?"

"Play along, Ajay. It's therapeutic for me."

He sat back against the bed pillows and contemplated her question. Finally, he answered, "I think Hope and Faith would be great names for twin girls."

Lizzy grinned. "Hope and Faith?"

"And since it's almost Christmas we could save the names Rudolph, Donner, Dasher, and Blitzen for those four boys!"

Lizzy laughed until tears rained out of her eyes. "I don't think so," she said.

Ajay shrugged. "Then let's go with Matthew, Mark, Luke and John."

Lizzy wrapped her arms around his neck and pressed her lips to his. "Hope and Faith," she repeated. "Those names sound like something I might have dreamed."

"It was a good dream then."

"It was about you."

He kissed her again. "Then it was a dream come true."

"Yes, you are, Ajay Wright! Yes, you are!"

He smiled. "I love you, too, Lizzy Colton! I love you, too!"

\* \* \* \* \*

# COMING SOON!

We really hope you enjoyed reading this book.
If you're looking for more romance
be sure to head to the shops when
new books are available on

## Thursday 15th
## August

To see which titles are coming soon, please visit
**millsandboon.co.uk/nextmonth**

# MILLS & BOON

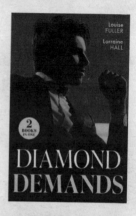

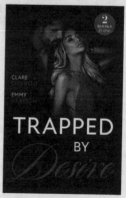

# LET'S TALK
# *Romance*

For exclusive extracts, competitions
and special offers, find us online:

- **f** MillsandBoon
- **X** @MillsandBoon
- **⬛** @MillsandBoonUK
- **♪** @MillsandBoonUK

Get in touch on 01413 063 232